TALES OF TREMORA

The Shimmering

William Westwood Jr.
AUTHOR AND ILLUSTRATOR

Book Publishers Network
P.O. Box 2256
Bothell • WA • 98041
PH • 425-483-3040
www.bookpublishersnetwork.com

10 9 8 7 6 5 4 3 2 1

Printed in the United States of America

LCCN 2011904805
ISBN10 1-935359-79-7
ISBN13 978-1-935359-79-1

Editor: Julie Scandora
Cover Designer: Laura Zugzda
Typographer: Stephanie Martindale

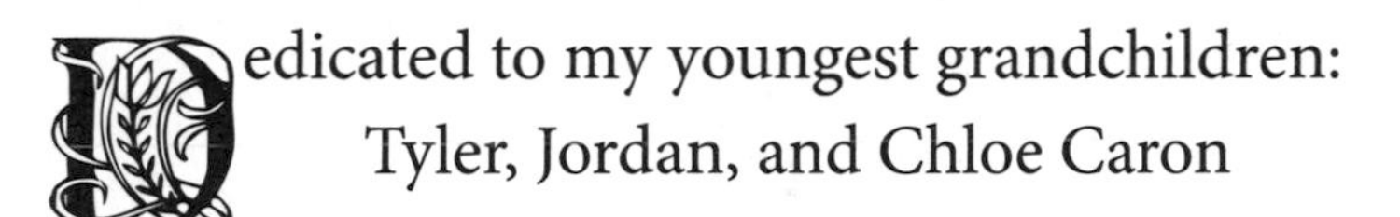

Dedicated to my youngest grandchildren:
Tyler, Jordan, and Chloe Caron

Contents

Acknowledgements

Thanks to all of my family: Especially my ever supportive wife, Heather, and my children Tonya, Jason, Tracey, and Garry. Special thanks to Steve Long, my Ideal Reader and mentor, whose help and inspiration were invaluable and kept me going during the dark hours, Christina Fossum (who just might be a Tremoran herself), ever encouraging and inspiring nephew Wayne Bailey, unshakably loyal cousin Sharon Goss, Sarah Gagnon (obviously a fellow boundary traveler), Kim a.k.a. Violet, who reminded me that grammar and character could not be ignored, and all those others who read snippets of the manuscript through eight long years and supplied the encouragement I so craved and needed. Finally, my thanks to Sheryn Hara and the talented group of editors and designers at Book Publishers Network who helped bring this project to fruition.

Prologue

Prelandora, the Witch of Spreten, entered the gates of Tremora Castle astride a magnificent black warhorse, resplendent in trappings of ebony and gold. She held the reins easily in one hand while the other rested proudly on her bulging belly. Six wisps armed with carved stone knives darted furtively in front and behind her—their polished black jackboots and fluttering leather capes flashing in the bright midday sun. The faces of the fearsome escorts were completely concealed by deep hoods with only the tips of long noses protruding as their heads swept side to side. From an overlooking balcony, the king, queen, and nobles of the court watched in stunned silence as the strange procession serpentined through the cobbled streets toward the main pavilion.

No one had seen Prelandora since the wedding between King William and Queen Lelana two years past. The witch's reputation for scandal and troublemaking had come to a head that summer when she had been caught practicing the dark arts in her bedchambers. As a consequence, she and the king's brother, Lord Pratt, were exiled to the distant island of Sitka for *high crimes against the state*.

Now, here she was, attending the celebration of the birth of Cedric, the new crown prince. On the surface, she appeared to be taking advantage of the liberal terms of her banishment that allowed her to enter Tremora during official holidays and public festivals. But no one was fooled, not the king, not the queen, not the lowliest serf. She was not here to swear fealty to the new heir-apparent. No! Her real intentions were crystal clear. Everyone now knew that a second name would soon be added to the line of succession to the throne and title, High King of Tremora. And more than one person realized a more chilling fact: Only Cedric would stand in the way of Prelandora's child one day becoming the most powerful person in the world.

Chapter One

The Shimmering

Michael awoke early. He lay still, listening to the rain falling on the tin roof of the family's small cabin. It was one of his favorite sounds and he would have normally just snuggled down and let the patter put him back to sleep. But not today! It was his fourteenth birthday, and he had a long day ahead of him. His mother was taking him to a Seattle Mariners baseball game and then to dinner at the Space Needle, so he only had a couple of hours to get in his morning hike before he had to be back. Guess I'll be getting a little wet, he thought, as he threw back the covers and jumped out of bed. It didn't matter. As his father often said, "Never let a little rain change your plans."

He brushed and flossed quickly and then splashed water on his face and wetted the unruly crop of thick black hair that fell to just above his shoulders. He ran a brush through the mop and checked his chin closely for whiskers, but found none. "Someday," he said to his reflection wistfully. He then crept into the kitchen and changed into warm hiking clothes and waterproof boots that were kept near the back door. He didn't want to wake his mother.

He smiled, though, when he picked up his daypack and fished inside—it was already filled with energy snacks and bottled water. He also found, neatly folded in the bottom, the hooded cloak his mother had made for him that was shaped like a poncho. It was reversible, with one side dark green and waterproof and the other lined with wool as colorful as a Mexican serape. "I don't want some hunter taking you for a deer, *dear*," his mother always said in response to Michael playfully crinkling his nose when she made him put it on, bright side out. In reality, Michael didn't mind wearing it at all. It was another way to show his mother how much he loved her, and besides, it was rainproof *and* warm! And, as usual, his mother was spot on—it would come in handy today if the showers outside turned into a downpour.

It's scary how she knows my thoughts sometimes, he mused as he removed his hunting knife from a hook on the wall. In spite of all the birthday plans, she knew he would still be going out this morning. He shook his head and smiled as he threaded the knife's leather sheath through his belt and buckled up. Next, he put his arms through the straps of the backpack and shrugged it snugly in place. Then he grabbed his Mariner's cap and favorite walking stick (the one with a carving of Gandalf) and eased the porch door open just enough to squeeze through. Once clear, he carefully closed and locked the door behind him and leapt down the wooden steps, two at a time. The rain had turned to a light drizzle, and he could just make out the light of the sun crowning the Cascade Mountains to the east.

He set out on the path bordering their property and fell into a comfortable but careful pace; it was still dark, and the going was muddy and slippery. In spite of the slow going, his heart beat fast with excitement. He was taking a new trail today—he was going to explore Baker's Wood!

The reclusive Mr. Baker had unexpectedly called yesterday and given permission to enter the forest that covered Founder's Peak; something that had been forbidden as long as Michael could remember. His mother said it was a birthday present from the old hermit, but Michael suspected something different. *A spell, perhaps?* After all, when in a lighter mood, his mom always claimed she had been a witch in another life.

He smiled again at thoughts of his eccentric mother. She was a middle school teacher and also taught ancient Greek literature at the University of Washington. Even though she refused to wear makeup or have her hair cut in a salon, the world still thought her beautiful. And, of course, so did Michael. She typically wore her graying hair held back with leather hair clips and dressed in layers with hoops and stone jewelry as accessories; a look she described as a little gypsy, a little hippy, a little witchy. Michael loved her dearly.

So why did Mr. Baker make that strange phone call? Michael wondered. His mom still could have been responsible—she could be very persuasive when she had her mind set. He shook his head to clear the conundrum and raindrops flew from the bill of his cap. *Well, no matter,* he thought. It was still one of the best birthday presents ever. Because now, out of nowhere, there were miles and miles of new trails open to him. He could hardly contain himself. *Perhaps today would be the day ...*

Michael's mind then turned to the mysterious disappearance of his father. One year ago this date, his thirteenth birthday, his father, a Washington State forest ranger, simply vanished. He'd been called out to investigate a cougar sighting in the early hours of morning and was never heard from again. Poof! The police, fellow rangers, volunteers, dogs—all spent weeks combing and searching the heavily wooded area around the cabin. Nothing. Michael's mother was even questioned as *a person of interest*. He shook his head in disgust, and raindrops flew again. Eventually, though, his mother was cleared (*of course she was!*), and the search was reluctantly called off. But the sad fact remained: His father was gone. No trace. Poof!

Michael, though, didn't care what anyone else thought. *He* wasn't going to stop looking for his father—ever. And gratefully, his mother was ever supportive as he continued to blaze new trails almost every day in hopes of finding his own clues. Why? Because the last image he had of his dad was of him waving goodbye from this very path.

His dad had shaken him awake that morning, wished him a happy birthday, and then put a big, new, fixed-blade hunting knife on the pillow next to his head. Michael remembered reaching back clumsily and grabbing it by its handle and holding it up to his sleepy eyes. The leather sheath was embossed with a large silver M, and the handle was inscribed: *To my intrepid son, Michael, love Dad.* His father, then, had smiled down at him, ruffled his hair, and apologized for leaving him on his special day, but said there was rumor of an errant wild cat prowling nearby that had to be checked out. "It shouldn't take too long," he'd said.

Michael remembered his disappointment. It wasn't so unusual for his father to be called out at odd hours, but did it have to be on his birthday? Michael had watched from his bedroom window as his dad had tipped his Smokey Bear hat before disappearing into the woods. Michael had waved back belatedly, clutching his new birthday present to his chest. And that was the last time he saw his father.

He shook off the sad memory and came back to the present. His hand went fleetingly to the hilt of his dad's gift. He thought again of the new trails at his disposal and hurried on with new conviction. *Yes, perhaps today would be the day …*

After a short spate of rain and drizzle, the wet weather let up, and the sun broke through the cloud cover in isolated shafts of gray and white. Michael stopped at a clearing to gaze back across the Snohomish Valley, taking in the breathtaking display. "Thank you," he whispered. His parents told him these moments were sent as gifts, that he should absorb them and take time to wonder. And he always did—especially when he saw the sun rise on a new day. But he was in a hurry *this* morning. He took only a moment before he set off again, heading toward the mountain.

After a half hour or so, he branched off the main trail and fought his way through thick wet patches of blackberry brambles and huckleberries to a stile in the fence that bounded Baker's property. He used his knife to clear the thorny canes imprisoning the wooden gate and scrambled through the narrow opening. The path was more overgrown on this side, and he followed it with some difficulty in the poor light. He spent the next half hour in heavy woods, skirting large sword ferns, navigating old cedar stumps, and circling shallow pools of water bordered by giant skunk cabbage. Gradually, the trees got bigger (much bigger), and more and more of the sky became blocked by a soaring canopy of green. He was in a tract of old growth forest now where the trees were hundreds and hundreds of years old.

But Michael didn't marvel at their majesty this day—he was on a mission. His eyes missed little as he scoured his surroundings. *Had dad come this way? Those vine maples look like they've been cut by someone. And it wasn't recently either. It could have been a year ago …*

"Hey! What the …?" Michael suddenly blurted. He'd just experienced the strangest sensation—like being sprayed all over with a mist of ice-cold water. But he wasn't wet! He rubbed the back of his neck and looked around in confusion when, there, about fifty yards off the left of the trail, he saw someone hurrying toward him. Michael watched warily as a wizened old man with a tall staff, backpack, and lighted pipe approached and hailed him by name. The man was very short and had skin the color of pistachio pudding.

"Michael! I've found you at last," the man cried as he rushed up and looked at Michael's astonished face. "Just where they said you'd be."

"I, I beg your pardon."

The stranger hardly paused. "I can track a flea for a hundred paces, and yet I couldn't find a trace of you anywhere. I must admit I was beginning to have my doubts. But here you are! Though, I think you must have just now arrived in Tremora, eh?" He tilted his head and raised an inquisitive eyebrow. But, seeing only Michael's bewildered look, he shrugged and continued on. "Well, never mind. Come along, come along. We can't wait another minute. We must be off if we're going to make the wizard's gathering. We only have a fortnight!"

Childhood alarms went off in Michael's head. *Stranger danger! Call 911!* He gripped his walking stick with both hands and held it out menacingly. "You just stay where you are, mister," he said. "You must be crazy if you think I'm going anywhere with you."

The old man opened his eyes wide in surprise. Then he laid his staff carefully on the ground and held up both hands in apology. His right hand still gripped his smoking pipe. "No, no, it's nothing like that. My goodness, I mean you no harm!"

Michael scowled for a few moments longer, and then, not really feeling very threatened, curiosity got the better of him. "You do know you're green don't you?" he asked finally.

"But of course! Many Tremorans are green."

Michael wasn't sure what answer he was expecting, but that wasn't one of them. It wasn't very helpful either. "OK, look. I don't know who you are, and I don't know what you're talking about. Is this a practical joke or something? Because if it is, you're obviously mistaking me for someone else, and," he paused, "uhm, wait a minute. How did you know?" His voice trailed off.

" You do know you're green, dont you? "

Relief crossed the man's face in a wave. "That's better. That's better. No need to be hasty!" He lowered his hands and retrieved his staff. When he straightened back up, he gestured with his pipe. "Now, first off, this is definitely *not* a joke. And secondly, if you think about it, I just told you quite clearly what I'm talking about. However, you *are* correct on one point: Indeed, you don't know me—yet. And fourthly, even if it's not obvious now, I assure you I've made no mistake. Finding people after all," and here he made a deep sweeping bow, "*is* one of my specialties. My name is Fremoran Tremelan, son of Miriam and Mendelan of Gondalor, Land of the Stalwart. I am a true Tremoran. But you may call me Tracker." He gave a satisfied nod. "There! Now you know me. I am your escort. And, of course, it was the Magus, Megan, who told me your name."

Michael stared, even more dumbfounded than before. *Magus Megan? Who's Megan?* He shook his head. *This can't be real. I've been out a couple of hours, and maybe all the rushing around ...* He reached out to touch the man's sleeve, and Tracker readily extended his elbow. *No, this guy is very real. Not only can I feel him, I can even smell his pipe tobacco.* His eyes caught a curling wisp of smoke, and he followed it upwards. It was then Michael noticed Tracker wasn't the only strangeness in the woods. *The trees!* The once familiar trees and shrubs looked completely different—they were shaped different, greener, larger, taller … *Taller*?

"What in the world?" Michael said as he turned in a circle. "Where am I?"

"Ah yes, well, that's the rub, isn't it?" Tracker said. "You see Michael, you're no longer in *your world* at all; you're in Tremora. Tremora is a neighboring world to yours; you might say—a neighboring world that has a few leaks in it. You entered through a big one just back there. And this was no accidental meeting either. You are needed, Michael. You have been summoned." The sounds of the forest seemed to pause.

Michael started. "Summoned? Summoned by who?"

But Tracker waved him off with a quick flick of his pipe. "Sorry lad, but that's enough for now. King's business! And this is, after all, the Age of Secrets. The most important thing is you're here and I've found you. All else will be revealed in its own time. As you will soon find out, secrets are closely guarded in Tremora. Come along, come along. It's a long way to Mesmer Henge, and we have more than one stop to make along the way."

The forest returned to its busy hum. Tracker turned, beckoned with his staff, and trotted off with puffs of smoke in his wake like a tiny steam engine—completely confident, it seemed, that Michael would follow.

But Michael hesitated as he watched Tracker weave his way through the huge trees. He wasn't sure what to do. Should he really follow a stranger he'd just met into the forest? A stranger who was green, barely as tall as his shoulders, and claiming to be from another world! Or should he get the heck out of there while he still had the chance because he was beginning to feel really uneasy? *What if it was true? What if this really isn't Washington? And did he say "King's business"?*

Then Michael looked back in the direction of his cabin. "What the …?" he exclaimed for the second time that morning. For there, just a few yards behind him, was a wall of shimmering air. It was like looking through the back of a thin waterfall.

His brow furrowed. "Well, that could explain the water-that-wasn't-really-water feeling on my neck," he muttered as he studied the gently undulating air. *Is that what Tracker meant? Am I looking at a 'leak'? Seriously!* He turned again in the direction of Tracker, but the little man was out of sight now. Michael could just make out a last puff of smoke floating over a rise in the trail. Then a new thought struck him like a clap of thunder: *Wait! Is this what happened to Dad?* His heart leapt into his throat. *Of course!*

Reflexively, he jumped to follow Tracker and then stopped dead in his tracks. For one thing he had jumped at least a foot or two farther than expected, and for another he was suddenly awash with an overwhelming sense of dread. *What am I doing? What about Mom? What will she do if I disappear without a trace like Dad?* He saw a picture-clear image in his mind of his mother looking anxiously out their kitchen window for his return. He reeled and stumbled and dropped to one knee. "I can't leave her all alone like that," he moaned as he bowed his head and struggled not to be sick. More images of his mother, grieving now, bombarded his mind, and an ethereal female voice suddenly filled his head: "Go back, go back!" it demanded. "You don't belong here. Leave! Leave before it's too late!"

He let go of his walking stick, and held his head in both hands. The voice droned on relentlessly. But just as he felt he couldn't stand it any longer, that he *had* to return to his mother, he heard another voice call out faintly.

Now what? He cleared tears from his eyes with the back of a hand and looked around angrily, but didn't see anyone. And yet, with the emergence of the new voice, the nagging one in his head stopped abruptly, and his feeling of nausea and images of his mourning mother also disappeared.

Still shaky, he gathered himself and, using his walking stick as support, pulled himself slowly to his feet. Although he couldn't explain what had just happened, it was obvious that someone didn't want him to follow Tracker. As if he needed proof, just the thought of the first voice caused angst to reappear and bile to enter his mouth all over again. He removed his hat and wiped his brow with his sleeve, then looked in both directions, completely torn between following Tracker or rushing back home to his mother.

"*Michael.*"

His head snapped up. The second voice again. Only this time he knew who it was—it was his mother! He looked around anxiously, and there she was, standing in the middle of the path, on the other side of the shimmering. She had one hand at her mouth and was watching him as if he were a small child teetering on the sill of an open window.

He took a half step toward her, but she shook her head and emphatically motioned him back. He heard the jangling of the bracelets on her wrists.

"*Michael, it's OK. Don't come any closer. Just listen!*"

His jaw dropped. Her lips weren't moving. He could hear her thoughts!

When she was sure she had his attention, she dropped her hands to her side, and her face became calm. "*Michael, there is little time. You must choose and choose quickly whether to stay in Tremora. The shimmering won't last much longer. It's important that you alone decide. I can't help you. Just follow you heart, Michael, as we've always taught you. And remember your Homer: Am I not Penelope awaiting her Odysseus? Are you not Telemachus?*"

She continued to hold his gaze as the shimmering suddenly became more active and opaque. Then—she was gone.

Michael stood agape. *How did she do that?* he wondered. *She was talking to me without talking! What in the world? No, wait, we already tried that. I'm not in my world*, he confirmed by looking again at the enormous trees around him. He then played his mother's words over in his head. She was trying to tell him something—that was for sure, but what? For one thing, she actually knew he was in a place called Tremora. He shook his head. *How could she know that?* He began slowly to adjust the straps on his backpack—his arms and body strangely detached as his mind whirled. ... *and remember your Homer? My Homer?* He patted himself absently, feeling for his knife, checking his pockets. Of course his mom had brought him up on the classics, and *The Odyssey,* the story of Odysseus's twenty-year journey home from the Trojan War to his faithful wife Penelope, was one of his favorites. His mother knew that. And Telemachus was their only son who aided Odysseus in his return … *Well, it must mean she thinks Dad is alive and he's coming back; that's what it means. And she's telling me he's here in Tremora and I have to help him!*

His excitement was reaching a crescendo. He put his hat back on his head, quickly knelt down and retied the laces on his boots while staring off into space. *And what was it Tracker had said? That someone needs me—that I was being summoned …*

He stood up and pulled down hard on the bill of his cap. *And now I'm supposed to decide whether to stay here or go back home? Are you kidding me!* He made one final adjustment to his backpack and then gripped his walking stick in his left hand. His bewilderment was completely gone, replaced now with the same resolve that had fueled him for the past year when looking for his father. There was no question of what he was going to do, regardless of that enigmatic voice. He gave a nod to the spot where his mother had stood just moments before. The disturbance in the air was barely visible. "Thank you, Mom," he said, hardly able to contain his eagerness. "And don't worry—I'm staying. And if Dad's here, I'll bring him back. I promise! And, I love you."

Then he turned and, with a hasty wave behind him, took his first steps to follow Tracker. But the same thing happened as before; he traveled farther than expected and nearly fell down. Tentatively, he took another couple of steps, and images of men walking on the moon came to mind. Although not nearly as pronounced as theirs, his step definitely had a spring to it that wasn't there before. *Could it be that Tremora's gravity was somewhat less than that of home?* A smile came to his face. *Well, this should be fun!* Then, with his newfound speed barely in control, he set off to follow Tracker.

❧

The last remnants of the shimmering veil vanished with a snap. Michael's mother stood looking at the spot where she had last seen her son. "Oh, Michael," she whispered. "Now, you're both gone. I knew you'd choose to stay of course—it's in your blood. And Megan assures me Tremora needs you … But, please be careful and come back to me safely. And please, please, Michael, don't kill your father."

Chapter Two

The Messenger

Michael hurried along the narrow trail as best he could. He was having difficulty avoiding roots and stones and trees with his newly discovered strength and speed. "Hey! Hold up! I'm coming! I'm coming!" he shouted ahead, after stubbing his toe and stopping to hop painfully up and down on one foot. But, Tracker apparently didn't hear him. Michael righted his hat and limped off as fast as he could, mumbling beneath his breath. Eventually, he caught sight of the diminutive green man and hurried to close the gap.

"Well?" Michael gasped as he got nearer. "I've decided to follow you! Wasn't that what you wanted? And where did you say we are going?" Michael was right behind Tracker now. "Come on, hold up a minute. I need to know if you've seen my father. And who is Magun and where's this messy hedge place, anyway?"

That did the trick. Tracker pulled up, and Michael just avoided bowling him over. "Harrumph, well yes. I guess I could explain a little more clearly—now that you've decided to stay in Tremora!" Tracker gave Michael an approving look. "But first," he said, holding up a finger, "you'll have to excuse me." He put his staff under one arm and walked over and knocked his pipe on the trunk of a huge cedar tree and then put the empty pipe in his vest. Next he reached into a pocket and took out a piece of blue cloth and tied it loosely around one end of his staff.

Michael watched him, exasperated.

"Just watch," Tracker said as he pointed to an enormous blue-grey goshawk perched high in one of the tallest trees. Tracker then put two fingers to his mouth and whistled shrilly while waving the cloth high in the air above his head. With a loud scream the hawk launched itself right at them, talons extended. Michael reflexively ducked, but when he raised his head back up, the bird had already grabbed Tracker's cloth and was gone.

"Just a quick message to the king," Tracker said. Then his brow furrowed, "Now, I know you'd like to talk, but time's a-wasting, and there's the gathering, and we have to get Waz and pick up supplies—"

But, Michael had stopped listening. "King? A message to the king!" His patience was finally gone. "OK, OK," he said, grabbing Tracker's shoulders. "I don't care about all that. You said you'd explain, remember? So, give me something. Anything! I mean, what was that back there?" He gestured backwards with his head. "Was that the leak you were talking about? And, do you really expect me to follow you, a complete stranger, into god-knows-what-or-where, just like that? ***AND HAVE YOU SEEN MY FATHER?***"

Tracker was startled. Not so much by the outburst, but because the boy's grip was so strong. "Okaaaaaay …" he said slowly. Then he scrunched his face as if about to do something unpleasant. "But first off, lad," he said as he dipped and dislodged Michael's hands from his shoulders, "***NEVER MANHANDLE A SERVANT OF THE KING!***"

In an instant Michael was flat on his back and the sky was spinning. "What the …?" Tracker's face appeared above him like a craggy shape in a kaleidoscope.

"Sorry," Tracker said, offering a hand. He pulled Michael to his feet and helped brush leaves and dirt from his clothes. "I believe some lessons are better learned with a bump or two, and there are rules and customs you must learn rather quickly if you're going to survive in Tremora. Understood?"

Michael nodded slowly while fingering dirt from his ears. Though not hurt, he was keenly aware that he had just been knocked to the ground by someone half his size and many times his age and wasn't quite sure how that happened. He didn't even see Tracker move, and the next thing … *I'm going to have to learn how to do that*, he told himself.

Tracker was talking. "I've been sent by King William and Megan to find you and bring you to the wizard's gathering at Mesmer Henge. That's it Michael. Those are my orders. I can't give you any information at all about your father—or much else, for that matter." He gave Michael a questioning look to make sure he was following. "From now on, you need to trust me and follow me or you may never see your home again. I'm sorry to be so short, but there is a missing prince, a kingdom in peril, and lives may depend on us. And, as to Megan, he is a wizard and a magician. In fact he is the most famous and powerful wizard in the entire world. He is the Magus of the Age of Secrets!"

"What? No, wait!" Michael held out both hands (carefully this time) and shook his head in confusion. "*Now* what are you talking about? Lives may depend on us? Princes, kingdoms, wizards!" He became increasingly incredulous as each revelation sunk in. "And the king has sent for me?"

Tracker nodded. "Yes, Michael, the *High* King. He is also known as the Augur King because he is a great seer. But these things are really best left to ..."

Tracker stopped. A movement caught his eye. A girl was rapidly approaching along the path and was using that strange gait that power-walkers use when their feet never really leave the ground yet are moving at a very fast pace.

"Hallo!" Tracker called out. It didn't seem necessary that he indicate their whereabouts, however, as the walker was already coming directly toward them.

Tracker grabbed Michael's arm. "Listen up," he whispered. "It's a king's messenger. His majesty must have had a vision. Don't talk to this girl unless spoken to, but don't hesitate to answer any of her questions either. She likely carries something very important."

The messenger stopped abruptly in front of them, and Michael studied the new arrival. She was very tiny in stature (even shorter than Tracker), slightly hunched over, green skinned, and had short severely bowed legs. Up close she wasn't nearly as young as she had first appeared. She was dressed in a leather jerkin and carried a bow and two quivers on her back. In addition to arrows, the quivers held two rolled parchments. The girl's brow was creased, and her expression was one of puzzlement and suspicion. She gestured at Tracker.

"Greetings, messenger," Tracker said, bowing low as he did when he first encountered Michael. "Can you illuminate our way?"

Without acknowledging Tracker at all, the girl looked at Michael. "Are you a boundary traveler, boy?" Her voice was very low and gruff.

"Well, err; I don't know what you mean. What's a boundary traveler?" Michael asked. At the same time, he couldn't help but grimace. The messenger's breath smelled like compost. He also now thought the girl had the ugliest face he'd ever seen. He looked to Tracker, bewildered.

The messenger also turned to Tracker. "And you're a Mazalon Warrior!" She was incredulous. "Who are you *really*, old man?" she demanded. "And where are you going with this boy? What's your business?"

Tracker's demeanor immediately changed. He crouched low and took a slow, deliberate step backwards, while motioning for Michael to do the same. His face was as fierce as a cornered animal. He pointed his staff at the girl. "That's hardly a proper greeting for a messenger of the king. What's your purpose in accosting us? And be quick, or you'll soon find out that this old man's business is about you," he growled.

The girl looked startled. Then she held up her hands and also stepped back. She obviously didn't want any part of Tracker now that she saw he wasn't intimidated and, indeed, just might be a warrior after all.

She wasn't the only one surprised at Tracker. Michael's mind flashed to his recent take-down at the hands of this little man. *What happened to the kind, friendly, little old green guy who spent his time tracking fleas? And the messenger just called him a warrior?*

"OK, don't get excited," the messenger mumbled, still showing attitude. "I needed to make sure I had the right pair of travelers, that's all." She stood up straight, adjusted her garments, and shook her head to untangle her curls. Then she bowed her head so her face was mostly hidden, and Michael got the distinct impression she was trying to avoid eye contact. "My job is to deliver important messages to you both," she said as she very carefully removed the two rolled parchments from her quivers. "With your permission ..."

She stretched out her arms, still keeping her head down, and gave them each a scroll. Michael noticed that her hands were old and wrinkled and the knuckles were covered with hair.

"The king desires to communicate with you both," she said. Then, as if reciting from memory and in a great hurry lest she forget her lines, "Umm, my name is Tralana, and I am a messenger of High King William. I am to deliver these messages to a Mazalon Warrior known as Tracker and a boundary traveler named Michael, who are traveling to Mesmer Henge. That's you two, right? And you are going to Mesmer Henge aren't you?" She barely raised her head to look from one to the other.

Neither said a word.

She smiled grimly. "Well, never mind. Keep your secrets if you must. But I'm sure you're the ones. Although you seem old for a warrior," she added, looking at Tracker.

Tracker growled.

"OK, OK, sorry." She pointed at the scrolls. "Don't open those until I'm gone. The future of Tremora may depend on what they reveal." With that she turned and disappeared into the trees. She couldn't get away fast enough.

"Now that was very strange," Tracker said. "No signing … confrontational …" He stared long and hard after the messenger while Michael examined the parchment in his hands, turning it on its end, looking through it lengthwise as if it was a telescope.

"What was that all about, Tracker?" Michael asked. "Was that really a messenger of the king? And why was he dressed up like a girl?"

Tracker abruptly returned from his pondering. "What was that you say? You saw a man?"

"Well, yes, only not really a man, kind of man-like, you know, and he was pretending to be a girl, kind of, and talking but not really, like a ventriloquist's dummy sort of … Sorry, but none of it seems very clear now, kind of like a dream where trying to remember only makes it harder to remember." Michael became silent.

Tracker looked at him as if seeing him for the first time. "Well done, Michael!" he exclaimed, slapping him on the back. "You've just confirmed my suspicions: A shape-changer!" Then thoughtfully,

"And you weren't fooled at all. Yet I only saw a young girl the whole time ..." Tracker considered this fact for a long moment. Finally, he pointed at the scroll in Michael's hand. "If you don't mind, I think I'd better take that. It could be dangerous."

He took both parchments and tucked them carefully away in his backpack. "No, that was no messenger of the High King, Michael. That was an imposter. They are called shape-changers. I'm guessing these scrolls aren't what they appear to be either. Overall, a very poor attempt at deceit, I'd say. The enemy has been careless in its haste to find and waylay you."

"Enemy? What enemy? How can I have enemies?"

"I'm afraid you do, indeed, have enemies. The king's enemies are *your* enemies, and they are already on your trail. Now, we really must hurry. Your presence in Tremora was supposed to be secret. I fear the worst: There's been espionage in the king's court." Tracker turned and hurried off again down the path with Michael following.

"Well, the good news is you're not easily fooled," Tracker said over his shoulder as he quickened his pace. "The bad news is, as I said, your presence in Tremora is obviously no secret, and since we never mentioned Mesmer Henge, our destination doesn't seem to be much of a secret either. I need to get this news to the king and Megan right away!"

✠

The shape-changer sat straddling a branch high up in a big leaf maple tree as Tracker and Michael passed by beneath him. He was seething. Earlier, he'd watched helplessly as the two had set off down the trail without opening their scrolls. *They had to have been on to me*, he thought. *It was that dratted boy—he saw right through me.* He waited till they were out of earshot, then pulled out a small piece of parchment and a pen and inkpot, and wrote a hurried note:

The boy is here.
Plans 1 and 2 have failed.
I go to Bearcamp.
Malif will take care of them at the fords.

He tied the message to the leg of a large crow perched by his head and sent it flying. He then motioned to a wisp that was also hiding in the branches and leaves of an adjoining tree. They both descended.

The shape-changer whispered, “Listen, Malif; all is not lost, but we must re-think our plans. Get some help and wait for these two at the fords. You can’t do this alone, but you must keep them from crossing into Havenland at all costs. Otherwise, it’ll be your head. Your task is simple: Kill the old one and capture the boy. Rest assured you’ll be well rewarded. I’ll be waiting at Bearcamp in the tent of Kalib.”

“What? I do not have the skills of an assassin,” hissed the black hooded figure angrily. “I was sent to assist *you!*”

“Were you not watching, you fool!” screamed the shape-changer. “They didn’t fall for the ruse!” His face contorted and turned beet red. “It should have been easy—the powder in the parchments would have knocked them out, and then—” He spat on the ground and leapt up and down crazily. Then he kicked up dirt and only stopped when he was completely out of breath. He stood bent over, panting, bracing himself against a tree with one arm. Slobber drooled down his chin and onto the ground. He was a frightful sight; part girl, part something reptilian and hideous.

Malif wasn’t impressed. He’d seen it all before. He waited.

The tantrum was over. When the shape-changer was again in control, he straightened up and continued on as if nothing had ever happened. Using a persuasive voice, he said, “Besides, Malif, it’s still just an old man and a boy. And I have urgent business with the merchant that cannot wait. If you question me, you question our master. Is that your intention?”

There was an unintelligible snarl but no further comment.

“Good,” the shape-changer growled in return. “Then those are your orders. Now, go!”

The wisp gathered its cape, turned defiantly, and climbed again to the treetops. Once there, it moved off effortlessly through the canopy, appearing as nothing more than a fleeting shadow.

The shape-changer watched the wisp disappear. Then, satisfied, he quickly bound off and also vanished into the dense forest.

Chapter Three

Of Wazalops and a Little Fenn

Tracker and Michael hiked several hours through the heavy woods without further incident or much conversation. Michael's ability to jump higher and run faster was already becoming second nature. At first, he tried to get Tracker to talk about enemies or the shimmering or the fact that the shape-changer called him a warrior.

"Mazalon Warriors are a race of men who have served the kings of Tremora for all of history. I am fortunate to be one." Tracker didn't elaborate further. As to any other questions Michael asked, "All will be revealed," was his constant reply.

Michael then tried to concentrate on what he had learned so far on his adventure, but in the end, there were just too many distractions. He had spent a lot of his childhood tromping through and exploring the forests of the Pacific Northwest, and he always carried the Audubon books his father had bought him. He could identify most of the myriad trees, plants, animals, and insects he encountered by the time he was ten years old. But being familiar with the ecology of old growth forests in Washington didn't quite prepare him for the woods of Tremora. The trees were enormous, far larger even than the giant redwoods of northern California. As he walked, his head turned side to side, hardly believing the wonders of his new surroundings. He constantly stopped to turn a leaf, smell a blossom, or look up at the towering canopy of giant trees, exclaiming at their majesty or at the sight of a new creature jumping limb to limb. One in particular looked like a huge bat. But rather than flying, it moved tree to tree in a blur, swinging hand to hand from limbs and vines or racing along branches almost faster than the eye could see. *There's a virtual highway up there*, he thought.

They came upon a cluster of giant mushrooms with yellow-green caps the size of seat cushions. Michael was again reminded of his father. His dad often accompanied him on his hikes and was careful to show him the plants that were edible and those that weren't, saying, "You never know, Michael, when you might be forced to eat something picked in the wild for your dinner, but you don't want to die from it!" When it came to wild mushrooms, the advice was simple: If you don't know it's edible, don't eat it. It didn't help that wild mushrooms were especially tricky to identify. Michael was sure he wouldn't want to eat the ones he was looking at though; they looked suspiciously like death caps, a particularly poisonous kind of mushroom that humans needed to avoid, and they smelled awful.

Tracker swerved far wide of the group of toadstools and crossed his pointing fingers in the universal sign of danger.

Michael smiled. His father would have been proud of him. But then he became somber. *And what about my father?* His initial euphoria was now replaced with doubt. Did his mother actually say his father was alive—or that he was even in Tremora? Was it wishful thinking? Did he have his hopes up for nothing? Tracker was no help. Michael stayed lost in thought for some time, but eventually, his senses brought him back to the adventure at hand.

The going was pleasant, though a little close, and it was obviously early spring in Tremora. The forest was alive with new growth, the sounds of insects, spots of sunshine, and earthy smells. The path they were following wound its way gently up at times, but mostly down, loosely following the meandering of a mountain stream that occasionally crossed their way, requiring jumping from rock to rock or wading knee deep through icy water. Michael laughed as he leapt across gaps that would have been impossible back home. But the novelty soon wore off, and after several hours of hiking without a break, he looked forward to making camp.

Tracker must have been of the same frame of mind because, even though the sun was still an hour from setting, he stopped and said it was time to rest for the night.

Around the early evening campfire, as they chewed on food from their backpacks, Tracker said, "We'll be keeping watch at night from here on in. That shape-changer will surely report our whereabouts and—"

"Report to who, Tracker?"

"An enemy that is both elusive and cunning. For now, suffice to say there are sure to be other spies afield and we must avoid them if we can. You'll learn more about these things at the gathering."

Michael gave him a withering look.

"Sorry, Michael, but I have my orders. Now, by chance, have you ever ridden a camelop?"

Michael stopped with an energy bar half way to his mouth. "I don't even know what a camelop is," he said, still irritated. He then finished the bar off and took a swig from his water bottle. As he brushed his hands on his pants to get rid of the crumbs he asked, "Is it anything like a camel? Because if it is, I've read that riding a camel is pretty uncomfortable. I've seen them at the zoo and heard a lot of people get seasick if they ride them for very long. Why?"

"We're going to cross the Asyr Desert after visiting the wazalops, and you most certainly won't be able to walk in all that sand and heat. We'll be securing you a camelop at Bearcamp, and it would have been better had you some experience 'in the saddle,' as they say."

Michael sat quiet for a long time. Tracker wasn't answering many direct questions, but either by design or carelessness, information *was* coming. If he could just keep Tracker talking … He took a stab. "OK, I'm getting the message about your orders, but still, there must be *some* things you can tell me? And maybe a favor?"

"Perhaps …"

First a little flattery. "Tracker, would you show me that move you used back there? It was amazing. I actually did a little wrestling in school, but I've never been thrown like that! And, er, what's a fortnight anyway and what's a wazalop?"

To Michael's surprise, Tracker nodded his head, "Yes, yes, of course. In fact, I'll be teaching you a lot of self defense—and maybe even show you how to use that staff of yours as a weapon—and that knife, too! Now, as to your questions …" He paused. "The first one is easy: A fortnight is two weeks, of course. However, as to wazalops, well, that will take a little longer. It's a rather lengthy story. Perhaps you're too tired?"

"Oh please," Michael said. He wasn't going to pass up a chance to hear more about Tremora. "With all of the excitement of today, do you think I'm going to go to sleep any time soon?"

Tracker smiled and gave a grudging grunt as he put more wood on the fire. He threw Michael an extra blanket from his backpack.

"Thanks," Michael said, gratefully. He'd noticed the temperature had been dropping pretty fast with the setting of the sun, even with the heat of the campfire. He took off his boots, propped himself against his own backpack, wrapped himself in the blanket, and then looked at the old man expectantly.

Tracker removed his pipe from his vest. "It's interesting that you asked about the wazalops, Michael," he said as he sat down cross-legged on his own blanket. "Megan wanted me to tell you their story before the gathering and also, just as important, something of the legend of Fenn. I was only waiting for the opportunity."

Tracker carefully filled his pipe with a tobacco that smelled like apple, tamped it down, lit it, and puffed contentedly before continuing. "What I tell you next is a closely guarded secret, and has been for hundreds of years. It will be your first secret in this Age of Secrets, Michael. You must keep it safe.

"Wazalops live in the foothills of the majestic Seven Sage Mountains that circle the top of the world. They live in a country called Fenn, named after a young shepherd girl who once saved them from certain death. Their home was originally called Farland and was famous for heavy garments made from the wool of llamas and the thick shaggy hair of highland cattle. Merchants once made the trek to Farland each summer to barter for its valuable clothing and bolts of fine cloth. Today, however, only decaying ruins and overgrown cobbled roads remain of the once prosperous kingdom. Wizards renamed the country Fennland at the beginning of the Age of Secrets, and for reasons that will soon become evident, the entire region is now protected by a wizard's spell.

"So, what are wazalops you ask? Well, at first glance they appear to be nothing more than miniature sheep. They are tiny grazing animals, most no larger than a child's kickball, covered with a remarkable coat of thick woolly hair. The density of their coats is so thick they can bob along on a body of water like a cork and never feel the wet or cold. And the colors of their coats span the rainbow. Each family, and there are many families, has its own distinct hue. Garments made from wazalop wool were even said to be fireproof! Unfortunately, it was these remarkable qualities that nearly caused the creature's demise.

"In the halcyon days of Farland, wazalops were raised and bred to clothe Tremora's royalty. Their wool was never used for the common garment trade like that of the llamas or the course hair of the cattle: It was too rare and valuable. Its popularity with the ruling families of Tremora brought great profits, and all of Farland's citizens prospered.

"However, over time, demand for the colorful garments far exceeded supply. Greedy merchants snatched up entire inventories and clamored for more. Wazalop wool was more valuable than gold! In response, Farland shepherds and farmers tried to increase the yield of each tiny animal through experiments, like selective breeding and such. The tragic result was that, through their ignorance, they bred out the entire species' ability to survive being sheared. There came a time when a wazalop actually had to die to give up its prize!"

Tracker got up, put more wood on the fire, and checked that Michael was still listening. He needn't have worried. Michael was wide awake, and the fire reflected in his eyes.

"I'm still here *and* awake, Tracker," he said, smiling.

Tracker returned to his comfortable pose. "When the last of the wazalops were about to be sacrificed for a prince's cloak, Fenn performed a daring rescue and whisked the condemned creatures off to the highlands. Their whereabouts were never revealed, and legend has it that the wazalops went the way of the dodolop bird: They were never again seen by the people of Farland.

"But as you've probably guessed, this was not exactly true. After Fenn hid the wazalops in the mountains, the animals adapted quite well under her protective eye: They quickly became feral and multiplied prolifically. Fenn watched in fascination as each season brought new revelations about her little friends.

"One of her first discoveries was how the wazalops get their amazing colors. Wazalops eat a tundra-like mixture of plants, collectively called svelten. Svelten is found above the frost line and is made up of three leafy plants: red venegard, blue trefin, and yellow mendolin. Wazalops rip it up and chew it as cud. But she noticed that they didn't eat everything in sight as they grazed; rather, they selected and ate specific amounts of each plant as if mixing paint on a palette. Then they would spit their cud into their tiny paws until the mixture exactly matched their family colors before swallowing."

"That makes sense, Tracker," Michael said. "Svelten has the three primary colors in it, right? All the colors of the rainbow can be mixed if you start with those."

"Exactly. Fenn also found that wazalops were not as helpless as they first appear. They had a very effective method of protecting themselves. At the first sign of danger, the wazalops would jump and bounce wildly around, never landing in one spot for more than an instant before taking off again. In no time they were widely dispersed, and a would-be hunter or predator was left with no prey in sight."

"Like colored ping-pong balls in a bingo machine," Michael said, sleepily.

Tracker looked at him curiously. "If you say so."

"Sorry, Tracker. It was such a vivid image. Something from my world … Please, go on. I won't interrupt again, promise." He yawned.

"At least you're still awake," said Tracker, gesturing with his pipe. "But you're obviously fading. I'll just finish up, and then you can get a good night's sleep." He gathered his thoughts and continued. "During the first lambing season, Fenn discovered another of the wazalop's secrets: There was another type of wazalop, one she had never seen before. And they were real ugly ducklings. The other animals, however, welcomed the first one of them born with great enthusiasm. Once Fenn discovered the new wazalops' functions and importance, she named them *sentry-herders*, and they soon became her favorites. Mine also, I might add, as you will someday see.

"Sentry-herders are incapable of surviving captivity and are never born outside the highlands, which is why Fenn had never seen one before. They are very intelligent and develop quite differently from their brothers and sisters. They are much bigger and stand upright on long spindly hind legs, which they use to constantly circle the highlands and leap in the air to get a view of the surrounding land. And all of their senses are highly efficient. They spend most of their time with their larger ear aimed away from the flock and nose elevated, listening and smelling for the slightest sign of danger. Their eyesight is particularly sharp. They can easily pick out an unusual movement miles away.

"But protection is not their only function. If a small wazalop becomes frightened or falls ill, a sentry-herder soothes the animal and any others nearby by making a melodic twirling sound with its mouth and lips. Often this wazalop-lullaby permeates the entire highlands as other sentry-herders join in the chorus. This ability to ease pain and anxiety is part of a large arsenal of magical gifts that sentry-herders have at their disposal. They are slightly stooped over and have large hands shaped like paddles that are used to urge and push their small charges back to safety.

"Now, Michael, we come to the most amazing part of the wazalop's story and the reason the wizards protect them so fiercely. It has to do with another secret Fenn discovered quite by accident. Are you up for just a little more?"

"Yes, of course," Michael said with another yawn. He rolled on his side and faced Tracker.

"Well, one of Fenn's favorite pastimes was watching the wazalops from high on a hill and musing aloud about her life and dreams as if confiding in her closest friend. As the flocks grew steadily each year, she noticed an intriguing effect: The combined movements of the different families through the meadows made the countryside come alive with swirling colors and shapes. Like a constantly changing finger-painting, it was quite spectacular. Similar to watching large puffy clouds become fantastic animals and sailing ships, she spent many hours watching the swirling canvas from her lofty overlook.

"On one such occasion, Fenn was agitated as she gazed down on the meadows. 'Surely, saving the lives of the wazalops was not the only reason I was called to this world,' she lamented. She—"

"Wait a minute, Tracker!" Michael sat up on one elbow. "Are you saying Fenn wasn't from Tremora, either? Was she a boundary traveler or something, like me?"

Tracker gave Michael a long thoughtful look. "We don't have time for the story of the wazalops *and* Fenn, but, yes, that is what legend tells us. Her story would fill a large tome, and it's for another time. You'll just have to be patient. Shall I continue?" Tracker chided.

"Sorry," Michael said softly. He lay back, but his mind was racing. *What isn't he telling me now?*

"All right then, as I was saying. One day, Fenn was looking down on the wazalops from afar and talking out loud. Rumors of an impending war with the Giants and Trolls hung heavy in the air in Farland. She had grown into a strong young lady, and she wanted to fight! At the behest of a wizard friend, she'd been training secretly and had already mastered the sword and lance and could ride any animal with skill. And she was apparently just as strong as any man. But still, few looked on her as anything but a shepherd girl; hardly a candidate for going to battle. She stomped her foot in frustration.

"It was then that a motion below caught her eye. A sentry-herder was guiding a wayward group of dark red wazalops up a long crooked path towards the meadow. As the animals joined the main herd the swirling colors and shapes of the animals started to shift and form into a startling image. Similar to the tapestries on the walls of the castle, a stylized vision of battle emerged. The main warrior was an armored woman with long flowing blond hair riding a white horse, sword raised in defiance. A warm feeling engulfed her, and she knew with certainty that the image was of her.

"Indeed, Michael. Fenn's deeds and skills as a field commander in the battle of the Trolls and Giants are legendary. When you hear the full story of Fenn, you will hear the story of a true heroine. She fought alongside the bravest of Farland warriors, and had an uncanny knack for anticipating the enemies' every tactic and strategy. Could it have been her secret trips to the highlands that helped her? The wizards think so.

"After the war, Fenn returned triumphantly to the people of Farland. They even made her an honorary queen. She was very popular and became an important member of the royal court. Over time, her visits to the highlands necessarily became more infrequent. She still mounted her horse and rode alone to visit the wazalops but often only had time to watch them from afar for a few precious moments before returning to the castle. Even so, armed with these brief visions, Fenn influenced the prosperity of Farland for many years.

"And now, to answer *part* of your question, Michael, and to bring our story to an end," Tracker said kindly. "We know Fenn really existed in the Age of Conflict, but like those of most heroes and heroines, her exploits have been retold so many times they have become more legend than fact. And part of her mystique is no one really knows where she came from or where she went when she disappeared from Farland forever; no one but the wizards, that is. And it is this part of her story I have been given the freedom to reveal to you. On her last visit to the highlands, Fenn was met by her wizard friend who showed her the way back to where she came from. And yes, she did come through a shimmering veil just like you. But, even to her final days in Farland, Fenn never revealed to anyone except the wizard the secret of the wazalops—or the fact that she herself was of another world."

Tracker stood up and again tended to the fire. He pulled Michael's blanket up tighter and Michael rolled over on his back and smiled up at him. "Thanks," he mumbled. An instant later Michael was asleep.

"The end of your first day in Tremora," Tracker said, quietly. He sat back down, relit his pipe and wrapped his blanket around him. Then he looked at Michael curiously. The boy was very young; much younger than Tracker thought he would be. Yet his strength had surprised him. And no matter how fast Tracker walked or ran on the trails, Michael easily kept up with him.

I wonder how many other surprises you have in store for me? Tracker thought as he puffed on his pipe. *Well, no matter. You'll need all your faculties, and more, before this adventure is over, I'm sure.* Then Tracker pulled his blanket tighter and scooched closer to the fire. A long night was in front of him, and he wasn't going to get any sleep. He was under king's orders: He would be keeping a close and careful watch over Tremora's new visitor until they reached Mesmer Henge.

Chapter Four

Tralana

Early the next morning, just before daybreak, Tracker nudged Michael with his staff. Coffee was steaming, and a type of gruel that didn't taste much like porridge was cooking on the campfire. Michael's head was full of wool, but it wasn't from dreaming of wazalops. He wasn't happy that he was yanked to the surface from such a deep sleep. He was sure that if he could have dreamt just a little longer, Fenn would have given him an important clue about his father. But, by the time he'd opened his eyes and remembered where he was, even the memory of why he was angry was completely gone. He was in Tremora! And there was Tracker … and, yep, he was green.

While eating breakfast, Michael thought about the story of Fenn and the wazalops and asked, "Do you think Fenn was from my world, Tracker?"

"So, you were still awake at the end?"

"Mmm, I think so. I remember that she kept a secret."

"Yes, she kept the secret of the wazalops and the fact that she was from another world to herself. Only the wizards know the full story. Maybe Megan will shed some light. But for now, enough questions!" The old Tracker was back. "We must be off," he said, gruffly.

Michael had no time for disappointment, though. The excitement of the adventure overtook him, and he leapt to his feet. But he immediately found himself sprawled on the ground with a mouth full of wet ashes (fortunately, Tracker had doused the campfire with water).

Tracker stopped what he was doing and looked at Michael curiously.

Michael raised his head. "Oops, forgot about that," he said, sheepishly. He then slowly got up, brushed himself off and spit and wiped the dirt from his mouth. "I can't explain it," he said, shaking his head. "Other than, I think I must weigh less here in Tremora than at home. I mean, everything I do is kind of easier." He shrugged his shoulders.

Tracker looked thoughtful. "I think you also might be a lot stronger than you think," he said, remembering Michael's grip on his shoulder. "Well, be careful Michael. Some of these cliffs are pretty high, and if you trip and fall off one of them, in spite of your feeling so light on your feet, you probably can't fly."

Michael laughed and started gathering his things. "I'll try and remember that."

They broke camp and set out at first light.

After a couple of hours, Michael began talking about his father's disappearance and seeing his mother beyond the shimmering veil. Tracker listened intently, but when asked what his thoughts were, he was again strangely curt. "You were right to choose to stay in Tremora," he snapped. Michael gave up and continued on, alone with his thoughts.

By mid morning, the going was more difficult as the path plunged steeply. The sun beat on their heads, and the air was thick with insects that Michael kept swatting to no avail. Tracker stopped and removed something from his backpack. It looked like a small section of bamboo that had a stopper in both ends. "This should keep the skeeters away," he said, as he handed Michael the makeshift medicine bottle. "Use only a little on your exposed skin and try not to get any in your eyes."

As Michael removed the cork a pungent odor that could only be described as *overpowering* filled the air. Holding the container at arm's length Michael dipped a finger into the slime-green salve and carefully dabbed some on his cheeks. Insects dropped from the air all around him.

"See, it works! And it's my very own concoction," cried Tracker in delight. "It's called Bonzo Bugger Gook. A Mazalon Tracker of course has no use for such protection, but most people do. This will come in handy when bartering in the market at Bearcamp. But you have to be careful with it, Michael. Once you've put this on, no one will want to come near you, and there's always the chance you could go blind."

But Tracker had a smile on his face, and Michael was sure the unction was quite safe.

They were making slow headway through thick underbrush and brambles when they suddenly emerged from the thicket to a breathtaking view. "You're looking at the country of Charn," Tracker said, sweeping his staff from side to side. The flat land spread out as far as the eye could see in a patchwork of bright colors. "Daffodops and tulipops," explained Tracker. "A wonderful time of year to cross Charn. And there to the north you can just make out the islands of Havenland and Bearcamp, our next destination. We should arrive at the fords sometime late tomorrow afternoon."

Later, they found themselves on a narrow rock-strewn path that turned sharply left and downward, hugging the contours of a large wall of granite. A sheer drop-off of dizzying height lay to the right as they slowly descended the cliff face. At times, Michael had to inch sideways with arms spread wide, facing inwards, feeling the rock face for balance. Once, while spread eagle against the wall, a small hummingbird hovered a few inches from his face and studied him intently.

When Michael brought this to Tracker's attention, he wasn't pleased. "It might have just been a curious bird or perhaps it was protecting its nest. Maybe we disturbed its area. But these types of birds also make excellent spies. The sooner we get off this exposed rock face the better."

After a couple of hours they reached the bottom of the cliff, and the going became much easier. They soon found themselves hiking along a well-traveled country road, bordered by the huge tracts of the brilliantly colored flowers they had seen from the mountain. The red, yellow, purple, and white squares looked like a vast multicolored carpet. The fields were dotted with stooped-over workers in straw hats harvesting the flowers for market. The air was full of song as the pickers filled waiting wagons with tied bundles of color. In the distance Michael caught sight of the occasional thatched-roofed farmhouse, snuggled comfortably beneath a whirling windmill or cluster of shade trees. It reminded Michael of the tulip fields of Skagit Valley back home.

Tracker was just discussing plans for dinner at a local inn when he stopped abruptly in the middle of the road. In the distance another king's messenger was rapidly approaching.

"Quick Michael, tell me what you see."

"A young *and pretty* girl is coming toward us, walking in that same strange way we saw before. She's green just like you and a bird is flying along with her," he said, tenting his eyes with both hands.

"Ahh. Now hold your tongue, Michael, and we'll see what *this* visitor brings us."

"Greetings, travelers!" hailed the young girl as she rushed up to meet them. "I am Tralana, and I have urgent messages from the king." The bird landed lightly on her shoulder. It looked exactly like the one that had studied Michael on the cliff.

"Tralana?" Tracker said. "That's strange. We just met a messenger named Tralana and have already received scrolls from the king. Are you saying there are more missives and that all of you messengers are named Tralana?"

The girl looked astonished. Then she glared angrily from one to the other of them and then back at Tracker. "There is no other Tralana," she hissed. "Quickly, you fool. When and where did you meet this imposter?" The bird leapt up excitedly and hovered above her head.

Tracker stood silent for several moments. "I would not be judged so quickly," he said in a measured tone.

Tralana stamped her foot in anger. "Surely you are a Mazalon Warrior. You've received messages from the king before. You know the signing, the greeting … How could you be fooled by such an obvious trick?"

"I've already warned you not to judge too quickly," Tracker answered. He was fairly certain they were in the presence of a real messenger of the king now but remained cautious. Besides, he thought she was over reacting just a little. "Indeed, it *was* an imposter that we met on the mountain top yesterday. We were not fooled then, and we won't be fooled now. How do we know you are who *you* claim to be?"

The messenger suddenly went for her knife, and Tracker quickly raised his staff. Michael leapt between them. "Good grief, hold on a minute. It's okay Tracker. It's just a girl!"

The messenger looked at Michael, startled. So did Tracker.

Seeing that both were now staring at him, Michael stammered, "This is definitely not a man, err I mean, not a man dressed as a girl. She's just a girl, I mean a *real* girl that is … err …" Michael's face turned red, and he suddenly found his shoes immensely interesting.

Tralana slowly re-sheathed her knife and adjusted her bow and quiver without taking her eyes off of Michael. The tension in the air was replaced by a palatable awkwardness.

Finally Tracker had had enough. He stepped back and bowed. "Tralana, please accept our apologies. Let's start over shall we? You can't blame us for being wary. We were approached yesterday by someone who was also claiming to be a king's messenger; claiming to be you, in fact. I'm sure it was a shape-changer. Its powers were somewhat muted though, and its disguise was pretty transparent. The king's wishes should be our first concern now, don't you think?" He took another abbreviated bow. "Greetings anew, Tralana. My name is Tracker and this is Michael. Can you illuminate our way?" He straightened and looked at her expectantly.

Tralana stood arms akimbo, and the bird returned to her shoulder. She did not answer immediately. Perhaps it was her training, or her personality, but she was not quite so quick to forgive and forget. "Yes, I suppose you are correct, but a king's messenger should never be treated in this way. And it's troubling to think there is an imposter out there pretending to be me."

"I, too, am a servant of the king, Tralana," Tracker reminded.

She turned slightly pink. "Of course," she said. But her anger lingered. She straightened and crossed here arms. "Well, I'm glad to see I passed *your* test," she said, giving Michael a withering look. "And to be cautious in these times *is* proper and wise. But I warn you, this messenger is much more than *just a girl!*" She stood as tall as she could and again grasped the hilt of her small dagger. "I am a special servant of King William and have been sent to deliver his personal messages to you both." She then stepped back and, with a sweep of her arm, bowed.

She straightened up and looked at Michael again. "I must confess. I've never met a boundary traveler before. I was expecting something more, I think …"

Michael blushed and uttered something unintelligible. Tracker started to interject, but Tralana held up her hand to stop him. "I'm sorry. That was uncalled for. You might just say it was a little test of my own." She then smiled sweetly at them both and addressed Michael.

"Welcome to Tremora, traveler. As you've already learned, it's extremely important to determine a person's true identity in these troubled times. I won't ask your mother's maiden name or what town you were born in or your favorite pet even. After all, you might not know who your *real* mother is; therefore, you wouldn't know where you were *really* born, and a ferret doesn't actually count as a pet, now does it?"

Michael's eyes went wide. "Of course I know who my real mother is! She's Ria Tull. She's right back there in the cabin where I was born," he said waving behind him, "and I have a *dog* named Bandit, not a ferret, and …" But the messenger was no longer listening. Michael glared defiantly at her, then at Tracker, but the two were exchanging their own looks.

"You have a lot of work to do with your young cub," the messenger said smugly.

Tracker turned a darker shade of green. "Now, you know darn well that a traveler has to answer your questions in order to receive a king's message."

"Ah, but I haven't even asked the first question, now, have I?" She scolded. She then inclined her head slightly toward Michael and added with a voice as silky as a lord's kerchief, "And yet, without effort, I now know your family name, where you bode from, even that you have a favorite pet dog; information that could make your journey more difficult before it even begins."

Michael was dumfounded. *How could I be so stupid? Of course she's right. Have I put my mother in danger?* An uncomfortable silence ensued. Michael looked at Tracker, finally following his warning to talk only when spoken to.

Tralana seemed at last to be appeased. She softened. "It's OK, Michael," she said. "There was no real harm done. You've just arrived, you're very young, and fortunately you don't yet know anything of importance." She held up her hand to stop Michael from responding angrily. "But you must be careful from this moment on. Be less forward and heed your guide's warnings at all times. There are many secrets and dangers in the land of Tremora."

The messenger shifted her attention to Tracker. "And now, please forgive *my* rudeness, father. I'm afraid, in haste, I called you a fool, and for that I am sorry." Tracker waved her off, and she continued. "A Mazalon Tracker is also a rare sight in this part of the world ... and without your familiar, Waz. I trust your *frenada* is vital?"

Tracker hesitated. "Quite," he said slowly. He started to ask his own question, but Tralana left no opening.

"I'm one of several messengers of the High King. It's been six days since I was sent out to find you and your traveler. You of course know the proper responses?"

"I do."

"Any untruth or hesitation on your part and my message will be left undelivered. Do you understand Fremoran Tremelan, son of Miriam and Mendelan of Gondalor, Land of the Stalwart?"

Tracker again answered slowly, "Yes."

"As you mentioned, we're both servants of the king," she said. "Knowing your given name can hardly be a surprise to you. And of course I know you have a companion named Waz. You're both quite famous, you know. However, even you must prove you are a loyal citizen of Tremora. All subjects of the Augur King have a unique air sign. Show me!"

Tracker handed his staff to Michael. Facing the girl, he slowly raised his left hand to cover his heart and swiftly completed two quick movements in the air with his right before returning both hands to his side.

The messenger also described a complicated sign in the air before her and returned both hands to her side.

For a long moment nothing happened, and then a small dot of light appeared between them that grew slowly, bathing them in a soft blue glow before disappearing in a puff of twinkling dust.

Michael stood staring at the diminutive girl and the gnarled old man before him. "What the …?"

"Shhh," Tracker warned in an aside as the odd pair bowed solemnly to each other and stepped apart.

"Well met Tremoran!" Tralana said. "Now, father, what is the purpose of your journey? Of course, it is already known to me. I only wish to confirm."

"By order of the High King, I was to meet a boundary traveler named Michael at a secret location in the mountains of Golan. I am now to pick up a camelop in Bearcamp and then travel to Fennland to reunite with Waz. Along with Michael, we will then all travel to Mesmer Henge and the wizard's gathering that begins in less than a fortnight."

Tralana nodded her head. "And so, the adventure continues," she whispered, again signing in the air in front of her.

"What I deliver to you may or may not be of consequence, but the king has had a vision," she said. "He is sharing it with you in these missives. It may affect your very lives and the lives of others or matter no more than a breeze in your hair. The Augur King is a mighty seer, but the future can never be entirely known. Follow your heart when deciding whether to heed what is written."

Michael recognized his mother's advice in Tralana's warning.

Two rolled parchments sealed with wax appeared magically in the hands of Tralana. She handed one to Tracker and one to Michael.

"As you can see, it's the king's personal seal. These are to be opened once I leave," she said. "Messengers carry the king's secrets in their quivers, not their heads. Now, keep your messages safe and remember they are purposely vague in case they get stolen or intercepted."

She then took a quill and inkpot from her pouch.

"Wait! Tralana, are you sending a note to the king?" Tracker asked.

"Yes, of course."

"The shape-changer knew more than he should about my orders. He knew I was to meet a border traveler named Michael and also knew our destination. We need to let the king and Megan know that the meeting of the wizards has been compromised."

Tralana nodded her head. "Of course." She first scribbled her own note on a piece of parchment and tied it to one of the legs of her feathered companion. Then she handed the pen and another small parchment to Tracker.

When Tracker finished, Tralana attached the new message to the fluster bird's other leg, and with a gentle nudge, it flew away. "She will deliver your news to the king and also inform him that his own messages were received as intended."

Then she smiled and waved goodbye. "We just might meet again. It should start out friendlier next time, don't you think?" She winked. "Good luck, Michael!" With that she set off across a purple field of tulipops and quickly disappeared.

Neither Tracker nor Michael said anything for several minutes; each absorbing what had just occurred. Finally, "This is getting complicated," Michael said.

Tracker looked at his scroll. "Michael, as we both told you, the High King is an oracle. He perceives the future in the form of dreams. However, as vivid as the dreams might be, their meanings are often obscured, and their events occur in no particular order. Experience has shown these visions can be of immense importance or mean nothing at all. But they always, always, involve subjects of his realm. Thus, the king relays his visions to his people through a group of specially gifted messengers like Tralana."

Michael continued to turn the parchment over in his hands. "But, I'm not a subject of the king," he said.

"It's not wise to question the ways of kings and wizards," Tracker said with a flash of impatience. "A bit of advice that should be remembered! The king can communicate with whomever he chooses, subject or not, don't you think? I'd guess the king has had a vision about our coming quest and you, of course, were involved."

"Coming quest? Is that why we are going to a wizard's gathering? A quest?"

"Ahh, yes, well … You weren't summoned for a picnic, now were you? Even you could figure that out." Tracker was angry at himself. There were secrets that were supposed to be kept until Michael met the king and wizard: It was for the boy's own protection. But it wasn't Michael's fault he had slipped up and mentioned the quest, and he felt even worse that he had snapped. "I'm sorry, Michael. But I can't reveal any more. You must understand that by now."

Michael stood silent, pensive. He decided to give up the battle—at least for the moment. "All right then, what about the air signing?" he asked. "And that strange blue light? Those aren't secrets, are they?"

Tracker gave Michael a thankful look. "No, they're not. There is no question that evil exists in our world. There are those that envy the freedom and prosperity of others or feel threatened by another's faith. These people would have us all marching lockstep or, even worse since their beliefs are non-inclusive, have us all killed. But evil's not as obvious as a name on a marquee. Long ago, the king realized he needed help in identifying friend or foe, especially when sharing his visions, a way to tell a loyal subject from his enemies. He knew that portents in the wrong hands could do incredible harm. With the help of Megan, the High King has assigned a unique magical air sign to each of his subjects. And from the very early years of every new child born in Tremora, a sign is assigned and practiced until perfected. As you saw, any citizen can confirm another true member of the kingdom by following the same sequence of signing you observed between Tralana and me. It's a very valuable gift. Loyalty to the king and love of Tremora is the only price. And if a once-loyal subject decides to walk on the dark side or show allegiance to an enemy? A poisoned heart can never create a blue flame."

Tracker then looked at Michael and his scroll. "Shall we?" He broke the seal on his own message and read it to himself, then out loud to Michael:

Congratulations on finding the boundary traveler,
Fremoran Tremelan.
He is your charge until you reach the Gathering.
His training is of utmost importance. But also know,
A second prince is in need of rescue at the Inn.
Listen for a familiar name.
Avoid bloodshed, but save the prince and return
him to his people.
Continue to protect your charge at all costs.

"Another prince? Training and bloodshed?" Michael's voice trailed off. He looked at his own message warily.

"Remember, the messages are purposely vague," Tracker said. "Now, what about yours?"

Michael broke the seal on his parchment. He read his message and then looked in bewilderment at Tracker as he handed the scroll over.

Tracker read the note intently.

Welcome to Tremora reluctant traveler!

You've chosen to stay ... you've passed your first test.

Now, know this: From now on, your journey will be fraught with danger, and you will make other choices at every turn. But, there is a purpose. All will be revealed in its own time.

This night we've had a vision.

A companion must die willingly to complete your quest. Will this life be lost for naught? Will you keep secrets in this Age of Secrets? Will you choose the prince or the worm?

Know this:

All gifts have a purpose; use them wisely.

Trust your guide and follow his directions.

And, lastly, when there is no help or hope, always follow your heart ... it is your one true beacon, for good and evil are deceptively clothed in Tremora.

"Well, Michael, there's a lot yet to be revealed it seems. Even I can't decipher most of this. But you did get the meaning of 'trust your guide and follow his direction,' didn't you? Just keep this close. I think we will be rereading these messages many times before this is over. Don't worry for now about what you cannot know."

"But, 'a companion must die,' Tracker?"

"You will have many companions on this adventure, Michael. And remember, not everything comes to pass that the king foretells. The reality might be something quite different from what you think. I'm sorry, but the advice again is: be patient. All will be revealed in its own time."

Chapter Five

PATTERSLING

They reached the tavern near dusk, and it was hopping busy. The building appeared warm and friendly with its long, low, thatched roof, smoking chimneys, and glowing stained glass windows. Adjoining stables were full of animals, and heavily loaded wagons lined both sides of the road. The smell of baked bread and grilled meat made Michael's stomach grumble.

"It's busy because everyone's on his or her way to Bearcamp," Tracker said. "I doubt we could get a room tonight even if we wanted to, but this may very well be the inn the king was talking about. We have no choice; we have to find out. We were going to eat here anyway. So, what say we get a warm meal, shall we?"

They heard the sounds of clinking glasses and voices raised in song as they swung open the carved wooden doors to the Flying Fare Inn. Once inside, they passed through a mudroom full of cloaks, hats, and overboots, and then entered a long crowded rectangular room running lengthwise left to right. The ceiling was low and crisscrossed with heavy wooden beams. A stone fireplace with all the trappings took up the entire right wall, and a well-stocked bar took up most of the left. The facing wall of yellow plaster and straw was covered with copper plates, buckles, and sundry wood and leather farm tools. Three long rows of wooden tables, all full to capacity with boisterous patrons, stretched from the bar to the fireplace.

Michael's attention was immediately drawn to a much smaller table, sitting in the far left corner of the room. It had a mounted leather hood at one end like a baby pram. Ten wooden pins stood in the hood's opening and he was reminded of a miniature bowling lane. In fact, it was a bar game called Skittles and Cheese. The "skittles" were the pins, and the "cheese" was a thick wooden disk that patrons took turns throwing to knock down the pins. It was a loud and raucous game, and more often than not, the game ended, not with the pins being bowled over but, rather, when someone was *cheesed* in the face or back of the head.

Sitting on the small table with its legs dangling over the edge was a tiny male elf with large hands and feet. One leg was shackled and chained. He had a brass and leather helmet on his head and was absently throwing a cheese up and down, catching it with various parts of his body: back of hand, top of foot, forehead … He yawned and appeared completely bored until he caught site of Michael and Tracker. Then he suddenly stood up and stretched to see over the crowd, following the pair's every move with great interest.

Barnabas, the publican and inn's owner, also saw Michael and Tracker as they entered the room. He was an enormous man, yet moved effortlessly behind the cramped bar. He was busy pulling pints from wooden casks and pouring two fingers of liquor from strangely shaped glass bottles into pewter and earthenware mugs that were lined up on the back counter in front of a large etched mirror. When he saw the two in the mirror's reflection, he reached back and held up one pudgy finger, indicating they should wait one minute. Then, with a sweep of his hand and the same pointing finger, he turned and launched his concoctions into the air and sent them flying down the rows of tables. The drinks bobbed, weaved, and slopped frothy beer and alcohol onto the tables and floor before landing in front of a group of waiting, clamoring customers.

Barnabas gave a satisfied nod and then threw a towel over his shoulder. He leaned forward with both hands on the bar and yelled over the din, "No rooms left, but there're two seats against the wall by the stairs if you're hungry." He pointed toward the far corner at the end of the third long row of tables.

Tracker gave a thumbs up.

Barnabas then reached up and rang a copper bell mounted on the ceiling over his head. "Two more, my love!" he bellowed in the direction of a Dutch door with its top half open. An answering *two bells* came from somewhere deep within the kitchen. He smiled and waved them through.

Tracker and Michael waded through the people standing at the bar and then sidled along the far wall to the right until they reached the corner where Barnabas had pointed. They found two roughly hewn chairs backed up to a heavy wooden door with leather hinges and a twisted iron handle. Over the door was a carved sign that said ROOMS with an arrow pointing upwards. It was ajar and they could see stairs leading to the second floor through the opening. They stored their backpacks and staffs beneath the table by their feet, and no sooner had they sat down than two plates with cloth napkins came whizzing through the opening in the door to the kitchen and landed in front of them, followed closely by knives, forks, spoons, and a basket of warm bread and butter.

"Saves on labor," Tracker explained to Michael as he reached for the bread. "It's the "flying" in the Flying Fare Inn!" A pint of beer and a mug of sweet mead arrived next, both sloshing liquid all over the table.

Michael laughed, broke off a chunk of bread, and spread it with a big dollop of dripping butter. He looked around the room as he chewed. It was the strangest gathering of people and creatures he had ever seen. Sitting across from him was a sour looking man who looked as if he was made of wood. His skin looked like bark, and his hands and fingers looked like branches and twigs on a tree.

The tiny elf on the skittles table jumped up and waved at Michael. Michael smiled and acknowledged him back with a hand full of bread and a nod of his head.

In the background, most of the crowd was singing bawdy limericks to a song being banged out on an old piano by a thin man in a tweed jacket. There were several verses to the catchy tune, each getting ruder as it went along. Michael didn't really understand most of the humor, but he laughed along with the crowd anyway. Suddenly, the piano player pointed at him and called out that it was the new folks' turn to rhyme. Michael shrunk down in embarrassment, but Tracker jumped up at once. Without hesitation, he heartily belted out:

> There once was a satyr from La Belle
> Who loved a trollop named Nell.
> She could contort like a pretzel,
> Which excited his wetzel,
> So he overlooked her propensity to smell!

The crowd whooped and hollered and Tracker sat back down with a pleased look on his face. "I've been to a pub or two in my time," he said in response to Michael's questioning look. "And don't go asking me what a wetzel is either," he warned. They both burst out laughing. Not long after, two bowls of stew arrived, spinning and sloshing just like their drinks, and they dug in with gusto.

The rhyming finally came to an end, and without a pause, the piano player went into a new, livelier tune. Two tiny creatures that looked like meerkats quickly jumped up and started dancing on the tables. They were fully dressed in coat and tails and wore round spectacles. Similar to cloggers, they kept their paws hanging down straight at their sides as they traversed the tabletops with their lower limbs moving in a blur. Patrons flipped coins at them like tiddlywinks, and they were very deft at catching the coins in their hats and depositing them in their pockets. The crowd loved them.

"You can bet they'll be big hits at Bearcamp, too," Tracker said.

"Bearcamp? That's where *we're* going, right?"

"Yes, and that's why we have to leave soon. The sooner we get there the better. We'll just have to look for an open field to sleep in tonight. You'll have to keep watch for the first couple of hours, though, since I didn't have any sleep at all last night. I'll have time to tell you the story of the Bearcamp races while we're setting up camp. But for now, we have to stay sharp. We have to help a prince, remember?" Tracker turned and searched the crowd but didn't see anyone familiar or princely looking.

Just then the music stopped, and wooden spoons began to beat on the copper plates mounted on the wall. Everyone looked to Barnabas who had his hands raised in the air.

"Attention, please!" he shouted. "Attention, please! For the benefit of any newcomers, I am Barnabas, and as always, I am your happy host." The crowd cheered loudly. "Tonight, I will also be your race announcer and final umpire." More enthusiastic cheers. He reached out and put his hands on the shoulders of the elf that was now standing on the bar in front of him. It was the same elf that had waved at Michael. "As you all know, our very own Skittles and Cheese tender, Pattersling, is Charn's reigning table race champion." Several people applauded, but there was a healthy spattering of jeers and boos as well. Barnabas only smiled; he was in his element.

"Once again, in the spirit of the annual Bearcamp races, we are offering an open challenge tonight to any of Pattersling's kind that thinks it can dethrone the champ. The purse is one hundred silver knops!" He held up a cloth bag of coins the size of a good-sized apple. Everyone applauded enthusiastically this time and whooped and hollered. Pattersling, as if on cue, raised both of his tiny arms like a winning prizefighter and strutted up and down the bar, beckoning for any takers to show themselves.

Barnabas looked around the room expectantly. A giant bearded man seated at the first table pushed himself to his feet, and there, sitting on his shoulder, was a near exact copy of Pattersling. The man reached up and raised the elf above his head in one hand for all to see. The elf's leather and metal helmet was painted bright yellow. "I think the Beer, Beard, and Belch just might have this year's new champion!" he declared. He then addressed the room at large with flair, "The Three Bs gives you: Strutbeam!" Four or five enthusiastic cheers went up from his table, but the rest of the patrons whistled and catcalled in good humor. Strutbeam was the perennial loser in this challenge, and few thought he had any chance of winning—ever.

Pattersling bent over at the waist, with one hand holding his belly and pointing at poor Strutbeam with the other. He then rolled up in a ball and pretended to laugh hysterically. At the same time though, his eyes were looking anxiously around the room.

Next, a lady's voice rang out over the crowd, "This year, the Heifer and Hound might make the race a little more interesting." The voice came from the middle table. Slowly, a woman, who looked quite a bit like a cow wearing a flower hat, and a man with a long rubbery face like a bloodhound, rose to their feet. The room went quiet. This was something new.

Everyone stared at the odd couple. The silence dragged on as the two just stood, looking smug. "You don't look like no elf," someone finally joked. "Maybe her husband is going to race?" someone else piped up. "No dogs allowed," another added, and people laughed.

The couple just continued smiling. Barnabas finally asked, "Well, Daisy? This isn't a beauty contest you know. Let's see what you're so proud of."

The bovine-looking lady gave Barnabas one last wide grin and then, with exaggerated fanfare, removed her hat, and there sitting on her head was a fairy, half the size of Pattersling, and it was a girl.

Pattersling's concerned look changed to relief. He quickly gathered himself and jumped to his feet. "I can beat any girl, anytime," he bragged loudly, "but she'd better not use those wings!"

Barnabas made a show of squinting at the new challenger with one hand shielding his eyes. "He's got a point there, Daisy," Barnabas said seriously. Then, he waved his arms like a bird and made his audience laugh.

"Oh, don't be such a poo poo," Daisy said indignantly. "Those wings are so small they don't even flap yet. Why, she's just a baby! Look, they're only just starting to grow." Daisy made a circling motion with her finger and looked up toward to top of her head. The girl obediently stood and put her hands above her head and turned so all could see the barely visible wings sticking out of her back.

Michael studied the tiny creature. He thought she was every bit as cute as Tralana. Also, he didn't get the impression that this was a baby at all. Her eyes were very bright and intelligent, and they swept the room intently as she performed her pirouette. Suddenly, she saw Michael, and her eyes opened wide. So did Michael's—hers in recognition and his because he heard her thoughts!

"I see them, Priam! You were right; they're here. It must be the boundary traveler and the warrior."

"*Yes, just like the king's message said.*"

Michael put out his hand and jostled Tracker's shoulder excitedly. Tracker looked at him in surprise. Without taking his eyes off the girl, Michael said, "Tracker. You won't believe this. But I can hear them, and they're talking about us. And Pattersling has another name I think."

"You can hear who ..." Tracker began to ask and then stopped. The wooden man had perked up. He was obviously trying to overhear Michael and Tracker's conversation.

"Hold on a minute, Michael," Tracker warned. "There are unfriendly ears here, and they are very close ..." He indicated the man across the table with his head. The wooden man quickly glanced away.

Meanwhile, Daisy took her hat and shooed the fairy from her head. It jumped down and landed lightly on the table. It too wore a tiny shackle on its ankle with a chain. The end was tied to Daisy's wrist. "And now," the cow lady said dramatically, "let me introduce you all to Blingtrail!" With that, the tiny girl rose high on her toes like a ballerina and performed handstands, somersaults, flips, and splits up and down the table to the delight of the crowd.

"Very well, very well," Barnabas said, using his hands to quiet everyone down. "I see no real problem with your entry, Daisy. But, it is obvious that she is not a pureblood wood elf." He turned to Pattersling. "Do you object to this little girlie, Pattersling?"

The elf put a look of scorn on his face. "Hardly!" he said. "*But little do you know, Barnabas, you great fat git. This 'girlie' is destined to be the queen of the entire elfin world!*"

Michael heard Pattersling's thoughts as if he were standing right in front of him talking out loud.

"So be it," Barnabas declared. "That makes three then. Now, are there any other comers?"

Six other patrons lifted elfin creatures above their heads to the delight of the crowd.

"Well, that makes nine! A fine turnout it is, a really fine turnout. I think we may have every elf in the whole country this year." Barnabas's face beamed. "It's exactly enough for three legs and a final! So, now, everyone make sure you stay back from the tables. No hands to help or hinder, please. Those in the end seats, please grab the copper plate on the wall nearest you marked with an x."

Michael realized he was being looked at expectantly by the wooden man. They were both seated in end chairs. The man pointed at a plate hanging on the wall behind Michael's head. Michael got up and brought it back and sat down.

"Now, hold your plates up between you and the person across from you," directed Barnabas. "Make sure you hold on steady. Don't want the racers shooting off the end of the tables into the fireplace, now do we?"

Michael and the wooden man held the large plate up between them, forming a barrier at the end of their table.

Michael looked at Tracker, wondering what was going on. Tracker just shrugged his shoulders.

Barnabas came from behind the bar with a large metal spoon and made his way slowly (and painfully from the grimacing of his face) to the end of the first table. He struck the copper plate that the end people were holding. It was the smallest of the three plates, and it resounded with a dull *plink.* "Now that's the sound of a winner at this table," he said. He then moved to the middle table. He again struck the copper plate that was being held between the two end seats. It was the middle-sized plate, and a loud *plank* reverberated around the room. "And that's the sound if the winner is from this table!" He then went to where Michael was sharing the holding duties with the bark man. Their plate was the largest. "And finally," Barnaby said, as he hit the third plate squarely with the metal spoon. A loud *plunk* filled the room. "Right. Now, there should be no problem in determining the winner of each race."

He returned to the bar.

"Based on the order of entry, Pattersling, Blingtrail, and Strutbeam will each race two challengers. First off we'll have Pattersling, Ingorsnot, and Raightlog!"

With that, three very tall men in striped pants and stovepipe hats jumped up and moved between the tables, taking bets and noting them with pencil and pad.

"These men will take care of all your wagers, and remember, although side betting is allowed, the house still gets its 20 percent," Barnabas said, sternly. The announcement was met with more grumbling than anything else, but Barnabas didn't seem to care.

Soon, all the money was collected, and the room quieted with anticipation. Pattersling and his two opponents took up starting positions at the bar end of their respective tables. Michael looked to where Pattersling was stooped over at the end of his table and noticed there were remnants of beverages and food strewn everywhere on the tabletop, making for a very slippery and treacherous surface for racing.

"Owners, please remove the restraints," Barnabas said, as he unlocked Pattersling's chain. "And, please, everyone, watch all the doors and keep an eye on these little buggers. Don't want them scampering off, now do we?" He returned to his position behind the bar.

"Ready … steady … go!" Barnaby rang the bell.

All three racers shot forward, and everyone else jumped to his or her feet. It was impossible to see all three elves at once. Michael saw Pattersling slip in a puddle of beer and land on his tiny toosh. Everyone at his table groaned in unison. But the other racers must have met similar fates out the gate because there were lots of groans and laughter and cheering and encouraging shouts from the other tables as well.

Meanwhile, Pattersling quickly leapt up, regained his footing, and dashed off down the table. He dodged a pat of butter, caromed off a wooden candlestick with a heavy pewter base, and plowed through a plate of mushrooms, sending them flying. Then, when about ten feet from Michael and the wooden man, he launched himself into the air with his hands held straight back at his sides and helmet pointing forward.

THUNK, PLINK …PLANK. All three racers finished with their helmeted heads crashing into their copper plates. It was a close race, but the sounds told the tale.

"Pattersling, first, with Raitlog a very close second," announced Barnabas. "Nice effort Ingorsnot." The three tall men hurried down the rows paying out the winning bets and collecting for the next leg.

While the end-of-race folderol was going on, Pattersling took off his helmet and wiggled his fingers in his ears, trying to un-ring the bells that were tolling in his head. When his eyes finally focused, he looked up at Michael and Tracker and quickly jumped to his feet. "Hah, you're here to help us, right?" he rushed in a whisper. "You must be Tracker. Megan said you were our friends." His large eyes were anxious.

Suddenly, the wooden man reached over and grabbed Pattersling by the shoulders. "Hey, what are you saying there?" he growled. "You know you can't talk to us folk." He turned to the bar. "Barnabas!" he shouted. Barnabas heard him and hustled down the wall to the beckoning man. "Pattersling here, he's fraternizing with this lot, he is."

"No, no," Tracker said quickly. "He's hit his head so hard he's talking gibberish to everyone, that's all. Look." He pointed to the elf, hoping he would follow his lead. Pattersling caught on immediately and walked off down the table spouting nonsense to anyone in earshot.

Barnabas looked at Tracker and Michael suspiciously and then at the disappearing elf. He looked back at Tracker. "Well, they do rattle their pate a bit at the finish line, don't they," he said finally. "But, they're a bit dim and really aren't here to strike up a conversation, you understand." He turned to the stick man. "I'll take care of it, Mr. Crabapple," Barnabas said in an assuring voice. He shuffled back to the bar and deftly reached out and grabbed Pattersling by the scruff of the neck as he passed by him on the way. He put the chain back on the elf's ankle and set him down roughly on the skittles table.

Tracker nudged Michael and whispered, "Well, that's put a stamp on it. You heard Pattersling mention Megan. And he knew my name! But, where's the prince?" He again searched the room to no avail. "Keep a sharp eye, Michael."

Mr. Crabapple was trying to hear Tracker's conversation again, but there was too much noise. He scowled into his beer. He wasn't happy.

"Tracker, these elves received a message from the king, too," Michael said behind his hand. "That's what I was trying to tell you. I overheard Pattersling and Blingtrail. They think we are here to help them escape. Tracker, I can hear their thoughts just like I heard mother's!"

Tracker tried to hide his surprise. Then he looked around warily to make sure no one was watching or listening. Crabapple was collecting a bet from one of the money-men and was preoccupied.

Michael had watched as Pattersling was unceremoniously dumped on the table and re-shackled by Barnabas. "I don't know about any prince, Tracker, but I do know that these elves are nothing more than slaves and are being treated like performing monkeys. Even in

Tremora, that must be wrong. We have to help them!" Michael said in earnest. "Did you see his eyes?"

"Yes," Tracker said, giving Michael another appraising look. "And I noticed those shackles too. I have every intention of investigating these elves some day. And yes, and yes again because slavery is evil anywhere and in any form; even with performing animals." Tracker then creased his brow and looked concerned. "But the king's mission comes first. And, of course, there is the riddle of the prince. Let's be patient and see where this leads us." Then he whispered, "And, let me know if you *hear* anything else." Michael nodded his head.

Tracker then looked over and gave a big smile to the woody Mr. Crabapple.

Barnabas returned to the front of the room and again took over his duties. "Attention, please. Attention, please. Now to the second of our three preliminary races..." He looked to the heads of the three tables. "Owners, remove the constraints!" Then he turned and, without warning, rang the brass bell.

The next leg wasn't even close. *THUNK ....PLANK, PLINK.*

"Blingtrail, first; Stinglebat, second; and Rougeknot, third," Barnabas declared enthusiastically. "Wow, that girl can *skedaddle*! I think our Pattersling might have some competition after all," he said, turning to the elf in the corner. Pattersling scowled, and Barnabas laughed. Either way, Barnabas was going to reap a fine profit from this year's races.

"As to you two," Barnabas said, turning to the losers, "perhaps you should stick to retrieving cheese and setting skittles for a couple more years." He got a few scattered claps and laughs, but the audience wasn't happy. It was understandable. Not many people had bet on Blingtrail to win and the house had just made a killing.

Blingtrail gave Michael and Tracker a nervous look and a small wave as she recovered from her winning, head-first lunge. She scurried off up the table, and Mr. Crabapple snarled after her. He was one of the ones that bet against her, and he'd lost heavily.

Next up was Strutbeam's race. Unbelievably, he won his leg more easily than either Pattersling or Blingtrail. His opponents both slipped and knocked themselves out cold before they even finished.

Barnabas was beside himself with glee. The house had just made another very large take on the upset. "Well, Strutbeam, you've outdone yourself this year. Your very first win!" he shouted as he enthusiastically clapped his hands. Then he awarded Strutbeam's owner with a flying cigar and mug of beer.

"And now, to the final race!" Barnabas announced. The crowd cheered raucously. He climbed up on the bar to better see and be heard. He made sure that all of the wagers were made and that the tables were clear of any unexpected (or illegal) obstructions before continuing. He held up a small cup-trophy and the bag of coins. "Will the champion's cup and purse move to another pub this year?" he asked. Shouts, boos, cheers, whoops, and hollers all exploded at once. "We shall see, we shall see," he said. "Racers, please take your marks." He turned in the direction of the kitchen. "And now, here to do the honors; my wife, Bella!"

Out of the kitchen stepped a short, rotund lady that matched Barnabas's shape and girth. She was dressed in white kitchen garb with a chef's hat. With some difficulty, she sidled sideways through the door and turned and continued crablike until she was standing beneath the bell. Then she turned her head to the crowd and smiled, showing gaps in her tegs. Suddenly, she reached up with a set of tongs and clanged the bell long and hard.

The racers shot off.

This was for all the marbles, as they say, and the noise was deafening. Everyone was on their feet. Blingtrail's owners were mooing and howling. Bella climbed up on the bar and jumped up and down with Barnabas. The piano player struck up another lively tune. Poor Strutbeam was so excited and befuddled he couldn't run more than two or three steps before falling or slipping or tumbling head over heels on the slippery tabletop.

And then, half way through the race and half way down the tables, something incredible happened with Blingtrail. She suddenly stopped in her tracks, jumped straight up in the air, almost to the roof, and screamed so loud it got the attention of everyone in the room. Then she landed and immediately bounced to the side onto Strutbeam's table. She landed in front of the startled Strutbeam, grabbed him in her arms, and gave him a loud kiss on the cheek. The outrage was instantaneous, and everyone hollered at once and craned to see what she'd done. "She can't do that," the people on Strutbeam's table yelled. "She's disqualified," more people hollered in protest from across the room. But Blingtrail wasn't done yet. In the midst of all the shouting, she jumped high in the air and screamed again. This time she landed on the middle table again and, with hardly a pause, bounced a second time over several heads and landed on Pattersling's table. Once there, she took a triumphant stance with one hand on her hip and the other pointing up and down the table. "Voilá!" she said in a triumphant tiny voice. The people at the table didn't get it at first. They looked at each other confused. But eventually it sunk in: Pattersling was gone!

Table three exploded in loud shouts of outrage and anger. Now all three tables were in chaos. Barnabas tried to be heard and everyone was up, waving betting slips and utensils, even weapons. In the middle of it all, there was a loud *PLINK.* Another reality sank in to the collective consciousness of the crowd. Strutbeam had just won the race! His table broke out in screams and hollers and loud applause, and for a while, all attention was on table one. Strutbeam was the new champion! The giant man who owned Strutbeam picked the elf up and held him high in the air, while jumping up and down with Barnaby's cigar bouncing crazily from his mouth. But that caused table two to raise even angrier shouts of protest. And when people looked for Blingtrail at table three, there was another, shock. She had vanished, too!

Now it was pandemonium times ten. Tables were overturned as people tried to find the missing elves and a huge fistfight broke out. Barnabas yelled to close the doors, that there was a reward for the capture of the racers, but it was all falling on deaf ears. Heads were being cracked, and bedlam was in the air.

"Tracker!" Michael yelled over the noise. "Grab your bag. We have to get out of here. We have to help Pattersling!"

Instead, Tracker pushed Michael rudely to the side, and lunged to grab the copper plate that Crabapple had just raised above his head. Tracker then smashed the man square in the face with it, and Crabapple fell just like a tree and bounced and crashed across the table. The man had been just about to clobber Michael in the back of the head.

Michael looked down numbly at the stick man draped over the table. "Whew, thanks, Tracker," he mumbled. Then he started as if suddenly remembering something and reached out and grabbed Tracker's shoulder, but just as quickly drew his hand back. "Oops, sorry, no offense meant," he said, quickly. "But, we really, really, have to get out of here. Now, Tracker! I'll explain later—come on, come onnnnn!" He grabbed Tracker's backpack and staff and threw them at him and then turned to the door leading up to the second floor and dived through.

Tracker didn't hesitate. His instincts told him he needed to follow Michael, and besides, the king's message had told him to avoid bloodshed. He shrugged into his backpack and followed Michael through the door. He pulled the door closed behind him and then darted up the stairs two at a time. Michael was waiting at the top. They ran to the end of the hall and unlatched a window that led out onto the roof of the stables. Then they climbed through the opening, ran crouching along the ridgeline of the thatched roof, and slid down into a wagon full of hay.

Tracker put a hand on Michael's chest and a finger to his mouth, indicating he should stay quiet. They then listened intently to make sure they hadn't been followed or seen running along the roof. After a moment, Tracker gave the all-clear, and they jumped down and crept behind the stables. Tracker peeked around a corner and looked back toward the entrance to the inn. There were shouts and screams as the fight poured out into the road.

He pulled his head back. "Well, Michael," he whispered, as he spit hay from his mouth, "we haven't saved a prince yet, and we haven't helped any elves out either. So, what was that all about back there?"

"Tracker, you're not going to believe this, but we've helped the elves more than you know. And, I think I know who the prince is."

"Well, it's time you let me in on your little secret, then," Tracker said, looking at Michael suspiciously, "because, I sure haven't seen him yet."

A tiny voice came from somewhere behind Michael's back. "Are you sure about that?"

Tracker grabbed Michael by the shoulders and quickly turned him around. And there, peeking out from beneath the flaps of Michael's backpack, were two sets of lamp-green eyes. Tracker used his fingers to increase the opening just a bit, and there were Pattersling and Blingtrail staring back at him.

Tracker started with surprise and then amusement. "Well, Pattersling," he said, "there's certainly more to you than meets the eye."

"Even more than you think," said the elf. "Because if you're looking for a prince that's not Prince Cedric, that is, then you've found him. I am indeed a prince. I am Prince Priam. Pattersling is my slave name. I'm surprised Megan or the king left that bit out. But, if you don't mind, we'll just stay in here for a while where it's safe. Could you maybe carry us on down the road a bit farther?"

Just then Tracker felt movement in his own pack. He turned and looked over his shoulder the best he could. "Uh, oh," he said, guessing the truth. He told Michael to have a look.

Four more pairs of frightened eyes peeked out of Tracker's bag back at Michael. "Good grief, are you *all* stuffed in our bags?" Michael asked. "I thought it was just the two of you."

Tracker turned and gave Michael a questioning look.

"I overheard Pattersling and Blingtrail talking of their escape," Michael said. "I didn't have time to tell you back there, not with you banging heads and everything."

"*He overheard us. How could that be?*" Blingtrail's thoughts were incredulous, and Michael, again, heard them.

Michael was just about to answer her, when … "Excuse me, but those of us on the bottom here are pretty scrunched," came a tiny voice. "Could you please hurry up and get where you're going?"

Tracker looked at Michael and shrugged his shoulders in resignation and humor. "Nothing left for us here. Looks like we've followed all of King William's wishes. Let's be off then."

They struck off across a field of yellow flowers that glowed faintly in the light of the moon. After an hour, they settled in a small copse of trees on a slightly raised hilltop. When Michael and Tracker set their packs on the ground, Michael was immediately reminded of the circus; just like clowns that keep coming and coming out of a tiny car, nine elves emerged from the bags.

"How in the world did you all fit in there?" Michael asked.

"Well, we can roll up into pretty small balls," said the prince. "But, we have to apologize. You might be missing some food and maybe some bottles of water."

"Those can be replaced easily enough, Pattersling, er, I mean Prince Priam," Tracker said.

"Priam, if you please," said the prince quickly. "The name Pattersling is gone for good now, and we certainly won't stand on ceremony here after all that you have done for us."

"So be it, Priam. But, I think it's time you told your story, don't you? We were only told to look out for a prince in trouble and to avoid bloodshed. It's clear now what the king's vision was about, but now that you've escaped, I feel our paths may be parting ways again very soon."

Priam stood next to Blingtrail with his arm around her waist. He looked around at his group. They were stretching, doing handstands, and lying on the ground waving arms and legs as if making snow angels. He smiled.

"We are wood elves and fairies from the forests of Golan, but our kingdoms stretch to the Mishtock and Aloman mountains. It all started at our wedding rehearsal, Tracker. Not only were Blingtrail and I to be married, but it was to be a marriage between the faeries and elves, as well. It would have been a first, and there was much anticipation and excitement between the two peoples. Members of our wedding party were on a boat, floating down the Trallsbone River, when a storm suddenly appeared. The downpour was torrential and caused a flash flood that carried us all out to sea. Sadly, a number of our friends and family perished that fateful day." Blingtrail's eyes welled with tears, and Priam hugged her more closely. The other elves stopped what they were doing and also stood and hugged, giving comfort to each other. It was obviously a very painful memory for them all.

Priam gathered himself and continued. "Those of us who survived spent days afloat at sea and were about to give up all hope when a ship came to our rescue. Unfortunately, it was a pirate ship; instead of a rescue, we were all put into cages and transported to a remote island called Coriss. There, we became slaves to the island's royal family. We may as well have been in a prison. There was no way to get off the island, even if we escaped.

"Then, one day our fortunes took another terrible turn. The older daughter of the king and queen of the island, Princess Leonie, got married. Her new husband was a merchant from the mainland and deeply into the slave trade. When he became aware of us, not surprisingly—he is such a vile creature—he contrived a unique way to make money off of us and still keep us as slaves: He took us all to Charn and meted us out, one at a time, to the local country inns as indentured servants. He's been drawing a fee from each pub ever since."

"I think I may be familiar with this merchant," Tracker said with a frown.

"His name is Kalib."

"As I suspected."

"Then you know there is no end to his evil. And he is very clever. By separating us and spreading us all over Charn, he knew we had no chance of organizing or escaping. We were no better off than when we were on Coriss. We've been slaves in these ale houses for over three years ..." Priam's voice trailed off as he recalled some unpleasant memory.

Michael felt a small hand grab his own. It was trembling. He looked down and the youngest of the elves, a girl, was looking anxiously up at him. He noticed the rest of the elves had gathered around him and Tracker as well. He looked down again and whispered, "Don't worry, you are free now. You are all going home."

Priam heard Michael and was brought out of his reverie. He also looked around at the worried looks on his friends' faces. "No, no, friends. Don't be afraid. We will never again be shackled as slaves. The traveler is exactly right. We are free, and we are going home!"

The mood of the group again changed. It was obvious that Prince Priam was their leader. Collectively, they were still very fragile. Priam knew they needed his direction and strength in their newfound freedom.

Michael gave his elf's hand a squeeze.

"That's better," Priam said. "Now, to quickly finish our story, Tracker. I shouldn't be so easily distracted. It must be all that head banging through the years." He looked around and was pleased to see everyone smiling again.

"One night last winter, the wizard Megan stopped by the inn. Normally, Barnabas would have had me locked away if there was a king's man in the pub. Slavery among men has been outlawed for many years, and even though we elves are considered nothing more than clever animals, it's still a form of slavery; so he always avoided the issue by keeping me out of sight. This time though, he must have overlooked me in the excitement of having the world's most famous wizard in his house. Megan announced that he was traveling on king's business and was offering huge rewards to anyone with information about the missing Prince Cedric. In an opportune moment, I whispered, 'Please help me, Megan. I, too, am a missing prince.'

"He looked at me and then at my shackles and evaluated my plight in an instant. He knew that if I was really of elfin royal blood, then I would be able to receive his thoughts. He reached out with his mind and said, *'If that is true, then tell me your story, quickly!'* At the same time he casually looked around the room as if he'd never spoken. I shouldn't have been surprised; of course he could communicate with me with his mind. He was the Magus, Megan!

"I told my story. When I was finished, Megan stayed silent for a long time. Then, "*Priam, your story, at least in part, was already known to me. Unfortunately for you, no one thought you survived the storm.*" He said that both the elves and faeries had given us all up for lost long ago. They had searched the Trallsbone for days, and when the bodies of some of our party washed up on shore, it was believed the rest of us were lost at sea.

"Megan would have rescued me that night, but I wouldn't agree to any plan that didn't include us all. He thought long and hard before he agreed to leave me. 'I respect your wishes, Priam,' he said, 'but this will take some time.' Before he left, he told me not to despair, just to stay ready.

"About a week ago, Blingtrail and I both received mysterious messages from King William. He said to look out for you, Tracker, and a young companion; that our rescue was at hand. We were instructed to create a diversion during the table races. Blingtrail came up with a way for us to disappear into the crowd, at least for a while, but we had no idea what we were to do from there on. Then, this evening, you walked through the door with two bags on your back, and we had our answer. And, sure enough, there you were, and here we are."

"The king's messages are always vague, Priam," Tracker said. "We were only told to give aid to a prince in trouble and avoid bloodshed. At first, we had no idea it was you. It seems my 'young companion' had a unique way of figuring it out, though. Perhaps you should explain, Michael."

"Well, yes. Yes, you see, I don't know how, but I, too, can hear you both when you're thinking at each other … just like Megan." He looked embarrassed. "Sorry …"

Blingtrail looked up at Priam and then at Michael. "Do you hear everything?"

"I, I, don't think so … Just when you need me to, I think, " Michael said.

"Well, are you of royal blood, Michael? Only those who are have this power in our world," Priam said.

Tracker interjected suddenly. "No, no, it's not the same outside the world of elves. Is Megan royalty? No, something else must be at work here." He changed the subject quickly. "But that means *you* are both royalty then?"

"Yes, Tracker. Blingtrail is the daughter of the king and queen of the faeries. And I am the oldest son of the king and queen of all Elfland." Priam looked at Tracker curiously. Tracker obviously didn't want any more questions about Michael's surprising ability, and Michael seemed as perplexed as anyone that he even had it. The prince decided to let the subject lie. A secret was a secret after all.

"You're right about our paths leading in a different direction," Priam continued. "We are desperate to get under way. The king's note said that my father was seriously ill and that I needed to get to him as soon as possible. So, we must hurry and return to our home, Tracker. We will be forever grateful to you both, but we must be off immediately."

Just then a figure stepped out from the shadows. It was another male elf, only he was much bigger and wilder looking than Priam or any other of his group. He had a hard look and wasted no time with niceties. "And, I have come to escort you, Priam," he announced. "The High King's message told me to watch for you this night."

Priam and Blingtrail both rushed forward and hugged the newcomer. "This is my brother, Persus," Priam said turning to Michael and Tracker with a huge smile.

However, Persus barely acknowledged the two's existence as he studied Priam at arm's length. "But what is this, my brother? You are so much shorter! And you Blingtrail," he said, turning, "where are your beautiful wings?"

"Hello to you as well Persus! And so nice of you to notice," Blingtrail responded, but there was a lilt in her voice that said she wasn't offended at all. She was obviously used to the elf's candor.

"Yes, Persus, it's an unfortunate truth," Priam answered. "It's like we've been disappearing a little each day. Another reason we were desperate," he said, turning back to Tracker. "Some of us hardly have the strength to care anymore. We can only hope the effect reverses now that we are free again."

"Perhaps the Healer can cast a light," Persus said. "She is with Father now. Regardless, Priam, now that you *are* free your duty is clear. Father waits," urged Persus. "I think we have little time." He beckoned with his bow for them all to follow.

"Just one other thing, please," Michael suddenly interrupted. Everyone looked at him in surprise. "Before you go—I need to ask you … We are on a king's mission, to be sure, but I am also looking for *my* father. Have any of you seen another traveler that looks like me, maybe a year ago?"

All of the elves, even Persus, looked long and hard at Michael. Tracker pursed his lips. But, there was only silence.

"We are sorry, Michael. But, we will keep watch," Priam said finally. His expression was sympathetic.

Michael's face fell.

Blingtrail went to him and put her hand on his arm. "It's unusual for travelers such as you to go unnoticed for long," she said softly. "And we understand the bond between a son and father. Can you not sense it with Persus and Priam and their father? Have heart, Michael. Not much escapes us if we have a mind to care. We will keep an ear. You've earned a spot in our hearts forever."

With that, the elves, each in turn, hugged Michael and Tracker goodbye. Then they vanished.

❧

"And that was pure genius, the planning of that escape," Tracker said later after the elves had gone. They were settling in for the night, and Tracker still couldn't get over Blingtrail's cleverness. He propped his head against his backpack, laid his staff next to him, wrapped himself in a blanket, and curled up to go to sleep. "That was a masterful diversion that was that she pulled off, just masterful …," he continued, as he closed his eyes and fell asleep.

Michael, too, was taken by Priam and his people. "I hope we meet them again," Michael said wistfully into the night. Their memory lingered. Was this part of their enchantment? He could still see them plainly in his mind. In the dark, their skin became the color of a softly glowing watch dial, and every movement they had made left a fine trail of sparkling dust …

He was standing, looking out over the moonlit countryside from the vantage point of the raised hill. All the different colors of the flowers glowed softly under the quarter moon, and he could just make out the orange light of the windows in the inn and a few lit windows in scattered farmhouses. The wind had started up, and it was chilly, but Tracker said it was too exposed on the hilltop to light a campfire. Michael felt guilty that he was wrapped in Tracker's extra blanket; the old man must be cold with only the one thin cover.

Suddenly he remembered his mother's cloak. "Of course," he whispered. Then another thought. *I hope the elves didn't remove it from my backpack when they were making room for their escape!* But no, when he found his bag and opened it, the poncho was still folded in the bottom. He pulled it out and, after removing his hat, put his head through the opening and let the material drape down over his clothes to his thighs. Then he replaced his hat and pulled up the hood. Almost immediately, he felt the warmth of the fur lining throughout his body and whispered, "Thanks, Mom." Then he took his blanket and threw it over Tracker.

Tracker's eyes opened at once. He took in Michael's new garment, glanced down at the second blanket that now covered him, deduced what had awakened him, and went back to sleep.

Michael smiled. His new friend was sure a light sleeper! He went back to standing watch and, to keep his mind occupied, looked up and studied the strange night sky and moon. *Not unlike my own*, he thought, *but not the same either. Way more shooting stars …* He passed the time counting them.

Hours later, Michael watched the setting of the moon. Tracker said that would be a good time to change the watch. To Michael's delight, Tracker was talkative once nudged awake. As promised, Tracker told him the story of Bearcamp, which wasn't long, but just like the tale of the wazalops, Tracker's voice was the last thing Michael heard as he dropped off to sleep at the end of his second day in Tremora.

Chapter Six

Bjorg

As Michael helped break camp the next morning, he tried to recall all that he'd learned the night before about Bearcamp from Tracker. *What a wonderful place it must be!* Bearcamp was a tiny island located off the northeastern coast of Charn and Tremora's mecca for all things commerce; from the business of imports and exports to trading and bartering to gambling and gaming. They had actually seen Bearcamp in the distance from the cliffs yesterday. What made Bearcamp especially unique was it was an island on an island; the only such formation in the entire world. The larger island, Havenland, was heavily wooded and separated from the mainland by a treacherous channel of water known as the Gush.

Bearcamp sat in the middle of Havenland's Lake Shampore and was reached on foot by crossing one of four cobblestone bridges located at each of the island's cardinal points. From a distance, the island looked like a gently rising cone, circled by myriad small buildings and spiraling streets. And at the top of the island sat tiny Castle Logan; a small fortress that became the royal residence during festivals and stately visits. The castle's main purpose, however, was to serve as a treasury annex to Tremora Castle and a prison for local criminals. Circling the island and closely following the shoreline was a wide, flat thoroughfare called Reverie Way. Seven days a week, merchants set up tents, tables, and carpets along its length and breadth to create the largest free marketplace in Tremora.

After Tracker described the different people that made the market possible, Michael remembered being surprised. He hadn't really thought about how big or how diverse the population of this world must be.

Every day, a steady stream of Tremorans traversed the choppy waters of the Gush using rope-drawn rafts and boats. Balanced precariously, these brave souls pulled themselves hand over hand along cable-ropes that stretched from the mainland to Havenland. Wagons and livestock were transported by larger rafts and ferries, piloted by trolls who gave assistance for a hefty price. Once reaching the big island, there was still a day's journey through thick forest to the bridges of Bearcamp.

Merchants and farmers brought vegetables, fruits, flowers, and native arts and crafts to market from the south. From the north, exotic plants, animals, and wares originating in the distant Orient came to market from cargo ships that arrived almost daily at Havenland's seaport, Stern. West of the islands were the Pishtock Mountains and beyond them, the vast Asyr Desert. Large caravans braved the difficult trek through the Sherkan Pass to bring sundry items of cast copper and bronze, water pipes, fine musical instruments, and oddly shaped knives and swords. But more important, these desert nomads supplied another essential commodity to Bearcamp: racing camelops.

Finally, from both the Pishtock Mountains to the west and the Serka Mountains to the east, the sometimes large, always strange, and most definitely dangerous mountain folk descended from the hills. In addition to demonstrating their strength and other physical skills in lively competitions, they traded hand hewn wooden furniture and animal skins for items they might desire. They never accepted currency; only gold, silver, and precious stones. The mountain folk reveled in the art of bartering and intimidation.

Then Tracker smiled and told Michael how fortunate he was to be visiting Bearcamp at this time of year because, even though the free market he described so vividly was lively and exciting and drew most Tremorans to the islands at least once a month, nothing compared to the crowds that invaded the area each spring. For seven straight days, as the fields of Charn became colored blankets of flowers, Reverie Way was transformed into a gathering place for the largest spectacle of the year: the Bearcamp Races. Whether it was snails, frogs, hounds, or horses, a race and wagering could be found somewhere along the Way during this festive week. And the meet ended on day seven with the most famous race of all, the Running of the Lops.

❧

Michael and Tracker reached the fords of Havenland by late afternoon, the day after rescuing Prince Priam. They joined a long line of people waiting to use the boats, ferries, and rafts needed to cross the Gush. Great hubbub was in the air; the Bearcamp Races were under way, and tomorrow was day four.

They were standing near the docks where large fishing nets and sheaves of bulb kelp hung drying between tall wooden poles when a deep voice boomed out, "Hallo, you two!"

A pile of rocks with a yellow patch of weeds on top lumbered up and engulfed Tracker in a crushing hug. It was a troll. He was as much taller than Tracker as he was shorter than Michael and just as wide, with huge hands callused from continually grabbing the ropes that pulled the watercraft to the island and back. His small eyes were not quite centered in an otherwise kindly face, and his thick yellow locks were similar to those of Tracker, Tralana, and many others queued up at the docks.

"Bjorg, my friend," gasped Tracker as he dangled off the ground.

The troll laughed loudly and put him down. He then put heavy arms around both Tracker and Michael and shooed them into a small wooden shack. Once inside, he latched the door and the outside world vanished. They found themselves in a surprisingly large makeshift office with a stone fireplace.

"Sit," said the troll, pointing at a roughly hewn table up one corner. His voice sounded like gravel turning in a cement mixer. Michael and Tracker grabbed a wooden chair each and dragged it across the floor to the table. Sunlight filtered through two dirty glass windows, and a kerosene lamp cast an orange tinge on a countertop strewn with papers.

Once Bjorg saw Tracker and Michael comfortably seated, he grunted in satisfaction, bent down behind the counter, and grabbed three earthenware mugs and a dusty green bottle. The mugs he held up in one great paw to show they had glass bottoms. "To watch for enemy even while drinking!" he declared. He then filled the mugs from bottom to brim with a liquid thick enough to eat with a spoon.

He sat the mugs on the table along with a pile of what Michael thought looked like Brazil nuts. The troll then pulled up a heavy stool made of stone and sat down. He shoved the drinks toward Michael and Tracker and picked up a few nuts, cracking the shells between thumb and finger before popping the seeds into his mouth. "First, grog and troll nuts for long life," he grated while chewing noisily.

TROll NUTS AND GROG. . .

Michael thought this was very funny and stifled a laugh, but neither Bjorg nor Tracker saw the humor. Bjorg stopped chewing and eyed him curiously while Tracker raised a questioning eyebrow.

Embarrassed, Michael shrugged his shoulders and mumbled a quick apology, but he was still trying not to laugh. "Just something we'd consider funny back home is all—sorry." Then, he quickly reached out, grabbed two of the nuts, cracked their shells with one hand as Bjorg had, and popped the seeds into his mouth.

This drew a new, even more surprising reaction from the two: Tracker's eyes got big and round and the troll's mouth suddenly widened into a toothy grin.

"Michael, I've never known anyone outside of a troll or maybe a mountain man who could crack a troll nut with his bare hands," Tracker said in awe. "You really don't know your own strength do you?"

"I, I guess not …," Michael stammered. He hadn't noticed anything unusual at all.

"Boy must have troll blood in 'im," Bjorg said, still smiling. He held up his mug in a salute to both Michael and Tracker and drained it, with no small amount of liquid running down his chin. This he lapped up with an enormous tongue. Then Bjorg cracked more nuts in his giant paws and shoved the seeds toward Tracker. "You next!"

Tracker gave Michael one final bemused look, then turned, took a deep breath, and shoved the nuts into his mouth. He grabbed his mug and downed his grog in one go; only with a lot more difficulty than Bjorg. When finished he licked his lips and raised his empty to Michael. "Now it's your turn!" he said. "Don't worry. It's quite good once you get to the bottom."

Michael hesitated.

Tracker leaned over and whispered behind the back of his hand, "You've got to do it, Michael. It's extremely bad form to refuse an invitation to quaff from a troll. Even a friendly one!"

Bjorg grunted in agreement. Trolls have excellent hearing.

Michael looked from one to the other and shrugged his shoulders in surrender. Accepting his fate, he raised his drink slowly to his lips and sipped the thick mead-like concoction with eyes closed and a grimace. At first he had a hard time not gagging and almost stopped, but the drink was layered, and as Tracker promised, it actually went down quite smoothly in the end. When he slammed down the mug with more force than intended, Tracker and Bjorg nodded their heads at each other knowingly.

Tracker stood up and did the introductions. "Michael, I want you to meet Bjorg, a northern troll of few words and a trusted friend.

Bjorg, this is Michael. We travel on urgent king's business. It seems you have news for us."

Bjorg became serious and stared at them, nodding slowly. "Danger. Wisps wait for you both. Pay much for information."

Tracker furrowed his brow and muttered, "So much for traveling in secrecy …" He looked at Bjorg. "Wisps, you say? Looking for *both* of us?" He continued on as if talking to himself. "First the faux messenger on the path and now this. The enemy is determined to block our way—or worse."

Michael raised his head and looked at Tracker with eyes not quite focused. "Emmennee? Annn, whass a wisp anywaee?" he slurred. "Come on Trackerrr! Isss time you tell me why I'm heeer doan you tink? Maybe I can ashually hewp …" Michael tried to stand up but ended up just sitting down again with arms spread wide as if the table needed bracing.

"Indeed," Tracker sighed. "That *is* what you were summoned for. However, Megan thought it best to wait till the wizard's gathering …"

"Boy no secret," Bjorg reminded. This time his voice sounded like a box of rocks being dragged across the wooden floor.

Tracker looked at the troll for a long time. "Perhaps you're right," Tracker said. He went and gazed out one of the windows. "Circumstances have definitely changed. It seems only fair that Michael knows the danger he's in and where his loyalties must lie. But, I wasn't to reveal so much …" Darkness was approaching, and the light from the lamp was taking on a more dominant role in the small room. Tracker appeared to make up his mind. He turned to Bjorg and said, "You'd better get some coffee for our friend here. I fear the night ahead will require all of our faculties. It looks like we'll be crossing the Gush sooner than we thought."

It was dark outside and the last of the rafts and ferries had finished depositing their burdens on the shores of Havenland. Michael was finishing his second mug of coffee. It was as thick as the grog and tasted terrible, but it did clear his head. He was anxious to hear Tracker's story but knew by now his companion wouldn't be hurried. Bjorg, in the meantime, had finished off two more mugs of grog and the rest of the nuts and seemed content to wait. But he, too, wanted to know why the wisps were at his door.

Tracker lit his pipe, opened a window a crack, and sent a blue-green stream of smoke out the opening. Then he returned to his chair, crossed one leg over the other, and began.

"It all started when the High King's son and heir, Prince Cedric, was kidnapped on his twelfth birthday. One moment he was leaning out over a parapet in broad daylight, waving to a crowd of admirers, and the next a dragon swooped down and carried him off before everyone's very eyes. Knights quickly stormed out the castle gates in the direction of the creature's flight, but efforts to follow the dragon were futile. The prince was gone. Mazalon Trackers of Gondalor, of which I am one, of course, have since searched Tremora far and wide, but to no avail. Cedric had vanished."

"Dragons?" Michael asked in astonishment. "Tremora has dragons?"

"Well, yes and no … we suspect *a* dragon—singular. Until that day, dragons hadn't been seen in Tremora for hundreds of years. We think some form of black magic must have been used to conjure this one up from the past. And we believe the same magic may be keeping the prince hidden. Lord Pratt, the High King's brother, along with his concubine, Prelandora, were suspected of course. After all, they were both banished to Spreten for practicing the dark arts, but there was no proof they had anything to do with kidnapping Prince Cedric. Besides, there was an even larger groundswell of suspicion aimed at the guilds of white wizards and stargazers."

"Why?" asked Michael.

"Wizards and stargazers are notoriously mysterious and strange and reclusive, you see—perfect scapegoats for any unsolved crime. In other words, no good reason," he added sarcastically.

Tracker shook his head. "It's been sad times for Tremorans since that day. As I told you, King William often sees the future through dreams and visions, but no visions or dreams have come to him this time. Until recently, that is … But I get ahead of myself."

Tracker got to his feet, puffed on his pipe, and again blew smoke out the window. He listened intently for a few moments and then returned to his seat. "It's been well over two years year now, and still no news whatsoever of Prince Cedric. Spreten continues to deny emphatically any responsibility, and there have been no sightings or clues; or a body thank goodness. But that's no surprise. It's why we believe he's being hidden somewhere. Everyone knows it's fatal to spill the blood of an heir to the throne. Tremoran royalty has been protected thusly since the beginning of kings. Anyone trying to kill an heir-apparent simply bursts into flames and dies. Why, it's even written in the tablets of the moon in the onyx garden! The prince was kidnapped for some wicked purpose, albeit not to kill him; and it wasn't to demand some outrageous ransom either. That's clear now. No, the true purpose of the kidnapping was to create chaos—and it's been working brilliantly."

Tracker's voice saddened. "We don't have time to go into details, but the grabbing of the prince was only the beginning of Tremora's troubles. With every resource searching for Cedric, there weren't enough knights or sheriffs or soldiers remaining to enforce law and order. Suffice to say the kingdom has been in turmoil ever since, and our king and queen are withering before our very eyes."

Bjorg nodded sadly and grunted.

"Then, late last year, the day came that the king had been dreading for months—the winter solstice. By law, the official succession to the throne is announced annually at this mid-winter celebration by the king himself, and then confirmed six months later at the summer solstice festival by Tremora's parliament. Since Cedric had been missing for over two years, the king was forced to acknowledge publicly that the new heir to the throne was going to be Myrdain, his brother's son. It was an emotional day for all of Tremora."

Tracker stopped and removed a handkerchief to wipe his eyes. "You must excuse me, Michael. The king and queen are much loved, and the memory of that day is still painful to recall."

Even Bjorg used a finger to wipe away a tear.

Michael was struck. He knew these men were not showing weakness: Why, either one could fight off a dozen men all by themselves! No, they were what his father described as the "salt of the earth," profoundly good and loyal people who make up the strength of a country. He was suddenly humbled even to be in their presence. How could he possibly be any help to these men—and this king?

Tracker returned the handkerchief, cleared his throat, and continued; this time with a hint of anger. "Having to make the announcement was bad enough, but even more upsetting to the king was Prelandora's behavior. Just before the proclamation, the witch of Spreten and her entourage showed up at the castle gates demanding an audience. This was the second time the witch had taken advantage of the terms of her banishment. The first was when Prelandora showed up at the celebration of the birth of Cedric to show the world that she, too, was pregnant with a royal child. As on that occasion, she was mounted on a large fierce warhorse decked out completely in black, and although Lord Pratt was again not with her, their son, Myrdain, now eleven years old, sat proudly at her side on his own black charger.

"Prelandora was obviously there to show off her young prince, but more important, she was also there to plead her case in front of Tremora's parliament as to her and Lord Pratt's exile. And this she did. She argued that since, in only six months time, it would be official that Myrdain was the new heir to the throne; Tremora should also end the banishment of his parents!

"King William was not surprised. In fact he had anticipated this very demand. Even he had to admit that it was not unreasonable to expect an heir-apparent's parents to live with him in Tremora Castle. In the end, Tremora's Parliament also agreed and decreed that the banishment should end at the close of the month of Jenetta—the summer solstice. Prelandora celebrated the victory by parading her son before Tremora's curious crowds, and then, after leaving the castle, she continued to showcase Myrdain at every major township and village on their return trip to Spreten.

"The situation could not have been more desperate. Lord Pratt and Prelandora had made their move, and the king only had one hope left: Cedric had to be found before the end of summer—and time was running out! But how? There was nowhere else to look for the prince; even Spreten Castle had been scoured top to bottom! I myself took part in that search," Tracker said, shaking his head as if to clear an unpleasant memory.

"So, in desperation, the king began searching the ancient tomes in the Great Hall of Knowledge; specifically ones that dealt with witchcraft and sorcery. The king was so fraught with despair he was willing to walk in the darkness if it meant he could find his son. Was there some black spell or incantation that could help him? Perhaps the same power that summoned the dragon? But this was very dangerous. Black magic is forbidden in Tremora today, and the few books that exist on the subject were banned and locked away at the end of the Age of Magic by the white wizards.

"The use of all but the simplest forms of magic is forbidden in this, the Age of Secrets, and the punishment for practicing witchcraft and sorcery, especially, is severe—even for a king! Once, long ago, black magic was used to rule Tremora, and those were the most terrible of times. The world was very nearly destroyed. After the W Wars between witches, warlocks, and wizards, leaders of Tremora banned all black magic in hopes of preventing evil times like those from ever happening again. You see, black magic always requires some form of sacrifice; mostly animals, but the worst kind requires a person's life. It is evil incarnate.

"But the king was beyond caring. He thought; 'What's the worst that can happen? Sacrifice a goat to get my son back?' And, after all, he was the High King! His brother and his witch were convicted of practicing the vile arts, and they were merely banished; why, they even ended up with their own island! And now they were about to come back and take over his kingdom. Thus was the state of King William's mind. So, in spite of the danger, he searched for and devoured any references to ancient script, runes, and the dark arts—barely eating or sleeping for days on end. Many close to him, especially the queen, feared for his health, both physical and mental—he was consumed.

"Then, late one night, the king found a thin book wedged between two large leather bound volumes on necromancy. It was like finding a misfiled book in a library. It was bound in white leather, and the one-word title written in flowery gold script on the cover said *Fenn*. When the king tried to examine it more closely, he found it would only open to two pages containing crudely drawn maps of Farland Castle. The notes on the pages were written in the same hand as the title. It appeared to be a personal journal."

"Fenn?" said Michael in surprise, "Farland Castle? Wasn't she—?"

"Yes, Michael, it was probably written by Queen Fenn herself while a young girl growing up in the castle. The king suspected as much from the childlike quality of the drawings and writing. I've seen the diary myself and studied the pages. Since I am something of an expert on Queen Fenn, the king showed it to me just after he found it. I agreed with him that it was probably written by the young Fenn that I told you about your first night here. The two pages were labeled 'Secret Passages and Other Forbidden Things,' and the drawings were highlighted with illuminations and bright colors showing dotted lines, circles, red and green Xs, and such. A legend down the left page had entries like: 'SP to Queen's Qtrs,' 'K's escape rte,' 'Spare Key to Larder,' 'Hiding places,' 'Treasures,' 'Tunnel to Wazalops.' But what really caught the king's eye was an entry at the bottom of the second page. It was there that Fenn noted there was a 'Room of Glimpses' hidden in the catacombs, and it held the 'secret of the veil.'"

Michael sat up straight.

So did Bjorg. This was obviously a surprise to him, too.

"Yes, Michael, the veil—your veil, or the *shimmering* veil you came through, to be more precise. But, at the time of the king's discovery, there was just one problem. The king was familiar with a Room of Glimpses, of course. Every castle has one. It's a private sanctuary used by royalty for reflection and devotion. But what was this about the veil? It's true that a handful of children's stories exist where kings and queens of old, when their kingdoms were in desperate need, would turn to their wizards to conjure heroes from another world through shimmering veils in the air. The heroes were called boundary travelers. But everyone knew these were just far-fetched tales of the imagination. So, how could there be a *secret* about something that wasn't real?"

"But, surely … I mean, didn't I —"

"Yes, yes, you did come to Tremora through a veil," Tracker agreed. "But Michael, until I met you on the paths of Golan, even I had doubts such a thing really existed—regardless of what the king or Megan said. I've lived my entire life, as have most Tremorans, knowing of the shimmering, but as a superstition, not a fact. Only stargazers and wizards have ever given any credence to such things."

"I don't understand."

"Well, you see, the veil is Tremora's pretend answer to all the mysteries of the world. If someone is acting strangely, he has 'a touch of the shimmering,' or if you find a shiny stone in the road, it must have 'come through the veil.' And, since there are stories of creatures and odd mechanical things coming through the openings too, it's a catchall for anything unexplainable. But these are only old yarns told around campfires or at bedtime to children. Are you getting the picture, Michael? You're not supposed to be real. You're a character in a made up story!"

Michael's brow furrowed in confusion, and Bjorg stopped midway through lifting his mug to his mouth. He looked at Michael anew. "This very, very, big secret," he said.

"Yes," Tracker nodded. "Very. And it was supposed to stay that way. But somehow Spreten found out about you, Michael. The secret of the veil lasted one day!" He looked earnestly at Bjorg. "I've notified the king, but the fact remains; I still have to get Michael safely to the Mesmer Henge, and the way is far more dangerous now than before. I'm afraid we're going to need your assistance, my friend."

Bjorg's eyes glistened bright in the lamplight. "Bjorg help!" he thundered as he pounded the table with a huge fist.

Michael jumped. He'd only been half listening. He was still trying to understand. "So, the king found out the veil was real … and you're saying he summoned me?" he said slowly. "But he didn't call me, Tracker. I was just following a new trail, looking for my father—"

"Yes, well, regardless of what you think happened," Tracker said, "Megan and the king sent me to fetch you. And they knew when and where you were coming, even your name."

"But why me, Tracker?"

Tracker looked at Michael for a long time. He wondered how much more he should tell now. His orders from the king and Megan were clear: Bring Michael to the gathering without drawing attention; tell him of the wazalops, but little else. Already he'd told far more than he was supposed to.

"Too late to change mind," Bjorg said, reading Tracker's hesitation correctly. "Still hours before can leave." He gestured with his hands to carry on.

Tracker looked at Bjorg, exasperated. But once again his friend was on point. Michael still needed to know what this had to do with him—why the wisps were after him—why someone might want him dead!

With a sigh, he continued. "I still can't answer everything you're asking, Michael. I myself was only told so much. But it's obvious the king followed the lead in Fenn's journal and found the catacombs and the Room of Glimpses and, yes, solved the riddle of the veil. But he couldn't have done it without the help of the wizard Megan. But, we need to get back to the story.

"As I was saying, in spite of thoughts to the contrary, wizards and stargazers have always believed the stories of the veil had more than a grain of truth to them; that the veil was possible, even logical. They believe there are occasional rifts in what some people call 'the luminiferous aether' that separates the world of Tremora from other worlds and that some of these openings even happen at regular intervals—like geysers and comets. They also believe that ancient stargazers knew where these weak spots were going to occur by interpreting the stars through openings in the stones of Mesmer Henge; knowledge once hidden in the onyx gardens, but now apparently lost. So, with journal in hand, the king sought Megan, the oldest and wisest living wizard in Tremora.

"And, as you can readily see, together, King William and Megan solved the riddle of the veil! But I know very little of this. What did they find in the catacombs or at Mesmer Henge or in the onyx gardens? I can't say. Perhaps the king or Megan will share that part of the story with all of us at the gathering. But I can say this: Whether through a vision or something foretold in the Room of Glimpses, the king was convinced that you, Michael, must be found and summoned. Once again, the old adage, it's never wise to question the wisdom of kings and wizards, as your presence here so aptly proves."

"But, I'm no hero … I don't have any powers. Tracker, there's some mistake …"

"There's more to you than you think, Michael. Were you fooled by the shape-changer? Could you hear Blingtrail's thoughts? Not to mention, by the way, you are very strong and move faster than most. Haven't we just witnessed some of this? I think we are only just beginning to learn who you are. But you'll just have to wait. Answers will come. As I told you before; I've made no mistake."

Michael groaned and slumped back in his chair. Hero from another world! Me! Bjorg reached out and put a huge hand on Michael's knee. It was meant to console, but he almost buckled Michael's leg.

"Sorry," the troll rumbled in apology.

Michael only nodded back numbly.

Tracker went on. "We are finally coming to the end of all that I can tell you for now. After the king found Megan, they disappeared on their business for a long time. When the king returned with Megan to Tremora Castle, he saw at once that the situation at home had grown considerably worse in the time he'd been gone. He was at the helm of a floundering ship. A new royal family was about to take over, and the court was rife with squabbling, bickering, and jostling for power. The enemy was walking among them."

Tracker suddenly stood up and stretched. It was time for a break. Bjorg poured more coffee and offered crumb cakes and beans. "Need strength tonight," Bjorg said. Michael pecked at his plate and stayed silent.

Tracker ate a cake while standing near the open window. When he finished, he restarted his pipe and returned to the table and sat down. Then he suddenly went still. He cocked an ear and held up a warning hand to the others. Just then a mouse's tiny face appeared over the edge of the table. No one moved. The mouse's black shiny eyes darted from Bjorg to Michael to Tracker as its nose and whiskers twitched excitedly. Then it slowly pulled itself up on the table and cautiously crept forward, all the while watching the three giants from the corner of its eyes. When it got to Michael's plate, it grabbed a piece of cake, squeaked, darted into Bjorg's lap, ran down his legs, across the floor, up the wall, and disappeared out the window.

"Friend hungry," Bjorg apologized.

Tracker shrugged it off with a grim smile. "A reminder that not all creatures are caught up in the affairs of the more evolved. I think you'd better eat your food up, though, Michael, while you still have some left!"

Michael quickly grabbed the cake and took a bite, but only to end the distraction. He wasn't hungry at all. He only wanted Tracker to continue.

"As I was saying," Tracker said, "the king's court was in turmoil, and the nefarious plot was ripening. People were asking: 'What if, in spite of it all, no one finds Prince Cedric? What if the king continues on with his obsessions, loses his mind, or dies?' 'What if, overnight, he becomes a dark king ... requiring sacrifices?' The people's paranoia was even causing whispers of rebellion. It might be wiser to put Myrdain on the throne now under the guidance of Lord Pratt. Wouldn't that be better than a mad monarch? The intent and truth of the evil plot lies in the answers, of course—if Cedric was not found, then the next king of Tremora was going to be the son of a witch!"

"Then that *has* to be the reason for the kidnapping," Michael blurted. "Surely there's no doubt the king's brother is behind all of this!"

Tracker looked at Michael grimly. "Yes, Michael, you're most certainly correct. Of course, the High King and Megan were convinced of this long ago. Blaming the white wizards and stargazers was only a smoke screen, and a clever one at that. Tremorans are only now beginning to realize their plight. And the shape-changer and wisps only provide further proof. Your presence in Tremora threatens the master plan, Michael. That's why Spreten's special pets are looking for you."

Michael's mind was racing, but he remained silent, fearing that if he even breathed wrong Tracker would stop talking. *But, still, why me?* he thought. *How can I threaten anyone's master plan?* He didn't understand. *And, what in the world are wisps?*

Once again, Tracker got up, put an ear to the window, and then returned to his seat. "The king, of course, saw his plight quite clearly. But contrary to before, he himself now had newfound hope—and a plan. Armed with the knowledge of the veil, the king summoned what few loyal noblemen were left in his court to a secret meeting. He was dismayed at how few the numbers were. He sent Megan to the dungeons in search of any friends that may have been wrongly imprisoned, yet still alive. Many things were discussed that night: the kidnapping and its motive, corruption in the court, Spreten, the gathering at Mesmer Henge, weeding out evil in the land, calling a hero through the veil and finding Cedric."

Tracker's voice trailed off, and he leaned back, becoming silent. He exhaled a long stream of smoke toward the ceiling, lost in thought.

Only the slight hiss of the gas in the lantern could be heard as the gravity of what he said hung heavy in the air.

Finally, Michael asked quietly, "But, Tracker, how do you know so much about the King's meeting?"

Tracker gave a start, surprised at the question and then became embarrassed. "Well, I was there, of course," he said. He gave a depreciatory shrug. "I am but a humble servant, Michael."

Bjorg snorted loudly and then sat back with a blank innocent look on his face.

Tracker dismissed Bjorg with a wave of his hand, but Michael suddenly remembered. *Of course! Didn't Tralana say something about Tracker being famous? Tracker must be someone very close to the king.*

Tracker's face became serious. He leaned forward and looked Michael in the eyes. "For now, know this, Michael. At the meeting, I was given orders to find a young boy named Michael at a certain time and date along the paths of Mount Trey in the Mountains of Golan. The information was accurate because I found you almost exactly when and where Megan said you'd be. Do you understand now, Michael? You have been summoned to find and fight the dragon and rescue our prince."

Michael went numb. The silence was broken when someone coughed outside the window.

"Quickly, Bjorg!" Tracker was out of his chair in an instant. He held his finger up to shush Michael even as he grabbed him and pulled him to his feet.

The Troll jumped up and shoved the table to the center of the room. He motioned for Michael and Tracker to place the chairs around it as he put the lamp and papers on top and stashed the mugs on a shelf. Bjorg then bent down and swung open a trap door in the floor in the very corner of the room that had been hidden by the table. The coughing became louder and someone banged on the door. "Down," Bjorg said, pointing.

Tracker grabbed his staff and backpack and jumped into the hole. Michael grabbed for the lantern but Bjorg shook his head and pushed him none too gently into the opening. "No need," Bjorg said, as he threw Michael's walking stick and backpack after him. It was the last thing Michael heard as he fell into the darkness. He dropped about four feet and landed on his hands and knees. Then his backpack clobbered him in the head, and he fell forward onto wet sandy ground. Above him, the trap door closed silently, followed by a sound of something heavy being dropped on the lid. Michael thought it sounded like a sack of potatoes. He turned toward Tracker and discovered another odd but welcome fact about his new friend. Bjorg had been correct; Michael didn't need a lantern to see. Tracker's hair was glowing in the dark!

"It happens in time of need, Michael," Tracker whispered. "A true Tremoran is never in want of light."

Meanwhile, above them in Bjorg's office, a thin, pale hand reached through the gap in the cabin's cracked window and unfastened the hook that kept the frame from swinging open. The same hand then opened the window all the way, and a black hooded head poked through the opening into the room. The only facial feature visible was the blunt end of a nose that shifted back and forth, sniffing. It was shiny and wet like a pig's, and mucus dripped in globs onto the floor.

The wisp had heard voices and movement in the troll's office earlier but was now confounded by the total silence and strange odors coming from within. The lamplight in the room showed little else but a counter, table and chairs, and a fireplace with a stone hearth in one corner. Seeing and hearing no one, the creature climbed through the window effortlessly and unlatched the front door to let in another wisp.

"The room is empty, sir," the first wisp said meekly as Malif brushed past him. He sounded like someone with a nasal condition.

"And yet, Bardak, they were just here with the troll," Malif growled as he stood, legs wide apart in the center of the room. "We both heard them!" Malif flung back his hood to expose a frightful sight. His large head was nearly hairless with a row of bumps that ran back from his forehead to the nape of his neck. He had an emaciated and sallow face with a protruding prehensile nose and rows of sharp needlelike teeth. His long, bowed neck made him look like a vulture. Malif turned and scanned the room with wet, black, shiny eyes. Then he stomped across the wooden floor with his jackboots pounding to the stone hearth in the corner. He bent over and picked up a coffee pot with one hooked skeletal claw. "See!" he hissed. "This pot is still warm, Bardak."

"But no one is here *now!*" Bardak whined. "And I still only smell the hateful troll and perhaps a rodent." He raised his head and his wet, dripping nose, jerked in all directions. "Although, something else that is not alive is stinking up this place pretty bad. It must be what's making my nose run."

Malif threw the pot against the wall. "What has that got to do with anything?" he shouted angrily. He looked up and closely scanned the ceiling for any sign of an exit and then stomped on the floor in several places looking for a trap door. But the floor was solid. "Yes, they are gone," Malif spat. He turned and gave Bardak a dark look. "And it's your fault. You would have spooked a room full of snoring sows with your coughing, you fool!"

Bardak looked down at his boots. He couldn't explain his sudden fit outside the window, nor his gooey nose. He was sure to be whipped and beaten when they returned to Spreten. And that's if he was lucky. He remained silent.

Malif growled again. "You'll answer soon enough if I have my say. Regardless, we have little time left. We need nourishing. If we don't find those two and stop them tomorrow, we'll *both* pay dearly when we return to our master." He raised his head and howled in frustration. "I can't breathe in here!" he said suddenly. With that he plunged back through the open door into the darkness. Bardak wiped his nose on his cape and, with a final sniff of the air, followed Malif, grumbling.

After several minutes the stone hearth that was covering the trap door to Tracker and Michael's hiding place slowly transformed back into the troll, Bjorg.

As the lid lifted on their hideaway, Michael and Tracker looked up anxiously. Bjorg motioned that the way was clear and then lifted them both out onto the floor. Tracker crossed over and locked the door the wisps had opened and then closed and locked the window. Then he turned and held up his pipe and pointed at its smoldering bowl. "It seems one of our willowy friends is a non-smoker," he said, chuckling, "and especially sensitive to my *skulker-finder backy!* And Michael," he added, as he reached into a vest pocket and pulled out a familiar section of corked bamboo, "it appears our Bonzo Bugger Gook has come in handy, too! I certainly didn't know it would cover our scents when I mixed this batch, and to our good fortune, it seems a wisp's nose is also rather sensitive to its properties!"

"But, who were those guys, Tracker?" Michael asked as he brushed dirt and sand off his trousers. "Were those the enemies you were talking about? Wisps? And … wait a minute … Bjorg, how come they didn't see you?"

The troll shrugged and looked away. "Not hard. They see what I want." He motioned for Michael to help move the furniture back in place.

Michael frowned, but before he could ask Bjorg what he meant, Tracker interrupted. "I'll explain it later, Michael, but yes, those were *some* of our enemies." Tracker then turned to the troll. "Bjorg, as you can see, it's more important than ever that we get across the ford tonight. You heard those two. They'll be on the lookout tomorrow. The wisp called Malif is convinced that you were hiding us. Is there any way to cross the channel at night?"

"Fly," responded Bjorg.

"Did you just say fly?" Michael asked, astonished.

"Fly," Bjorg repeated.

"Yes, I was afraid you were going to say that," said Tracker.

Chapter Seven

Trebuchet

It looked like a huge insect silhouetted against the moonlit sky. "Is that it?" Michael asked as he, Tracker, and Bjorg approached the strange wooden contraption.

"Yes, it's called a trebuchet, or thingy flinger—a kind of catapult," Tracker said. "The trolls use them to move goods quickly across the fords. They also come in handy when the waters are too rough or at night when the channel is full of flesh-eating greels. Those fish are so voracious; they'll jump into your boat to get you."

"But, you don't mean—er, he can't mean—not us …"

"It's the only way, Michael. The rafts are too dangerous at night, and those wisps will be watching tomorrow. We'll never get by them without being seen. Besides, they'll be returning to their master soon, and we don't want them to have any more information than they already have. We have to get to the other side tonight."

Michael's thoughts turned quickly to his and Tracker's conversation earlier. Bjorg had briefly left the office, and while waiting for his return, Tracker told the story of Bjorg's amazing ability to turn to stone and then the story of the wisps.

Tracker had no doubts about how Bjorg had kept the wisps from seeing him as they had entered the room. All Tremorans know secrets; some more than others. But very few, other than Tracker and his countrymen, know of a troll's ability to take the form of stone or earth at will. At night, out of sight of any witnesses, a troll simply falls into a heap of rocks to sleep, or he takes the form of a large boulder or a section of cobbled road. It's very useful when avoiding danger or spying on an enemy. Mazalon Trackers have known of these abilities for many years and have used the trolls' special powers in times of war or conflict to great advantage. Tracker told Michael it would be wise for him to keep this secret to himself.

Then Tracker told of the wisps. Michael shuddered involuntarily as he recalled the frightful tale. Tracker said the creatures were personal servants of Prelandora, the witch of Spreten. And, although Prelandora adamantly denies it and there is no proof of it, wisps are thought to be the result of the witch's dabbling in dark magic. Megan and the king were sure of it.

"It took an evil mind, indeed, to create such creatures," Tracker said. Prelandora apparently took existing, already nasty, carrion-eating scavengers and created her own monsters. Then she molded them into something almost unrecognizable and dressed them in jackboots and hoods! "Picture the naked bald head and drooping neck of a carrion-eating bird," said Tracker. "Combine that with the short flexible proboscis of a tapir and the razor teeth and black beady eyes of an opossum, and you'll know what they look like. Just hope you never have to look one in the face in person; they're hideous. It's thought that the rest of their bodies must be bird-like because when they spread their arms within their capes they can hop along the ground like a crow and even glide short distances when needed, using their capes as wings. But no one knows for sure, because no one has ever seen a wisp without its long black leather cape or black boots.

"Only a couple dozen ever exist at any time," Tracker continued, "and, although they can be dangerous—they carry stone daggers that can render a person unconscious with just a nick—their main job seems to be to roam the lands spying or acting as escorts for their master, not to do battle. Although, there are rumors of extortion and murder and torture in the darker provinces ..."

"But if that's true," Michael asked, "why haven't they been arrested? And why are they allowed to roam so freely? Tremora must have laws against these things!"

"Yes, well, Michael, no witness has ever lived to tell the tale or come forward to testify against any of them, have they? There has never been any proof of any foul deeds. And besides, as I told you, all of the king's men have been otherwise engaged for over two years in their search for Cedric."

Michael involuntarily shivered again when recalling the rest of the wisps' sordid story. They sustain themselves by feeding on the offal of the world: waste, rot, slop, or swill. And when afield, their insatiable appetite keeps them foraging in garbage heaps, bogs, cesspools, and even cemeteries! "It's why they have the heads and necks of vultures; that way they don't get the mess and gore in their hair!" said Tracker.

Michael believed he must have turned white when Tracker described this part because Tracker reached out and patted him on the back, saying all of the news wasn't quite so bad. "For one thing, they can only survive in the world outside Spreten for about a week before their bodies start to decline and lose mass and strength—eventually fading to a weak, wispy, ghostly form. To survive any longer, they need to return home and dine on a rancid concoction the witch prepares in troughs in Spreten Castle. So, they have to return every ninth or tenth day for this meal or die."

"What happens when they've eaten?" Michael asked, sure now that the "not quite so bad news" was over.

"Well yes, there is that. When finished with their feast, they become solid forms again, armed with sharp claws and teeth and stone knives dipped in their own vile gruel; ready to return to their duties. Unfortunately, that means there is always a constant supply of revitalized wisps. Oh, and they also have a keen sense of smell and can track a scent like a hound," Tracker added.

Michael guessed as much. He remembered feeling the same shiver of fear go up and down his spine then as now. It didn't help that they were sitting in almost complete darkness as Tracker told him the wisps tale. "Tracker, what can we do against something like that?" he whispered.

"It's not as hopeless as all that," Tracker assured him. "Remember, they're basically spies, not killers. When they've been away from Spreten for more than ten days, they're at the end of their strength and weight almost nothing. They must return quickly to their master with any information they've gleaned. When they do, they float on the wind with black capes flying, smelling putrid, and barely touching the treetops. If for some reason they don't reach their home in time, their bodies simple vanish into thin air, with their clothing falling to the ground and knives crumbling to dust. From what we overheard, the two that visited our cabin are obviously nearing their "wispy" stage," opined Tracker, "but they still have time to spy and attack."

"Can *anyone* stand against them?" Michael asked.

"Yes, but it would be very difficult. They seem impervious to pain and can take a lot of damage. There is one way to get to them, though, and that's to clamp their snouts shut! You see wisps are like horses and a lot of other small mammals; they are obligate nose breathers—they can't breathe through their mouths! So, with their nose passages closed off long enough, they will faint or even die. Of course, you could also keep one prisoner long enough for it to 'evaporate,' but they're very fast and evasive and are almost impossible to catch and detain. And anyway, no prison or chains could really hold one for long because it would eventually lose substance and simply float out a barred window or under a door. Since a wisp always has its poisonous daggers and claws or its face buried in its hood, no one has ever suffocated one either."

"Great," was all Michael could muster. He came back to the present.

Bjorg was pointing to a sling dangling high in the air. It was attached to the end of a long pole sticking out from the wooden frame. "You sit there," he called to Michael, as he pulled on a long rope that lowered the sling and, at the same time, raised a large loosely swinging box attached to the opposite end of the pole. He told Tracker to place a short wooden dowel with four feet of chain into a notch that locked the pole in place. Bjorg then produced two large round leather bags.

"To keep the profile of an aerodynamic projectile?" Tracker guessed.

"Don't want arms and legs flying all over place," Bjorg agreed with a smile.

"But where are we going to land?" Michael asked in dismay.

"These on other side," Bjorg said, pointing to the large hanging fishing nets. "Hit target almost every time," he added, deadpan.

Next, Bjorg cupped his hands together, threw back his head, and called into the night. A few moments later a troll that could have been Bjorg's twin, only taller and bigger, came waddling toward them from the shore.

"Counterweight," Bjorg said. "Brother, Fjorg."

Fjorg waved a huge hand to them and then climbed nimbly to the top of the creaking trebuchet. From there he jumped into the swinging wooden box and gave them a thumbs up.

Tracker and Bjorg decided that Michael should go first. Michael was pretty much numb by now and gave little argument. Besides, after Tracker's story, he agreed that they needed to put as much distance between them and the wisps as possible—and quickly. He tried to ignore the fact that he was about to be launched into the night sky across choppy waters teaming with piranha-like fish into hanging nets and seaweed that *might* break his landing.

At Bjorg's bidding, Michael stepped into one of the leather pouches and pulled the sides up and over himself and his backpack. He then crouched down and surrounded his knees with his arms as instructed. Bjorg pulled on the drawstring and the projectile took on the appearance of a big bag of grapefruit. Michael could just see a patch of starlit sky through the small opening left at the top of the bag. Bjorg and Tracker then tied several layers of the bulb kelp all around the bag before shoving everything snuggly into the sling ("to soften the impact," explained Tracker through the opening). The bulbs on the seaweed were the size of a fist and the bag of grapefruit now looked more like a bunch of very large grapes. Bjorg motioned Tracker to stand far back and then went to grab the chain attached to the wooden dowel.

"Are you ready ...?" Bjorg started, but at that very moment, a dark billowing shape suddenly rushed up from behind him. At the same time, another dark shape with a raised knife charged Michael's bag from the opposite direction.

"Pull pin!" bellowed Bjorg to Tracker as he grappled with the arms of the wisp that had jumped on his back. Tracker ran, lunged, and stretched out full length for the chain. He frantically yanked the pin free, but not before the second wisp leapt and plunged its knife deep into Michael's bag. Tracker watched helpless as the trebuchet's arm shot upwards, launching its cargo high into the sky.

Bjorg angrily flung his wisp far out into the water and turned to attend to Michael's attacker too. But the second wisp was gone. Tracker pointed upwards. The wisp could be seen trailing behind the ball of seaweed like the tail of a comet with its cape fluttering in the wind. The bag was swinging wildly, and the wisp was holding on with one outstretched arm. Tracker and Bjorg both watched helplessly as the bag and the wisp and Michael kept climbing and climbing, higher and higher into the sky. The whole tangle reflected in the moonlight and looked like a shooting star. Then, just as it seemed to reach its highest peak, a blood-curdling scream pierced the night; moments later, a faint splash. Next, a larger splash farther out across the water; then silence, broken only by the sound of lapping water at Bjorg and Tracker's feet.

Chapter Eight

A Wet Landing

Michael crouched inside his tiny capsule, waiting anxiously. It was dark and cramped, and he was starting to think that this whole trebuchet-thingy-flinger thing was a very bad idea. He heard Bjorg's muffled voice ask, "Are you ready?" but before he could answer, Bjorg frantically bellowed to Tracker, "PULL THE PIN!"

Michael heard more yelling and felt a jolt of panic. "Hey, what the ...?" he shouted as he struggled to untie the drawstring holding him inside the leather ball. Before he could fully loosen the opening, however, he was slammed hard from behind and then the arm of the trebuchet jerked him violently upwards. His heart leapt into his throat as, feet first, he was hurled high into the sky in the direction of the far shore. Unfortunately for Michael, his troubles were just beginning.

Once launched, the bag started wobbling crazily and Michael was struck instantly with vertigo as his head whipped back and forth and side to side. He was so dizzy he didn't know which way was up. He knew one thing for sure, though: If he didn't orient himself pretty quickly, he was going to fill his small enclosure with something very unpleasant. Hoping to get a glimpse of the ground, he strained backward to look out the opening above his head (which was pointing downwards!), and there, to his horror, he saw a hand with long sharp claws gripping the collar of his bag. Then, even more horrific, at the other end of the outstretched arm, he saw a skeletal face with a large wriggly snout sneering up at him.

In a heartbeat he knew: A wisp! But, how? His mind raced as he watched the beast struggling to gain a better purchase on the gyrating bag. *I can't let him get me!* He reached down and frantically tried to unpry the creature's bony fingers from the bag, but its grip was very strong, and even though Michael thought he could actually feel some of the bones breaking, the wisp only laughed at him and lurched with even more effort until it got hold of the bag with both hands. That must have put everything in balance because the wobbling of the bag lessened dramatically. The wisp grinned. Then it pulled itself up until its head was only inches from Michael's downturned face.

"When we land, you'll be mine!" it snarled, showing rows of sharp yellow teeth beneath its long, prominent snout.

Michael stared wild-eyed. He had never felt more afraid in his life. Then he flashed on Tracker's story about how to kill a wisp. Without another thought, he grasped the creature's rubbery nose midway along its length and squeezed with both hands.

For a second nothing happened—then the wisp's eyes grew wide, its mouth gaped open, and it went berserk. It was like a dog on the end of a rubber pull toy and Michael held on for dear life. As the wisp thrashed around crazily, it tried to bite Michael's hands and grab at his arms while still holding onto the bag with one hand. Michael felt a sharp pain in one wrist where a claw drew blood, but he knew he'd better not let go.

Spittle and mucus were flying everywhere! *Oh, gross!* thought Michael as his face got splattered. He scrunched his eyes shut and turned his head to the side the best he could. Then his ears popped and his head got as light as a helium-filled balloon. He was going to faint! The effort to hold onto the fleshy nose of the frantically, jerking wisp was sapping his own strength faster than the other way around! In a last ditch effort he redoubled his grip and felt something give between his hands.

The wisp gave a blood-curdling scream, and the crazy jerking suddenly stopped. Michael unclenched his eyes as the wisp's body went limp. When the wisp's hands slipped off the bag it was left dangling by its nose; the nose that Michael was still holding! Their eyes met for a frozen moment. Then the wisp made one last feeble effort to claw at Michael, but it only resulted in a fist full of bulb kelp. Michael let go and the wisp fell fluttering to the waters below.

Michael's eyes followed the wisp's fall in astonishment. *If Tracker hadn't told me ...* However, he had no time for further thought because he himself was now descending at an alarming rate.

He braced himself for the landing in the netting on the other side of the water. But, unknown to him, the weight and antics of the wisp had sent him careening far off course, and instead of reaching the array of fishing nets on the shore as intended, Michael fell far short of the target, and hit the teeming waters of the Gush with a huge splash. His last thoughts before losing consciousness were that the bulb kelp hadn't softened his landing all that much because he felt a sharp pain in his back and ... *Why am I so wet? And, hey, if this is the Gush, aren't there piranhas in this water?*

Chapter Nine

Flotsam and Jetsam

Tracker and the two trolls stood silently gazing out across the water. Finally Bjorg said, "Bulbs keep him afloat."

"Yes, but is he still alive?" Tracker asked, barely loud enough to be heard. "He was stabbed after all, and what about the fish …"

"Greel no eat kelp," Fjorg said. "Eat wisps though." He pointed toward a frenzy of activity churning on the surface of the water where Bjorg had thrown his attacker.

Tracker watched as the moonlight reflected off the silvery backs of the ravenous fish. Another secret revealed, he thought grimly.

"Now know another way kill wisps," Bjorg said, echoing Tracker's thoughts.

"Where will he end up Bjorg? And when can we go after him?"

"Not yet," Bjorg said, as they continued to watch the spectacle in the water. "Greel hunt with moon." The wisp's cape surfaced and slowly floated away with the current.

"But where will he end up?" Tracker asked again.

"Float many miles," said Bjorg.

Fortunately for Michael, the wisp's attempt to stab him at the fords was blocked by layers of bulb kelp and his own bulky backpack.

Unfortunately for Michael, the knife remained imbedded in his bag during his flight over the water. When he splash landed, the impact drove the tip of the knife into his back and sliced him badly. And, although the wound wasn't fatal, the poison on the wisp's knife blade left him unconscious.

As the current carried him downstream, an occasional school of curious greel fish swam by. But, being meat eaters, they weren't drawn to the bulb kelp that kept Michael afloat, and the scent of blood mixed with poison and Bugger Gook didn't appeal to them either. Finding nothing of interest, they continued on their hunt, unaware that a tasty dinner had been just inches away.

Several hours later, long after moonset and sunrise, Michael came to. He was lying on a sandy beach, head to one side, on his stomach, wet, and shivering. His backpack was caddywhumped (a strap was broken), and his bare back was exposed by a long tear in his shirt. He was vaguely aware of being jostled.

He slowly opened one eye and saw a large animal's head and muzzle only inches from his face. He quickly scrunched his eye closed again. *Ohhh, let me be dreaming*, he prayed. But no, it was a real animal all right, and it was sniffing and snorting as it prodded and nudged him: first his backpack and then his whole body, head to foot. The creature then licked at his back with what must have been a huge tongue, rocking him back and forth with the force.

Oh, yuck! Michael grimaced. *What should I do?* He stiffened his body, not knowing whether he should play dead, jump up and run, scream …

The licking suddenly stopped, however, and in the next moment, "*Yes, I thought so. It's awake. And, my goodness, I think…could it be?*"

The voice was garbled as if coming from under water, and it filled Michael's head. *Oh no, not again … Mother? Blingtrail?* No, this was a new voice invading his mind, and it was the voice of a young girl.

He daren't move, but the impulse to get up and run overtook him when he next heard heavy breathing and footsteps approaching. He started to rise, but immediately felt excruciating pain in his back and shoulders and fell back to the sand, groaning.

"You must lie very still, young master, if you please," called out a high-pitched, lilting male voice. "You will not be harmed. A camelop's saliva is most healing, and you've got a nasty looking cut there, I see."

Michael lay motionless, but his mind reeled. He didn't know where he was and couldn't get up; his back was on fire, an animal was about to eat him, and a new voice had invaded his head; and now, yet another stranger's voice was apparently talking to him. *And, where was Tracker?* He risked another cautious peek, and this time he saw a very fat man with short stubby legs coming toward him. The man had a large curling mustache, a dark turban, and several layers of flowing robes. He was breathing hard from running in the sand and was holding out both arms and hands towards Michael, motioning for him to stay down.

"Luckily the salt water has also washed your wound very clean," the man said, as he knelt and examined the gash on Michael's back. Sweat dripped from his brow, and he was still panting and puffing. He carefully removed the tattered backpack from Michael's shoulders and then gingerly held up the wisp's stone knife between a fat thumb and finger. His expression turned to one of surprise.

"Why, my goodness, look at this, will you … but surely … no, this can't be a wisp's dagger." He looked back at Michael, incredulous. "If so, you are so very fortunate to be alive—this blade is soaked in a most unsavory potion." He flung the knife away in disgust, and it stuck fast in a piece of driftwood. He then looked around and spied the leather bag and pile of bulb kelp. Curious, he heaved himself to his feet and walked over to take a closer look. "This," he said, probing with his bare foot, "is surely a cargo bag with the symbol of the handlers at the ford …" He then put a finger to his lips and looked thoughtful. "And, by the marks in the sand, you crawled out of this bag …" He paused, and then his eyes opened wide. "Ooooh, by the great beard! Of course! All that bulb kelp. Why, I do believe you have floated here from the troll's crossing!" He looked back expectantly, but Michael still lay unmoving in the sand.

Michael heard everything the man said, but he wasn't about to strike up a conversation. And anyway, he couldn't say if the man was right or wrong, even if he wanted to: He couldn't remember! The poison was still at work. He felt very weak, and his head was completely muddled. When he tried to remember anything, he had glimpses of the trebuchet, the launch, the in-flight tussle … even the wisp dying, but then nothing. He had no idea how he got there.

Suddenly, the girl's voice echoed in his head in disbelief, "*You rode the trebuchet! You killed a wisp!*"

At the same time the man was continuing with his speculations, "and since you are a young boy, could it be that you are Tracker's companion? But, by golly, where then is Tracker? Is he alive then? Has he …" The voice droned on, but Michael had already lost consciousness.

Chapter Ten

Novalena

Michael felt himself being jostled again. This time, he was sure he was in the middle of an earthquake. *I've got to get out of here*, was his first frantic thought as he opened his eyes. But, as before, when he tried to rise, he couldn't move. This time it was because he was lying on his side, wound tightly in a blanket, and strapped to a stretcher. He also realized he was being dragged along the ground behind a plodding animal. *Well, that accounts for all the bouncing*, he thought, relieved. Making sense of anything was a victory in his drugged state of mind. Then, another incongruous thought: *This is a travois*, he said to himself, smugly. *I learned all about these in US History while studying the Great Plains Indians.* He was so pleased with himself for solving such a difficult puzzle that he drifted back off to sleep without considering the more serious fact that he was obviously the fat man's prisoner.

Much later, he again opened his eyes. He vaguely remembered someone pouring a warm liquid down his throat while he was half awake, but the memory wasn't unpleasant. The liquid tasted good, and he felt better for it. He was still being bounced and dragged along behind some kind of pack animal, but his arms were outside his bindings now, and he realized he was lying on his side to protect his bandaged back. *Well, he must want me alive*, Michael thought, as he wondered about his captor.

Then he heard a familiar snort. He looked behind him and there was the animal with the long face that had nudged him awake on the beach. This time he wasn't frightened at all: It was a friendly face and looked a lot like a camel. It was leading a long caravan of similar animals that were draped in all types of colored blankets, dangling silk ropes, and sundry frippery and fanciness. Interestingly, though, this one only had a plain length of rope wrapped around its nose. The face was all the more friendly because of its large brown eyes and extremely long lashes. *Could this be a camelop like Tracker was talking about?* he wondered. He thought the animal looked intelligent.

"*Why thank you, young master.*"

It was the girl's voice from the beach! With a wave of comprehension Michael realized it was this animal that was sending its thoughts, just like the elves and his mother.

"*Let me introduce myself,*" the voice continued. "*My name is Novalena, and, yes, I am a camelop. A very famous camelop, I might add. You may call me Nova. And, yes, you are correct again; I am considered quite intelligent. But! I must correct you on one thing. I wouldn't be so sure about Kalib's intentions. The only reason you are alive is because he thinks you might be valuable.*"

Michael stared. Then, tentatively, "*Ahmmm, OK …*"

"*Very good, very good! Now, what is your name, young master?*"

"*M-m-michael …*"

"*Well now, M-m-michael with three Ms,*" she said, amused, "*first off, we have a little secret, you and I. Quite appropriate, this being the Age of Secrets. It would not be wise to let anyone know that I, too, am a Grock. No, that would not do at all. If Kalib—*"

"*Grock?*" Michael interrupted, frowning.

"*Yes, Grock. Surely, you know of your gift?*"

"*Err, well, yes, I guess I do, but …*"

Nova started in surprise. "*But aren't you a wizard's apprentice or a prince or a young knight, or, or, someone …?*"

"*No, I'm none of those people,*" said Michael, suddenly uncomfortable.

"*But, don't you know Tracker, and, and my goodness, you've killed a wisp!*"

Tralana's warning came into his head. How much should he reveal? He played it safe. *"I am just a boy who was in the wrong place at the wrong time, and I barely know Tracker."*

Nova hurried to his side. *"Michael, I don't know if all of that's true, but you are in grave danger, in any event. Do not be fooled by Kalib and his affable ways. He is a very unpleasant man. You will be talking to him soon, and I see I must tell you a few things first—and quickly. Your life will be worthless if Kalib thinks you are merely a common peasant. He believes you are under Tracker's protection. And yet, even this would not save you if he found you could communicate thusly; you would be sold and shipped to Spreten in a heartbeat."*

"Spreten!" More danger signals, and the name Kalib also sounded familiar. "*Nova, my head is splitting, and I can barely follow you. Whatever are you talking about?"*

She slowed her pace and fell back behind Michael again.

"You and I can send and received thoughts, but only with other Grocks," she said carefully. *"We are unique. In fact, I myself am especially unique. Animals are almost never full Grocks—there is perhaps no other in all of Tremora!"*

Michael's head nodded to his chest.

"*Michael!"*

His head snapped back up. *"Yes, yes, sorry, but I'm very tired. Go on, go on, you were saying?"*

"I was saying," she said, with concern in her voice, "*it appears you, too, are blessed but have no idea how to use your power.* She held his gaze as she plodded along. When Michael didn't respond, she assumed she was correct.

"So, I'm guessing this is your first voluntary exchange. Michael, I'm so excited! You're only the third Grock I've ever met. I didn't know I could read minds either. Then I met two elves on the island of Coriss who introduced me to my gift and taught me all the languages of Tremora. But that's a sad story for another time, I think…?"

"Yes, Nova, another time," Michael half thought, half mumbled out loud.

Nova took note. *"You'll eventually learn not to move your lips, as it is completely unnecessary. And you'll also learn when to speak out loud and when to read and send using your mind."*

"Er, OK …"

"Very good, again. It can create awkward moments, as you can well imagine. You'll catch on though, with my help. Very few can do it better. And now, more about me! I'm not one to brag, you understand, but as I said, I am a very famous racing camelop," Nova bowed her head modestly and flapped her ample eyelashes. *"I've never lost, you know. But sadly, now I'm on my way to my last race."* Nova pulled a gloomy face.

Nova's constant talking was making Michael's headache worse, and weariness was rapidly overtaking him again. He was poisoned, tired, strapped down, uncomfortable, apparently a prisoner, and not in the best of moods. But in spite of it all, when he looked at Nova and saw a long face pulling a longer face, he almost laughed. He thought she looked rather silly. *And, "not one to brag"? Oh, please. Who's she kidding? She is totally self-centered!* He was soon sorry for being so candid and tactless. Nova was still reading his mind.

"No need to be so judgmental! I'm only stating facts. The king himself has summoned me, you know. That's why it's my last race," she said, indignantly. *And if you don't want another Grock to read your thoughts, then learn to flag them first as private,"* she snapped.

"Sorry, I'm not used to …"

"*Not out loud!*"

"Oh, right. Sorry again. Just not used to having other people … er animals ... er Grocks, I mean, invade my head. Look, I don't want to be rude again or interrupt, and I'm terribly interested in your personal story, but could you get to the point and at least tell me where I am? And who is Kalib anyway? And where are we going? And, could you maybe teach me that 'flag' thing before we go too much farther?"

✠

Michael once again woke from a deep slumber to jostling and bumping. He was still being dragged behind a pack animal. He immediately flagged his thoughts. He wasn't going to forget that lesson for a long time. He kept his eyes closed and pondered what Nova had told him before he dozed off. She had first noticed him lying on the beach while swimming across the shallow animal crossing at Neerwood and decided to veer off and investigate. When she reached him, she first checked the three Bs (breathing, bleeding, and bones) and was administering a camelop's standard treatment for an open wound (licking) when Kalib arrived, puffing and out of breath. The merchant got very excited when he discovered it was a young boy lying there in the sand. Kalib hurriedly bandaged the boy's knife wound and, then, with the help of a servant, carried him back to the path and strapped him behind a pack mule. There was little time to spare as they were all on their way to the Bearcamp races.

Michael slowly opened his eyes and this time noticed a young, brown, turbaned boy walking at his side with long dreadlocks almost to his waist and carrying a leather flask around his shoulder. "Soon, we will be stopping for the night," the boy said when he noticed Michael looking at him. "Drink this. It is most medicinal, and it will also keep your stomach happy until evening meal. You must be hungry, and Sahib Kalib is anxious to talk at you. We will all meet in the tent after the tethering and feeding of the animals." The boy then dashed off.

Nova listened to the exchange intently. When the boy left, she moved forward and nudged Michael with her nose to let him know she wanted to talk. "Oh, right," Michael said.

He unflagged and Nova warned, "*Remember; be wary of Kalib, Michael. He would normally have stolen all of your possessions and left you for dead back there.*" She paused. "*But, he has acted very unKalib-like with you. I think the king's message has really undone him. He's still unsure of just who you are but fears you are indeed Tracker's companion. Regardless, please remember he is a merchant first and friend last … very last. He would sell your story, your possessions, and your very soul for a gold coin. And he must never, ever know that you are a Grock.*"

"*Yes, yes, I know, and I'll remember. But, so what if I am Tracker's companion? And what's that about a king's message?*"

"*Well, Kalib is very much in fear of your friend. You see, he owes Tracker a huge debt. Years ago, Tracker saved Kalib's entire caravan from being savaged by wolves in the Pishtock Mountains. To show his gratitude, Kalib offered the next newborn calf of his famous racing camelops as a reward, to be claimed at some future date of Tracker's choosing. Since that first born turned out to be me, and I am the most famous camelop of all time, Kalib is understandably reluctant to pay off this debt. But now, he has no choice. He must give me up after the last lop race in just a few days."*

"But what about the message from the king?"

"Well, that's just it, isn't it? The king himself is the one demanding that Kalib give me over to Tracker. Kalib was awakened in the middle of the night just a few days ago with a bird hovering in his face. The message from the king was very clear: Kalib was to honor his debt to Tracker after the Bearcamp races because I'm needed for king's business." Again, Nova bowed her head modestly. "*As I think I have already mentioned ... And since Tracker is a Mazalon Warrior, then I am obviously going to help perform some very important task that will probably save the world."*

She paused for effect. However, Michael appeared more distracted than impressed. After a few moments of plodding, she chose to forgive him for his insensitivity and continued, "*Oh, and there's also mention in the king's note of a young boy who would be accompanying Tracker as well. And that, my dear, is what probably saved your life."*

Michael stayed silent. He wanted to ask more questions, but weariness again overtook him, and he drifted off into a fitful sleep.

Later, as evening approached, the procession came slowly to a halt, and the turbaned boy reappeared. He nudged Michael awake and freed him from the travois. His name was Falin, and he said he was a camboy whose duties were to keep the master's famous racing animals groomed, fed, and happy. Since he had need of the pack animal, Michael would have to walk the rest of the way to the camp.

"*Humph*" and a lot of snorting was Nova's response. "*He's also one of Kalib's lackeys. Nice enough young fellow when alone, mind you, but he's a slave and serves only one master. Kalib's every wish is his command. He's also a thief and a spy and can't be trusted, Michael. Check your pockets!"*

Meanwhile, Falin was pointing ahead. "Please, go to the striped tent, and do not stray from the trail. Kalib would be very unhappy if he had to send someone to find you."

Falin then turned and took off in the opposite direction, dragging Michael's reluctant mule behind him. Another, similar looking boy with dreadlocks appeared and grabbed Nova's halter. He nodded at Michael without comment. Michael acknowledged and then stretched painfully. He took a few unsteady steps in the direction Falin had pointed and suddenly stopped. His bandaged back ached a little, but overall he was just stiff from being bound like a piece of luggage for the best part of a day. No, that was not it. He stopped because he realized his backpack was gone and, indeed, even his buck knife and belt was missing.

"*Lucky you still have your boots,*" said Nova over her shoulder, as she was being led away by the rope that circled her muzzle. "*And, Michael?*"

"*Yes?*"

"*Be careful! What you see may not be what you think you see. Kalib has many tricks.*"

Michael broke a branch to use as a walking stick and limped slowly along the road until he topped a rise and saw the evening camp being assembled below. The procession had halted in a large meadow just shy of an opening in the forest where the road continued on into the shadows. Bales of hay and bags of oats were being unloaded from the back of carts, and as the camelops arrived, each was tied to a line of heavy rope that was staked in the shape of a large half circle. A group of brightly colored tents stretched in a straight line from one end of the meadow to the other, making the camp look like a giant protractor. The largest tent stood in the very middle of it all. It was decorated with thick black and white stripes, golden flags, and long silver flowing banners. Smoke rose from a hole in its roof, and an orange glow spilled out onto the ground through the open flaps at the entrance. A flurry of activity inside the tent was evidenced by shadows dancing in the light.

Michael followed the trail down to the main tent and was immediately accosted by a large black man. He was sitting at the entrance of the tent on a stack of cushions. He was naked from the waist up and dressed in satin pants with pointed shoes that curved upwards with gold balls on their tips. He was completely bald and was picking his teeth with a large curved scimitar. Michael had never seen a more ferocious face in his life.

Pointing the blade at Michael, the sentry raised an eyebrow as if to ask, “What do you want?”

“I’m, I’m here to see Master Kalib,” Michael said. “I think he is expecting me.”

The giant continued to eye Michael. Finally, he grunted and drew a line in the dirt with his sword. He gave a warning look as if to say, “Cross this line and you die!” He then turned and disappeared into the tent, closing the flaps behind him.

Good grief, doesn’t anyone in this world just have normal conversation? Michael wondered.

Michael didn’t have to wait long. The giant soon returned. He threw back the flaps of the tent and, glowering, reached out and grabbed Michael’s walking stick and crumbled it into sawdust. He then smiled wide, showing gleaming white teeth. He bowed low at the waist and indicated with a sweep of both arms and a tilt of his head that Michael should enter.

Michael sidled through the gap between the tent and the giant, who seemed quite happy to make it difficult to slide by. Once inside, Michael was startled to see the tent was much larger than it appeared from the outside. *Was this what Nova was talking about?*

The floor was covered with straw, ornate rugs, and satin cushions. Fires flickered from low metal braziers stuck in the ground around the inside perimeter, and there, reclining in the center of it all, was Kalib. He was attended by two brown, veiled, dark-haired servant girls that looked remarkably like Falin. One was painting Kalib’s toenails, and the other was serving him peeled grapes from a silver tray. A third girl entered the tent from behind Michael and went to Kalib and began to primp the merchant’s locks, mustaches, and beard. The pedicurist had glanced up as Michael entered, and the other two girls also now watched him curiously. Michael noticed that the source of the smoke he had seen coming out of the top of the tent earlier was a large elaborate brass water pipe. Kalib puffed serenely on the hookah while lazily eyeing Michael.

“Welcome traveler!” Kalib said, with the same high-pitched voice Michael first heard on the beach. “I seem to have saved your life today.” He took a long drag on the pipe through a hose and mouthpiece and exhaled thick blue smoke through his nose. “And yet, I don’t even know your name. Please sit, be comfortable, have a puff. Tell me your tale—everything! Surely your story is remarkable." Kalib's demeanor was languid, but his eyes betrayed a much keener awareness.

The smoke in the room was palatable and the effect on Michael was almost immediate. At Kalib's invitation, he knelt on a pillow and then melted into a reclining position that mirrored that of his host. Michael had never smoked anything in his life, but readily took the tip of the hose offered by the young girl kneeling closest to him. When he inhaled deeply, all contact with the real world vanished.

Kalib smiled.

Chapter Eleven

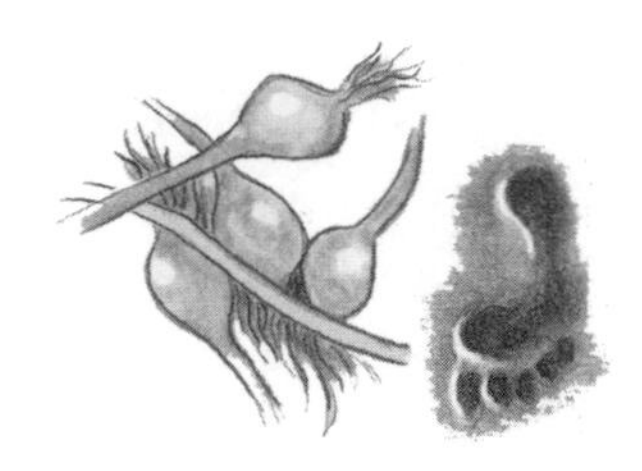

A Bit of Tracking

Tracker and Bjorg stood balanced, legs wide apart, on a small raft, grasping and pulling a thick rope connecting Charn to Havenland. The sun had hardly peeked over the horizon when they had set out in earnest to find Michael. The water was choppy and there was still the possibility of a rogue greel fish in the water, but Tracker would wait no longer. They finally reached the island, and Tracker quickly leaped ashore. Bjorg stayed on the flimsy raft. Tracker reached out with his staff and roughly pushed the outstretched fist of his friend. "The adventure continues," he said.

Bjorg acknowledged and pointed in the direction Tracker must go. With a grunt, he then turned and, hand over hand, started his return trip to Charn.

Tracker knew Michael had fallen far short of the nets when he heard him splash into the water. The layer of bulb kelp would have softened his landing, but did the wisp kill him before it, too, fell into the deadly waters? Bjorg said the bag would float north on the current and eventually wash up ashore, but when and where? Tracker could only hope that Michael was still alive, but of course he could also be dead and swept out to sea. With that sobering thought, Tracker bound off in earnest carrying both Michael's staff and his own.

The Mazalon Trackers of Gondalor have powers of direction and observation without equal. Magnetic north? Without effort they can tell you the exact direction you are heading at any time. Perhaps it's the sprinkles of iron that their mothers put in their food during their first years of childhood. Does an infinitesimal amount stay in the bloodstream, forever signaling north like the arrow of a compass? And, as to their powers of deduction, it is near magic. Thus it was, with little conscious effort, that Tracker observed the speed of the Gush's current, factored Michael's approximate weight and that of the bag and kelp, and calculated how far he might have floated downstream from the moment he first hit the water. Even though the current was running slowly, he knew he had hours of hiking in front of him.

He hurried along as best he could, but his progress was hampered by driftwood and brush that reached right to the water's edge. After three or four hours, Tracker's senses peaked. He was in an area where Michael could have come ashore. Ahead of him where the shoreline jutted out sharply into the channel, the sand was strewn with jagged rocks and debris. *Looks like that promontory catches a lot of floating stuff,* he thought. He carefully leapt from rock to rock keeping his eyes peeled. As he rounded the point, he jumped down onto a small sandy stretch of beach and saw a large mound of bulb kelp that had recently washed up on shore; it was still being jostled by the tide. *Michael's cushioning!* He was sure of it.

He rushed up and immediately started to piece the story together. *Michael crawled along the beach here—but, what is this? Camelop toes? Two sets of bare feet, one large, made by a very heavy person, one light, younger—and there, heavier steps yet, leading into the brush … They carried Michael away! And there, a wisp's knife buried deep in a piece of driftwood.* It crumbled to dust when he tried to pull it out. *Would anyone have carried Michael off if he wasn't alive? I don't think so!* That was the good news, but an uneasy feeling started to materialize: *Camelops—a very heavy man—could Kalib and Michael's paths have crossed? That would be very bad, indeed.*

Tracker followed the footprints easily to the Neerwood crossing. There he read signs that showed Michael was transferred to a travois. This was easily deduced by the footprints in the soft soil and two deep grooves split by the hooves of a pack animal (a mule according to the scat present) that led away toward the road to Bearcamp. Tracker became even more convinced that Michael was in the hands of Kalib when the trail joined a caravan of camelops and wagons.

He had to hurry now because Tracker knew Kalib very well. Kalib was a merchant of sordid reputation; the same merchant that enslaved the elves and faeries. But he was even more famous as a dealer of information. Anything gleaned from Michael would soon land in the hands of Spreten. Kalib had no scruples when it came to questioning an unsuspecting victim, and he always sold his knowledge to the highest bidder. In this case, that would be the agents of Spreten. His methods have never been revealed, but it was said that one conversation with Kalib will expose a person's very soul.

Tracker had to reach Michael soon, or the king's quest would be doomed. Not to mention, Tracker also had some personal matters to take care of with this merchant of questionable character …

Chapter Twelve

Kalib Revealed

Someone was asking him a difficult question. But Michael's mind was as foggy as the smoke in the tent. And an image was flickering in his head—a small person, a girl, her name was Tralana—and she was shaking a finger at him. *Why is she stomping her foot?*

"Surely you can remember your name, young master," a high-pitched voice was saying.

Michael gave a weak laugh. He licked his lips and mouthed a response, but nothing came out. He laughed again. Then he managed to mutter, "Yes, yes, of course. Of course I know my own name. It's just ...well, I must be careful, you know ..." He creased his brow and waved a warning finger back and forth at Kalib like the hand on a metronome.

"But you have nothing to fear from us!" Kalib cried out with his arms stretched wide to include the three young servant girls attending him. One of them pushed a pipe stem toward Michael, and he inhaled again, causing a fit of coughing. Kalib looked at him expectantly.

"My name ..." Michael said and then stopped. His head swayed back and forth as he looked from one servant to the other to the other, confused. Then with great effort he straightened his shoulders and slurred, "My name is Mmmmmichael ... And that's with three mmmms!" This set him off giggling, and he grabbed his stomach as tears streamed down his face.

Kalib watched Michael in disgust. "The leaf in the pipe is obviously too strong for a boy this young," he said to no one in particular. "Bah!" he spat. Kalib then tried another tactic. "Well Michael, let's start with your friend Tracker then, shall we? You do know him, don't you?"

Suddenly, the flaps of the tent entrance were thrown back, and a figure stood silhouetted against the evening sky. It was holding a staff in one hand and a large blade in the other. Kalib shouted. In an instant his three servants transformed into giant black guards, one of which was Michael's original greeter, with scimitars raised. Michael's mouth fell open in disbelief.

"Is that any way to welcome a friend, Kalib?" a familiar voice drawled. The mystery figure stepped forward into the reflected fire light, and the three guards moved in sync to form a barrier in front of Kalib.

"Peace, my moppets," whispered Kalib, never taking his eyes off the intruder. The guards lowered their weapons and recognition registered on their faces. "Very few have witnessed the Tres transformation and lived," Kalib said softly. "This is the second time you have been privy to my little secret, Tracker."

"Yes, well, I'm thinking there are several dead wolves in the snow that belie any regrets you might have from the first time," Tracker said. He gestured toward Michael with his staff. "I see you've been enjoying the company of my friend."

Michael's head lolled backwards. "Ello there, Trackerrr … We were just talkin' about choo! Hey, did you shee that just now?" he asked incredulously, as he pointed at the giants. "I mean, wowww …" His hand flopped back into his lap, and he went back to staring at the trio.

Kalib gestured to the guards to stay calm. "No harm's been done here, Tracker. He has no tolerance for the hookah, your friend. That is all. I doubt that he'll remember anything of our little talk."

Tracker's demeanor suddenly changed. He lowered both weapons, sweeping them back and forth. The air crackled with static as he growled. "Enough, Kalib. Your methods are known to me. If anything said today gets to the king's enemies, you will be hunted and tried for treason." Tracker turned to one of the guards. "You! Go and get

Novalena. Now!" He pointed his staff menacingly. The guard looked at Kalib for direction. "Go!" shouted Tracker again.

Kalib gave a barely noticeable nod. The guard stood up straight and transformed into the camboy Falin. Michael gasped again … then clapped as if watching a magic show. Falin disappeared through the flaps at the entrance to the tent.

"And you," Tracker said pointing to a second guard with his staff, while keeping his blade pointed at Kalib's throat, "retrieve all of the things you have stolen from Michael and bring them here. And, if you forget anything—anything!—your master will be very sorry." This guard, too, looked at Kalib for a signal. Kalib again barely nodded. The giant transformed into another small turbaned boy and hurried through a second opening in the tent behind Kalib.

"Now, for some fresh air," Tracker said. "Michael? Stand steady. Kalib? After you."

"But, what about the wishp, Trackerrr …?" slurred Michael.

"It's dead, Michael. It's OK. I'll tell you all about it later."

Tracker stood aside and waved the huge merchant out the door. Kalib waddled forward, followed closely by his third servant. Tracker grabbed Michael's elbow and helped him to his feet. Then they followed Kalib and his guard out the door, closing the flap behind them.

Unnoticed, another small servant girl emerged from the shadows. She crept to the tent flaps, made a small opening with her hairy hands, and watched intently.

Kalib was talking with his hands waving, even before he turned around. "You can't take Novalena yet, Tracker. I'll surely be ruined," he whined. "She's the main attraction, after all. She has a huge following. By the beard, Tracker, I didn't learn anything from that boy, and of course, we were only keeping his belongings *safe*. I didn't even know who he was. And didn't I save his life?" Kalib went to his knees with hands pleading.

"Get up, Kalib," Tracker ordered. "Fortunate for you, I am a servant of the king, and his wishes are my command. You were instructed to hand over Novalena *after* the last race, and I won't interfere with that directive."

"Oh, Tracker, you are a most admirable fellow. I am again in your debt!" Kalib wrung Trackers clothes. His relief was immense.

"Thank you, thank you. Of course I have no camelop to give you this time," he joked, nervously. "But, I am your humble servant, and all I have is yours until we part ways again." He patted Tracker's arms and stepped back bowing.

"Hmm, you may live to regret that commitment, too, Kalib. For now, though, we just need food and a safe place to rest."

"Fortina will make the preparations," Kalib said, as he dispatched his third servant with a sharp gesture. This giant changed into a servant girl and quickly disappeared.

Just then, Falin arrived, leading Nova. Then the second camboy rushed up and dropped a sack in front of Tracker and Michael. He backed quickly away with his nose to the ground.

"Michael, go through your belongings and make sure nothing is missing," Tracker said as he reached out and caressed Nova's muzzle. He gently touched the piece of rope surrounding her nose. "I see you still wear the reminder I left with you." He'd attached a length of magical hemp rope to the young camelop years ago to ensure he could always identify his prize.

"Didn't have much choice did I?" Nova shot at Michael. *"Clashed with everything I've ever worn."* Nova tilted her head and looked at Michael with concern. *"Michael, your mind is as fuzzy as a peach. What has that slug done to you?"*

Michael sat down heavily on the pile of cushions by the tent entrance. *"I'll be all right, Nova. The air is clearing my head."* He fumbled absently at the knot on the burlap sack. Then he poured its contents out on the ground in front of him. There was his hat, knife, belt, and ripped backpack. The contents of the backpack had also been removed: travel mix, one plastic bottle of water, energy bars, bug repellent, mirror, matches, poncho, and the king's scroll ... Even his cell phone—which he had completely forgotten. *Wonder how many bars I've got?* he thought wryly. Then, there amid the pile, something unfamiliar: an envelope addressed to Michael in his mother's hand. He picked it up slowly and looked quizzically at Tracker. "I don't remember this," he said. "It's from my mother."

Tracker took the envelope from him and looked closely at the writing. "I think you should wait before opening this, Michael. Is there anything missing?" he asked with a nod to the items on the ground.

"No. It's all here. But I think I left my walking stick back at the beach …" Michael looked around helplessly, still dazed.

"No, here it is. I brought it with me," said Tracker as he retrieved the staff from the grass where he had left it before entering the tent.

Michael took it absently. He had gone back to looking curiously at the letter from his mother that Tracker still had in his hands.

"Now, Michael, I think we should talk before you read this," said Tracker. "There's, ahem, there's more to your story than I've been able to tell you. As I said earlier, there were things Megan thought better to hold until the meeting of the wizards. But I fear any hope of that coming to pass has just been dashed. And, I fear this letter is going to leave you in a very bad mood."

Chapter Thirteen

Kalib's Good Fortune

Kalib lay reclining once again on his satin cushions, pipe stem in mouth. A servant fanned him slowly with a large colorful feather. His eyes looked up, unseeing, as he pondered his recent luck. One moment he was in danger of losing his guards, his best camelop, the biggest gambling score of his life, and the next moment that stupid oaf Tracker lets him off the hook.

No, that's not quite right, is it? he corrected himself. Tracker was in fact a very dangerous adversary—on all fronts: He couldn't be beaten in combat (he was a Mazalon warrior, after all), you couldn't hide from him (he was a Mazalon tracker), he was a confidant of the king, he had a mind as sharp as his blade, and, most dangerous of all, he knew secrets. No, Kalib would have to be very careful with this unexpected reprieve, very careful, indeed.

This was Kalib's second recent brush with disaster. When he had been rudely awakened by the king's fluster bird just days ago, he had been sure his life was over. *A personal message from the king? It has to be a summons to the gallows,* he had thought as he had gingerly unrolled the small scroll adorned with the king's coat of arms. But he couldn't have been more wrong. His past hadn't caught up to him, after all. But it had not been good news either. It had been an order from the king to meet Tracker and a boy companion at the annual Bearcamp races and surrender the camelop, Novalena, immediately after the final race. *After the race!* If he did not, he would be in violation of the WOR (Wishes of the Realm), which could carry a very severe sentence, indeed.

The king had demanded a response in writing, so Kalib had scribbled a note saying he understood and would, of course, honor his king's wishes. As he tied the message to the tiny bird's leg, he suddenly had realized he had a fluster bird in his hands. *A fluster bird!* Then Kalib had done a very strange thing. He had quickly reached under his mattress and retrieved a Y-shaped twig. He had held it up to the bird expectantly. The bird had done nothing at first, then had relieved itself on his hand, yanked its leg free, and flown out the tent door.

Kalib had laughed. *Well I tried*, he had said to himself as he had wiped his hand on a pillow and returned the twig to its place beneath the bed. He wasn't going to let a little bird doo dampen his mood, though. The warning he had received from the king would normally have a sobering effect on anyone unlucky enough to receive it, but not Kalib. *Another opportunity to put a little jingle in the old jangle* was all his twisted mind could see. For, being Kalib, he had sold the king's missive the very next day to a wisp for a handsome fee. And now, he thought with glee, he could officially hold on to Nova for the final race at Bearcamp; a race that was sure to put huge amounts of money in his coffers.

He took another long drag on his water pipe and grabbed a peeled grape. He popped it into his mouth and further contemplated his plight. He'd been in constant fear that this would be the year Tracker claimed his reward, and he was right. How did he get into this mess in the first place? *A lapse in judgment*, he admonished himself for the millionth time, *a terrible lapse in judgment*. His mind wandered to that fateful night.

Years ago, he was camped high in the Pishtock Pass with his three servants and band of racing camelops. They were bedded down for the night beneath a full moon that made the freshly fallen snow sparkle. In the early hours of morning, a pack of wolves attacked the camp.

They were wolves of the fiercest kind. The camelops bellowed in terror as the pack came in, howling and snarling. Kalib and his guards scrambled for their weapons and put up a brave fight, but soon all three guards were bloodied and weak, and Kalib was making a last stand with the alpha beast snarling in his face. It was then that Tracker and his familiar (a strange looking animal named Waz) suddenly appeared. Tracker first slew the leader using his staff as a spear and, with incredible speed and skill, used his knife to kill several other beasts. At the same time, the remaining wolves were sent fleeing into the night, driven mad by the high-pitched whistling of Tracker's companion. Tracker and Waz had saved Kalib's life.

Later, in the light and warmth of a campfire, Tracker attended the wounded servants. It was then, quite by accident, that Kalib's most closely held secret was revealed. Tracker was bandaging an ugly gash on the forehead of one of the giant guards when the wounded man began to change shape. Tracker jumped back, and Waz leapt ten feet in the air.

"What is this sorcery, Kalib?" shouted Tracker as he drew his blade. He looked down in astonishment. The deep wound he was attending looked even worse on the young girl that now lay before him.

Kalib groaned. "Oh no, not now," he whined. He jumped to his feet and held out his hands to assure Tracker things were OK. "Please, please, kind sir … I can explain!" He motioned for Tracker to put away his sword as he came around the fire and then tented his hands as if begging. Inside, his mind was racing. He had to think quickly. This secret had to be protected at all costs.

Both Tracker and Waz were now staring at him wide-eyed. *Both Tracker and Waz?* In spite of his angst, an odd thought crossed Kalib's mind: *Did that animal actually understand what he had just said?* He looked from one to the other. "Ah, yes, well. You have perhaps never seen a Tres?" Kalib asked feebly.

Tracker slowly resheathed his blade, never taking his eyes off the merchant. "I don't know what you're talking about," he said. Just then the young girl moaned. "Keep an eye on him, Waz," ordered Tracker, pointing at the merchant. He then quickly bent back down to administer more salve to the girl's head wound.

Kalib watched helplessly. Now he had no choice. The secret was revealed. And he simply had to find a way to protect it. So, he began to spin his tale. "Well, I must admit, sahib, kind sir; I had not heard of a Tres either, myself. A Tres is a group of three individuals linked by a magic spell. Something left over from the ancient world,

I think. You see, at first I was given these servants as a kind of reverse dowry—more of a bribe if the truth be known—by a mighty king. 'They were mine, given as a gift,' the king said. I need only marry his oldest daughter. "But, oh, what a beast she was!" Kalib cried as he framed his face with both hands and raised his eyes in despair. "A Minotaur was not as ugly," he added for effect.

But his antics didn't seem to be working. Tracker didn't look like he believed *anything* he was saying, and Kalib watched as Tracker gave Waz a skeptical look.

"No, no," Kalib said, "I'm telling the truth!" A man pleading for his life could not have looked more sincere. He then continued earnestly. "In spite of all the riches that went along with the slaves—I mean servants," he corrected, giving Tracker a wary look, "I was the most miserable man in the world. What had I done? For a few pieces of silver …" His face became distraught and tears actually ran down his cheeks. He was really working hard.

Then Kalib told of a surprising discovery. The servants were more valuable than he ever imagined. They were a group of servants called a Tres! With just a thought from their master, each individual took on one of three forms, depending on the needs of the moment: a young boy, a servant girl, or a fearsome giant guard. "Very handy for a merchant, I can tell you," Kalib said, smiling. "I became a new person!" He had three of them, and they were his to keep. He only had to stay married to the princess. "She's home right now; doesn't like to travel," Kalib added as if he thought he needed to explain her absence.

It was the best he could do. There were obvious holes in his tale *and* lies; but that was to be expected since he was making most of it up on the spot. The truth about how he actually took possession of his "moppets" would not do, especially to a member of the king's court. No, this was a secret about a secret that must never be revealed—ever.

But Kalib, exhausted and exasperated now, could tell Tracker was still having none of it. Kalib stood sweating profusely before the warrior, and it wasn't from the campfire. And it didn't help that Tracker's strange animal friend was making low growling sounds in its throat like a watchdog giving a warning.

So Kalib was completely surprised when Tracker said: "Lucky for you there's no time for more questions, Kalib. I think your story is mostly rubbish, and my companion, Waz, thinks you're blowing smoke too, but we have to go. Your brave servants will live, Kalib. But the king's business can't wait. We must go."

Relief crossed Kalib's face like an ocean wave coming ashore, and then, quickly gaining control, he assumed the most innocent look he could. *By the beard!* he thought. *I knew that weird creature could understand me!* But he still had a problem. They couldn't leave—not like this. Tracker still knew the secret of the Tres! He started to panic. He had to do something!

"You do me an injustice, Tracker," he whined to gain time while his mind worked frantically. Then—was it the full moon? Perhaps he, too, was driven a little mad by the frightening whistling of Waz. Regardless, in a moment of extremely poor judgment (at least, in his opinion), Kalib said, "Wait, wait. Tracker, you've saved my life—and the lives of my servants—my camelops! Please, please, let me reward you."

Tracker and the Waz exchanged looks again. "What do you have in mind, Kalib?" Tracker asked, suspiciously.

Kalib wrung his hands, grimaced as if in pain, and then went on in a rush, "I have made up my mind, sahib. The first newborn camelop of my string of racing animals is yours to keep!" Kalib then bit the back of his hand. The immensity of what he said took his breath away. But, before Tracker could respond, he hurriedly pronounced his caveat: "In return I must ask only one small favor ..."

Tracker slowly turned and fully faced the merchant. "And what would that favor be, Kalib?" he asked menacingly. "You do remember you are talking to an agent of the king?"

"Yes, yes, of course. But, well ... you know this *is* the Age of Secrets. And we all have them, Tracker; we all have secrets." He raised an eyebrow as if looking for agreement.

Tracker remained silent.

"OK, OK. Never mind. It's really nothing, sahib, I assure you. You only have to promise to tell no one about my servants—that's all!" Kalib shrugged his shoulders and raised his hands, palms up. "And, nothing about my marriage, of course," he added quickly. "But that's not such a huge request, is it? You see, it all relates to my business—who I am, my mystique!" His high-pitched voice was about to exceed the hearing limit. "Do we have a deal? Please?"

But his worries again were for naught. Tracker acquiesced at once. "Your secrets are safe with me, Kalib. Secrets revealed are no longer secrets. And good luck with that bride thing, if it's true. But remember, if it's ever found that your 'wedding gifts' have a more sinister story behind them ..." Tracker let the warning linger.

Kalib shook his head, gesturing emphatically to the contrary.

"Well then, for now—" Tracker unexpectedly stopped. He wrinkled his brow and seemed to be thinking. "But that does create something of a dilemma," he said finally. "Since this animal has yet to be born, I have no idea when or how I might claim this reward. We're on a mission for the king right now, and I can't be sure when I will see you again. And I may never be in the position to be hampered with the care and safekeeping of a newborn camelop ..."

Kalib couldn't believe his ears. He already knew it was a massive mistake to offer up a racing camelop as a reward, and now, unbelievably, he was going to get out of it! And he had Tracker's promise not to reveal the Tres's secret to boot! What luck!

But then, at the very moment Kalib thought Tracker was going to graciously turn down his offer, a baby camelop cried out mournfully in the night. Tracker gestured to Waz, and the animal immediately jumped off to investigate. Waz soon returned with a newborn camelop cradled in its arms and the calf's mother following close behind. It seemed, in the horror and excitement of the wolf attack, a pregnant camelop had given birth to a young female. Waz was making another strange sound with his mouth, but this time it was to comfort the baby camelop.

"Well, Kalib, part of my problem has been solved," Tracker said, laughing. He reached out and caressed the baby's tiny muzzle. "I will call you Novalena after the brightest star in the sky tonight." Even Kalib looked up at the constellation of the Lantern.

Tracker then reached into a pocket and took out a small length of thin rope and a bag of coins. He threw the bag of money to Kalib. "Gold coins," he said. "There's enough there to take care of her until she's grown. You may even race her and realize greater rewards for keeping her safe for me." He then took the length of rope, which emitted tiny sparkles when handled, and tied it around Novalena's nose. "This will serve as a reminder of our agreement, Kalib. As you can see it has some minor magic. It'll remain there and grow along with her. It is elfin made. It will bring her luck. I'll remove it when I come to retrieve her."

Tracker then looked sternly into Kalib's face. "Now, this time we really must be off. But remember, there is a difference between servants and slaves, Kalib. Slavery is forbidden in Tremora. You would do well to remember that."

Kalib returned from his daydreaming, dismissed his servant, and lay back with a smile on his face. He drifted off to sleep, thinking what a fortunate and clever man he was.

Chapter Fourteen

The True Tremoran

My Dearest Michael,

If you're reading this letter, then you're in Tremora. You chose to stay as I knew you would. Yes! Tremora! I've also been there. In fact, I met your father there. Your father, dear Michael, is a true Tremoran. And, it's also where I was a warrior princess, a queen, a witch ...

There is so much to tell you. But tales of Tremora are never revealed easily on this side of the shimmering. Alas, my quill pen resists me even as I write ...

It's been a whole year since your father disappeared. There is no question in my heart that he went through the veil. You must bring him back, Michael. It breaks my heart that you are both there without me. But it is you who has been summoned, not I.

And now, while the magic in my nib still holds: It was Megan who called you ... Find him and, bewar of the dra , you mustn't bel

Michael turned the letter over excitedly, looking for more writing. "Tracker, my mother's been here! And, and, he's here, Tracker! I knew it! My father's here! And, Tracker, he's a Tremoran. A true Tremoran, just like you." He suddenly stopped. He dropped the hand holding the letter and looked up at Tracker, confused. "But, how can that be?"

Tracker didn't answer, but his face became grim. "May I?" he asked, reaching for the letter.

Michael nodded, numbly.

Tracker took the letter and moved his pipe to the side to see better in the flickering light. They were sitting around a campfire not far from Kalib's tent, preferring to eat and sleep outdoors where the air was fresh, rather than in the tent Kalib had offered. Nova knelt nearby, chewing her cud. The yellow-orange light of the fire reflected brightly in her large glassy eyes.

"I think the magic of your mother's pen kept you from finding this till you passed through the veil," Tracker said, thoughtfully. "But the magic may have been too weak, or the water from the Gush seeping through your backpack …" He too turned the paper over, looking for more writing. "Whichever or whatever caused it, what was written last is lost, I'm afraid." Tracker handed the letter back. "I'm sorry you had to find out about your father this way. Megan wanted to speak with you first, but I'm afraid he didn't factor in the wiles of your mother."

Michael shook his head. He took one last look at the letter, then folded it, and put it back in his backpack. *Was this ever going to end?* "How can any of this be true, Tracker? My mother—a warrior princess? And she knows Megan? Megan!" He became angry as he repeated the wizard's name. "Tracker, if you don't tell me what's going on, I'm leaving right now. I don't care about your orders! I'm going right back down that road, and, and—" His face turned red, and he stopped in frustration.

"I'm afraid that's not possible, Michael," Tracker said, softly.

"Maybe so, but I'm going anyway." Michael stood up and strapped on his backpack, steadfast and determined.

Tracker sighed. "Michael, that way is no longer safe, and besides, the shimmering is long gone."

Michael stopped, stared blankly at Tracker, and then dropped heavily back down on the ground. "OK, Tracker. But whether you can tell me or not, don't you see that I'm finding things out, anyway? Please, just tell me about my mother. Surely, you can do that now."

Tracker looked uncomfortable. Michael couldn't possibly know the struggle he was going through. As a soldier and servant of the king, he was bound by his orders, but the original scenario had changed so dramatically. And wasn't the bigger mission still intact? To get Michael safely to Mesmer Henge? Besides, hadn't he already told Michael more than he was supposed to back in Bjorg's cabin?

Tracker put both hands on his knees and rose. "Well, they can only hang me once," he said. He lit his pipe and blew smoke into the night sky before saying anything more. "OK, Michael, you win." He returned to his seat.

Michael waited.

"As I told you before, Michael, other than wizards and stargazers, no one today believes the veil is real—not even the king, until recently, of course. But there are plenty of heroes and heroines who, legend says, did come through the shimmering. So, your presence here not only proves that the veil is real, it also shows that some of those legends could be true as well. And that brings us back to King William and Megan. What they uncovered while searching the catacombs and stones of Mesmer Henge was incredible. Michael, not only did they find evidence of your mother coming through the veil to Tremora hundreds of years ago, she has come through twice! And both times she helped save Tremora: once as a queen and once as a witch. Just as her letter says."

"Hundreds of years ago? That's impossible ..." Michael's voice was barely a whisper. He was beyond astonishment now. He might as well have been smoking Kalib's pipe again.

"Yes, Michael, it is possible. But it's nothing I can explain. For that you really must talk to Megan. He only told me that 'when traveling between worlds, time is no companion.'"

Michael's face went blank, and he began to swoon. Tracker quickly leapt to his feet and grabbed Michael's shoulders as he slumped toward the fire. Nova grunted in surprise, heaved herself up, and moved quickly to Michael's side where she licked his face copiously as Tracker laid him gently back on his blanket.

"What a fool! The boy's been flung and stabbed and drugged ... and a letter from his mother that obviously upset him. This could have waited till morning. What was he thinking?" Nova raised her head and glared at Tracker.

"That's the second time I've been called a fool in two days. I'm afraid I deserve it this time, though."

Nova's eyes became as big as the moon above her head. She dropped back on her haunches, and a bewildered look crossed her long ruminant face. She finally managed, "*Not you, too!*" Then she immediately flagged her thoughts.

Chapter Fifteen

Megan and the King Confer

At the same time Michael lay unconscious on the shores of Havenland, King William stood gazing out a window of the Tremora Castle keep. He was absently watching the sun rise over his kingdom. More than two weeks had passed since his return with the wizard, and there were many issues on his mind, not the least of which was the rescue of Cedric, treachery, and the assault on the throne. However, most pressing this day was his need for more news of Tracker and Fenn's son, Michael.

The goshawk, Ka, had arrived the day before with the blue cloth: It was a prearranged signal. It meant that Tracker had found Michael at the shimmering and they were now both on their way to Bearcamp. The King's relief had been immense. Not that he had any doubt the veil existed, especially after what he and Megan had seen in the catacombs and experienced at Mesmer Henge and the onyx gardens, but now there was confirmation: He and Megan had successfully summoned a hero from another world to find and slay the dragon!

But that was yesterday. This morning, the king was looking for news of another kind—he was waiting for word from Tralana. The night after Tracker had left the castle to meet Michael, the king had had a vision. Not so unusual for a king who was known as a seer and an oracle, but it had been so long since his last vision he feared his gift had left him. He was never sure when these visions were going to appear or how; sometimes they took the form of a dream or dancing images in a fire, or he would go into a trance while meditating, and some strange event would unfold before him like an elaborate stage production. They were both a gift and a curse; useful as warnings, but also confusing, enigmatic, and sometimes very dark. This latest vision, however, was different and came to him like no other.

It was late at night, and the queen had already retired. The king quietly eased into the royal sleeping chambers, trying not to disturb her. With a movement of his hand he dismissed the queen's two ladies-in-waiting and motioned for his own guards to leave and stand watch in the hall. When the door closed behind them with a resounding clunk, the king shucked his royal demeanor and became the old man behind the mask, the old man his subjects would never know. After changing into nightclothes, he sat on the edge of the huge canopied bed and sighed heavily. Months of grief and angst had taken their toll; sleep and rest were still elusive. But the wheels were in motion! Tracker was on his way to meet the boy. Perhaps now he could finally rest, knowing there was new hope in rescuing Cedric. Wearily, he reached out and patted his dog, Aster, where it lay sleeping on the bed.

"That I could so easily slumber without a care in the world like you, my old friend." Aster opened his eyes, gently licked his master's hand, and then dropped his head back down on his paws and returned to his dreams. The king smiled and turned to blow out the candle by the bedside when he heard a strange sound; like the crunch of boots on gravel. He looked around the room curiously. No other person could possibly be in the room at this hour, not with the dog and the guards. He saw nothing. Aster hadn't even raised his head.

He shrugged it off and puffed up again to blow out the candle when the same sound, only louder this time, made him stop and sit bolt upright. It came from the direction of the wall. He grabbed the candle and held it out to see better, then gasped as what the light revealed. The wall was moving! *No, it's the stones that are moving*, he marveled. He could only sit and stare. The stone blocks that made up the wall were grinding and tumbling in place as if caught in a giant mortar and pestle. He continued to watch, hypnotized, as the stones split, cracked, smashed, and crumbled into smaller and smaller pieces. And all the while, the noise grew louder and louder until it became a deafening roar; and then the whole room started to shake like an earthquake. He could hardly hold on to the bed.

He quickly snapped out of his trance. *We have to get out here!* He leapt to his feet and looked toward the door. *The guards!* "Where are my guards?" he growled, angrily. He was about to call out when he noticed his queen and dog out of the corner of his eye. Astonished, he cried, "What trickery is this?" They were both still sleeping! Then he crouched and spun back around—the noise had changed. Now it sounded like a gale wind blowing. He looked to see a spinning vortex of rocks and debris; and the room's drapes, tapestries, paintings, and torches were all being pulled into the maelstrom. Too late, he realized his danger. He fell back on the bed and raised his feet, but it was a futile effort. He was pulled off the bed and into the tempest like a leaf caught up in a dust devil. The candle flew out of his grasp, and his arms and legs flailed wildly as he spun and caromed dizzily toward the whirlpool where, with a loud pop, he was sucked into the eye of the storm.

Once his senses finally returned, he didn't know if he had blacked out or had simply spent a long time in pitch-black darkness. He kept his eyes shut as he took a mental inventory. He was lying on his back with his hands folded on his chest. *Am I dead?* He reached up and stroked his beard. No. But he didn't feel quite alive either. *At least I'm not spinning out of control anymore.* He then realized he felt rather damp. Slowly, he opened his eyes and saw a blue sky full of spectacular cumulous clouds above his head. *Am I floating on the ocean, then?* he wondered. *Well, there's only one way to find out …* He rose to a sitting position and immediately pulled up his legs and grabbed his knees. No, he couldn't have been more wrong. He was flying!

The sensation was giddy and fantastic and breathtaking, all at the same time. After several minutes of the wind blowing in his face, he felt brave enough to look down. With a start, he saw he was high above Tremora and watched in awe as familiar landmarks rushed by beneath him.

He was keenly aware now that his body had no substance, that he was as insubstantial as a ghost. But he wasn't alarmed; he knew what this was—he was in a dream. And he was going to be shown a vision. So he relaxed. *Might as well enjoy this*, he thought. He knew his sole purpose for being there in those clouds was to observe and listen.

At first, it was exciting, cruising along on his bed of air, and he did enjoy himself for quite a while, but eventually he became bored. So he began to entertain himself. He leaned back with his hands behind his head, one leg cocked over the other, and studied the billowing clouds above his head. Soon, preposterous creatures and humongous, gnarly faces appeared and glared down at him. *Enough of that!* Next he lay on his stomach and flung his arms out wide and pretended he was an eagle. *That's better!* Then he turned summersaults—many, many, summersaults. It was as if he was a young boy again, without a care, and his imagination soared with the clouds. However, he was soon reminded that, at the same time he was reliving his childhood, he was also being transported somewhere at a rapid rate, and he had no idea where that somewhere was going to be.

It happened while he was pretending to be an intrepid adventurer, perched high in the crow's nest of a three-masted galleon ship. He stood heroically posed with the wind blowing his hair and his nightshirt billowing like a sail when he suddenly started to lose altitude. In an instant, the childhood game was over. He fell to his knees and pitched forward to lie flat with his arms stretched out straight in front of him. The wind contorted his face and caused his eyes to water as he sped toward the ground at an alarming rate. Then, to his immense relief, his speed slowed, and just above tree level, he leveled off and began to follow the contours of the land. Everything passed by in a blur as he dove and swerved and climbed over hill and dell.

Eventually, the topography changed from mountains and hills to a vast flatland; first desert, then grassland, then tilled and cultivated fields. His speed and altitude reduced again, and he saw a small village looming in the distance. As he reached the outskirts of town, the speed of his air chariot died down to nothing more than a gentle breeze. He was then carried slowly down the main street. As he passed by each building, he darted from window to window like a hummingbird feeding flower to flower, catching glimpses of people, hearing snippets of conversations, experiencing strange smells and tastes; he actually felt the people's emotions for the fleetest of moments before he was whisked away to another building and another street. In a short time, he became aware of a certain truth; his people were anxious and afraid.

He wasn't sure how long this went on before the scenarios and sequence of time itself changed. It was as if time no longer had meaning; he traveled miles in an instant and was shown things past, present, and future: landscapes, buildings, people, places, all aged or regressed before his eyes.

Now he was approaching a country inn. Suddenly he was inside in a large room with a crowd of people. The scene before him moved in slow motion. Tracker was there with a young boy and there were elves … *Wait, didn't Megan say something about an elfin prince and an inn …? Was that the boy, Michael?* More snippets of conversation … Megan's name ... then, in an instant, he was gone again. Another flit. Now he was crossing an ocean and approaching a long rocky shoreline. There were tall cliffs and caves … and, in the mouth of the largest cave, a dragon! And behind the beast, in the shadows, a boy—*Cedric? Was that Cedric?* The scene faded, and he was gone again. *No wait!* It was all happening too fast. Now he was flying over the henge. A battle was raging beneath him. He recognized his own banners … He panicked. He had to remember … he had to remember …

"William?'

With a shock, the king was sitting back on the edge of his bed, shaking, and wringing wet. The queen's hand was on his shoulder.

"William? You're trembling."

"How long have I been gone?" he gasped.

"Gone?"

The king looked at his wife, first in confusion, then with clarity. He quickly grabbed her hand. "I've had a new vision, Lelana." He looked around at the walls and trappings and everything was just as it should be. Aster cocked his head to one side and looked at him quizzically.

The king turned back and looked earnestly into the queen's eyes. "He's alive," he said, "Cedric is alive. And I know where he is!"

The queen gasped. "Are you certain? Was your vision so clear?"

The king hesitated, then, "No, no … but yes, I'm sure of it. I've been shown the future and, and …" He jumped up. "I must write it all down before it's gone!"

He hurried to his writing desk and cleared everything away with a sweep of his arm. He picked up a writing quill and dipped it clumsily into a recessed ink well and frantically started to write down all he could remember. Ink spilled and splattered as he wrote, and he swore under his breath; he couldn't keep up with the images in his mind. Then the queen came and rested her hand once again on his shoulder.

"Let me," she said softly. She removed the pen from his trembling hand and nudged him so she could sit next to him on the small bench. He looked at her in a daze and then gratefully scooted to the side. William then described his dream, and the queen transcribed everything he said in her delicate hand. Her only pause came when the king said he saw Cedric in the cave of the dragon. Tears welled in her eyes and fell on her parchment as she asked, "Did he look …?" She grew silent. She couldn't bear to think her son was in pain.

"He was alive, Lelana," said the king, grabbing her hands in his. "That's what's important. And, don't you see? Now I can direct our hero to him!"

It was hours before they finished.

"I must get my messages out this morning," the king said as he rifled the pages the queen had written. "I can't rest until I do." He turned and kissed his wife on her forehead. "Have heart, my queen. The winds have changed. Now, quickly, go and assemble the messengers while I prepare the scrolls and parchments."

The queen returned the king's kiss and gathered her nightgown around her. She then wrapped herself in a cloak, swept through the door, and called to her maidens to accompany her down the hall.

Presently, the king finished his writing. The scrolls held information that could cause great harm to Tremora if they fell into the wrong hands; they had to be delivered to the proper recipients by a troop of the king's own personal couriers. The smaller parchments contained messages that were less sensitive or very brief in nature and would be delivered via fluster bird; a bird noted for its speed and ability to avoid capture.

He stood up wearily, stretched, and yawned. When had he slept last? He was so tired he didn't even want to expend the energy to change out of his nightclothes, but not even servants should see their monarch in nightcap and slippers! So he donned a purple robe and sandals and removed his cap. Then he gathered the rolled scrolls and exited the chambers. His messengers were lined up in the hall.

Tralana, his favorite, was dispatched first. She was given the task of delivering his visions to Tracker and the boy. The king knew it was no coincidence that Tracker and Michael would pass by the very inn where the elf prince was being held captive. Tralana would have to hurry to get his directions to them in time.

He spent the next hour dispatching the remaining personal notes to other subjects he had seen in his dream. Later, his shorter messages were sent to other folks including the elf Pattersling and the fairy Blingtrail. Finally he was done. The remaining remnants of his dream were for him alone. He reentered the chambers, closed the doors, and fell exhausted onto the bed next to his queen. She turned and held him in her arms. Finally, he dropped off into a deep sleep.

❧

So King William was now standing at the window of the keep, patiently waiting for word from Tralana that she had successfully delivered his scrolls to Tracker and Michael. He didn't have long to wait. Just after the sun cleared the horizon, Tralana's hummingbird flitted in the window and landed on top of the map that he had been studying earlier by candlelight. He'd been looking for caves. The bird looked exhausted. "Looks like you've had to do the work of two," the king said, as he untied the pieces of leather attached to its legs. He scooped the tiny bird up in his cupped hands and carried it carefully to a perch that had seed and water waiting, the resting place for all the feathered carriers that visited the king each day. He then unrolled the tiny notes and set them down on the table, weighing down their corners with items from a small glass cabinet. He then read the messages with a magnifying glass in the light of the candle. When done, he sat for several minutes staring out the window. Then he sent for Megan.

Megan scaled the ladder that was the only access to the king's retreat and nimbly climbed through the opening in the floor. He approached the king and bowed. "Your majesty," he said. The king looked sharply at the tall wizard. "No need for formality, Megan. It's only us two." Then his face turned grim. "We have a spy in our midst."

The king gave the messages to Megan to read and strode to the window. He stood with his hands clasped behind his back and waited for the wizard to read Tralana and Tracker's accounts of the encounters on the mountain.

Megan tapped his wand to the side of his head, and half-moon reading glasses appeared. He held the swatches of leather to the light. "Yes, I'm afraid you're right," Megan said, finally. "How else could the shape-changer know so much? Spy birds or wisps, either way, someone took little time to expose our plans. It wasn't only loyal followers that answered the call to the conclave, it seems." Megan laid the notes on the desk and looked warily at the king. "We must think on this, your majesty—"

"Our carelessness almost cost us any chance of rescuing my son, Megan," the king said crossly. "We are not happy. When the spy is found, he will be hanged!" When angered, the king often reverted to the "royal plural," representing himself and all his subjects in his unhappiness.

"Yes, but think on this," Megan said quickly. "Michael and Tracker are safe. In spite of this breach, the boy has survived his first encounter with the enemy." Megan searched the face of the king. Friend or no friend, wizard or no wizard, a fuming monarch was extremely dangerous. And royal plural or not, "our" carelessness could also mean "your" carelessness, meaning the wizard. "It is a good sign that he was not harmed," Megan continued. "Michael will have to weather more dangerous storms than this before his task is over. How else can he succeed?"

The king looked at Megan intently. "Perhaps you're right; it might show the boy's resilience, but his presence was supposed to be kept secret just so we could prevent these encounters from happening so quickly. He's young. He needs weapons and training! It was part of our plan, remember. But now, because of this," he motioned to the pieces of leather, "we already have to change our strategy. Do you have any ideas?"

"Yes," the wizard replied with relief. "First, Tracker's directions were to train Michael in the arts of self-defense. Perhaps a stronger request is now in order. It may be helpful if the boy knew the sword and staff now, rather than later. Then we should consider using our knowledge of the spy to our advantage. Maybe fog the air with an untruth or two … and, I think the meeting at the henge should be rethought." He took his wand and described a square in the air in front of him. A piece of parchment appeared and gently floated to alight on the surface of the table. "With your permission," he said, as he pulled up a chair.

It wasn't long before the king heaved his seat back and looked at Megan with approval.

Chapter Sixteen

Treetop

Tracker was right about the letter. Michael woke up really angry. He wouldn't talk to anyone and glowered if anyone ventured near him, especially Tracker or Falin. Nova tried but couldn't get through to him; he was flagged private. He was angry at his mother, at his father, at Megan (whoever that was!), the whole world; both worlds! He could hardly contain himself. He finally stormed out of the camp.

He struck out blindly, roughly following the route of a shallow stream. He hadn't hiked long before he found what he was looking for. Before him loomed the biggest tree he could see. It was huge and heavily limbed with branches that hung far out over the water. *Perfect!* he thought. Then he took refuge the same way he always did at home; he climbed the tree to the very top.

The tree swayed gently. He'd reached the height where his weight just barely made the tree trunk bend and found himself high above the forest's canopy. As Michael leaned side to side, rocking with the breeze and listening to the rustle of the leaves and buzz of busy insects, he felt the anger gradually drain from his body. Calmness slowly replaced the angst as he bathed his face in the wind and rays of the early sun.

"These things are sent to try us," he sighed—an old adage repeated many times by his mother.

Mother? Yes, what about his mother? he wondered. *A warrior! A queen! A witch!* He couldn't grasp it. *And what about his father? He was from here, is here, and is in trouble or perhaps dead here! And I'm supposed to fix everything! Even rescue a prince from a dragon!* His pulse raced. He closed his eyes and again tried to meld with the serenity of his high perch. He breathed deeply. When he opened his eyes, he reached out and broke off a small twig that was too near his head. He absently trimmed off the excess with his teeth, creating a tiny slingshot, and twirled it between the fingers of one hand as he tried to recapture his feeling of calm.

As he gazed east, toward the morning, he noticed two very tiny birds flying to and fro near a scraggly treetop. Its highest branches also reached well above the forest's canopy, and he could see it quite clearly. After watching for a time, he could see that the birds were making a nest. He was marveling at their brilliant colors when one of them struck a beeline straight for him. He grabbed at his tree in reflex, still clutching the slingshot shaped twig in his hand.

The bird stopped abruptly in front of his face and hovered, studying Michael for several ticks. He had never seen a bird quite like it. It suddenly shot to the hand that held the twig, floated there, and then returned to Michael's face. It repeated the same thing two or three times and then hovered again, expectantly.

Was it trying to …? Michael slowly held out his hand with the twig resting in his open palm. "Looking for more nesting material, little friend?" he asked.

The bird went berserk. It waved its wings wildly, turned summersaults, blustered, and sputtered—feathers flew everywhere as it chirped, whistled, and spun like a spinning wheel firecracker. It then plopped down with a thud on Michael's upturned hand, legs splayed, eyes crossed, and small tongue hanging to the side. Even so, in the midst of it all, it still managed to grab the twig with one small foot.

Michael carefully balanced himself to free up both hands, and gently stroked the small bird's head. "Well, that was something to see," he said. "I'm sure your little brain is scrambled like an egg after all that!" The bird slowly calmed. It cooed softly and pressed its head against Michael's finger like a cat or dog would do to a master's hand. After a minute or two, the bird opened its eyes, looked at its wings and feet as if to take inventory and, with a final chirp, flew off with its prize clutched tightly in its tiny claws.

The bird didn't return and Michael finally decided it was time to go. He dropped to the ground, brushed off his hands, and made his way toward the stream he'd followed earlier. It took him past the tree where the birds were nesting and something there caught his eye. He went to the base of the fluted trunk and found three round stones lying in the dirt between its spreading roots. They were small, about the size of his thumb, and gave off a dull glow, like pebbles he'd once found along the beach. He picked them up and examined them more closely. They were hard and smooth and egg shaped. His examination was interrupted when he heard someone coming along the creek, so he put the stones absently into his pocket and immediately forgot about them.

It was Tracker. "I wouldn't normally follow you, but the caravan is on the move, and we really need to join them," Tracker said. "This is no time to let Kalib out of our sight." He threw Michael his backpack and walking stick. "And anyway, it's a day's journey to the bridge—plenty of time to talk. I think I owe you that."

Michael held his backpack to his chest and looked at Tracker in surprise.

"Well, you do have more questions, don't you?" Tracker asked. He then placed his pipe in his mouth and scampered off, jumping from stone to stone down the course of the shallow creek.

Michael watched him disappear. Soon, he found himself again scurrying to catch up to the small, green, wizened old man with a staff, backpack, and lighted pipe, much the same as he had done that first day in Tremora.

Chapter Seventeen

Questions Answered

Michael and Tracker returned to camp and hailed Nova, who was waiting patiently by the fire. She was relieved to see that Michael wasn't angry anymore. They quickly broke camp and set out to catch Kalib's slow-moving caravan. Tracker jogged on one side of Nova, and Michael on the other. Each tried to have a conversation with her, but her thoughts were still flagged private. Even though she was very excited, she wasn't ready to talk to either one of them. Why? Because Nova possessed a brand new secret!

Now, isn't this interesting, she thought to herself. *Should I tell them I can meld with them both? No. Everyone knows a secret revealed is no longer a secret, and once revealed the power is gone. I think it must be why the king chose me—I'm sure I'm the only Grock animal in the whole kingdom. Or the whole world maybe! I think I'll just keep this to myself. The king would want that ...*

"Nova looks quite pleased with herself this morning," Michael said.

Tracker leaned forward and looked back to better see her face. "Yes, she does look rather smug."

Nova looked back at him, even winked, but just kept plodding along.

They passed by the long line of pack animals and wagons in Kalib's caravan and then caught up to one of the strangest sights Michael had ever seen. A very large elephant was supporting a platform that was at least eight feet off the ground. It was covered with ornate rugs that hung down over the sides nearly to the ground, and strapped securely on top was a massive carved and gilded chair adorned with silk braids and cushions. And perched on those cushions was the rotund Kalib, holding a tiny parasol!

The animals walked in step so the whole ensemble swayed back and forth, causing tassels to fly and wood and leather thongs to groan. Two of Kalib's servants occasionally flicked a switch across the rumps of the poor beasts as they toiled along.

"At least he's out of mischief up there," Tracker observed.

They slowed and got in line behind Kalib and his strange entourage. Michael reached into his shirt pocket and removed his mother's letter. He studied it again and said, "I can't believe my father's here in Tremora. Everyone thought he was dead ... I have to find him, Tracker. I promised Mother. He must have got in trouble, or he would have come back to us. But, where is he? Where do I start?"

"Where you start is remembering why you are here, Michael. You've been summoned by the king to save the prince," Tracker said, sternly. "It's your first priority. It's why you were called. You can't forget that. As to your father, Megan has great wisdom. I'm sure he'll have more to tell you at—"

"I know, I know, 'wait till the wizard's gathering, and all will be revealed.' I thought you were going to answer questions." Michael snapped.

Tracker remained silent.

"Anyway, the last lines have completely disappeared now," Michael said, holding the letter close to his face as he walked. "But Mother was trying to warn me of something, and there was a mention of Megan. How could she know of him? And do you think she was warning me against the dragon? That seems hardly necessary ..."

"Not only do I think your mother knows *of* Megan, I think she might actually know Megan! He's a wizard, Michael. They can live a very long time and can even have more than one life. And couldn't the traffic through the veil go both ways? As to the dragon, I agree, that's more of a riddle. She had something more to say about that …"

"Michael was silent for a long time. Nothing was adding up at all. Finally, "I don't understand anything about my dad being a Tremoran," Michael said. "And, Tracker, my mother is obviously younger than you! How could she have visited Tremora all those years ago? Twice! And that's how she met my father?"

"Ah, yes." Tracker paused. "But, remember. This is where we, again, get into Megan's territory."

"Oh, please."

"It's wizard's business!" Tracker said, sharply. Then, relenting, he continued with a sigh. "I must be careful. A wizard's wrath? You don't want to know. Megan thought it better to keep certain facts from you. Yes, Michael, until the gathering! And for good reason, I'm sure. However, in spite of his wishes, there are things you just need to know, now that your presence in Tremora is known to the enemy. After all, your life is in danger every day, and you should at least know why!"

Nova snorted in agreement, and Michael reached an arm around her neck and gave her a hug.

"Remember when I told you about how you were called to save the prince—that it was a vision of the king or something he and Megan found out in the Room of Glimpses? Well it was a little more specific than that. What they found out was, for Cedric to be rescued from the dragon, a boy must be called through the veil and he must choose to stay on his own accord. But, more important, he *had* to be the son of Fenn."

"Son of Fenn! There, I told you this was a mistake. I'm no son of Fenn. I mean, I did choose to stay and all that, but—"

"Yes, that does appear to be a problem," Tracker said. But his voice had a hint of expectancy. He remained silent.

The longer he was silent, the more Michael felt uneasy. "Tracker? Tracker, what are you saying? That my mother is Fenn? Was Fenn, I mean … But, but, that's ridiculous."

"Have you forgotten what she said in her letter? Look, King William and Megan saw the same problem but for a different reason. Queen Fenn of Farland has been gone for a thousand years, and Fenn the Warrior Witch for half of that: And they had no children! It was

Megan who found the answer. It appears that Queen Fenn and Fenn the Warrior Witch are one and the same person, and she came through the veil twice from your world when Tremora was in grave danger. Your letter only confirms he was right: Fenn is your mother. You *are* the son of Fenn, Michael, and that's why the king summoned you."

Michael stopped in his tracks.

As did Nova. *"You ARE of royal blood!"* Nova was incredulous.

"I, I just don't know, Nova. I mean, Mother's letter does say she was a queen … and a witch. Michael looked at Nova helplessly. *Nova, is it possible that I'm actually who they think I am?"*

"Why yes, I think you are!" she said, proudly. *"In fact, I always suspected something like this about you! And, of course, I was right …"*

Tracker motioned for them to keep on moving. Those behind them were starting to catch up. "We know something of the first Fenn from ancient tapestries hanging in the castle," Tracker continued, as Michael and Nova caught back up to him. "They tell of her deeds as a knight in the Great War against the giants and trolls in the Age of Conquest. They are part of the story I told you in the mountains, Michael.

"Then, in the Age of Magic, it seems Fenn returned to Tremora. She had only aged ten years in her own world; she was now a young girl of eighteen, but five hundred years had passed in Tremora since the life she had known as queen in Farland.

"Her adventures were again legendary. We know a lot about this second Fenn because they are among Tremora's most loved stories. They are tales of war, love, revenge, and sorrow. Fenn helped defeat a gang of witches and warlocks, this time by becoming a powerful witch herself. During her adventures she met and fell in love with a young Tremoran knight named Paladin. But she also met her nemesis, the sorceress Ohndrea. At the end of the war, Ohndrea and her minions escaped to the caves of the Cyclops. In revenge, she came out of hiding and kidnapped Paladin on the day he and Fenn were to be married. Fenn mustered an army and, in another famous battle, killed the one-eyed monster of the caves and Ohndrea as well. At the same time, wizards helped find and rescue Paladin, but he was barely alive. Fenn tried to nurse him back to health, but found that Ohndrea had cursed him with a debilitating spell. The story ends with Fenn, in a desperate attempt to save her husband's life, taking Paladin with her back to her own world.

"No Tremoran had ever left with a boundary traveler before, that we know of. Even the wizards didn't know what happened after that. Neither Fenn nor her knight was ever seen again. But, we now know that Paladin recovered from his ailments in your world, and that you are, in fact, his son. Again, it was Megan who discovered this secret."

"My father is a Tremoran knight," Michael whispered in awe.

"And you're the son of a queen!" added Nova.

Tracker raised both his hands as if to say, that's it. "And now I've told you as much as I know, Michael. I really don't know anything more. And only Megan knows how time is explained in all of this. So, we really *must* wait for the wizard's gathering now. Besides, I think I see the bridge to Bearcamp just ahead."

Chapter Eighteen

Bearcamp Races

The eastern stone bridge connecting Havenland to the isle of Bearcamp appeared in the distance. Kalib's caravan came to a halt, and a well-orchestrated flurry of activity began. The elephant carrying the corpulent merchant atop his perch dropped to its knees and then eased slowly to the ground. Servants unloaded pack animals and wagons and quickly hung copper wares, musical instruments, water pipes, and other sundry items from every available spot on Kalib's traveling throne.

Other servants attacked an even bigger job—Kalib himself. Young girls combed and slicked back his hair, beard, and mustaches with shiny scented oil, and adorned his hands with huge rings on each finger and thumb. Then they dressed him in striped silk robes and ostrich feathers and set a huge red beaded turban on his head. Others put bracelets and bangles around his arms and then painted his nails to match his headwear and added bands of golden anklets and ornate toe rings to his bare feet. A large scabbard with a protruding jewel-encrusted hilt and a lethal looking short blade were added to his waistband as a final touch, perhaps as a warning to all that the merchant was armed and not as soft as he might appear.

Novalena also went through a transformation. Camboys dressed her anew from head to toes with colorful blankets, tassels, ringlets, jeweled livery, and scented perfumes. She became the stunning lead in a string of lops; all decked out in their individual racing colors and gear. The servants themselves changed into silk garments and turbans of matching colors and took up cymbals, trumpets, lyres, and various other stringed instruments.

When preparations were complete the elephant beneath Kalib's tower started its laborious journey back to standing. It was a slow process. The entire affair teetered, tottered, leaned, and swayed as several camboys threw ropes and tied knots furiously to keep Kalib and his throne from crashing to the ground. In the end it reminded Michael of a huge layered ice cream sundae covered with way too many toppings.

Kalib turned to survey his troop. With a grunt of satisfaction, he gave the signal to proceed. The servants moved to the front of the line and set off, dancing and prancing to the sounds of their own music. The arrival of Kalib and his camelops was heralded, and the procession advanced with great flourish across the bridge to Bearcamp. Kalib entered Bearcamp fashionably late, as was his custom, and with pomp and ceremony, as was his wont.

All along Reverie Way, the onlookers cheered. Kalib threw small clay images of himself to the crowd and many hands reached out to touch Novalena as she passed. Her head turned slowly side to side acknowledging her admirers with a humble nod and smile. Other camelops had arrived over the last couple of days but with much less fanfare. After all, Nova was easily the most famous racing animal in the world. Many fortunes would be wagered on whether she would continue her incredible winning streak. Kalib could hardly contain his glee.

It was the fifth day of the weeklong Bearcamp races. Nova would be racing on the last and seventh day. Typically, the smallest races took place during the opening day, with the size of the racers and excitement of the crowds growing through the week. Everyone was welcome to take part. If a person with an adventurous soul noticed a roly-poly bug scooting across the floor, it would be scooped up and brought to Bearcamp where that person could easily find an equally enthusiastic owner of a cell-bug or inchworm that claimed his or her creep-crawly was the fastest. Or those who thought their hound ran faster or frog jumped higher or duck waddled waddlier would also pack their dreams, and off they'd go to seek their fortune. Racing tracks of all sizes and shapes were elaborately constructed or hastily thrown together to accommodate any and all types of competitions. Wherever and whenever a race materialized, enthusiastic punters soon gathered to cheer and place their bets.

The wide thoroughfare of Reverie Way was normally lined with vendors hawking their wares peacefully on market days. During racing week, however, the vendors competed for less space, and the atmosphere was often raucous, wild, and very, very, rowdy. Touts were everywhere, selling their questionable insider information—racing forms and hot tips—to unwary bettors. Turf Accountants dressed in bright red costumes walked through the crowds on tall wooden stilts. Their job: to collect wagers and pay the winners before and after each race, pocketing a small percentage off each bet. The rest of the profits went to the royal vault in Castle Logan.

The chaotic conditions offered tantalizing opportunities for pickpockets and petty thieves, but the risk was great. The crowds had a way of pouncing on and holding court for any careless thief caught "with the goods." And justice was meted out swiftly. The prisoner's fate was decided with loud shouting and a show of hands. If convicted, the offender was quickly thrown far out into Lake Shampore by accommodating mountain folk who were only too willing to hone their skills at "shucking shysters."

Unfortunately, the popularity of watching and betting on how long a crook stayed in the air caused the occasional innocent bystander to fall victim to one of these hastily formed courts, and he, she, or it also ended up in the lake. Since there were no dangerous fish lurking in the lake's depths, most ejected folks ended up swimming to the far shore relatively unharmed; the occasional broken arm or leg being the worst of it. Even so, it would have been extremely unwise for any of them to return to Bearcamp once convicted and ejected. Second offenders were sent to the island's prison and rarely ever seen again.

The most popular day of the races was the last, and the most popular race was the Running of the Lops. Camelops in a hurry are something to see. A camelop runs with an extremely awkward gait: its long neck stretches out, tongue lolling to the side, and it constantly brays as if being chased by a nightmare. And to see and hear a dozen or so loping, braying camelops coming around a turn with their tiny jockeys wildly waving riding crops to no avail whatsoever simply raises the adrenalin levels to heights not achieved in any other racing event. The carnival atmosphere of the market and seven days of racing culminated in this final day of the "sport of kings" and was unequaled in excitement anywhere in Tremora.

The High King once attended the Bearcamp races faithfully. But since the disappearance of his son, the Tremoran flag over Castle Logan was flown at half-mast, indicating the sovereign was not in residence.

Kalib's procession continued on until it reached the stables where the animals would be quartered for the night. The area was cordoned off with ropes to afford some privacy and for the protection of the camelops and their jockeys. Tracker and Michael helped strip Nova of her colors and led her through the doors to the largest stall where they gave her water. Leather straps, reins, and bridles hung from the walls, and a lantern created highlights and deep shadows in the cozy manger setting. The floor was covered with fresh hay, and there was plenty of room for both Michael and Tracker to spread out their cloaks and blankets to sleep.

Tracker grabbed a pitchfork and casually leaned one boot on the back of the tines. Nova had yet to send a thought to him since the campfire that morning. *"You sure have a following Nova!"* Tracker tried again. *"Only the king could cause more excitement out there. Come on. You must be bursting!"*

Michael was preparing his sleeping area and not paying any attention to the two. Since Tracker's revelations about his mother and father, he had been mostly silent, alone with his thoughts.

Nova's head was in a leather nosebag full of oats that Falin had tied around her head earlier. *"Without them I am nothing ..."* Her watery voice came to Tracker but seemed different than before. *"I'm sorry, but I am feeling very tired right now. Must be the ..."* Her head sagged down, bag and all, and she appeared to have fallen asleep standing up.

In alarm, Tracker threw the pitchfork to the ground, grabbed Nova's head and tore off the feed bag. He raised one of her eyelids with his thumb, and looked anxiously at the pupil in the lantern light. Michael heard the commotion behind him.

"What's wrong Tracker?" he asked, looking back over his shoulder.

"I think Nova's been drugged. Quick, throw me my backpack, Michael, and fetch some fresh water from the lake." Tracker was holding Nova's head up with both hands now, trying to make contact, but to no avail. "It's straight across the way. Empty that bucket. The lake's the only water we can trust. Be careful Michael. There are enemies in this camp."

Nova's thoughts were invading again, *"I'm f-fine, Tracker ... Just dozed off there for a moment ..."* But her eyes were barely open, and her thoughts were very faint.

"I fear it's more than that, Nova!" Tracker fished in his backpack. *"Here, sniff this."* It was Tracker's Bonzo Bugger Gook.

Michael hurried out the stable and headed across Reverie Way. He darted between two of Kalib's tents in the direction of the lake, but suddenly came up short as he saw the shadow of the merchant and a servant dancing on the canvas to his left. Kalib was listening to Falin. "Sahib, the camelop will be much slower by race day, yes?"

"That's the plan. Just make sure you empty the exact amount of my juice in the oats tomorrow like you did today," answered Kalib. "I don't want her to die, do I? We've already lost one camelop testing the correct dosage. I just want her to lose by a nose or two. Hah! A half a nose would be best! But that would be cutting it too close. Keep a keen eye on her tomorrow, Falin. She should be showing very little effect by morning. But it will be in her system. She should feel it again by the second leg and then, by the beard, I'll be the richest man in Tremora, I swear!"

Michael sped off. He had heard enough. He retrieved the water from the lakeshore and returned via a different route. He again crept across Reverie Way, stepped over the rope barrier and was about to enter the stable when a hand closed roughly over his mouth and the bucket of water was yanked from his grip. It was one of the giant guards.

"Nova!" Michael screamed in his head. He was struggling, but was no match for the giant.

Nova's head struggled to rise. *"Michael's in trouble, Tracker ..."*

"What? But, how do you know that? Where?" Tracker's head swiveled round, looking.

"He just called out to me ... he's outside." Nova's thoughts were barely strong enough to understand.

Tracker grabbed the pitchfork and rushed out the stable door. The giant heard him and swung around, one hand still around Michael's mouth and the other holding a scimitar to his throat. Then, unbelievably, he dropped Michael to the ground and slowly transformed into the servant girl that had offered Kalib's hookah to Michael only the night before. She went to her knees with hands tented and pleaded,

"No, you don't understand. We want to help. You must believe me. Water will only make her worse. You might kill her!"

Michael struggled to his feet and looked beyond Tracker's shoulder. His faced drained as a second giant stepped out from the shadows with a scimitar held tightly in its huge hand. Too late, Tracker swung around.

"You saved our lives once, perhaps twice. I return the favor," the giant said softly. He lowered his sword and went to the girl and pulled her to her feet. "We will not beg, Fortina." He glanced toward Kalib's tent and then at Tracker and Michael. "We will tell you our story, but first we need to get inside and tend to Nova."

The girl nodded. She picked up the bucket of water and grabbed the giant's hand. They both hurried into the stables.

Tracker and Michael just stood and looked at each other. "You can mind meld with Nova, too!" Tracker said.

"Kalib is going to fix the race tomorrow, Tracker."

"Yes, but, you can meld with Nova?"

"Well, yes. I guess I'm a Grock or something. But Tracker didn't you hear me? Kalib is drugging Nova so she won't win the race."

"Michael, I don't think you know how unique you really are."

"Tracker!!!"

"Very well, Michael," Tracker said, looking across the way to Kalib's line of tents. He then grabbed Michael's arm and led him towards the stable doors. "I heard you. But, these two just spared our lives, and it sounds as if they saved Nova's, as well. I think Kalib might be in for a surprise before this is over, regardless of his plans. Come, let's hear their story."

Chapter Nineteen

The Princess and the Tres

Fortina and Tarbak stood waiting in Nova's stall, and Fortina had one hand on Nova's neck. "Falin put something in Nova's oats today that will take her strength away," she whispered in a rush. "It's evil. Kalib has been using it forever to help us win races. The other owners suspect him, but Kalib is very clever!"

"Water will only help spread it through her system," said Tarbak. "She must empty her stomach, by force if necessary, or she will surely weaken, maybe even die. It's happened before!"

But it wasn't necessary to induce vomiting in Nova. As soon as she heard and understood what Fortina said, she began to retch. "*Kalib fixed my races?*" The revelation made her nauseous, and she moaned with the thought and pain of it. *"It's all been a lie?"* Large tears welled up in her eyes. Then she hung her head low and upchucked her oats on the floor of the stall. *"I'll never be able to show my face again,"* she thought miserably.

Both Tracker and Michael looked at her in alarm. She was a most pathetic sight. They were receiving her thoughts, but didn't let on to the two servants.

"But, it looks like the poison is disagreeing with her anyway, don't you think?" Tracker noted to Tarbak. Nova continued to barf profusely.

Tarbak looked pleased. "Well, yes, and that's a good thing. And right on cue. There can't be much left in her after all that."

Nova finally stood up a little straighter and shuddered. Fortina held the bucket of water from the lake in front of her and Nova took a long drink.

"The water won't hurt her now," Fortina said to Tarbak as she looked with sympathy at Nova. Nova licked her hand weakly.

Tarbak grunted but didn't interfere. He looked around and found a shovel. Michael retrieved the pitchfork from outside and the two of them disposed of the soiled mess at Nova's feet in the paddock behind the stall. Then they spread fresh straw on the floor.

Tarbak continued. "Tomorrow Falin is supposed to add more of Kalib's poison to Nova's food bag. He'll avoid it if he can, but Kalib is watching over this personally. She must not eat that meal!"

"Leave that to us," Tracker said. "She will not eat any more tainted food. Now, before we go any further, it's time you told us what this is all about, don't you think? What is your story? You are the most unique people I've ever seen. Was what Kalib told me in the Pashtook Mountains all nonsense?"

"Actually, the story Kalib told you wasn't that far off the truth," said Fortina. "He did marry a king's daughter, and she actually does look a little like a Minotaur." She pantomimed two horns on the side of her head and made an ugly face. Tarbak gave her a disapproving look. She stuck her tongue out at the giant and continued on, unabashed. "But they both married willingly, Tracker—she to escape a life of spinsterdom, and he to get his hands on us."

"Believe us, there is no end to this man's deviltry," Tarbak spat, angrily.

Fortina nodded her head in agreement and then put a comforting hand on Tarbak's arm. "We are all from the island of Coriss, and it's an evil, evil place. In the old world, it was the very center of the slave trade and home to the vilest of the vile. Today it remains a blight on Tremora; Coriss still trades illegally in slaves and other ugly business. So, is it any surprise that someone like Kalib found out about the island and exploited its people to his advantage? No! But, regrettably for us, he also discovered a very closely held secret of the royal family of Coriss: The legend of the Tres was true."

Fortina paused for effect. She looked from Tracker to Michael expectantly. However, there was no response from either one. They only looked back at her, blankly.

She shrugged her shoulders at Tarbak. "Looks like we're not so famous outside of Coriss, are we?" Then she turned back to Michael and Tracker. "Well, as you said Tracker, the three of us are indeed 'unique.' We are known as the Tres. The unfortunate truth is we are bound by a witch's curse. Among other things, that means Princess Leonie is our mistress, and we are her slaves. It was barely tolerable with just her, but when we were forced also to cater to the whims of this disgusting man ..." Fortina visibly shuttered. "He is evil, a cheat, and a liar. But soon we—"

Tarbak suddenly shot out his hand and covered her mouth. Fortina angrily shoved the hand away. "Oh, all right!" she said.

She looked at Tracker and Michael apologetically. "Secrets must be revealed in their own time, as you know. And our story is—well, secret *and* long, and Tarbak is probably right; it's better to follow the oral tradition and tell the tale in its proper order and way." She looked back at Nova and stroked her long nose. "And, of course, only a male can do the story justice." Her sarcasm didn't go unnoticed. Nova snorted at just the right time. Fortina looked with surprise at the camelop and then suppressed a giggle.

Tarbak put down his weapon and took a stance in the light of the lamp. Fortina then became serious, and she and Nova both turned to look at the huge man. First, Tarbak caught each set of eyes before moving on to the next. Next, he spread his arms wide, making sure that he was the center of everyone's attention. Then, he slowly transformed into a young boy with long dreadlocks and many bracelets and wristbands. With hands free to gesticulate, he took over the narrative, and the kerosene lamp needed refilling long before the tale was finished.

The Tres

"If you please, I have taken on the form of a camboy to appear less fearsome, and for other reasons that will become clear later. First, I will tell of Kalib, the slime, and how he won the hand of Princess

Leonie; literally. Then, I will tell the tale of the Tres. It is an ancient and revered story of revenge and tragedy. Finally, you'll be brought to the present, and we will then decide if we are to embark on a new story together. For our personal stories are but ripples on a large flowing river, and we are but brief passengers on its journey through time."

Tarbak motioned for all to sit, even Nova. She knelt obediently on all fours in the clean straw. Then he also sat and, with crossed legs, began.

"As Fortina said, we are from the small island of Coriss located in the Labath Channel. Coriss was once the slave center of the old world. Slaves of every kind were bought and sold there, and the entire island prospered greatly from its unsavory trade. The ruling families always had first claim when an unlucky soul stepped up on the auctioneer's block. Thus, the brightest, heartiest, most talented, and fiercest slaves always ended up working in the palace. Of course, owning slaves and slave trading is banned everywhere in Tremora today. The wizards officially broke everyone's mental and physical shackles at the beginning of the Age of Secrets. But the island's royal family always treated its slaves extremely well and, even though the practice was banished, not all servants on Coriss wanted their freedom. Entire families devoted to the royals still live in quarters on the castle grounds for very little if any wage. Whether they are free or not could be debated, but to what end? Most are living happily; those slaves living in the palace, that is. But the island holds many dark secrets. One you already know—slave trading never ended on Coriss. The wizards could hardly expel a way of life that goes back centuries! Many ships still come and go under cover of darkness and in the light of propriety. Perhaps it's fitting, then, that today Coriss is paying a heavy price for the evil character of its people: It brought Kalib to the island!

"It was a rueful day when Kalib's ship anchored and he and his hoard disembarked down the gangplanks. It only took him a few months. The people of Coriss had little defense against Kalib's devious mind. Through the cunning use of games of chance like cards, dice, and racing, where the odds were always in Kalib's favor, he soon had most of the island, most of the king's court for that matter, heavily in his debt. In a very short time, our kingdom was helplessly snared in Kalib's evil web.

"You see, it wasn't only through gambling that Kalib was able to work his evil. Even more insidious, Kalib had also grabbed the reins of the island's slave trade. The king didn't see it coming until it was too late. When he finally realized his kingdom was under silent siege, he actually entertained the black thought of imprisoning Kalib falsely or even having him killed, but Kalib was no fool. At just the right moment, Kalib boldly sent a message to the king stating that, in the instance of his sudden disappearance or untimely death, messages would be sent across the sea and through the air to Tremora Castle. The threat was real. If the true nature of his island kingdom got back to King William, the king of Coriss would lose his throne and then his head. There was no way out.

"Life on Coriss slid farther and farther into crime and decadence as Kalib became more and more powerful. Then one day, Kalib came to the palace and demanded an audience with the king. It was time for Kalib to spring his final trap."

Tarbak stopped and adjusted the jewelry on his wrists. No one else moved. He had them all hanging, wondering what Kalib was going to do next. Tarbak was indeed an accomplished master of the oral tradition.

When he was ready, he said dramatically, "Kalib offered to expunge everyone's debt in return for the hand of Princess Leonie."

Tarbak sat back on his haunches. He nodded and acknowledged the bewildered look on the faces of Michael and Tracker. "Yes, your reaction is the same as was all of ours on Coriss: The king was stunned; the princess was stunned; the people were stunned. Could this clever man be serious? After all, everyone knew that the princess was destined to stay an unplucked maiden forever. The king had given up on anyone wanting to marry her long ago. She was completely disagreeable, mean, incredibly unpopular, a major pain, and yes, very, very, ugly.

"The citizens were justly dubious. Many were living with the weight of looming gambling debts and fear of impending disaster, and along comes a chance to be rid of two burdens at once? Unbelievable! Besides, everyone knew there was another rather large problem:

Princess Leonie was the royal family's first born and couldn't be forced into marrying anyone. It was all up to her, and no one believed she would actually make a choice just for the good of Coriss!

"So, the hour was set. Everyone waited for the princess's appearance on the castle's veranda. Would she take the hand of the foreign merchant? Would the princess wave a white kerchief in her right hand, or raise a red kerchief in her left to signal the offer was not to her liking? Princess Leonie, however, wasn't stupid. She saw her opportunity and jumped at it with enthusiasm. That day, Kalib himself appeared next to the princess and raised her right hand much as a referee indicates the winner of a boxing match. The mob was ecstatic, and celebrations started immediately. The festivities lasted for days.

"The wedding was quickly arranged and took place with a great deal of fanfare. After all, everyone in the kingdom was also relieved of his or her gambling debts that day. The couple took up residence in the castle, and the island expelled a collective sigh of relief. But a gambler's way is as predictable as the rising sun. In no time at all, Kalib had most of the island back in his debt once again. And, if he was arrogant and incorrigible before the marriage? Kalib and his wife virtually owned the island after that. The king was nothing more than a puppet. Kalib was "King Kalib" to many a slaver and merchant during those days.

"Eventually, Kalib began to make long trips to the mainland to continue his trading and racing. At first, he took both Princess Leonie and the Tres along with him. Over time, however, he traveled mostly without the princess, and she became more despicable with each opportunity to lord over Coriss alone. Then, with the unexpectedness that defines him, Kalib made two incredible announcements: one, the princess was expecting a child and, two, he was leaving her, the child, and the island of Coriss for good and taking the Tres with him!"

Tarbak stood up and again adjusted the bands on his arms. Then he ran his fingers along and through a long strand of hair on top of his head. Then he unclasped one of several strands of tiny beads and stones that adorned his right wrist. He closed his eyes and passed the strip slowly through his fingers as he swayed back and forth to a private cadence.

Fortina explained. “You’ve noticed that we often weave our dreadlocks when alone or idle. We are actually recording the daily events of our lives. We later transfer the most important memories from our hair to knots, carved stones, and beads on our bracelets, using a secret code. In this way we record and store the important events of our lives around our arms and wrists and in our hair. Tarbak is merely recalling the next part of his story.”

Tarbak opened his eyes and, as he replaced his memory band on his arm, he explained: “This is the main reason I took the form of Falin to tell our story. As a giant, I have no dreadlocks to untwist or read!” He laughed, and then became serious again. “Now, do you doubt the evil character of Kalib?”

“Kalib and his reputation are well known to us, Tarbak,” Tracker said. “Even Michael, who has been in Tremora only a few days, has been exposed to Kalib’s wickedness.”

Tarbak sat back down and shook his head in disgust. He closed his eyes and took several moments to calm himself. “At this point, you need to hear more of *our* story,” he said finally.

“The ‘Princess and the Tres’ was once a well-known play, a tragedy performed often on the stages of the old world, but few remember it now. It is the story of three slaves that were owned by an evil enchantress who lived on Coriss long ago. One of the slaves was a huge black man named Tarbak, and the other two were a brother and sister named Falin and Fortina.”

Michael looked confused. “But those are your names. Are you named after them? No, wait, are you saying …?” Michael’s voice trailed off.

Tarbak held up his hands, “Patience, young master. Indeed, you have begun to guess.” He resumed. “The reigning king of the time had a first daughter named Corrine. She had an independent streak and sensitivity that caused her a lot of trouble in those days. Her idealism led her to despise injustice of any kind. This was, of course, difficult in a land noted for its evilness. As she grew older, she spent every waking hour, it seemed, denouncing slavery and cruelty to all creatures. She gave aid to runaways by giving access to underground passages in the castle and purchased slaves at the auctions just to set them free. She would have been better off living in another time. She was very unpopular and only lived in moderate safety because she was the kingdom's first child and princess. She had many enemies, including the island's resident witch.

"The princess and witch were foes from the moment Corrine was born. Their rivalry was legendary. The witch's hands were tied because her nemesis was of royal blood, and Princess Corrine had very little she could do against the powerful magic of the witch—stalemate! Yet, their hatred for each other festered as Corrine grew older, and every small opportunity to irritate the other was savored.

"One day the princess met the young slaves and their giant friend quite by accident while shopping for baskets of fruit. The three were a curious sight, and the princess took an immediate interest in who they might be. They were reluctant at first to talk at all and tried to retreat quietly into the crowd. But Corrine was persistent, and through a series of seemingly innocent questions, she eventually broke down their defenses. The young girl especially seemed to warm to the princess and, even though the scowling giant showed his displeasure"—here Tarbak gave Fortina an I-told-you-so look, and Fortina returned his admonishment with a derisive snort—"she eventually told the princess of their sad and sorrowful existence in the castle of the witch.

"Princess Corrine sympathized with their plight and, admittedly, also saw an opportunity to enrage the enchantress. You see, the boy and girl's futures were already planned by their mistress; they were about to be separated, perhaps forever, and the two were desperate. Fortina finally confided to Corrine that they were all planning on escaping the island. The princess, of course, readily volunteered to help. Eventually, they agreed on a desperate plan. The three were to slip through a gate left open and then disappear into the castle's hidden passages with the help of the princess. They would hide there until the time and tides were right. Then they would flee to the shore and swim to a neighboring island, kept afloat by pieces of driftwood. Once there, they would set out to sea and freedom on a small boat supplied by friends of the princess.

"The plan was going smoothly. The three slipped into the bowels of the castle and disappeared for several days. When the time was right, the princess led them to a secret exit and bid them an emotional farewell. But, just as they were within reach of their freedom, the witch surprised them in the very act of diving into the sea.

"She captured them and took them to a cave where she cast a spell that was both incredibly inventive and cruel. She pointed her wand at the girl, and she turned into the boy. She then pointed her wand at the boy, and he turned into the giant guard. Laughing hysterically, she continued to turn each into another until the three forms danced wildly wherever her wand pointed. 'And then there were nine!' she marveled, admiring her work. 'Yes, I think I have done quite nicely.' She then cast the most devious spell of all. They would become slaves to Princess Corrine. And the princess would not be able to free them because they would die if she did. They would be assigned work every day and take on the shape that best fit the task. And finally, displaying the cruelty of an enchantress scorned, her curse made it certain that the Tres would be slaves to the first born of all future royal families of Coriss, forever!"

Fortina bowed her head in tears, and Tarbak put an arm around her shoulder. "We have been slaves for hundreds of years," he said.

There was a silence for several minutes as the meaning of what Tarbak said sank in. Michael could hardly grasp it at all. *They must be older than Tracker!* he thought in awe. "But, will you never grow old? You don't look as old as I am! And, never be free?"

Fortina raised her head. "We do not change. We are even older than some wizards," she said sadly.

Tracker grabbed at his belt and fumbled to fill and light his pipe. "This is a most extraordinary story, but surely the wizards knew of your plight when they freed all of the slaves."

"Yes, they were aware," Tarbak said. "And, yes, they did abolish all slavery at the beginning of the Age of Secrets, but they couldn't completely remove the enchantress's spell. Her powers were too potent." He became silent again.

Tracker finally asked, "What do you mean they couldn't 'completely' remove the enchantress's spell, Tarbak?"

Tarbak's demeanor suddenly changed. He pulled Fortuna to her feet and with fiery eyes turned to Tracker and Michael. "Before I answer that, Tracker, we have to know: Secrets revealed are no longer secrets. Their power can only wane. It's time to know, Tracker. Do you swear to help us?"

Tracker remained seated and drew deliberately on his pipe. His eyes were as bright as coals. "I think we are, indeed, destined to navigate the same waters, Tarbak—at least for a while. We would have had a hard time stopping Kalib's devious plans without your help, I think. But it seems you may need our help and council as well." He gazed steadily at the boy. "Is the answer not obvious?"

Fortina pushed Tarbak gently. "See, I told you. Go on. You can hardly stop now."

Tarbak stood still for a long time undecided. Then he slowly fingered another strand of hair and sank down cross-legged on the ground, and Fortina sat down close by. "Forgive me. Only, it's been so long and now …" He became silent again.

Fortina gave his arm a reassuring squeeze, and he continued. "The wizards made every effort to help us. After much effort and many attempts by the most powerful wizards of the day, we were told we would remain shape-changers, at the whim of our masters, for a long, long time, maybe for the rest of our lives. The wizards had little power over such a dark spell. But they could at least give us some control over the changes when we were alone. Then they told us that the best they could do with the slavery spell was reduce its lifespan. Good news, right? Anything would be better than 'forever'! But the news became more sobering when they said we had to wait until the birth of the seventh first-born princess in a row before the curse would vanish. When we asked what the chances were of that happening, they answered that they were too small to believe it would ever happen at all …

"Even worse, we wouldn't be able to keep track of how many generations had passed anyway, because with the death of each master, our memories would be wiped clean and always revert back to the first day of the original curse with Princess Corrine.

"But a young wizard named Megan recognized our plight and taught us the secret of the memory locks. We have been tracking the history of Tremora and our past lives for over three hundred years!"

Tracker removed his pipe in astonishment with the mention of the name Megan. He answered his young companion's look. "Yes, Michael, it very well could be the same wizard."

It was Tarbak's turn to give a blank look.

"Sorry. It's not important for now. Please, please, continue," Tracker urged.

"Well, that brings us to the most incredible part of our story and why we are here in front of you." Tarbak's voice suddenly became conspiratorial. "You see, in spite of all I've told you, Princess Leonie's decision to marry Kalib was an incredible blessing to the Tres. Why? Because Princess Leonie is the sixth first royal princess in a row to be born on Coriss in the Age of Secrets!"

Tarbak paused to watch the expressions on Tracker and Michael's faces as they realized how important this was to the Tres.

"Yes," he said, nodding in agreement, "and we've been living with that fact for years. But, can you imagine our torture? Leonie was never going to get married; she was so revolting, and she would never have a child, and our enslavement would continue on and on until some far future date when a firstborn princess of Coriss would again come of age and wed and have a child that had to be a girl—It was excruciating to be so close. Yet, we saw no end. And then, incredibly, along came Kalib!

"From the beginning, we suspected Kalib knew of the Tres because he was obsessed with having us as slaves. He made outlandish offers to buy us, was forever following us, questioning, probing … But at every turn, he was blocked by Princess Leonie. And so, since he had no access to us except through her, he concocted the incredible solution I described: He married her.

"But he was in for a rude awakening. Because, married or not, we would still only serve Princess Leonie. You can imagine his frustration when we ignored his every command. However, there is no end to this man's resilience, as you well know. He needed the princess to give the order that we should obey his every command and whim. But, again, she was no fool; she refused his request for years. She just kept using her power over us to get her way with Kalib. It made for an ugly marriage.

"But Kalib's reputation as an unscrupulous character is well earned. How could he coerce the princess into doing his bidding and gain the power of the Tres for his own? In the end, the answer was easy: Give her what she wanted most, a royal child and heir!

"He really, really, wanted us bad," Fortina said, again pantomiming horns and an ugly face. Then she put her finger down her throat and pretended to gag.

Tarbak's face grimaced with embarrassment for his sister's crudeness. He gave her another disapproving look before continuing. "Can you imagine our feelings when the announcement was made that the princess was pregnant? What if it was a girl?"

He rose to his feet. "And now, I will tell you the biggest secret of all. We will soon leave this ogre forever because the princess has delivered a girl this very night! Kalib doesn't know it yet, but we do. When the girl was born the spell was broken. We were awash with the most indescribable feeling—free for the first time in our lives."

Fortina beamed.

"We all found each other, and the meeting was long and very emotional. But, what to do? We needed a plan. Our first thoughts were to flee. But where to and how? With what? It became clear that we had no resources other than each other. To return to Coriss was out of the question; the place is too corrupt, and we never want to see the princess again. In the end, we decided to seek out King William and offer our services. It's all we know, after all. We're sure the Tres can work for the greater good of Tremora, and besides, the true story of Coriss needs to be told."

"Perhaps we can even help with finding the young Prince Cedric," Fortina added.

Michael and Tracker both sat up straighter. Surely the mention of Cedric was merely a coincidence. The Tres couldn't possibly know of their own quest.

Tarbak continued, "Our original plan was to leave Kalib immediately, but we can hardly run away and let this monster get away with stealing everyone's money. Why, we even helped put his evil plan in place! No, Nova needs to win her race, and with honor. We agreed to act out a small ruse for a while and undo as much of Kalib's plan as we could before we leave. We also decided to come and seek your help. But the first thing was to get to Nova. She was poisoned, and we needed to get to her quick. When we saw you, Michael, with the water … well, you know what happened next."

The door to the barn of stalls opened and shut suddenly, and Falin stepped into the light. He was in the form of the huge black bodyguard and had his scimitar at the ready. He quickly looked around and acknowledged everyone with a quick nod.

"Kalib has a visitor," he growled.

Chapter Twenty

Kalib's Caller

Falin was in the middle of transforming Kalib's quarters into a lush boudoir for the evening. First he covered a huge round, down-filled mattress with garish red comforters and then arranged several plush scented pillows to make a headboard. Next, he draped the whole affair in mosquito netting and lit the incense sticks that were sitting on two carved wooden nightstands. The smoke drifted up lazily, spreading thick perfume throughout the room. Finally, he placed silk pajamas and slippers on a footstool by a large ornate blind, behind which Kalib was disrobing and attending his toilet. His huge shadow cast a grotesque image that Falin tried very hard not to look at as he collected the day's worn clothes draped over the screen.

A dark form silently entered Kalib's tent. The fires in the braziers danced. Falin was caught off guard. He whipped around to face the intruder. A tall caped figure stood facing him with arms crossed and a sneer on its face. It held two cruel looking daggers in hairy, skeletal claws. The wisp showed no fear—Falin had no weapon.

Kalib either felt the chill of the flap in the tent opening or sensed the silence. "Falin?" he called feebly, as his face peeped around the divider. His eyes opened wide as he saw the standoff. In his highest pitched voice he cried, "No, no. It's OK, Falin, it's OK." His hand shot out and grabbed the pajamas and slippers. "It's merely a messenger making another unexpected visit," he said, irritably. "Your master really must let me know when one of you is coming …"

The wisp stood unmoving. Falin scowled.

Kalib then knocked the partition completely over as he hastily tried to tie the silk rope of his nightgown around his enormous girth. "By the beard!" he swore. He angrily completed the knot and shoved his fat feet into the furry slippers.

The wisp was unmoved. He merely looked on, expressionless.

Kalib gathered himself. Then he hurried forward, the slippers flapping loudly as they smacked the bottoms of his feet. He got between Falin and the wisp and bowed slightly to his guest. He kept his eyes on the visitor while waving Falin back with one hand. He then pointed toward a chest at the foot of the bed.

"Falin? A carafe of mead, please. That's a good boy. No need for excitement. We're all friends here. Only one tumbler, though. Our visitor doesn't partake of this form of libation, I'm guessing?" He raised one eyebrow questioningly toward the wisp.

Nothing.

"No, I didn't think so."

Falin went to the chest. He opened the lid and removed a glass decanter with a stopper and a small jeweled chalice. He was seething inside. *'That's a good boy!' I won't be your boy for much longer, Kalib,* he thought as he angrily pulled on the cork of the bottle.

"Now, what brings you here at such a late hour?" Kalib asked the wisp as he took the drink from Falin and downed it in one gulp. Falin poured another.

"Dismiss your servant."

Kalib got very still. "Yes, well, sure," he said slowly. "Ah, Falin? Please …"

Falin gave the wisp a last hard look. He then bowed to Kalib and retrieved his sword and belt and left swiftly through the flap. *Something is up for sure,* Falin thought. It wasn't unusual for Kalib to dismiss him when doing business (most of it was secret and shady anyway), but to be asked to be left alone with a wisp? And something else wasn't quite right. It certainly appeared to be a wisp, but where was the smell, and there was something odd about the claws. He hurried to find his companions.

❧

Once Falin left the tent, the wisp slowly sheathed its knives and reached up and brushed back its hood. Then it grabbed at its neck with both claws and in one swift movement removed its face.

Kalib gasped and then stared, as the rest of the wisp crumbled into a pile. A fat reptilian creature hopped out of the black jackboots and thumped onto the floor. It then inflated like a puffer fish and grew taller and fatter until it was half as tall as Kalib. When the warty beast reached its full height, it sat back on a cushion and rested its large belly on the floor. Now there was no doubt—it was a big, fat toad. It had webbed hands and feet, a large head with slits for eyes, and a darting tongue that constantly flicked in and out of a wide mouth. It wore burlap pants and a torn and ragged sleeveless blue vest. Once settled, it sat and stared back at Kalib.

"A shape-changer," Kalib gasped.

"Flugbark, at your service," croaked the creature. "I'll have that drink now, thank you." It opened its mouth and a tongue darted across the distance between them, snatching the chalice from Kalib's hand. The tongue and drink retracted back into its maw in a flash. It then gulped, licked its lips, and spit the cup out onto the floor with a clatter.

"Your slave is very alert," Flugbark belched. "He would have found me out had he stayed much longer." The shape-changer then rocked forward and picked up the pieces of the wisp disguise. It rolled the facemask, cape, and even the knives and boots into an increasingly smaller and smaller ball, then dropped the wad, now the size of an orange, into a pocket in its vest.

Kalib hardly heard a word. He stood speechless; mesmerized like a rat in a python cage. And for good reason: Shape-changers were assassins, and Flugbark was the most famous. Kalib was sure he was a dead man.

Although a shape-changer's weapons were deadly, its most effective weapon had nothing to do with knives and such. A shape-changer's ability to become someone else rivaled nature itself. A tadpole becomes a frog, a catersnork becomes a butterlop, and a toddler becomes an old man. Transformations like these would be even more remarkable if they didn't need such a long time to complete. Not so for shape-changers. They transform at will: Add a little magic, some sleight of hand, theatre makeup, a costume, more magic, and voilá, the disguise is completed. Very useful when stalking and getting close to your intended prey. Then, a shank and flit. The deed is swiftly done, and the assassin is gone.

Kalib knew there were only a couple of defenses against these assassins, but they involve more luck than skill. For one thing, a shape-changer's disguise is never completely on the mark; a mismatched boot here, a hairy knuckle there, or light lipstick on a bearded face. An alert person can catch the flaw, but the creatures rarely give their intended victim that much time. Kalib hadn't seen anything unusual about the wisp earlier. If he would have seen through the disguise, he wouldn't have dismissed Falin so quickly. Because another thing about these hideous creatures—they happen to be consummate cowards. Once exposed or even suspected, a shape-changer quickly flees the scene, its resolve and disguise evaporating as it jumps away to fight another day.

Flugbark watched Kalib intently. "I see you have heard of me," he said laughing. "But, you have no need to fear me. No, you are safe this time. I have a message for you, though, Kalib. Unfortunate for you, two of master's real wisps have been rather careless. It seems they are dead. So that brings us to you and me and why I'm here. You'll be happy to know that we are our master's backup plan."

Kalib blanched.

"But first, some old business. It's time to give up your Tres, Kalib. They're needed to capture the boy. And then they're to take their prisoner with them to their new home and master in Spreten. You are to give them the proper orders to obey master's every command from here on."

"The Tres?" Kalib squeaked out. "But they're mine. Whatever would Spreten want with my slaves?"

"The Tres were never really yours, Kalib. You didn't even know they existed until the master told you. Surely, you knew they would be claimed some day?"

Kalib wrung his hands. He went to the decanter in a daze and removed the stopper. "But what about Tracker? He's a Mazalon warrior, and the boy is his personal charge. By the beard! The Tres would never get away with kidnapping the boy!" He chugged from the bottle in huge gulps.

"Leave Tracker to me," Flugbark said. "It's my specialty. And, hey, leave that to me too!" The tongue darted out again, and the bottle was wrenched from Kalib's grip. This time when Flugbark finished, he spit the empty bottle at Kalib's belly. It hit and bounced across the floor. The shape-changer again belched loudly and laughed.

"Now, it's time we put our heads together. I haven't thought much on this yet, but these two are more resourceful than we imagined. And, by the way, one small thing you might keep in mind. For you, all is not lost. With Tracker gone, doesn't that mean that your precious Nova remains in your stable? "

"But how did you know that?" Kalib asked, taken aback.

"I've been traveling with you for two days, and you didn't even know it. Some of my finest work, I might add. Even posed as that big fellow once. I overheard your conversation with Tracker, Kalib. And, I also know of your plan to fix Nova's race. I look forward to my cut of the take."

Kalib appeared defeated and in a daze. He heaved himself heavily up on the bed and sat with his slippered feet dangling off the floor. But Kalib's mind was racing furiously. It didn't look like Flugbark was interested in assassinating him, after all, thank goodness. *And I'm not going to lose Nova!* That meant he could still fix the race. But now he'd have to cut this disgusting creature in. *Well, we'll see about that*, he thought. *There's more than one way to count money. He could still become fabulously rich. And Nova would still win future races for him. And couldn't having the Tres as spies in Spreten be a good thing? Technically, they'll surely still do my bidding if I play this right.* He hid his growing excitement.

Flugbark perched himself on top of a pile of cushions. "I can't be seen around here tomorrow. That dratted boy can see right through me. They nearly had me on the mountain top!" he said. "I still can't understand that—must have been the hairy knuckles. Hands are getting harder and harder ..." He turned his webbed hands over absently, examining the bumps and warts on their backs.

"Anyway," he said, coming out of his reverie, "it wouldn't be good if Tracker finds out I'm here. And your slave was getting suspicious—I'm staying out of his sight, too. Make sure that at least one of the Tres is watching Michael at all times tomorrow. It wouldn't go well for either of us if he and Tracker disappeared and again escaped capture."

He looked around and spied the hookah.

❧

Much later that night Flugbark was still sitting in the same position atop the stack of pillows in Kalib's tent. Kalib had retired and was snoring loudly in his canopied bed, but Flugbark paid him no attention. He was smiling to himself. His orders had been simple: Kill Tracker, kidnap Michael (preferable to killing, but killing was acceptable if all else failed), and get the Tres back to Spreten. Just one small problem was all: He couldn't easily get at Michael because of Tracker, and he couldn't easily get at Tracker because of Michael. But now he had a plan worked out that should accomplish all three of his master's wishes. Not surprising. He was, after all, Spreten's best. How else could he have become Queen Prelandora's own personal killer?

Chapter Twenty-one

Plans Aplenty

"How's Nova?" Falin asked. He looked anxiously at the camelop kneeling on the stall floor.

"She's fine," answered Fortina.

"She's been sick to the point of dry heaving," Tarbak added. "But, I'm sure we were in time."

Falin knelt and stroked Nova's nose. "I'm sorry, proud beast. I was still a slave. He bowed his head and touched his forehead to Nova's neck. He then quickly stood and, gripping his weapon, turned again to Tracker and Michael.

"It's OK, Falin. These two now know our story," Fortina said. "All of it."

"Then you will help us?"

Tracker tucked his pipe away. He then stood up and brushed off his pants. "Well, hmm, yes, but you see, that creates something of a problem. I must say, yours is a truly remarkable story." He turned so he could see all three faces. "But we're on a king's mission, Michael and I. We can't easily stray from its purpose, even for a cause such as yours."

Nova gave a snort and rose to her feet. Tarbak and Fortina looked at each other in surprise, and Falin quickly re-gripped his sword.

"But, I thought you said …" Fortina looked at Tracker, not understanding.

Tracker held up his hands. "Hold on, hold on. Please let me finish. It's very important that you know Michael and I are servants to the king. Our priorities are with his wishes—always. You must remember that."

Even Michael wasn't sure where Tracker was going with this. Didn't he just say they were all going to help each other?

Tracker then spread his arms and smiled. "However, if you truly plan on staying, then our paths, indeed, seem to be merging. It is noble to keep Kalib from fixing Nova's last race. You will be correcting a serious wrong. As to your plan to seek audience with King William, in this, I also applaud you. So, since Michael, Nova, and I must stay till after the Running of the Lops, anyway, we would be remiss if we didn't help to bring down a criminal like this who is loose in our kingdom. We will be only too happy to help you."

Fortina ran and gave Tracker a huge hug. "Thank you, thank you!"

Falin's deep voice interrupted. "But you might need our help as well, Tracker."

Everyone turned.

"Kalib's visitor appears to be a wisp. The two are together now, and I'm guessing they're discussing something other than the races."

Michael gasped. He saw a vision of the wisp's wicked, leering, face.

"This is indeed heavy news," said Tracker.

"It seems you have your own story to tell. Does this have something to do with your mission?" asked Tarbak.

"Yes, we're being followed. But there's little more I can tell you. Wisps attacked us at the ford, and a shape-changer has also crossed our path. And now, another wisp has followed us to the island." Tracker relit his pipe. "I need to think on this," he said slowly. "And, you're right, Falin. We may very well need your help. Whatever Kalib and his friend are up to, it's sure to involve us—possibly the Tres as well.

"For now, all of you please keep your ears open and be careful. Find out what you can. In the meantime, we'll take turns standing watch over both Nova and Michael. Tomorrow we'll make our own plans."

Chapter Twenty-two

PRELANDORA

He lay sprawled out on an ornately carved obsidian throne with a strip of black silky cloth draped across his lap. It was his only clothing. His arms and legs were stretched wide, and his long white hair and beard cascaded down the dais and across the black marble floor. A single globe of blue light floated above his head, casting a dull glow that created ominous shadows. The rest of the vast hall lay in darkness.

He'd been in this position for years. His face was so deeply etched he looked to be a thousand years old. His eyes stared blankly, and he barely breathed; taking only one shallow breath after unbelievably long intervals. But today, for the first time in a long time, he was showing signs of life. His fingers and toes were splayed wide, and every hair on his arms and legs was electric with static. He was sensing Prelandora's world.

An extremely thin woman leaned over and put an ear close to his mouth. Then she rose up and, without taking her eyes off the man's face, held out an impatiently gesturing hand toward her sister who was standing opposite. "It'sss true, Riella," she hissed. "He is consciousss again … but jussst … and isss trying to ssspeak." A small black forked tongue darted in and out between her lips as she spoke. "Quickly," she said, snapping her fingers.

Riella took a folded white cloth from a small table at her side and draped it over her arm. Then she carefully lifted a shallow silver basin with both hands and held it out over the prone figure's chest. The bowl contained a glowing green liquid that reflected off her face. "Let's hope she isss happy thisss time, Twyla," she whispered.

Twyla sneered and inhaled through clenched teeth to show her distaste. She reached out and took the cloth from Riella's arm and dipped it in the liquid. Then she wrung it out over the man's parched and cracked lips, and waited. To her relief, his tongue soon appeared, reacting greedily. After further administration and several anxious minutes, the man began to speak, laboriously croaking out one word at a time.

The two sisters spent the next several hours scribing his every utterance. It was long grueling work to make sense of the ramblings. Regardless, these moments of clarity were occurring less and less frequently, and Prelandora would be livid if they didn't capture every word. Today, though, even if it was tortuous work to understand him, they were lucky. Not only was Lord Pratt talking, but he was downright loquacious.

◈

Twyla knelt with head bowed and hands extended in submission before her mistress, who was peering imperiously down her nose with one eyebrow raised in query. Prelandora too was draped back on a black obsidian throne, but her eyes weren't staring out blankly at the world like Lord Pratt's; they were alive with fire. She leaned back casually with one leg extended, showing a bejeweled sandaled foot. Her bare arms, white as alabaster, were draped languidly over armrests carved in the images of fire-breathing dragons. The flames exploding from their mouths were inlays of yellow jade and red carnelian stone. She was dressed in raiment of green gossamer, and on her head she wore a simple silver circlet set with emeralds. She held a matching silver wand in her left hand, and her long pitch-black hair, parted in the middle, fell straight down and over her shoulders.

Prelandora was a witch. She was also an enchantress, but she was not a queen. It was true she called herself queen and demanded that her underlings call her queen, but she was not a queen. She could never bring herself to marry that poor creature in the adjoining hall. At one time she thought it possible. After all, he had been strong and virile and in succession to the throne … but, no, she knew he was also spineless; he would never have stood up to his older brother, William. She only stayed with him because she needed him, because he would give her a son. A son, who, according to a long dead ancestor named Ohndrea, could become High King. Only, that didn't turn out so well …

"What brings your slimy, cold-blooded self to my chamber, Twyla?" Prelandora asked.

"He speaksss again, my queen." Twyla's tongue worked overtime, licking her own face and eyes.

"At last!" Prelandora cried and leaned forward. "Out with it then! I'm growing old, waiting for birds and wisps to bring me news."

Twyla rose to her feet and bowed her head. Then she took a deep breath. "My queen," she said, still looking at the floor, "The assassssin is ssshaken. Malif and Bardak are dead. The merchant is gloating. He hasss a daughter. The son of Fenn growsss stronger. And the dragon is in danger." Twyla looked up fearfully. "The old man hasss been repeating thessse things for the last ssseveral hours, my queen."

Prelandora sprung to her feet and stood with fists clenched and arms ramrod straight at her sides. She glared down in disbelief. "He said what!"

Twyla bowed her head again and started to repeat the message. "The assasssin—"

"Enough, you fool!" Prelandora screamed. Then she raised her wand to strike, but dropped her hand back down to her side. "No. If I keep killing the messengers, I won't have any left," she reprimanded herself. "Besides, I need *all* my creatures right now." Prelandora often spoke to herself as if no one else was in the room.

She then turned her head and took a pensive posture, raising her chin, and staring off into space. *This is dire news, indeed*, she thought. *But, I must think on this calmly. And give thanks; at least now, I have some timely news to contemplate!* Her eyes refocused. "Just when I thought his usefulness had come to an end," she said softly. She then turned and walked to the back of the throne. Once there, she carefully struck another pose, grasping her sceptre and leaning it out at an angle with one stiff arm. It was her habit to move continually from one statuesque pose to another.

She looked again to her servant. "Are you sure you have everything correct? That there's nothing more?"

"Yesss, my lady," Twyla hissed. "Every word isss exact."

Prelandora studied the figure before her but found no signs of deceit. She wasn't surprised—Twyla and her twin were her most trusted creatures. "Then you and Riella continue to monitor him day and night. I want to know anything new—anything! Your duties with the boy can discontinue for a day."

"Yesss, my queen," Twyla said, breathing a long sigh of relief. She wasn't going to be beaten! Or worse. She'd been fairly certain she was going to be safe from Prelandora's wrath, but you never knew with a witch. She'd seen heads roll many times. Then, feeling emboldened, she raised her head and looked hopefully at her mistress.

Prelandora looked at her with surprise, then angrily, and then laughed. "Well, I give you kudos for audacity." She reached into a leather pouch hanging on the side of the throne and threw something quivering and dripping to the woman. Twyla's face suddenly distorted, piranha teeth gleamed, and her neck extended to catch the morsel in mid air. The witch dismissed her with a wave of her hand. Twyla hurried from the great hall with blood running down her chin and her reptilian tail dragging across the floor.

Prelandora stood unmoving as Twyla disappeared. She was deep in thought. When she first cast the spell that bound the High King's brother, it was important that he willingly succumbed to her entreaties. It was a requirement of the enchantment. But that was hardly a problem; he was already a quivering wreck of a man. He was enchanted without her even enchanting him.

She found the spell in a book of black magic in the Great Hall of Knowledge while they both still lived in Tremora Castle. *Before their exile,* she thought bitterly. It was too dangerous to try on herself, of course. *Who better to bewitch then?* And it worked beyond her wildest dreams. Under the spell, Pratt was able to sense the moods and thoughts of all of her creatures and special pets. He received tremors like a spider at the center of a huge web; the slightest ripple told a tale. He was her connection to each and every one of her spies in every part of the world. *What exile!* she smirked. He could even sense, though not nearly as well, the moods and thoughts of her enemies. Slowly, however, the true nature of the spell became apparent: It took more and more strength and time to poll her "flock," and eventually the poor man ended up lying comatose in a near prone position on his throne. His life energy was drained to near empty. So, as time went by, his ability to sense her spies also declined and became sporadic at best. It had been a long time indeed, since she had last heard from Pratt.

She considered his latest revelations about her minions. She already knew that Flugbark had failed with the scrolls and had sent her wisp, Malif, to finish the job. *Didn't the crow's message say as much?* "Plans one and two have failed," the note said. She was furious when she read it. *That bird will never deliver another message! And now, Malif and Barak have also failed to kill Tracker and capture the boy—instead, it's them that are are dead.*

She didn't understand. *It is only one man and a mere boy! Albeit, a Mazalon warrior, but he is old!* She shook her head. She would have to work a little harder on her next batch of wisps …

And if that wily merchant is "gloating," then what is he up to? No good, for sure. Gloating because he now has a daughter? No, there's more to that story. But, no matter. She could always handle Kalib.

That left Flugbark. *And he was "shaken"?* She knew about shaken. When she received word of the king's plans to summon the boy through the veil from her spy in Tremora Castle, she was stunned. Another messenger died for that one. *The secret of the veil—uncovered by the king! Just what Ohndrea warned against. And the king was summoning the son of Fenn? Even worse! And on top of it all, the wizard Megan was also called to assist the king.* The only person alive as powerful as she … From nowhere, Tremora was fighting back.

It was astonishing that the boy was here at all. Her resolve-destroying spell at the veil should have sent him back home a quivering wreck, but he somehow fought it off. *Did that witch of a mother, Fenn, interfere?*

But Prelandora always, always had a backup plan. It was her mentor, the long dead witch Ohndrea, who gave her that bit of advice. That's why she also sent the shape-changer to intercept Tracker and the boy on the paths of Golan. Flugbark was her most lethal weapon. If the boy somehow made it into Tremora in spite of her efforts, then Flugbark was to stop him, and quickly. While disguised as the king's favorite private messenger, he was to give poison scrolls to both the boy and Tracker, and then he and Malif were to kill Tracker and kidnap the boy. Why not turn the tables and use the boy herself, was her thought. Simple enough. Then Flugbark would move on to Bearcamp and retrieve her new slaves, the Tres, from Kalib. With the Tres and Fenn's boy under her control, not to mention Prince Cedric and the dragon … her head reeled with the thought of it. The power!

Then reality sank in. Flugbark failed in the mountains, and the wisps failed at the fords. She was incredulous. The boy had already escaped three times from her snares! Once again, she was forced to make new plans. *If the two are in Bearcamp now, in spite of efforts by the wisps at the fords, then aren't Flugbark and Kalib also in Bearcamp?* she reasoned. *And aren't the Tres there, as well? Surely, with Kalib and the Tres to help him, Flugbark will not fail again. It's such a simple task. Once Flugbark and the boy and the Tres are on their way to Stern, I can send new wisps and soldiers to escort them all back to Spreten.*

But, what if Flugbark fails yet again? she asked herself. *What if Kalib snarls up my plans with his own web of desires? He was gloating, after all. No, I cannot depend on this plan to work any better than the others. And the son of Fenn must not make it to the gathering. Ohndrea made that quite clear. He must not succeed in finding the prince … ever. But, he is getting "stronger."* She felt doubt for the first time.

Yes, it's clear, she decided. *The boy is stronger, stronger than I ever imagined. Well, we shall just have to send reinforcement of another kind*, she mused. *And who better? It seems only appropriate that we, once again, release our special friend!*

Chapter Twenty-three

Bearcamp—Day Six

It was the busiest day of the week along Reverie Way. The island would empty out pretty quickly after the Racing of the Lops on day seven. Revelers, of course, would drink and celebrate into both nights, and most of the seedier businesses would continue, but legitimate commerce peaked on day six.

Kalib's servants, including the Tres, woke up before sunrise to start their preparations. First they unrolled huge hand-woven carpets and spread them on the ground at intervals along the thoroughfare. Then they unloaded Kalib's wagons and laid out sundry items for sale in lavish displays on silver- and gold-threaded rugs. They added sweet smelling incense, water pipes, and more miniature statues of Kalib to entice further the pedestrian traffic. As an added attraction, baby camelops were decked out in miniature racing gear and hobbled within petting distance of passers-by.

Tracker also woke early and was in a grumpy mood. He'd taken his turn at watch, and then couldn't sleep much when given the chance; he was too preoccupied with the events of yesterday—especially the appearance of the wisp. Michael was curled up asleep on a pile of hay, and Tracker nudged him awake rather rudely with his boot.

"Get up, Michael," he growled. "Falin stopped by earlier but had nothing new, and there's no sign of the wisp. Kalib is in a jolly good mood, though; more indication that he's up to no good."

"*Good morning, Michael!*" It was Nova.

"Are you feeling OK, Nova?" asked Michael out loud as he wiped sleep from his eyes. He ignored Tracker altogether.

"*Yes, Michael. And, by the way, Tracker knows of our special way of communicating.*"

"*Yeah, we had that conversation last night. He couldn't get over it.*"

"Ahem," Tracker said. "If you two are quite through?" He looked at both of them impatiently. "Look, this is going to take some getting used to. I'm sure it'll prove useful some day, but for now, let's keep it to a minimum, shall we? Oh, and for your information, Michael, I can also meld with Nova. Mazalon warriors can normally communicate with animals on at least some level—it's one of our gifts. Only," he scratched his head, "I don't do it in the same way or same *something* as you. It's like you and I send different languages, and only Nova knows them both."

Michael looked up at Tracker and then at Nova. After a pause he said, "Tracker, do you know how special you are?"

Surprise crossed Tracker's face. Then he reluctantly smiled and kicked Michael again with his boot. "Very funny. Now, let's go. The sun is up, and we've let you sleep long enough. I have a plan, but I fear nothing is going to prepare us completely for what's coming in the next two days. I'll meet you outside."

Michael hurriedly pulled on his boots, washed his face in the waterbucket, and ran a comb through his hair. "What now? What plan? It's time someone started asking what I thought," he muttered to himself. He had had a lot of time to think during his turn at watch. If there was going to be another wisp attack, he was going to be ready next time. He patted the hunting knife hanging from his belt. He wished it was bigger.

It seemed to Michael that everyone was waiting for Nova's race to be over with: Kalib … the Tres … Tracker … everyone—maybe even the wisp. Then he and Tracker were to go and pick up someone named Waz and get to the wizard's gathering where a bunch of other stuff was supposed to happen. And, as Tracker said, the king's quest must come first … But Michael had his own agenda, too; he still had to find his father! He hurried out the door of the stable adjusting his backpack.

"We don't know all of it, but we know part of Kalib's plan now," Tarbak was saying to Tracker in a whisper. Michael hurried up to join them. There was an awkward silence.

"Go on, Tarbak," Tracker said. "We're all in this …"

Tarbak crossed his huge arms and looked first at Tracker and then at Michael. "It seems you are to be kidnapped tomorrow, Michael."

Michael's face went pale, and his hand went involuntarily to his knife. "How—," he started to ask, and then stopped. Tarbak was smiling. "Why is that funny, Tarbak?"

"Sorry, Michael," he said, but he continued to look pleased. "It might be true, but you don't have to worry. And you won't need that toad sticker you have there, either. See, it's the Tres that's going to do the snatching!"

Tracker quickly grabbed Tarbak and Michael by their elbows and pointed them toward the stables. "I need you to start at the beginning, Tarbak. But we need to go inside, away from inquiring eyes and ears. It's crucial I know everything. *Everything!*"

They gathered in front of Nova's stall—it was no accident. Tracker wanted Nova to hear everything too.

"Kalib called us in to his tent this morning to give his orders," Tarbak began. "As expected, Falin is to poison Nova again this evening to ensure she won't win the final race tomorrow. But then he said something completely unexpected: We are to kidnap you, Michael, at tomorrow's race, and then take you to Stern, where we will be met by soldiers who will escort us by ship to Spreten. There, we're to turn you and ourselves over to someone named Prelandora, our new master."

"Prelandora? Why, that's Prince Pratt's witch! That is strange news, indeed," Tracker said. "I think the king will find this very interesting."

"Well, we don't really know anything else about her. At the end of the race, we're to grab Michael, bind him, and throw him in one of Kalib's wagons, then set off for the seaport. We're to wait there until we receive further orders. Kalib must owe someone a big debt to give us up so easily. Anyway, we don't care. After the race we're going to discard our yokes forever! And I guarantee, a trip to Spreten won't be in our plans!"

"What about the wisp? Was it there?" Michael asked, anxiously.

"Yes, it was standing away from us, silent as ever, not moving. I think the plan is for it to report back to Spreten, too. But Kalib said his 'friend' had some business to attend to first. And Tracker, I think that business is with you."

"Of course, it is. They know you won't get away with kidnapping Michael right in front of my nose. But, little do they know …" Tracker stopped and pondered. "They'll need to separate Michael and me somehow; probably use a diversion … That's where the wisp will come in, I think. We'll just have to keep our eyes and ears open. I think it's best that the Tres continue its ruse and actually kidnap Michael, Tarbak. We need to keep your secret as long as possible. We'll have to come up with a plan where we can all meet up later."

"Yes, I agree," the giant said slowly. Then, "By the way, I'm not supposed to let either of you out of my sight today. In fact, I'm supposed to take you to the market. As for Falin and Fortina, they're to keep their eyes on Nova today, and then Fortina and Falin will ride in both halves of the race tomorrow as usual."

Tracker lit his pipe, walked off a few paces, and stared into space. Michael and Falin waited patiently. Abruptly, Tracker turned and said, "Well, let's go shopping then, shall we?"

Just then Falin came in to get Nova. All of the camelops were going to be on show for the morning. Catching the three standing inside, he said, "I see Tarbak has talked to you. As I said this morning, Tracker, Kalib has given orders to poison Nova's meal this evening. But I'll pour the poison on the ground. If only she could be less excited this evening. Kalib may come in to check on her."

Tracker patted a pocket on his vest. "I think I might have something here, but much milder in nature than Kalib's concoction. It'll do the trick. Nova will need to relax tonight, anyway, with the big race tomorrow. Don't worry. She'll pass any test."

"Well, we're off then," Falin said. "Nova is Kalib's main attraction today, and we can't be late."

"Are you going to poison me, too?" Nova's question came sharply into Tracker's mind.

"No, no. It's something I use myself to relax when I can't sleep. It has a little toad, a little whistle wart, and some other stuff. Quite pleasant, I assure you. Your eyes will even dilate slightly!"

She gave Tracker a stern glance backwards as Falin led her out the stable door. *"It'd better wear off before tomorrow! I have a race to win, you know."*

No sooner had they left than Kalib appeared next at the door. "Ah, Tracker!" he hailed. "And Michael, too! Good day to you both. I hope you've accepted my servant's invitation to spend the day at the open market? It's a wonder of the world. And Tarbak is an excellent guide and protector. No pickpockets or thieves will bother you today," he said jovially, as he turned sideways to get in the door.

"Greetings, Kalib. Yes, thank you. It is most kind of you to release Tarbak from his duties today. But surely you need his services to prepare for the races tomorrow?" He wanted the merchant to squirm a little.

Kalib blushed. "But Tracker, it is a gift I give you. It is no secret that you and your young friend are traveling on king's business. And didn't I bandage a wound inflicted on Michael by a fiend I shall not name? You could perhaps do with the extra protection. I merely extend an opportunity to enjoy this wonderful day outside these meager quarters. You're staying until tomorrow, anyway. Why not show Michael the sights and let Tarbak be your guard? Why do you hurt my feelings this way?" he pouted.

"I think our business is none of your concern, Kalib," snapped Tracker.

Kalib looked alarmed. His mind raced. What if the boy had some horrible accident; died unexpectedly, disappeared, or stumbled into the water and drowned? Then she would blame him and come and kill him in some terrible way …

Tracker saw the distress in Kalib's face and wondered what he was afraid of. He decided not to upset the merchant any further; in the end it was better if Kalib felt he was in control. He pretended to reconsider.

"Actually, Nova, Michael, and I do have many miles ahead of us, and we do need supplies for our journey …" He slowly scratched his chin. "Kalib, I'm sorry. I misjudged you for a meddler. I see, now, you only had good intentions. We accept. But we'll not be gone long, and you'll have Tarbak's services back this afternoon. Thank you."

Kalib smiled ear to ear and bowed to Tracker. "Tarbak can stay as long as needed."

Michael and Tracker gathered their backpacks and other gear from the stable. Then, with Tarbak leading, they made a right turn outside the stables and soon came to the row of Kalib's lavish displays. Several people were gathered at one particular spot, and there was Nova. She looked splendid in her regalia. From her head to her tail and down to her toes, she never looked better, thought Michael.

"Why thank you, Michael. It's my favorite part of coming to the races, seeing my admirers. I'm quite over yesterday, by the way. Even without the drugs, I'm sure I would have won every race."

Michael just shook his head in admiration as he watched Nova project her most humbling and demure look on her admirers.

"If only I could sign autographs ..."

"She's certainly in her element, isn't she?" said Tracker, nudging Michael. "Someday, I hope to let her return to racing, you know. But don't let on. It will be another of our secrets."

They carried on in an easterly direction, following Tarbak through the crowd. Michael had never seen anything like it. He watched in amazement as bargain hunters jostled and pushed each other to get position at the different stalls and displays. There was hand gesturing, bartering, and offer-counter-offerings going on at every stand. And the bazaar atmosphere just kept growing with each passing moment as the throng grew; items were scrutinized, lifted, prodded, and poked; food was smelled, sampled, bought, and consumed. And at the end of every transaction, the lucky buyer scurried quickly away with his or her prize tucked under an arm, and another bargain hunter quickly took the empty spot; hoping to match or beat the last deal.

As they moved slowly along, Tracker took as much interest as Michael in the goods being offered. "We'll need supplies for our journey to Fennland," he said. "And I think it's time to upgrade your weapons, Michael. You'll be surprised what a stopper full of Bonzo Bugger Gook will get you here. Have you seen all of the different animals? Every one has its own brand of gnat or horsefly. People are being eaten alive!"

Several hours later, Michael was still wide-eyed with marvel. In addition to all the remarkable merchandise for sale, he witnessed a small sampling of the races and competitions that made Bearcamp famous. His favorite contest was a three-legged ostrich race where the jockeys were gibbons. During the race the huge birds ran with their wings spread wide, while the small apes leapt from pair to pair literally "jockeying" for position. The winning birds ended up with seven clambering, hairy jockeys clinging to their backs and necks as they crossed the finish line as one.

He also watched several contests between the giant mountain folk. Huge men threw axes at trees, stumps at wagons, barrels at each other, and boulders into the lake. In one contest, they threw whole trees like spears at blindfolded mountain maidens that were holding targets high above their heads (the maidens were the mountain folk without the beards). And of course, the occasional pickpocket was chucked out into the lake to the applause of the crowd.

Gradually, they began to make their way back toward the stables. Tracker was right; the Bugger Gook was very popular. Their backpacks were full of supplies, and Michael sported a much larger knife at his side. Tarbak had picked it out.

A brightly colored stall with blowing pennants and streamers caught Michael's eye, and he slowed. Tarbak and Tracker remained back, keeping a wary eye out while Michael wove his way to the entrance of the three-sided tent. Once there, he stopped and just stood, looking and listening in amazement. Myriad birds were chirping, preening, and singing in and out of ornate cages stacked on counters, on the floor, and hanging from hooks on poles. Several small birds flitted within the closure, and a flock of white doves circled, kettling above the roof. Hooded raptors were spaced throughout, leather thongs binding them to their perches. At the entrance, two talking parrots were arguing and cursing at each other in a constant stream of insults and obscenities.

Michael shook his head in wonder as he entered the tent and slowly walked around the enclosure, taking it all in. A grey-haired lady stood behind a wooden counter that displayed bird food, stuffed toys, and other avian accessories. Michael smiled when he noticed she had birds on her shoulders and on her head. When she saw him, she smiled back and put her arms to her side, elbows bent, and palms up. On cue, two budgerigars landed, one on each hand. "Which one should I wrap for you?" she asked, beaming.

Before he could answer her, a large brown pelican flew in through an opened flap in the back of the tent and landed clumsily behind the lady on a driftwood perch. The bird was dripping wet, and tail fins protruded from its long bill, indicating its pouch was full of fish. The lady quickly launched the small parrots from her hands and grabbed a bucket from under the counter. Then she turned and lovingly patted the pelican's head while gently prying open its bill. Next, she reached in and transferred the fish to her pail and emptied the contents into a bin labeled "Pelican's Pick of the Day" that was sitting on the counter top. She looked at Michael and pointed to a strip of cloth that was tied around the bird's throat. "This keeps him from swallowing," she said as she undid the knot. Then she offered up a couple of fish to the bird from the bin, and the pelican gobbled them greedily. Finally, she retied the cloth and pushed the bird in the direction of the open flap. The pelican launched itself clumsily, stirring up dust and feathers, and disappeared out the opening. "It keeps him coming back every time," she said. "Now, anything *catch* your fancy?"

He noticed a box full of small colorful stuffed birds and picked one up to look at it. It was the bird he had seen in the trees.

"Ah, the mystical, mythical, mysterious fluster bird, messenger of kings, escort to fortune. I'm afraid I only have the fake stuffed variety," she said. "A real one would be priceless."

"Why is that?" Michael asked absently as he continued to look at the toy. He noticed two small eggs attached to the feet, one very colorful and the second a dull white.

The lady looked mildly surprised. "You've never heard the legend of the fluster birds? You don't carry a stick shaped like a Y for good luck or just in case you see one?" She reached into her apron and pulled out a handful of twigs, all shaped like little sling shots. Michael's face was blank.

"My, my, you are a strange duck. And I know my ducks!" she laughed. "Here, take one. And if you find a stone filled egg, be sure and remember me!" She winked at him and returned the remaining sticks to her apron. She then picked up one of the stuffed birds and leaned both elbows on the counter, holding the toy up close to her face with both hands so she could point out its features.

"Now, this is all speculation, of course, what I'm going to tell you. No one knows if any of this is true. Probably just folklore. The royal family supposedly has the only living fluster birds left, being kept captive in their aviary and all. In fact, no one has seen a fluster bird in the wild for so long; they may not even exist anymore."

"But I ..." Michael began and then stopped. He saw Tralana in his mind stomping her foot at him and giving a warning look. "Never mind," he said, embarrassed. "The story started to sound familiar, but I was wrong. Please, continue ma'am."

"Ma'am?" the lady exclaimed. "Well. You may not have learned your fables, but at least someone taught you manners." She went back to looking at the stuffed bird. "See here?" she said, pointing a finger at the toy, "fluster birds are the same color as the rainbow, only dappled, not striped. Otherwise, they appear to be like any other bird, until it's time for the female to lay an egg, that is. As her time approaches, she starts to get quite flustered, thus the name, and begins making rapid twittering sounds that increase in pitch. Then, one of the many things that make these birds unique happens: The female lays an egg by standing on her head and spinning like a top. She spins faster and faster until the egg comes out of her mouth! Immediately after, she flops down on her little rump, reeling and dizzy, with intact feathers in disarray and loose ones falling all around her. And get this? The male hovers above her the whole time squawking loudly while copying her every behavior—without laying the egg, of course. He does this partly in sympathy for his mate, but more important, it provides protection for her during such a vulnerable time. She'd be an easy meal for a predator, if you think about it. So he offers himself up as a distraction. He also supplies all the squawking since the female's mouth is full." The woman smiled again at her own wit. "Anyway, the male also drops to the nest when the egg is laid, wings splayed and tiny tongue lolling out the side of its bill. And the egg? Well, it's the same color as a fluster bird's feathers; only this time, the colors circle the shell in stripes just like a rainbow."

The lady caught sight of Tracker approaching. She stopped her story and looked up from her prop.

"No, no. Please go on. I'm with him," Tracker said as he put an arm around Michael's shoulders.

She looked at them both curiously. "Well, I was just telling the tale of the fluster birds to your young friend. He doesn't seem to be familiar with it."

"Ah, yes, well. You see he was orphaned and raised by wolves and finally escaped only to be captured by pirates, and they put him on a slave ship, and he's hardly seen the light of day his whole life." Tracker stopped and smiled. The lady looked back at him, getting the point. She wasn't going to get any information about these two today.

"Very funny," she said. "Okay, keep your story to yourselves. I'm only a poor merchant, after all. What do I care about your secrets?"

She returned, unperturbed, to her story. This time she pointed her finger at the tiny plain egg. "Not all eggs are so beautiful, though. Every once in a while an egg is laid that is plain, the color of a dull white stone. They say it glows faintly, but who knows? This egg is the female's way of ridding herself of impurities in her body. It's the main difference between the male and female fluster. The female forages for bugs and insects in the mud of shallow streams so stones and such constantly mix with her food. The male eats berries and catches insects on the fly like a swallow, so it doesn't have the same problem. Now here's the biggest mystery. Where do these birds live? Where do they nest? Why does anyone care?" She paused for effect. "Because if you break open that dull, plain white egg, you'll find a small sampling of the most beautiful and precious gemstones in the world!"

Michael knew halfway through the story that he owned his very own Tremoran secret. He knew exactly where these birds lived! And even Tracker didn't know he knew! He forced himself to hide his excitement.

"But, but what about the twigs?" he stammered. "Where do they come into the story?"

The lady threw the stuffed bird back in the box and straightened up. "It's what they build their nests with, isn't it?" She again reached under the counter and brought up a very old wooden shoebox. She blew the dust off the cover. "Now, I'm not saying what I'm going to show you is real—no—but it's been in our family for many, many years. A severe windstorm supposedly bore this nest onto our family's farm, and a great-great-great-grand somebody found it. It's not the only one floating around, mind you. There're a lot of fakes out there that are used to send people on wild gooselop chases. But you have such an honest look about you," she said, looking at Michael.

She then glanced at Tracker. "You, though?" she said poker-faced. "Not so much …"

She laughed out loud and then set the box on the counter top. "Just kidding. But you deserved that. So, look at this." She raised the lid and carefully removed a bird nest from the box and handed it to Michael. "Notice how the twigs all interlock. And it's very strong." The nest was completely formed with Y-shaped twigs. "Legend says that if you see a fluster bird and offer it the right size and shaped twig, it will lead you back to its nest. And there you just might find a discarded dull white egg lying on the ground." She took the nest from Michael and put it back in the box.

"Who knows if any of this is true? I sure haven't seen any precious stones bartered about lately. But just in case, most Tremorans carry a twig or two for luck, anyway. Why I bet even your elderly friend here has one or two in his vest …" she gave Tracker an expectant look.

Tracker stepped back, crossed both arms, and reached into two vest pockets with opposite hands. "Voilá!" he said as he pulled out two Y-shaped twigs and showed them like cards in a magic trick. "Of course I do!"

Tracker and Michael bought two stuffed fluster birds and a few fresh fish to dry and smoke for their journey. They waved goodbye to the grey-haired lady and joined Tarbak outside.

"You're learning, Michael. It wouldn't have been good to tell her that the king, indeed, still sends messages via fluster bird. They have a way of causing a great ruckus when spotted. And anyway, part of the lore of the fluster bird is that the stones will only bring happiness to those of pure heart and dire need. Not many would pass that test in Tremora today!'

❧

When they returned to the stalls, Nova was there with Falin and Fortina. Fortina was giving Nova a slow rubdown with a currycomb. "Nova has eaten, and Kalib is sure to check and see whether she's been properly sedated," said Falin nervously. "I think you need to give Nova her potion, Tracker."

"No need. I can fake being drugged without your help, Tracker. I'm a good actress, too, you know."

"The fewer people that know you can understand normal conversation the better, Nova. Just take your medicine like a good girl ..."

Tracker set his backpack down. He fumbled through the pockets of his vest until he found a small glass vial. He handed the cork to Falin. He then found a piece of sugar cane in another pocket and dipped it into the bottle. "This should do the trick," he said. He walked over to Nova and held out the makeshift wick in the palm of his hand. She nuzzled it tentatively and then tongued it into her mouth.

"This should take effect pretty quickly. I think you'd better make room for Nova to lie down ..."

Fortina barely had time to back away before Nova flopped to the ground.

"Whoaaaa, Tracker."

"I thought you'd like it."

✥

It was the wee hours of the morning when Kalib crept into the stall. Tracker watched him with hooded eyes from where he lay on the ground in the hay. Kalib laid his hand on Nova's neck and lifted one eyelid to examine her eye. "Humph," he grunted. He left smiling.

Chapter Twenty-four

Flugbark Takes Command

"Wave Michael and Tracker up on the dais, and I'll take care of the rest," said Flugbark to Kalib the day of the race. "And keep them separated." He was sitting on the floor, hookah hose in one hand and a bottle of mead in the other. He wasn't going to give Kalib any more of his plan than he had to. The wily merchant was up to something, he was sure of it.

"If things go according to plan, you'll be in my debt for a very long time, my friend," chided Flugbark as he licked dribbles of drink from his chin and chest. "Remember, I expect a cut of every purse Nova wins from here on. And that includes today's purse when she loses!"

Kalib gazed back at the disgusting creature. *Maybe I'll root for Tracker today*, he thought. *No. The witch will send for the Tres regardless. And being able to keep Nova and also having Tracker out of my life ... that's a good thing. So, for now it looks like I'm stuck with this toad. He gave Flugbark his best winning smile.* "Truly, we were destined to be partners."

The shape-changer only laughed.

Chapter Twenty-five

The Running of the Lops

A camelop's racetrack is not circular, or even oval for that matter. It's more of a slowly winding obstacle course with two legs—each a mile long. In each leg, the camelops have to race to and around a half-mile pole adorned with flags that match everyone's colors. Each jockey is required to grab a matching flag as he and his camelop make the turn and race back to the start-finish line.

It sounds simple, but the challenge is to avoid the other camelops who are bearing down as a rider navigates the return trip. Trailing camelops and their riders purposely block the paths of the leaders or try and unseat their jockeys. It gets increasingly chaotic as the field divides naturally into two groups; the slower, bunched group and the fleet and agile leaders. The two groups typically meet head on at least three times in a race, coming and going in opposite directions. It then becomes a spectacle of multiple jousting matches and opposing lines meeting on the battlefield (without the weapons, of course); it is then that charging animals often collide and many a rider gets thrown, to the delight of the crowd.

Now, camelops bellow, bawl, spit, and grit their teeth even when in a good mood. In the mélée of a race, they go berserk. The crowds also go wild in the midst of it all with shouting and jeering and laughter and egging-on as jockeys try to remount and get their animals under control.

Marshals on foot enforce what few rules there are: No clubs or sharp objects (riding crops only), no biting (by the jockeys), and no ganging up (one-on-one confrontations only!). A marshal need only blow his whistle, point the dreaded colored flag of shame, and flip open his infraction book. A yellow flag is a warning (each jockey gets two), and red is immediate disqualification (mostly for drawing blood with an illegal weapon or ignoring yellow warnings). If someone is ejected, he or she must leave the track immediately. Giant mountain men are only too happy to remove a reluctant or defiant offender. Of course, when this occurs, it adds greatly to the spectacle. But what really makes the race interesting is, at the end of the first leg, each camelop must turn and do the whole thing again, only this time with a different jockey!

❧

It was day seven in Bearcamp. An extremely tall, thin man in top hat and tails stood atop an elevated platform overlooking the racetrack, staring intently at a large gold timepiece on a chain. He also held a white flag straight down at his side. After noting the time, he replaced the watch in his breast pocket and grabbed the silver whistle hanging from his neck. He then took in a huge breath and blew so hard on the whistle his cheeks puffed out like small red balloons and his eyes nearly popped from his head. The effect was immediate—the huge throng gathered below him noted the shrill sound and went silent. All eyes were on the man as he gave a satisfied nod and tipped his hat to the crowd. Reveling in the moment, he leaned over the railing of his perch and majestically scanned the line of camelops and jockeys stretched out below him. Then the starter straightened up, raised the white flag high above his head, and with a flourish, dropped it back down to his side—and with that, the biggest event of the Bearcamp Races, *the Running of the Lops,* began.

The crowd erupted as twenty camelops and jockeys burst from the starting line. All jumped to their feet, waving hats and enthusiastically calling out their favorite camelop's name. The field of loping animals kicked up large clods of dirt and turf as they raced down the track and disappeared around a bend in the distance.

Then the crowd's attention was drawn back to the starting line where more than a few camelops had stayed back, rearing and spitting and snarling and biting at their neighbors and anyone else in sight. Some were even sitting down on their haunches and bellowing mournfully in protest to the whole affair. It was comical entertainment to see the jockeys kicking and whipping their reluctant mounts to get them off the starting line. Some people, not quite so entertained, ran out onto the track to help pull on the reins or push the animal's rumps in an effort to get their favorites into the race. Many of these intrepid souls were kicked or knocked silly themselves, and the crowd jeered and laughed enthusiastically at them, as well.

Meanwhile, far down the track, Nova loped easily into the lead, even prancing to the side once to look backwards and appraise her competition. She was in her element, and the fans lining the rails hooted and hollered at her brazenness. Fortina had to urge her with her crop to pay attention to the fact she was in a race! Nova turned reluctantly and, with a snort, sped off again, leaving her closest rivals far in the distance.

Fortina and Nova easily reached the half-mile marker first. Nova was so naturally fast that Kalib had once bet a rival that she could beat any of his stable in a flat-out race—running backwards! Kalib had instructed Fortina to make sure the race was close so he could get the fool to wager again. Of course, Nova had won both races. It was part of her legend.

Fortina grabbed her matching colored flag as Nova whipped around the first turn. They knew the real race was now about to begin. As expected, the rest of the field was bearing down fast—at least a dozen closely grouped camelops were charging right at them. It was a daunting sight: Arms, legs, crops, and tongues were flying everywhere, and the sound of hoofs kicking up sod thundered in their ears. There was no gap to run through and no time to circumnavigate. But Nova and Fortina were prepared. The crowd was about to see why Nova and her jockeys were the most famous racing team ever.

Even as a young foal, Nova could always leap and dodge and run like a deer. Where other camelops couldn't even get all four feet off the ground at one time, she could leap effortlessly several feet in the air. But an even bigger advantage was having Fortina and Falin as her jockeys. After all, they'd spent part of several lifetimes as giant warriors! A riding crop was more than enough weapon for them to ward off any attack from other riders.

Nova picked out the biggest camelop in the bunch and swerved toward it while Fortina quickly put the flag in her mouth. She then grabbed a thatch of hair on Nova's back with one hand and leaned far out to one side with her riding crop balanced in the other. The gap between them and the horde closed rapidly. Fortina reared and threw the riding crop with all of her might at the camelop in front of her and hit it soundly between the eyes. The animal bellowed in pain and stumbled into the camelop next to it. Both combinations of rider and camelop spilled to the ground, and Nova leapt over and through the gap in a flash.

Fortina whooped and waved her arms to the crowd triumphantly as she and Nova sped down the track. The fans in turn gave the pair a resounding ovation. Then, to everyone's astonishment, Nova suddenly slid to a stop and turned around and raced back to the downed riders. A hush fell over the crowd as Fortina quickly dismounted and went and helped both shaken jockeys to their feet. She found they were dazed but not hurt badly. She then retrieved her whip from the churned up turf and ran to the injured camelop. She saw a huge lump on its forehead. "Sorry!" Fortina whispered as she held the animal's muzzle and rubbed the wound softly. Then she gave a quick glance toward the other racers that were just rounding the half-mile marker. It was time to go. She kissed the camelop on the cheek and ran and leapt back into her saddle, and she and Nova were off and running again.

The crowd exploded again in enthusiastic applause and shouts of approval, good sportsmanship being revered by the racing aficionados of Tremora.

The pair soon met a second group of stragglers, but easily dodged any attempts at blocking their way. Nova was flying. In the distance, Falin stood waiting. As they approached the start-finish line, Fortina jumped lightly to the ground before Nova came to a full stop. "Good luck!" she cried as she passed Falin the riding crop—the roar of the crowd was deafening. He saluted her, smiling, and swung into the saddle. Nova took the time to do a little prancing for her fans before turning and dashing off on the second leg of the race.

Fortina watched anxiously as they pounded down the track and then quickly ran off in search of Tarbak. She didn't want to be late. After all, she was about to help kidnap Michael!

Nova and Falin didn't get far before they again met up with the group of riders that were trailing behind them. This time, however, the slowest group of riders was also in the mix and the track in front of them was blocked by a wall of shear madness. Not one camelop was making progress because they and their riders were all stopped in place; kicking, rearing, and fighting with abandon. Marshals were on the field, frantically trying to bring order but to no avail. They were blowing their whistles and dodging in and out between flailing arms and legs while waving yellow and red flags and shouting warnings, but they were completely ignored. At the same time, two giants were wading into a group of camelops and battling jockeys who were using weapons that looked more like maces than riding crops. The roar of the crowd was as deafening as ever.

Nova and Falin surveyed the bedlam spread rail to rail in front of them, looking everywhere for an opening but seeing nothing. Falin then nudged Nova to one side, and they slowly started to creep forward—perhaps they could pass unnoticed in the frenzy. But the other riders were on the lookout. A rider saw them and shouted out a warning to the others and then rushed to pin Nova to the rail. Another jockey and mount joined in and attacked them from the front—Falin soon found himself fighting multiple riders with both fist and crop. A marshal screamed at the illegal tactics, whistled, and pointed his yellow flag, but no one paid him any attention. Out of the corner of her eye, Nova saw another jockey and camelop racing to join in, and she realized she was about to be completely blocked against the railing with no way to escape. In an instant she lowered her head and bunched her body. Falin started in surprise. He then realized what she was going to do and barely had time to grab on tight before Nova launched herself backwards and started backpedaling, butt first, in a long arc.

The blocking camelops and riders turned to chase her, but she could, of course, outrun them, even going backwards. Soon several other camelops joined in the race to catch her. She then put on the brakes by stiffening all four legs and digging into the soft turf. The followers had no time to react and rushed past her before they knew what was happening. Nova then jumped, pirouetted in the air, and hit the ground running. Since most of the field had moved to help trap her, there were now several openings to race through. She was gone before they realized she'd outfoxed them all.

"Nova, you're amazing!" shouted Falin in her ear.

"*Yes, yes, I am,*" she thought happily.

They raced to the half-mile pole, and Falin grabbed their second flag. He raised it over his head and waved to the frenzied crowd. Nova then turned and sped toward the finish line. The last and third meeting with the field was uneventful. Mountain men had removed the mace-wielding jockeys by tossing them over the railings into the crowd, and their mounts were wandering aimlessly across the track. More important, the other jockeys realized that second and third place was still to be determined and there was money to be won—even if Nova and first place were out of reach. They merely raised their crops in salute as Nova flew past.

Nova and Falin coasted across the finish line and pandemonium broke out in the stands as both were mobbed on the track. Nova looked up at the dais where Kalib had been watching the race and saw him topple over backwards in apparent shock at her winning. *Stay down, Kalib! You're not going to like your new world when you come to!* she thought happily.

Falin also looked up at the dais. But he noticed something besides Kalib's fainting—what were Michael and Tracker both doing up there? Wasn't Michael supposed to be kidnapped by now? Someone yanked hard on his leg and he looked down and saw Fortina's concerned face looking back up at him.

"I couldn't find Tarbak," she mouthed.

Falin reached a helping hand, and she jumped up behind him in the saddle. He shrugged—he could do nothing. He and Fortina and Nova were being led by the crowd toward the dais and the winner's circle.

Chapter Twenty-six

Fly Away—What Tracker Saw

Michael and Tracker took their positions along the railing about fifty yards from the start-finish line. The starter's flag dropped, and they cheered loudly as Fortina and Nova jumped out to an early lead. *Would they still be winning when the pack returned to switch jockeys?* Tracker wondered.

Tarbak stood behind them and combed the crowd for any sign of the wisp. He tapped Tracker on the shoulder. "Kalib is beckoning," he said, and pointed to the raised dais overlooking the track next to the starter's tower. "I think he wants you both to join him."

Tracker could just make out the gesturing merchant. He waved back with his staff. "Here we go. This must be part of the plan, Tarbak."

"Perhaps he wants to make it easier to grab Michael," Tarbak said. "We, too, are waiting for his signal. But he has not shared this particular strategy with us."

Tracker looked pensive. "Yes, it would be smarter for the wisp to make its move up there with Kalib," he said. "People don't take too kindly to their sort, and the crowd might turn on him down here." He put his arm on Michael's shoulder. "Well, the adventure continues! Shall we go? And remember, when the Tres come for you, don't go too willingly. Give at least some struggle. Kalib and the wisp must believe you're actually being kidnapped."

Michael nodded. "But, will you be safe, Tracker?" He didn't like the idea of Tracker facing the wisp alone.

"Only one opponent? That's no challenge for a Mazalon Warrior," Tarbak scoffed.

Tracker didn't acknowledge Tarbak's comment. He only answered, "I'll be fine, Michael. My biggest problem will be not to harm it too badly. And I need to do a little acting, too. I need to appear badly wounded myself. In fact, we'll all be doing a little acting before this day is over. A little fake blood should do the trick. We want the wisp to return to Spreten with the news that I'm out of commission and that you've been captured by the Tres and on the way. It'll keep the witch's brood off our tail for a while and help us get to Mesmer Henge in time for the meeting."

They made their way slowly through the crowd toward the dais. Tracker was in the lead, with Michael next, followed by Tarbak. Tracker held his staff high in the air as he plowed forward. The crowd was massive. All of a sudden, a roar went up, and everyone pressed to the rails to get a better view. Nova was just finishing the first leg of the race, and she was still in the lead.

Tracker had to steer away from the track to make any headway. The distance between Michael and Tracker increased, and Michael tried in vain to keep up. He could just see Tracker's staff. He looked back at Tarbak and yelled over the din that they should trade places. Tarbak's huge body could clear the path much better than he was doing. Suddenly, he was tripped up and knocked head first to the ground. Tarbak angrily threw people to the side and knelt down protectively to see if Michael was all right.

Sensing something, Tracker looked back over his shoulder. He couldn't see Michael or Tarbak at all. He started to turn, but then saw Tarbak raise up and motion to him that everything was all right and to keep moving. He saw Michael's hand rise and wave at him as well. Satisfied, Tracker then turned and continued pushing forward. He finally reached the stairs to the dais. He climbed a couple of steps and turned to see Michael swimming toward him as if fighting an ocean tide. But he was alone. Tracker scanned the crowd behind Michael and could just make out the giant, Tarbak, moving in the opposite direction.

"Tarbak went to fetch Fortina," Michael explained, panting and out of breath, as he climbed the stairs. "She's finished her leg of the race. They'll meet us up top."

Tracker took it all in in an instant. He was now sure that the Tres would seize Michael from the dais. He also knew he himself would be attacked up there as well. The plan was to defend himself against the wisp, then fake being seriously wounded, and let Michael be taken by the Tres. He might have to deal with Kalib, too, but it concerned him little. After all, the merchant would be watching his entire world crumble before his eyes as Nova won her race. "Be alert, Michael," warned Tracker as they ascended the stairs. "I think we'll be seeing all our friends shortly." Michael only grunted, still breathing hard. Kalib was waiting for them at the top.

Kalib led Tracker and Michael to the front railing overlooking the finish line and took a position between them. "You'll be my special guests on this glorious day!" he exclaimed. His face was beaming, but his eyes told a different tale. He was looking anxiously toward the track, wondering why Nova was in the lead. He knew she should be wheezing by now. Nevertheless, he spread his arms wide to embrace both Tracker and Michael. Flugbark had told him to keep the two separated.

❧

Nova crossed the finish line with no one else even close. Falin pulled Nova up, and the crowd poured out onto the track. The pair was quickly surrounded with jubilant fans, jumping and cheering and grabbing at them in wild celebration. Kalib stared down at Nova in disbelief. He then staggered back and raised his hands to his face. "Noooo!" he wailed. "Oh noooo!" He then collapsed dramatically onto his back in a dead faint.

Tracker quickly bent down to make sure Kalib was still breathing. He saw that Kalib had indeed hit his head and was knocked out cold. Probably a blessing, he thought, feeling sympathy for a brief moment. He then looked back up at Michael and got another surprise. Michael had drawn his knife! Did he see the wisp? Tracker spun around, jolted with adrenalin, but saw nothing. Then he turned back, and his eyes caught something in the sky behind Michael's head. A dot was fast becoming another shape entirely—a familiar shape. It was a dragon!

At the same time, the sound of the crowd below changed from jubilance to screams of surprise and fear. People pointed to the sky and ran wildly. The panic was contagious.

The dragon swooped down at a tremendous speed. It swept low, blowing fire and smoke, creating terror everywhere it looked. It followed the path of the racecourse straight to the dais. "It's a dragon, Michael, and it's coming right at us," yelled Tracker, pointing. "Get down!"

Michael leapt, but too late. The dragon reached the platform at just that moment, and with a high-pitched scream, it extended its claws, grabbing Michael in midair. Tracker threw his staff desperately, but the dragon was well beyond harm, and the would-be spear was knocked harmlessly to the ground by the beast's long spiked tail. Tracker watched helplessly as the dragon disappeared, clutching a struggling Michael beneath its wings.

Chapter Twenty-seven

Plans Awry—What Flugbark Experienced

The starter dropped his flag dramatically, and the race was on. Flugbark stood deep in the crowd between the tower and the starting line and watched Kalib beckon to Tracker and Michael from the dais. *Right on schedule*, he gloated. *The prey is falling into my trap.* He waited. Then, through the crowd, he saw Tracker coming toward him with his staff held high. *Why, thank you, Tracker! You've made it so much easier to see you and also keep out of your sight!* He lifted the hood of his cloak higher, hunkered down, and waited for the old man to pass. As soon as Michael came even with him, Flugbark rushed to him, stuck out a foot, and tripped the boy to the ground. As he fell, Flugbark hit him hard on the head and then jumped on his back and stuck a knife to his throat.

Tarbak saw Michael go down and quickly pushed people aside to get to his aid. When he reached the spot where Michael was lying, he bellowed in rage. Someone was on top of him! He bent to grab the assailant and then stopped and stared dumbfounded. The shape-changer slowly turned its head and looked up into the giant's eyes. It was the face of Michael!

The effect was instant. "It's time, Tarbak," Flugbark hissed, using his wisp's voice. "Now stand up and wave to Tracker that everything's okay!" He saw Tarbak look at the knife. "Do as you're told, slave, or you'll get a taste of this blade. That's an order from your new master!"

Tarbak slowly rose up and waved to Tracker.

Flugbark then leaned close to Michael's ear. "Now you stay put," he growled. Then the Michael-that-wasn't-Michael also stood up and waved to Tracker, motioning for him to carry on.

Tarbak stood behind Flugbark, staring, hardly believing what he was seeing. He'd never seen a shape-changer before.

"Take him to the stables. Your little helper should be waiting for you," Flugbark said. He continued to issue orders as he pulled the semi-conscious Michael to his feet and handed him off to the giant. "The wagon is ready. And don't tarry. Your master is anxiously awaiting her prizes! Now, I'm off to take care of Tracker. You don't want *him* following you now, do you?"

Tarbak grabbed hold of the sagging Michael, and Flugbark plunged into the crowd, aiming in the direction of the tower.

Tarbak stood flummoxed. He couldn't follow after the imposter and leave Michael bleeding. But Tracker needed to be warned! It wasn't a wisp he should be on the lookout for! Tarbak turned in the direction of the track with Michael in his arms. He had to get to Fortina and Falin.

❧

They were all three standing on the dais: Kalib, Tracker, and Flugbark-as-Michael. Kalib was in the middle. The shape-changer looked down on the course and saw Nova clearly out in front. *Now that's not part of the plan!* he thought. He looked at Kalib. Kalib looked horrified and was making a funny choking sound …

Nova streaked across the finish line to the tremendous roar of the crowd and fans. Everyone's attention was on the winner; except Flugbark. He was still watching Kalib. *My, my—not what you expected, huh?* Fleetingly, he wondered what had gone wrong but knew he had no time to dawdle.

Flugbark slowly pulled his knife from its sheath. He needed to get around Kalib to get at Tracker. But as he turned, he saw Kalib put both hands up to his face and moan in agony. *What now? Was he having a stroke?* Then, incredibly, Kalib fell over backwards with a huge crash. Flugbark couldn't believe it. And Tracker was actually bending down to help him! Not one to question a gift of opportunity

Flugbark crouched to pounce. But as he looked at Tracker, he saw the old man pointing to the sky.

"It's a dragon, and it's coming right at us," yelled Tracker, pointing behind Flugbark's shoulder. "Get down Michael!"

Flugbark turned and stared in disbelief. *She sent the dragon!?* Then, a horrible reality struck him as the nightmare raced toward him at an incredible speed. *It thinks I'm the boy!* He looked around in panic. In desperation he leapt at Tracker, still thinking he could do her bidding. He didn't finish his task or his thought, though. The dragon screamed in triumph and plucked him easily and cleanly from the air.

Chapter Twenty-eight

Leaving the Island

"*Tracker!*" It was Nova.

"*Tracker!!!*"

"*Yes, Nova. I'm here. The dragon took him, Nova. And, I couldn't stop it.*"

"*Tracker, that wasn't Michael*"

Tracker turned and rushed to the rail. He looked down and saw Nova gazing up at him with Falin and Fortina both straddling her back. Tarbak stood next to her. The giant held Michael in his arms.

Later they were all gathered in the stables. Michael's wound was bandaged, and he was sitting propped up against the wall. Nova stood in her stall, all wiped down, brushed, and curried. Fortina insisted she be pampered after her spectacular final win. Nova had regurgitated a tasty mix of oats and dates that Falin had prepared as a congratulatory meal and was chewing her cud, contented.

Tracker sat on an overturned water barrel, and Michael was just finishing relating what little he remembered about the attack. "I smelled his breath when he hissed in my ear, Tracker. I knew then that it was the same creature that we met on the mountain. The one that pretended to be Tralana; I'm sure of it. The next thing I knew, I was being carried by Tarbak ..."

Tracker listened to everyone's story in turn. He asked a question here and there but mostly just puffed on his pipe. When everyone was finished, Tracker stood up.

"It's time to share my thoughts," he said. "First off, this is an incredible moment for the Tres. You are finally free of the curse that bound you as slaves for centuries! In fact, you are the Tres no more. The yoke is gone. You are still bound together, of course, but as friends and family now, not someone's evil spell. May your futures be all you wish for."

All three mumbled thanks and looked back at Tracker with glistening eyes.

Tracker smiled at each, and then his face grew serious. "Now, to the moment at hand. Kalib is broken. The Tres is no longer his to rule, and his other servants are scattered. He'll sell what few possessions he has left and perhaps have enough to get back to Coriss—perhaps. But his fortune is most assuredly gone; his other racing camelops and even his elephants were all gambled away. He wagered everything against Nova and lost!" Tracker went and stroked Nova's nose affectionately. "Well done, Nova. You not only won your greatest race, but you also helped bankrupt one of Tremora's most dangerous villains."

He then turned back again to Falin, Tarbak, and Fortina. "And it was you three that let her earn her rightful victory. You were no longer bound as slaves this morning," he said solemnly. "You were free citizens of Tremora and your own masters. And yet … you chose to stay and fight Kalib and his evil. As a knight of the kingdom, I assure you, High King William will hear the true tale of your exploits from my very lips." He went to them each in turn and shook their hands. "Thank you for today," he said. Then, he turned away and seemed to wipe his eyes.

Tracker stuffed his kerchief in a back pocket and turned back to face them all with a different demeanor entirely. Michael had seen this face before when Tracker first confronted the shape-changer on the mountain. It was the face of a warrior! "Now," he said in a low, fearsome voice, "it's time we plan our next move." He looked at the three. "You *are* still offering your services to King William, aren't you?"

Tracker gestured for everyone to come closer. "There will be enemy eyes and ears everywhere soon," he said. "Be careful what you say, even to each other." He looked at Michael. "We—or more accurately you—have been either extremely lucky or, as I suspect, another force is at work here. Wisps, a shape-changer, a dragon; all have been sent to impede, kill, or kidnap you, and you've barely been in Tremora a week!

"And today the enemy's plans were again thwarted, but this time it seems by their own bungling. Why send a dragon to snatch you up when the plan to kidnap you was going so well? I should have been lying wounded or dead up there! There was too much confusion to see any flaw in the shape-changer's disguise. I only saw you Michael." Tracker's face became even grimmer.

"Did the Witch of Spreten get wind of or suspect that the curse of the Tres was over? No, I don't think so. According to your story, Tarbak, no one alive today could have known your curse would disappear with the birth of a baby girl to Kalib and Princess Leonie. It's more likely that, after her recent failures to stop Michael, Prelandora sent what she could muster to Bearcamp on short notice and hoped something would work. Like throwing more than one line in the water, Spreten most assuredly doesn't want us to make it to the wizard's gathering." Then he smiled. "And, I assure you, there's going to be one extremely angry witch when that dragon drops a pathetic shape-changer at her feet instead of Michael."

"She may finally realize who she is dealing with," Tarbak said.

Michael looked at the giant, puzzled.

"You could not be more protected if you had three Mazalon Warriors with you, Michael," Tarbak said, proudly. "Tracker is the most famous knight in the kingdom. And today he showed why."

Tracker quickly held up his hand. "Not a particularly accurate or current description, Michael." He gave Tarbak a withering look. "It's been many years since I was last summoned by the king, and do you forget I am traveling alone, Tarbak?"

The giant didn't seem fazed. "Deny if you will, Tracker, but you are who you are, and today's success was due in no small part to your planning and presence. I apologize, though; I seemed to have already forgotten your advice. I'm sorry; I'll be more careful."

"That was not advice, Tarbak; those were orders. Perhaps your newfound freedom has gone to your head. Don't forget you are now in the service of the king. And for now, I am the voice of that king!"

Tarbak dropped his massive arms to his side and nodded his head.

Tracker saw Tarbak's reaction and seemed to reconsider his admonishment. He reached up and patted the giant on the back. "Enough, Tarbak. Actually, we're just guilty of mutual admiration. Your help was essential today, and you performed your role brilliantly. No harm done, my friend.

"Now, let's get to our next move, shall we? Michael and I still have to visit Fennland. Then we're to meet with Megan at Mesmer Henge in just one week." He saw the surprised expression on the faces of the three. "Yes. I think it may very well be the same wizard that helped lift your curse and taught you the memory secrets. Wizards live a very long time, and Megan is without a doubt the Magus of this age. Each age has one, you know. And a wizard can live a very long time. But who can say? The ways of wizards and kings are not for the common folk to know or understand.

"Now, I think your plans to go to Tremora and gain audience with King William is still a good one," he continued. "But first, I believe a little more deception is needed. Prelandora will most assuredly send more spies to find us. It can't be helped, and there is little we can do to avoid her birds and wisps. However, for a while the witch will assume that Michael is still on the way to Spreten, a prisoner of the Tres. Her shape-changer won't know any different."

He drew on his pipe and then swept it in the direction of the three. "Together, take the wagon and head north, just as if you had Michael on board, but it'll only be a bundle of sticks and clothes made to look like him. A little crude, but we need plenty of people seeing you leave with him, and there isn't any reason for them to look too closely. Once you get to the docks at Stern this afternoon, sell or abandon the wagon and head back to Bearcamp. Keep the mule. You'll need it to pack your things over the mountain pass. Once there, take the western bridge to the Pishtocks and head for Tremora Castle, taking the northern route.

"The witch will be sending Spreten soldiers or wisps to meet and escort you to her island. And they'll look for you in Stern. There'll be plenty of stories of three slaves and a wagon and a boy for them to hear, but when they search and find the wagon sold and empty, they'll know their boss has been hoodwinked. At least it'll throw the witch off our scent for a while.

"The crowds are on the roads already, and we need the cover, so we should all leave right away. The wagon's already packed with plenty of supplies, and one of Kalib's mules is hitched and ready. Any questions?"

No one said anything. They were too excited. Fortina was working furiously on a lock of her hair.

"Good; then off we go. Have heart, my friends. I'm sure our paths will cross again."

✤

Falin and Fortina sat side by side on the front seat of the wagon, talking. The fake Michael—straw wrapped in blankets with one of Falin's hooded cloaks—was in the back, propped against the seat to appear as someone asleep. Tarbak walked by the head of the mule. They had crossed the northern bridge leaving Bearcamp and were headed for Stern.

"Falin, have you noticed?" asked Fortina suddenly, talking loud enough for Tarbak to hear.

"Yes, I think so," answered Falin. "I'm pretty sure I can change, but I don't have any desire to at all. I feel it would be wrong, somehow. I didn't want to say anything yet, though, for fear it wasn't true."

"Me too," Fortina said excitedly. "That means the changing curse may be disappearing. We'll live normal lives now, Falin. You too, Tarbak! You'll never have to look like me again," she called out, laughing.

Tarbak, completely uncharacteristic of the giant he really was, jumped up in the air and clicked his heels, which made them laugh all the harder.

Chapter Twenty-nine

Prelandora Throws a Fit

The weary dragon streaked toward the island of Sitka. The end of its journey was in sight, and it couldn't wait to be rid of its bothersome burden. As it neared Spreten Castle, it screamed a warning, and the front doors of the great hall creaked open in greeting. Then it swooped low, entered the cavernous chamber, and released its prize from its claws while executing a skillful landing on the slick marble floor. The limp figure spun across the polished surface and stopped abruptly at the base of Prelandora's throne with a thud.

"I hope you haven't killed him," the witch said nonchalantly as she looked down at the lifeless figure of Michael lying at her feet. "Although, it might be less trouble if you did." Just then, a groan emanated from the floor. "Ah, no fear. It seems our prisoner is still alive after all." She looked up and gave a silent signal to the guards standing in the shadows by the doors.

Four figures rushed forward with chains and quickly shackled the legs of the dragon. It threw its head back and roared but otherwise gave little resistance.

"Take him to his cave and feed him. And make sure the bars are chained shut. Wouldn't want him wandering off in the night, now would we?" Prelandora said, laughing.

The guards led the dragon through a huge dark stone archway and disappeared down a wide winding flight of stairs. The sounds of the shackles dragging and rattling on each step gradually faded away.

Prelandora was euphoric. She had captured the boy! She looked again at the pathetic figure lying before her. Then, she jumped to her feet and screamed. The groaning figure on the floor was transforming into Flugbark.

"*WHAT IS THIS?*" Prelandora shrieked. The hall lit up as if lightning was striking, and the witch's voice reverberated from wall to wall. Her slaves and servants all ran for cover; they had heard their queen throw tantrums before. Heads were going to roll!

She glared at the toad now cowering before her. "You bungling ass! *WHERE IS THE BOY*?!"

Just then, a servant made a move to sidle out a side door. The witch pointed her scepter, and he was struck dead on the spot. His head flew across the floor, through the arch, and thumped down the stairs.

The shape-changer squealed and dived to lie prostrate and trembling. "It's OK, my queen!" Flugbark squeaked. "The, the, Tres have him." His tongue lolled from the side of his mouth and slobber drooled onto the floor. He was still reeling from the painful grip of the dragon's claws, not to mention the complete terror of watching the murderous rage of the witch.

She bent forward so that her face was inches from the back of Flugbark's head. He could feel her breath on his neck. "What's that you say? He is captured still?"

"Ye-yes, just as we planned. But then, the, the, dragon snatched me." Flugbark kept his head down, not daring to look up. "Just as I was about to kill the warrior your dragon grabbed me out of thin air! I, I was disguised as Michael, and it must have thought I was the real boy." He was really squirming now. "But, but, the Tres are still bringing the real boy to you—just as you wanted," he whimpered.

The witch sat back on her throne and stared long and hard at Flugbark. Slowly the truth sank in, and her gaze drifted off into space. *Yes,* she agreed. *Flugbark's story is probably true; after all, I sent the dragon.* Then she got angry all over again. Another of her plans had failed, and this time it was her own fault! She flung her head up and to the side with muscles bulging in her neck, her mouth grimacing as if in pain, to assume another frightening pose. No one in the room dared even to breathe. Then, just as suddenly, her mood changed again, her body relaxed, and she smiled wickedly. *But it isn't a complete disaster; the boy was still captured, and he is on his way to Stern ...*

She sat back. She had to think. It was perfectly clear now; she had overreacted when she heard all of Pratt's warnings. It was as simple as that. She needn't have sent the dragon to bring the boy to her at all. The original plan would have worked out just fine. "Yet, who would have thought the dragon would snatch the wrong Michael!" she spat, like a cat cacking up a hairball. Her anger flared again as she blamed the dragon but then, "No, it's just an overgrown lizard. Let it be," she reasoned. She calmed and returned to her thoughts.

The boy was finally on the way to her, but even so, there was no guarantee he would reach Spreten safely. In her haste, she had actually created another most unwelcome scenario as well: The Mazalon Warrior was still alive and is surely on Michael's trail. *Did he think the dragon had the real Michael? No—maybe at first—but he wouldn't be fooled for long. He would eventually follow the boy's trail to Stern. She had to get to Michael before the old man. And, there was little time!*

Flugbark was kneeling with all the fingers of both reptilian hands in his mouth. Prelandora looked down with distaste. "Quit sniveling, Flugbark. The Tres have saved your sorry hide this time. But because of you, we still have work to finish. Gather a dozen of the guard and what wisps are healthy. We set sail in one hour."

Flugbark leapt up. His tongue worked overtime and spittle flew everywhere in his excitement. "Yes, yes, my lady." He started to back away, but Prelandora stopped him.

"Not before you cleanup all of that mess," she said pointing at the floor. She rose up from the throne and grabbed the material of her gown so it didn't trail. "And that one as well," she said, pointing at the body of the servant. "Put him in the trough—and don't forget the head."

She swept from the hall. Flugbark could be heard lapping at the floor.

Chapter Thirty

The Chasms of Dread

Bjorg was on the lookout. He'd been told that a boy had been carried off by a dragon when he ferried the first people fleeing the island. He suspected who it was. Just two days before, a young servant from Kalib's troop delivered a message from Tracker that Michael was OK and that they were both on their way to the races. Was Michael now kidnapped just like the young prince? This morning the same servant delivered another handwritten message. This time Tracker wanted him to meet at the Neerwood animal crossing and bring a boat big enough for four. Bjorg picked out a flat-bottomed skiff and paddled it up the coast of Charn to the crossing, arriving just after noon. He'd been anxiously watching for his friend ever since.

It was early evening before Tracker finally showed up, and as expected, he wasn't alone. He was accompanied by a camelop and rider and they were just joining the long line of people waiting to cross the shallow ford to the mainland. Bjorg watched them curiously. The rider dismounted with obvious difficulty. He had on the simple grey garment of a servant and had a hood covering his face. He was limping painfully. The camelop didn't look like it was doing any better; it was heavily ladened with supplies, and its head hung low. But Bjorg couldn't understand. Surely that was Michael who was standing next to Tracker! He stood watching his friends for some time. He decided not to bring attention to them, so he waited till they got closer.

"Prefer trebuchet?" he asked in a gravelly voice.

Tracker and Michael both turned in surprise. The troll was leaning on a long gaff, grinning.

"How can a pile of rocks be so stealthy?" Tracker said. He slapped his friend on the shoulder and then regretted it immediately. He shook his hand in mock pain. "I'll be taking a boat this time, thank you," he said laughing. Then hastily, "I've brought a friend with me. This is Parno and his pack animal, Rosy." Tracker said this last part loud enough for anyone nearby to hear.

"Parno and Rosy, is it?" Bjorg looked at Michael and noticed his skin looked more the shade of Tracker's. It didn't look like "Parno" was enjoying riding Rosy very much. He then looked at the camelop and grunted. Yet another disguise, he thought.

"Nice meet you, *Parno,*" Bjorg said, with emphasis to show he had tweaked on. Then, "Come talk." He motioned them all toward the waterfront.

Tracker followed the troll into a low building used to provide shelter to travelers in times of inclement weather. Michael tied Nova's reins loosely to a hitching post. "*Sorry, Nova. We shouldn't be too long.*" Michael limped inside.

"*Don't forget your Rosy's out here waiting!*" Nova scolded them both. "*And I'm hungry!*" She was tired and irritable. Trying to teach Michael to ride had been no fun for either one of them. Tracker said it was necessary because Michael wouldn't be able to walk in the heat and sand of the Asyr Desert. But a camelop walks with the two legs on each side moving in sync, like pacing horses in harness racing, so a rider constantly rocks back and forth like a ship on the ocean. Michael was basically seasick the entire time.

She was also carrying all of their supplies like a common ass. "To disguise your natural beauty and that you're a thoroughbred racer," Tracker had explained. "Not to mention," he added, "you are the most famous and recognizable racing animal in the whole world!" This last was Tracker's effort to placate Nova's sensitive ego, and it worked for a while. But now she very much needed pampering, and it looked as if all she was going to get was to be treated like the common pack animal she was pretending to be. No, Nova-come-Rosy was none too happy.

Meanwhile, Tracker was pointing out a window at Bjorg's boat. "Yes, that's perfect!" He then spent several minutes telling Bjorg all that had happened since he had struck out three days prior in search of Michael. Bjorg listened while sipping grog.

"Once Prelandora finds out her plans at Bearcamp have failed, she will assume that Michael and I are making our way directly to Mesmer Henge. But we have business in Fennland first. This should again throw her off the scent. With your help, Bjorg, and that skiff, we'll scull up the coast and enter the Pishtocks at the pass much farther north."

Bjorg stopped his mug in mid air. "That way not safe, Tracker. Much trouble."

"It can't be helped. Besides, no road is completely safe now." Tracker saw Michael's look of alarm. "Don't worry, Michael. I've traveled this path many times before. It's a shortcut."

Bjorg lowered his drink to the table. "When leave?"

"We'll leave tonight, of course."

Michael went and looked out the window at the tiny craft and had visions of greel fish teeming in the dark waters. Bjorg looked at Tracker and had visions of greel fish teeming in the dark waters. Tracker read their minds and said dismissively, "We'll just have to be extra special careful and not rock the boat."

✥

Around midnight, the foursome launched out into the channel. Nova lay splayed in the middle of the skiff surrounded by all of their supplies, and Bjorg sat in the back, using his paddle as a rudder. Tracker and Michael sat side by side in front with one oar each as they carefully paddled out into the current.

Nova couldn't have been more uncomfortable. At first, they tried loading her onto the boat with the supplies mounted and tied down on her back, but she was so top heavy they nearly lost everything before they started. Even kneeling, Nova couldn't maintain any balance and finally opted for the splayed position less the load. She wasn't even sure her legs would go in those directions, she had groused in anger.

"Remember you've been personally summoned by the king," Tracker reminded.

Nova blocked Tracker from her thoughts. "*Please tell Tracker to stop talking to me, Michael. I've never been so miserable in my life, and I deserve to be a little bitchy. How undignified. If anyone should see me …*"

They were barely on their way when Nova's legs started cramping, and she started to list to one side. She tried to adjust and then to her dismay—vertigo! "*Oh, when will this nightmare be over, Michael?*" she wailed.

Michael was concentrating very hard on keeping his oar in sync with Tracker's. "*We're going far upstream to a secret pass that Tracker knows. It will take a couple of hours. Listen Nova, you might try and lie very still. There are flesh-eating fish in these waters, and they're hungry. It wouldn't be good to capsize right now.*"

Nova groaned as only a camelop can groan and dropped her head to the deck.

Tracker looked quizzically at Michael. "I think she's seasick," Michael whispered. Tracker looked back over his shoulder at the wretched creature. "Here, give her a little of this. It helped her before when she needed to relax." Tracker reached into his vest and pulled out the small vial of liquid he had used the night before Nova's race. "And keep some for yourself. It might help your problems, too—like when you're riding!"

Much later, Tracker indicated a small confluence reflecting like a band of silver in the moonlight. They entered where it joined the channel from the mainland and continued upstream for about an hour. When the water became too shallow to continue, Tracker jumped out and pulled the boat to shore.

"Once again I thank you and say good-bye, Bjorg." Their supplies lay in the sand, and Michael was walking Nova in circles to help her regain her land legs.

"Not all trolls friends, Tracker," Bjorg said. He was standing close and looking intently up at his friend. "That, way to Chasms of Dread," he said, pointing upstream. "Not like you remember. Mountain troll blocks way. Need these for passage." Bjorg gave Tracker three green stones.

Tracker held one up to the moonlight. "But these stones are emeralds, Bjorg. And, yes you have guessed correctly; we are on our way to the chasms. But, what new mischief is this?"

Bjorg closed Tracker's hands around the stones. "Mountain troll controls bridge leaving Charn. It collect huge fee, but not for king—for witch!" He spit on the ground. "If must fight, remember; troll no good without head." Bjorg looked long and hard into Tracker's eyes and then turned and waved farewell to Michael and Nova.

Tracker watched Bjorg and the boat glide away downstream. As he disappeared, Tracker wondered out loud: "Now what in the world did that mean?"

Tracker went back to the landing spot and helped Michael put together a quick camp. He insisted they all rest until daybreak and quickly rolled up in his blanket and fell asleep. Nova welcomed the chance to rest and dropped to her knees where she was. She was snoring before Michael could make his own bed. *Well, I guess there's no need to pull watch*, he thought. *Tracker seems to think it's safe.* He looked at the sleeping duo and remembered advice his father had given him about traveling: "Never pass up the chance to take a nap or use the restroom." Michael pulled off his boots and stretched out with his hands behind his head staring up at the stars. Thoughts of his father filled his head as he drifted off to sleep.

The sun beating on his face woke Michael up. He was the first, so he made a fire and prepared coffee and breakfast. He took his father's second bit of advice a short way from the camp and then washed and splashed water on his face in the river. He returned to the camp refreshed and found Tracker and Nova both awake and eating.

While Michael finished tying down Nova's load, Tracker sat on a small boulder with his coffee and talked about the path ahead. "I expect to meet some mountain folk along the way and perhaps a giant or two, but they have all sworn fealty to the king and shouldn't cause us any trouble."

Michael and Nova exchanged surprised looks. "*Giants!*"

"The real challenge will be getting across the bridge that spans the deep chasms bordering Charn and the northern territories," continued Tracker, as if the giants were of no consequence. "It's the only way across for miles and miles, and Bjorg says the way is blocked.

The bridge that spans those canyons is like no other anywhere in this world, or any other world, I imagine. It's ancient and no one really knows who built it. It was built with magic, though, and it's counted among the true wonders of Tremora. There are no visible means of support, and it takes great courage to cross it. It once protected an ancient kingdom, and legend has it that any enemy that tried to cross was thrown to the rocks far below—thus the name—the Chasms of Dread. And now Bjorg has warned us of a mountain troll at the entrance, and that concerns me. We'll certainly have to keep our wits about us."

"Mountain troll!"

"No visible means of support!"

Nova and Michael eyed each other in alarm. "The adventure continues," Tracker said, giving his companions a wry smile. The he got up and hurriedly poured coffee on the fire and kicked dirt on the smoking ashes.

They broke camp and continued inland, following the banks of the small river until it became little more than a trickling stream. Tracker walked by Nova's side, and Michael followed behind. Along the way, Tracker took the opportunity to tell Nova an abbreviated version of the story of Fennland. "There is perhaps no bigger secret in Tremora than that of the wazalops, Nova." Tracker said, as he finished. This was the second time Michael had heard the wazalop story, but now he knew who Fenn was, and it was all the more fascinating. He was hearing a story about his mother!"

"If it wasn't for Megan, you wouldn't be able to enter into Fennland at all," Tracker was now telling Nova. "The way is blocked to all but wizards, witches, and border guards. It's folly to ignore the warnings of the men of Gondalor; the wizard's spell is very effective."

As midday approached, they began to climb, and the forest began to thin. The trail zigzagged back and forth as it gained altitude, and at times, they had to grab at roots in the ground to pull them up or tie ropes to trees to help Nova and her load. Nova surprisingly climbed like a goat, though, and actually had the easier time.

Michael heard a familiar sound off to their right—it was the roar of raging water. Tracker indicated with his staff that they should keep going, that the crest of their mountain wasn't too much farther. "You'll be rewarded at the top," he said.

They struggled up the last steep section of trail and emerged onto a flat ledge. And from there they saw a truly remarkable sight. All three stood and gazed across a deep ravine and up a massive wall of stone.

A mammoth waterfall cascaded down its face and plunged, churning, into a lake that overflowed in front of them, creating another waterfall that disappeared out of sight down another face of stone into mist and spray. The sheer scale was hard to embrace. The source of water for the first waterfall was a huge dark cave high up on the mountain.

As he tried to take it all in, Michael caught a movement directly across from him and saw two young children, a boy and girl, playing in the lake, splashing and running and throwing sticks. He pointed them out to Tracker and Nova and then stopped in mid sentence. "Those kids must be enormous," he finally finished in a hush.

"No, *ginormous* would be more accurate. Look!" Tracker pointed.

There standing in the waterfall were the adults. They were as tall as trees, and the water hit and ran down their huge bodies in white rivulets like the boulders they stood on. The giantess had long strands of hair as thick as vines that hung down to her knees. The giant himself was so big he dwarfed his mate. Michael could only imagine the strength in one of those huge hands that hung at his side. The female had a handful of tree limbs and was brushing the male's back. Only then did the trio realize that the couple and their children were probably bathing.

"Uh oh," blurted Tracker. "Quick! Avert your eyes and move on slowly. We don't want them to think we're spying on them."

But it was too late. The young girl saw them and, jumping excitedly, pointed right at them. The parents heard the commotion and looked back over their shoulders. The male giant's face became angry, but the female only smiled and looked amused. The boy, though, was the one who almost caused the whole adventure to come to an abrupt end there on that mountain top. He bent down and picked up a stone the size of a basketball and threw it right at where they were standing. The stone hit like a cannon ball and broke off part of the ledge. They ran for cover as more stones crashed around them, and debris and rubble tumbled loudly down the mountainside. They weren't safe until Tracker led them around a bend and out of sight.

"If it wasn't for that ravine …," laughed Tracker later. All three were huddled around a campfire, hunkered down and wrapped in blankets against the cold. "I don't think I could have talked our way out of that one. We'd have probably ended up on a spit over a fire."

"But I thought the giants were our friends," Michael said.

"Yes, well that's true, but giants have very poor memories—and eyesight for that matter. You're really never 100 percent sure of their loyalties or how long they'll last. King William has to send knights to their castle every year just to remind them of their allegiance. Fortunately for us, that giant family won't even recognize us if we ever run into them again. Giants take their privacy very seriously."

"So do we, traveler," boomed a deep voice. "What brings you to our mountain?"

Tracker put his hand on Michael's knee and kept him from jumping up. "Steady," he whispered. *"Don't be alarmed, Nova."* He looked beyond her into the night as three fierce-looking mountain men stepped into the light of the fire. They were armed to the teeth with bows, arrows, knives, and staffs that doubled as massive clubs.

"Travelers we are, but no threat," Tracker said. He held out his empty hands. "As you can see by our fire, we journey openly and without stealth. We are on king's business. But you have the advantage." Tracker looked at them expectantly from beneath his hood.

The largest of the three stepped forward and pounded his staff so hard on the ground it seemed the mountain shook. He wore animal skins from head to foot, and his hair and beard were black, thick, and wild. Only his eyes and teeth showed clearly in the light. "King's business, you say? Well, times have changed. No one can cross this pass without permission from the Trevor clan."

Tracker slowly stood and brushed his hood back off his face. "A Mazalon Warrior needs no such permission, Pashtook."

The mountain man's reaction was quite comical. His eyes opened wide, and he quickly bent forward. He put one arm on one thigh and held his club behind him out of the way with the other. He then stretched his neck and stared a long time into Tracker's face.

Tracker looked back unblinking. "Yes, Pashtook, it's me, Tracker. Shall I take you over my knee as I used to when you were a pup?"

Later they all huddled around a much bigger fire. Tracker and Pashtook had finally finished exchanging pleasantries (Tracker had lived with the Trevor clan for a time when Pashtook was a child), and they were now discussing the current situation in the Pishtocks.

"The troll at the bridge is no friend of ours," Pashtook said. His two companions growled and nodded in agreement. "He's part of a truce we now have with Spreten. The wizard hasn't been seen in our forests for a very long time, but one night about a year ago, our clan chief, Trevor, was visited in a dream by his mate. We don't know what was in that dream, but soon after, Spreten servants and creatures began to appear on our paths, and we were ordered to let them go unchallenged. Oh, they give us the occasional tributes. 'For your master Trevor, they always say.' But we've found these tributes are merely a portion of what the troll collects at the bridge. Spreten seems to be making out handsomely under this new agreement ..., and maybe Trevor is, too," he added bitterly, "both in his purse and his dreams." Pashtook's companions again growled and nodded in agreement.

"Regardless of the reason, it's obvious Trevor no longer gives sole allegiance to the king. Some of us think Trevor is under the witch's spell. But many don't, and the clan is divided. Perhaps the witch has enchanted more of our people than just Trevor. Some of us have stayed true to the king, but there is little we can do openly. Our numbers are too small, and we won't fight our own. But now, we hear the troll is throwing travelers into the chasm if they don't pay, and there are even darker rumors of wisps carrying children off to Spreten. We won't tolerate these abominations another day. My friends and I are headed in the same direction as you, Tracker. We plan on removing a troll from this world this very night. I do not think our meeting was just a coincidence, my old friend," he said grimly.

Tracker acknowledged the age reference with a derisive snort. "Indeed." He stood up and slowly lit his pipe. He puffed for several minutes in deep thought while gazing into the night. Michael recognized the now familiar pose and motioned for the three mountain men to be patient. Finally Tracker lowered his pipe. "You're right, Pashtook. We are also headed for that bridge and hope to cross it in the morning. And I agree. It may be more than a coincidence that we met because you definitely need our help. A mountain troll is not easily killed. Many have 'tried, died, and been fried,' as they say. Mountain trolls eat their enemies, you know …"

He looked around the campfire. Michael's face was pale, and Nova's eyes were as big as saucers. This was to be expected. But Pashtook and his friends merely looked on, unimpressed. "Good! You know something of your enemy then." Tracker took a few more puffs on his pipe. "But, there are things you may not know. A mountain troll's weakness is in its head." He paused and again looked out into the night. *Was this what Bjorg meant?* No insight came to him, though, and he continued. "That's the good news. They're dumb as stumps. However, the bad news is, physically they're almost impossible to defeat. They're made mostly of rocks. You'll need more than brawn to get rid of this beast, I'm afraid. But I just may have a plan."

The moon again leant its reflected light to the night. Tracker and Michael, along with the three mountain men, crawled up to the cliff's edge on all fours and peered down at the trail below. It snaked its way through the rocks and trees to the bridge. "That's it," said Pashtook, pointing. They looked hard but saw no sign of the troll. Two torches were burning at the bridge's entrance, and a large pile of rocks stretched between them, blocking the way.

Tracker grunted, and Michael, too, suspected the truth. "I'll now show you a troll's biggest secret," whispered Tracker. He gave Michael some quick instruction and told the others to stay put—only watch. Tracker then climbed soundlessly down to the path. Tracker was far back and out of sight of the torches but still walked very slowly toward the bridge, one careful step at a time. Michael stood at a vantage point where he could see both the bridge and Tracker.

Tracker took a cautious step forward on the trail and looked up at Michael expectantly. Michael looked toward the bridge and shook his head from side to side. This continued on for some time until, as Tracker inched his boot forward, Michael saw a few rocks move in the light of the torches at the bridge. Michael quickly raised both hands high in the air. Tracker drew back his boot. He then drew a line in the path with his staff and hurried back up to the overlook.

The mountain men looked at him as if he had lost his mind in the moonlight.

"The troll's there, all right," Tracker said. "You just don't see it." He indicated the pile of rocks at the bridge's entrance. "Believe it or not, that's our troll." They looked back at the bridge in surprise. "You see, trolls can't sleep when they're in troll form. They can only sleep when they change back into the pile of rocks they were made from, and that's their secret."

Tracker motioned them back from the edge. "Trolls need their sleep, and lots of it. So, for protection, they cast special stones far out from where they're going to rest. If anyone steps on even one of these pebbles, they wake up. This early detection gives them time to change before anyone sees them. Very few people have seen this and lived to tell the tale. Fortunately for you, I'm one of them."

Tracker then waved everyone up and pointed again at the bridge. "Now, listen closely. Do you see that big boulder sitting on top of the heap? That's the troll's head. Its eyes will open at the slightest movement. If there's a false alarm or no apparent danger, it won't bother to transform, like when I disturbed one of the stones just now; it would rather save its energy. If its eyes, ears, and nose determine it's safe, then it just goes back to sleep. Regardless, it's going to be impossible to approach that bridge without it noticing. So, we won't even try. But I think our knowledge of its secrets and your combined size and strength will be the undoing of this gatekeeper, Pashtook. Now, here's the plan."

✥

Pashtook and his two friends walked noisily down the trail. They passed Tracker's mark in the path, and Pashtook waved up at the lookout. Michael, Tracker, and Nova watched from above.

"Now, watch this," said Tracker. All at once the pile of rocks at the gate came alive. In a mad flurry of activity the stones shuffled and rolled and tumbled over each other to stack and become a much larger, more intimidating version of Bjorg.

Michael gulped and looked at Tracker. “That troll is huge!”

“Don’t worry,” Tracker assured him. “It’s in the plan.” Michael couldn’t help but recall they had a plan at the races, too.

“He’s just a big bully,” Nova thought at both of them. *“I’m not impressed.”*

The mountain men came in sight of the troll. “Halt!” a deep voice rumbled. The troll took up the entire breadth of the entrance to the bridge, torch to torch. It held a large mace in one hand and a leather bag by its drawstring in the other. Gnawed bones lay strewn at its feet. “You pay toll to cross bridge,” it demanded. If a dump truck tipped a load of gravel onto the ground, you would have the same sound as the troll’s voice.

Pashtook and his friends took no heed of the warning to stop and walked right up to the troll. They looked at the bones on the ground and remembered the terrible stories. Were those bloodstains on the bridge? The troll just smirked at them. As one, the mountain men forgot Tracker’s warnings, and anger took over their collective judgment. They were mountain men, after all! And this was three against one!

“We are of clan Trevor, and we’ve crossed this bridge many times,” growled Pashtook. “We’ve never heard of any toll. Maybe we don’t want to pay you anything. Do you think you can handle all three of us, troll?”

The troll laughed loudly in his face. “Me show you.” He dropped his mace and bag to the ground and put both hands on his hips. Then he pointed. “You! Big and ugly! Come. Hit me as hard as you want. Even use your little club if you like. First one free.”

Pashtook looked at his friend Teetook and said, “He must be talking to you.”

Teetook grinned and stepped forward. He looked back at his friends and shrugged his shoulders. “Well, he did ask for it.” He then turned without warning and took a mighty swing with his club. It hit the troll flat between the eyes, but the end of the club broke off like balsa. The troll smiled, showing horribly cracked and broken teeth. Teetook then took the stump of his club and rammed it into the troll's stomach, but the remaining wood only shattered, and he badly bruised his hand.

Quick as lightning, the troll grabbed Teetook's hurt hand and arm and hurled him back up the path with no more effort than if he was throwing a pillow full of feathers. Laughter again filled the air, and the troll's belly shifted and rattled with mirth as Teetook tumbled end over end. "That was for the cheap shot," he bellowed.

Pashtook and Joshtook hurried to Teetook's side and helped him to his feet. "Tracker's plan better work," Pashtook said in a low voice. "Because he sure was right about one thing; that troll wasn't even fazed when you hit him, Teetook. He's all stone!"

Pashtook stood up and returned to stand in front of the troll. "Okay, enough of this. Perhaps you can stand up to our combined strength—perhaps not. However, we are in a charitable mood and have important business to attend to. How much is the toll for all three of us to pass?"

The troll's laughter disappeared in an instant, and its voice was again demanding and menacing. "Normally, ten gold coins or an emerald *each* … but I don't like your friend. The price is double!"

Pashtook looked at Teetook in alarm. Tracker had only given them three emeralds and they didn't have any gold coins to barter with. After all, they had come to kill this beast not give him money. Pashtook had to think quickly. But first, he needed to get Teetook out of there. The troll was never going to let the mountain man pass by him now. He would probably kill Teetook for the fun of it *and* take the toll. Pashtook turned, furled his eyebrows, and looked sternly at his friend. "Now you've done it," he said angrily. "You'll have to go back to the castle and get more money. Because of you, I only have enough for me and Joshtook to cross the bridge. You'll just have to be late for our meeting. Go!"

Teetook looked at Pashtook, bewildered. "What? You want me to go back to the *castle*? What castle? I mean, er, yeah, the castle, but …" He was going to argue that he didn't want to leave them alone with the troll, but Pashtook's face made it clear he didn't want to hear it. Finally, Teetook took the hint. He bowed his head, grabbed his injured hand and retreated reluctantly back up the path. When he turned back to make a last minute plea, Pashtook was standing watching, still looking stern and pointing for him to go.

Pashtook waited till Teetook completely disappeared up the trail. Then he held both hands up in front of him, out of sight of the troll, to signal to Tracker that he had the situation in control. He then turned to the troll and brushed both hands off as if the incident was over. "Now that that's settled … I apologize for my friend's crass behavior. Could we maybe talk about that toll thing again?"

As mentioned before, mountain folk themselves are masters of intimidation and bartering. And Pashtook would certainly need to use his talents now. The problem was, with the troll's new demands, he didn't have enough money or emeralds for both him and Joshtook either. And Tracker's plan needed at least two of them to get through that gate and onto the bridge. It was time to find out how much of a stump this guy really was.

Without waiting for a response to his question, Pashtook sat down in front of the troll and crossed his legs. He looked up and said, "Coins of the realm or emeralds you say?" He reached into his pocket and pulled out a closed fist. "Well, we need to get across this bridge tonight, and here's what we have … emeralds!" He opened his hand to show three green stones and nudged them back and forth with a finger. The orange light of the torches danced off the many flat green facets of the stones. "As you know and can readily see, emeralds are certainly more valuable than Tremoran coins. In fact, in today's market, they're worth at least fifteen gold coins each due to inflation, and since you have doubled the normal crossing price from ten to twenty coins, meaning you want a total of forty coins, these three emeralds are worth forty-five coins, and that means if I give you all three emeralds you are making a twenty-five coin profit for your boss over your normal take for two very weary travelers in the night."

As hoped, the eyes of the troll stayed on the precious stones. "Of course, we could wait for my brother to get back from the castle tomorrow, but then we might as well go farther northeast to the next bridge where the gatekeeper won't be so upset and will take the normal toll of thirty coins to cross his bridge which means you would have cost your boss fifteen coins or *one whole green emerald*! And we know the queen won't be happy to find that out."

The troll gazed at the alluring green of the emeralds, only half listening to Pashtook's math. Its eyes glazed over at the word inflation and only wanted these two nuisances to disappear, with the three emeralds in its bag of course. The mention of the witch, though, brought it out of its trance. It reached out one massive hand, but Pashtook leapt to his feet and put the emeralds behind his back.

"Do we have a deal then?"

The troll was getting angry. "Be quick!" Its voice sounded like an avalanche. It knew it couldn't outrun the two mountain men. It couldn't even leave its post. The troll turned sideways and stuck out its bag. There was just enough room for one man to squeeze through at a time.

"Come on, Joshtook." Pashtook pushed him forward. The troll growled dangerously as each struggled through the small gap. Once they got through Pashtook very deliberately dropped the three emeralds into the troll's bag. *I'll remember that bag when this is over*, he promised himself.

The two men stepped gingerly out onto the bridge and carefully set off into the darkness. The troll held one of the torches high in the air so it could watch them disappear. Then it gave a grunt of satisfaction and returned the torch to its notch. After opening its bag and looking in at the emeralds as if to make sure they were all there, it turned away from the bridge and stood still for a long, long time.

Tracker, Michael, and Nova watched it all from the lookout. When Teetook was hurled down the path like a sack of potatoes, Tracker swore under his breath. "Mountain men's heads are as thick as trolls'," he snarled. Michael stood up, ready to rush down the mountainside, but Tracker held him back. All was not lost, yet. They watched as Pashtook sent Teetook packing. They also caught his hands signal. "Now what are you up to, Pashtook?" Tracker wondered out loud.

They watched Pashtook and the troll bartering but couldn't hear what was going on. They could see, however, that the troll was getting angry. So Tracker gave a sigh of relief when both men squeezed past the troll successfully and walked out onto the bridge. But only *two* of them. Doable, but it would certainly make things more difficult.

Teetook crawled up to the lookout and shame-facedly told his tale. "It can't be helped now," Tracker said. "Go back down to the path with Michael and wait for my signal. When I give the go ahead, you'll have to run hard to get to your friends. They'll need your help." Tracker wasn't happy and dismissed Teetook with a snarl.

Tracker and Nova continued to watch the troll. Finally, it turned its head side to side as if sniffing the air and set the bag of coins and emeralds down between its feet. "It's becoming sleepy," whispered Tracker. He was right. In no time at all, the troll completely collapsed to the ground between the two torches, creating the same large mound of stones they saw before. Tracker looked into the sky over the bridge. He then lit the end of an arrow with his pipe, notched it in Pashtook's borrowed bow, and let it fly.

"There it is!" said Pashtook, pointing. He and Joshtook were kneeling on the bridge about a quarter ways across the ravine, waiting for Tracker's signal. They dropped their weapons and removed their boots and began to inch back toward the entrance as quietly as possible.

Tracker motioned to Michael. Michael then barely nudged a stone on the path with his foot and quickly stepped back. The troll's eyes flashed open. A few pebbles rolled tentatively in front of him and stopped. No one moved. The troll's eyes looked left and right and up and down. Then the eyelids slowly drooped and closed.

Tracker waited for several moments and motioned to Michael again. Michael nudged the same stone, the troll's eyes snapped open, a few pebbles moved, the troll looked around, and then again went back to sleep.

Pashtook and Joshtook continued to move back across the bridge.

After the troll went back to sleep for the fourth time, Tracker saw that the mountain men were in position. "Here we go, Nova." He stood and shot another flaming arrow into the sky, and motioned to Teetook to get moving. Teetook took off running down the path. Michael held back and waited for Tracker and Nova.

Pashtook looked up and saw the signal. He patted Joshtook on the shoulder for good luck and then ran and leapt on the Troll's head. He grabbed the boulder with both arms and yanked it hard to the right with all his might. Joshtook jumped in and yanked the head in the opposite direction. The troll's eyes opened wide and rolled back its head to see what was happening. Then, its mouth gaped wide open as it bellowed in rage.

Stones started flying from all directions. The pair continued frantically to wrench the troll's head back and forth to separate it from the rest of the stones, but it stubbornly held on. Its body was taking shape, and the head was still attached! This was not part of the plan. They were losing the battle.

Teetook reached them and joined in the fight. "Help them with the head, or we're lost," yelled Tracker as he and Michael, too, rushed down the trail. The scene was pandemonium. All three mountain men grappled with the troll's head as stones rolled and tumbled and stacked one on top of another. Michael and Tracker fervently picked up stones that weren't too heavy and threw them as far away as they could. Michael especially threw stones far into the ravine, but they just came back as if magnetized.

It was looking bad. The troll's arms were almost formed and thrashed around wildly. Joshtook got slammed backwards onto the bridge and was barely conscious. Most of the rocks looked to be nearing their proper order and place.

"Nova, do something!" Michael screamed. He'd just been upturned by a thigh shaped boulder and was lying on his back.

"*Well, I thought you'd never ask!*" She was standing on the path, watching. Tracker hadn't included her in any plans, and she didn't know what else she was supposed to do.

"Tell them to stand clear!" she shot at Tracker.

Tracker looked up startled but didn't hesitate a moment. "Stand back, Pashtook! Let go, Teetook! Stay where you are, Joshtook!" he shouted.

Nova didn't hesitate either. She ran up to the now very confused troll, who was thrashing its arms wildly and spit in its face. It immediately bellowed loudly and rubbed at its eyes with partially formed hands and fingers. Nova then spun around and landed a two-legged kick squarely under the troll's chin. They all looked on in astonishment as the head detached and flew up, up, up, and away into the darkness and then down, down, down into the Chasms of Dread. For a moment there was total silence; even the stones in the troll's body stopped all movement, some of them suspended in mid air. And then, as if on command, all the stones took off and fell and rolled and tumbled along the ground and down the bridge and over the edge into the darkness, apparently in search of their head.

No one said anything; they just turned and stared at Nova. She merely blinked her huge eyelids demurely and put on her most humble face. After all, she was used to people looking at her admiringly.

"*Nova, that was brilliant! You saved our lives.*" Michael got up and put his arms around her neck and patted her nose with affection.

"*I'll never leave you out of my plans again, Nova,*" added Tracker in admiration. "*I had no idea you were so … so lethal.*" Tracker then went over and stood next to Nova as well. "*Please, don't be angry at what I say next. It's only to protect how special you are. Your secret is just too valuable.*"

"*Oh boy, here we go,*" Nova snorted.

Tracker turned to the mountain men. "Now you know one of *our* secrets. This is a truly a remarkable animal, our Nova. As you saw, she's trained to attack just like a guard dog." He also put an arm around her neck. "She was always our Plan B," he beamed.

Chapter Thirty-one

Abandon All Hope

Prelandora stood tall and regal in the front of her ship with the wind blowing her jet-black hair out straight in front of her. The boat's figurehead, jutting proudly out from the bow, was carved in her image, bare-breasted and fierce. Behind Prelandora, on the fo'c'sle deck, a dozen Spreten soldiers knelt on one knee with spears held in one gloved hand and black spiked shields in the other. Their heads were slightly raised, all eyes on her. From their armor to every whisker in their beards, they were exact copies of each other. Twyla was to one side of her master, facing aft into the wind, neck extended, comfortably straddling the ships railings with her tail resting on the deck for balance. They were making good headway as they sailed from Spreten Castle to the port of Stern on Havenland's north coast.

Flugbark sat cowering in the crow's nest, his huge eyes barely visible over the rim of the wooden basket. Helping round out the crew, aft, on the quarterdeck, stood a half dozen wisps shoulder to shoulder, legs wide apart, stoic and unmoving. Finally, at the ship's wheel was perhaps the most fearsome creature in Prelandor's arsenal: Captain Pus. The giant octopus was draped languidly over the helm using three of its eight arms to deftly steer the ship—the same lethal appendages that trimmed and unfurled the sails, meted out lashes when required, and weighed anchor; as integral a part of the ship as the sails themselves. And the monster's offspring made up the rest of the crew.

They had been at sea for several hours before the port of Stern came into sight. The ports of Tremora knew Prelandora's black ship very well: No pirate ship was ever as fearsome. Any merchant vessel foolish enough to sail alone could never outrun her or fail to relinquish its cargo. The *Abandon All Hope* was the terror of the Sea of Spreten.

So, more than a few ships struck out in panic when the shiny black sails of Prelandora's ship breached the horizon. Shop stores closed their shutters, dockworkers dropped what they were doing, and townsfolk took to the roads as if a hurricane was forecast. By the time the witch's ship arrived, Stern was a ghost town.

Once the ship was docked and secured, the soldiers marched down the gangplank two abreast and formed a double line on the wooden boardwalk. Next came Flugbark, hopping like the toad he was. The wisps jumped over the railings and descended effortlessly down ropes tied to the dock. All stood waiting for their mistress to emerge.

Eventually, Prelandora appeared at the top of the gangway with her reptilian servant, Twyla, at her side. With great aplomb, she struck a queenly pose and stood silent for several moments: haughty, nose aloft, scepter-like staff in one hand, wickedly shaped silver sword in the other. Pus draped himself over the bow of the ship with his long tentacles falling almost to the water and watched her intently. This was as far as Prelandora dared go. She was banned from even standing on the docks.

Finally, Prelandora addressed the wisps. "The slaves we are looking for should be easy to find. Look for a black giant … or three. They will have a companion with them, a young boy, who will be their prisoner. Question every weasely coward left in Stern until you find them. Then, bring them all to me at once!" The black-robed figures quickly scattered. She looked at the soldiers and motioned with her hand. "Sit," she commanded. As one, all twelve soldiers crossed their legs and dropped to their backsides with shields and swords held out in front of them. Prelandora and Twyla then disappeared into the captain's cabin to wait.

A couple of hours passed before two wisps were seen approaching the ship, pulling a wooden wagon by its tongue. Captain Pus banged a tentacle on the roof of the wheelhouse and Prelandora emerged with Twyla from the captain's cabin. The witch drew her cloak tightly around her and took her position on deck. Meanwhile, the remaining four wisps converged from side streets and helped push the wagon its final distance to stop in front of the ship.

The witch looked down at them expectantly from the railing of the quarterdeck. "Well?" Her voice echoed menacingly along the wharf.

The wisps looked at each other nervously. Then, one reluctantly climbed up into the back of the wagon and reached down and hefted up the straw Michael for Prelandora to see. He pulled the hat off the dummy and grabbed a handful of the straw and threw it up in the air. "This is all we've found. I fear you have been deceived. A giant and two children sold this wagon to a ship's carpenter for a song. The last they were seen, they were fleeing with the mule in the direction of Bearcamp."

In three loud explosions, the wisp, the straw Michael, and the wagon itself disappeared in bursts of flames and smoke. The other five wisps were blown onto their backs with their robes smoldering. Prelandora's scream of frustration could be heard as far as Bearcamp.

After several tense moments, Prelandora turned to Pus, gave the order to return home, and then disappeared into the captain's cabin, slamming the door behind her. No one moved. To have done so during the witch's tantrum would have meant death. Pus slowly raised his dangling arms and glided cautiously to the ship's wheel. From there, he cast his one good eye to the docks.

"Well, you heard the lady! Cast off the lines!" he gargled.

Immediately wisps, soldiers, and Flugbark sprang into action. They untied the ship's anchoring ropes and scampered up the gangplanks while half a dozen smaller octopi appeared from below decks and climbed the masts and set the sails.

Prelandora leaned back against the door, arms wide, hands reversed and splayed, as if to keep the entire outside world from following her into the cabin. She was panting. "He has escaped me yet again," she gasped. "How can this be?"

Twyla stood in one corner. The skin on her head and body matched the color and texture of the wood on the cabin's walls perfectly.

She was nearly invisible. Only her eyes could be seen clearly, and they were opened wide, watching her mistress's every move.

But she needn't have worried. Prelandora wouldn't have seen her if she stood in front of her, displaying the colors of the rainbow. The witch's mind was in another place, and her eyes stared into that void, unfocused. Prelandora maintained her position at the door long enough for her breathing to return to normal. Then she straightened and said, "I must think on this." She strode across the small room and took a seat on the sill of the captain's window. "Twyla, quit your silly game of hide-and-seek and come rub my feet ... and get me a pillow off the bed."

She was exhausted. It was happening every time she lost her temper now. She kicked off her sandals, and Twyla grabbed a pillow and a small stool and sat down in front of her. Twyla handed Prelandora the pillow and then lifted both the witch's feet into her lap.

"How did I get here—into this mess?" Prelandora whispered to herself. "Did it all start with that spider? I must think on this, Twyla."

Twyla began to respond.

"Don't talk to me; just rub," Prelandora commanded. Then she put the pillow behind her head and shoulders, leaned back against the wooden frame of the window, and closed her eyes.

Twyla bowed her head obediently and took one of the witch's feet in her chameleon-like hands, shaped like pincers, and began to massage away.

Prelandora grimaced slightly, adjusted her shoulders, and began to chant a series of magical words taught her by her grandmother long ago that always calmed her—first out loud, then in a whisper, then to herself. Presently, her mind journeyed back to where it all began …

Chapter Thirty-two

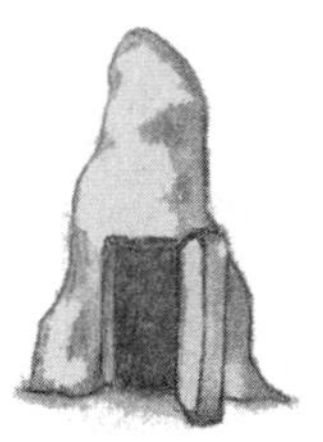

Prelandora's Story

She was a young girl, a young out-of-control witch. And she was going to rule the world. It was her destiny! She had known it from the moment she could form an independent thought. And her first conquest was going to be the country of Tremora. However, there was the small matter of High King William. An earlier strategy had been simply to marry the king and become queen. Simple? Not exactly. It was her first disappointment. In spite of her best efforts to enchant William with her bewitching ways, a commoner named Lelana won *that* battle and ended up the king's bride instead. Her consolation prize had been Lord Pratt. Lelana became her number one enemy.

But Prelandora wasn't going to let a little setback like that thwart her plans. There had to be another way, and she was going to find it. So it was no surprise to her at all when, on the very day of the royal wedding, she was struck with her answer: *Why not kill the king and queen and let Lord Pratt become king? Same thing! She'd still end up the queen. Of course!*

So, without hesitation, she set out to murder the new royal couple. Over the next several weeks, she tried poison, hired assassins, staged a hunting accident, even set off a landslide, but failed miserably each time. The royals, it turned out, were extremely well protected—or very lucky.

Then one day, while kicking a dog, she came upon yet another even more sinister idea: *Why not seek out the most powerful weapon of all? Why not learn black magic and use it to conquer the throne? Of course, again!* The thought was intoxicating. With all that power at her command, how could she fail? And once she was queen, no one could stand against her!

But right from the beginning, this plan also had its problems. If any black magic was left in Tremora after the wizard's purge, it was hidden in the deepest, darkest places in the world. She couldn't find a trace. And almost all the books and references to the dark arts had been banished or destroyed by the wizards long ago. Her search of the castle's Great Hall of Knowledge produced a few scant entries, which she absorbed greedily, but it was not nearly enough.

Then late one evening, after searching the darkest corners and recesses of the great library with no success, Prelandora found herself sitting on a low wooden bench between rows and rows of dusty scrolls and leather-bound tomes, head back with hands hanging down between her legs, totally frustrated. She couldn't understand it. If it was her destiny, why wasn't anything working? Black magic was such a good idea … But then a most opportune event happened that showed her she must, indeed, be destined to rule the world.

She opened her weary eyes, and there, just above her head, hung a red spider on a single strand of web. With little forethought, she reached up, grabbed the thread, and spun the spider around her head three times for good luck; then made a wish. "I wish to rule the world, of course!" Next, as was also the custom, she blew the spider into the air. She watched as it floated down the aisle and then, unexpectedly, turned sharply down another row of bookshelves. Curious, she got up and followed the spider with the light of her wand. She watched, fascinated, as it jumped from one side of the row to the other; first landing on a shelf or spine of a book on one side, then launching into the air to find another new surface on the opposite side farther on; all the while trailing a single fine filament of silk. Prelandora was now completely engaged. She continued to follow the bouncing arachnid down the row, around a corner, through a gap, and up several stone steps to a small circular room. The room's stone walls were lined with glass-fronted cabinets full of dark leather volumes that she had searched before. The spider came to a stop on top of one of the dark mahogany cabinets. Once there, it spent a couple busy moments scurrying around in circles, laying a heavier coating of web material, apparently to serve as an anchor. Then it turned and crawled back along its original strand dragging a second thread loosely behind. She watched as it disappeared back down the stairs. "That's going to be some spider web," she said. Then she looked more closely at the bookcase in front of her. *Was this spider-encounter some kind of sign?* she wondered. She carefully opened the lead glass doors of the cabinet and, as if guided by some invisible hand, found a thin black book hidden between two large volumes on necromancy. She had examined the two larger books earlier in her search, but the pages were blank. "Now this is new," she mumbled as she removed the smaller book and noted its cover. It was labeled *Ohndrea.*

The title was hand scribed, and she suddenly realized she could very well be holding a journal written by the most famous black witch in history. And she and this witch were related! She opened the book, and the first page contained an enigmatic warning:

> Wield these enchantments if you dare,
> But know they have their price.
> Use your power to feed the magic,
> Or it will be your own sacrifice!

Without a second thought, she turned the page. To her surprise and immense delight, it was a spell book. It contained detailed instructions on how to cast three different spells: The first showed how to create and bring to life a list of strange creatures; the second showed how to control and watch over them, and the third was a summoning spell for the ghosts of dead relatives. She scanned them excitedly. "Why these are easily doable!" she exclaimed. She closed the book and tucked it under one arm. She couldn't wait to try her hand at the spells, the book's warning being the farthest thing from her mind. And it was also of little consequence that each spell required something to die.

Her first attempt at creating creatures was successful beyond her wildest dreams. Wisps! And the castle hardly noticed the bats and cats that went missing. The second spell, of course, she used on

Pratt. It was a little trickier; the snake she used was poisonous, and the spiders were of a particularly nasty kind. And the third? Well, was it any coincidence that Ohndrea was in her own family tree? No—just as finding the journal was no coincidence either. Prelandora was certain that Ohndrea's book was not in that cabinet on previous searches. No, there was a tiny bit of black magic hiding in that journal—*and* in that spider!

When she realized what the third spell was for, she knew why she was led to the journal. The ghost of Ohndrea was calling! Prelandora wondered fleetingly what her ancient relative was up to, but she didn't really care. She only thought of what it meant to her. By using the spell to call Ohndrea, she could learn more about the forbidden secrets of black magic. And who better to teach her? Wasn't Ohndrea the most powerful witch that ever lived?

The first meeting with Ohndrea was like nothing she ever expected. She was sitting in her bedchamber in Tremora Castle, staring at her flask of potion. She was nervous. Were the ingredients correct? Was the incantation at the right pace and pitch? Was she a strong enough witch? It was time to find out. She took a deep breath, carefully unstopped the decanter, and stepped back. Then she watched, mesmerized, as green vapor rose from the opening in the bottle and spread across the ceiling. Slowly, a wavy form became visible in the rising pillar of smoke. Draped in a blood-red cape and sporting extremely long fingernails of matching hue, it was unmistakably Ohndrea's ghost, every bit as menacing as any picture ever painted of her. Prelandora had summoned the ghost of her great-great-great grandmother!

In spite of her success with the wisps and the enchanting of Pratt, she wasn't quite prepared for the apparition that appeared before her. Tall, intimidating, and wraithlike, the ghost hovered in the center of the room, staring at her an eternally long time before speaking. Then, "So, Prelandora, you'd like to rule the world?"

She was too stunned to speak. She swallowed and nodded her head.

After another long pause, the ghost said matter-of-factly, "Well, I think I can help with that."

She couldn't believe her ears. The ghost knew her name and her most coveted dream—right out of the bottle! "But, how—"

"We know your black heart very well, Prelandora," the ghost said, as if reading her mind. "We've been expecting you."

"We?"

"All of your past blood relatives have been watching you—only waiting for you to find the journal and seek our help. You're important to us! We will never die completely as long as our lineage survives. And, by the way, for that, of course, you must procreate; you need to get working on that … And you're right, Prelandora; it's time you took your proper place in Tremora. With my help, you can, indeed, become queen of the world!"

Prelandora collapsed back onto the bed, forearm to forehead, as if about to swoon, while Ohndrea's ghost hovered just above the flagon, waiting.

"If you are quite finished …," the apparition said, finally. "Really, there is no need for you to emote at every opportunity. It is quite tedious."

Prelandora sat up abruptly and gave Ohndrea a dark look, then regained her composure, and indicated with one hand, "Go on."

"That's better, but before I do, there is something you should understand. You did read the warning, didn't you?"

"Yes, something about feeding the magic …"

"Let me explain more clearly. It's *very* important! Nothing this powerful can be wielded without a price, Prelandora. Black magic is a living thing. It has an appetite! And once you start using it, there's no turning back. It's very simple, really. In exchange for its use, *you yourself* must grow more powerful and stronger. Then, through you, the power of the black magic will also grow. Thus the warning: 'You must feed the magic'. If you use the magic for naught, it will have no use for you. It will drain you of your very essence before leaving you a helpless heap. There is no compromise—" Ohndrea stopped. Prelandora was hardly listening.

"I have no concern with this," she told the ghost impatiently. "Of course, I'll grow stronger! Am I not going to conquer the world? Really …"

Ohndrea looked anew at Prelandora; at first surprised, then impressed, and then proudly. In fact there were tears in the witch's eyes. "Surely I am looking at a reincarnation of myself," she whispered.

"And so, the die is cast." She smiled down at Prelandora with affection. "We are pleased."

Then Ohndrea's face became stern. "Now! To the task at hand. The plan is simple: Get pregnant, build up your supply of creatures, spy on the land, and recruit the weak and wicked; introduce your son to Tremora, ensure he inherits the throne, and through him, conquer Tremora; and then, the world." Ohndrea rattled off the list on her fingers.

At first Prelandora was incredulous. *Could it be so easy?* She spent the next several hours with Ohndrea, discussing how she could become queen, and the witch was very convincing. It was so exciting!

First off, getting pregnant was not going to be a problem; after all, she had Pratt at her disposal, and he *was* a wizard. The next step was to create her creatures. It would take time, Ohndrea told her, and she needed to get started. Ohndrea also told her there was a way to create an army of soldiers from muggers and murderers and the criminally insane. "The dungeons of Tremora will be your cake mix!" Ohndrea had joked.

"But having a son—ensuring he becomes heir-apparent?" questioned Prelandora. "How can I—"

"A little trickier, I'll give you that," Ohndrea interrupted, "but don't forget—you'll be wielding black magic, and of course, I'll be there to help you."

After the witch disappeared back into her bottle, Prelandora sat on her bed and pondered the extraordinary meeting with Ohndrea. She accepted everything the witch said, and was excited at all the prospects, but she couldn't ignore the nagging thought that it sounded just a bit too easy. Especially when she considered her past failures. An unfortunate chain of events soon proved Prelandora's fears had some merit.

It all started with Queen Lelana's cat. For Prelandora just couldn't fight the urge to put the queen's tabby in her pot! It was the same night of her meeting with Ohndrea. Prelandora was still giddy with the thought that she was going to rule the world, so she decided to use her creature spell one more time on something called a shape-changer.

The cauldron was boiling. She had already sent the spellbound Pratt on a midnight mission for ingredients to a nearby swamp when the queen's mewing pet came clawing at her door. At first she ignored it, as she always did. But then a thought, evil and delicious, entered her head. Why not add a little spice to the soup? She crept to the door and quietly opened it a crack. The cat pranced in as if it owned the place. But before Prelandora could close the door or grab the animal up, it saw the boiling cauldron and smelled its contents. It immediately arched its back like a black Halloween cat and let out a high-pitched scream that resounded up and down the castle corridors. Prelandora quickly stunned the animal with her wand, but it was too late. In less than a minute, the queen burst through the door, followed closely by her personal guards. Upon seeing the state of the room, the cauldron, and her precious Puddles lying paws up on the floor, Queen Lelana immediately ordered the guards to "put that witch in chains!" Unfortunately for Lord Pratt, he showed up at that very moment with a dripping bag of toads.

It didn't take long for King William to find Prelandora and his brother guilty of practicing black magic. Fortunately for them, he showed mercy and only exiled them to Spreten; he could have sent them to the gallows.

You'll regret this, William, Prelandora swore, as the boat set sail to take her and Pratt to Sitka Island. For this only fueled her ambitions more. It also gave her all the freedom she needed to create her creatures, minions, and spies. Why, she would even have her own castle!

In no time at all, though, another event put a crimp in her plans: Queen Lelana announced she was pregnant. Lelana again bested her at her own game!

"Change nothing. Continue on," was Ohndrea's response upon hearing the news. "We must take the time to think on this, is all. For now, plan on visiting Tremora Castle when the new prince is born. It will be an opportune time to show the world we have an announcement of our own."

❧

After the birth of Prince Cedric and her dramatic visit to Tremora Castle, Prelandora returned to Spreten as determined as ever. During the next several years, under Ohndrea's watchful eye, she steadfastly built up her army and legion of sycophants, fortified

Spreten Castle, built the *Abandon All Hope*, and recruited followers and spies that permeated every corner of Tremora. But, there were other setbacks as well: Pratt had become almost comatose of late and getting pregnant and having a baby didn't work at all. But Ohndrea said she had other plans and Prelandora wasn't to worry. "There's always a backup plan, Prelandora," the witch had assured her. "And Pratt still has some usefulness—not to worry."

And so, Prelandora continued to build her world, and waited, and waited ... But inside, her frustration mounted with each passing year, and her hatred of Queen Lelana and King William boiled like her cauldron. And there was the uneasy feeling that she wasn't making any progress; that she wasn't *feeding* her powers as she was supposed to. Finally, one evening in the eleventh year of her banishment, she exploded.

It was midnight, and the full moon loomed, hugely, behind the black silhouette of Spreten Castle. A shiny black crow with a rolled parchment attached to one leg, winged its way toward the tower where Prelandora slept and landed on the sill of the open window. Two ivory white hands emerged from the darkness, grabbed the crow, and not too gently untied the scroll. In the next moment, screams reverberated through the castle, and the windows of the witch's chambers lit up with bright flashes of lightning. The crow burst into flames, and as its body fell from the sill, red embers and black smoke trailed its freefall down the face of the stone wall to the moat below. When Prelandora's tantrum subsided, she went to the window and glared out across the Spreten Sea toward Tremora. She held the notice of Prince Cedric's coming-of-age, twelfth birthday celebration in her trembling hands.

Her mind was raging. She was going to launch her ships, send her troops, invade Tremora, assassinate the king, the queen, the prince, and, and ... Suddenly, Ohndrea's spell book flew off the shelf and flitted and fluttered across the floor like a bird with a broken wing. Prelandora looked down at the book, not quite comprehending. Then, "Well, that's something new. But, you needn't have bothered, Ohndrea; I was going to summon you anyway!"

Later, Prelandora uncorked the glass decanter on a new batch of potion and stepped back. Ohndrea's voice came from the pillar of green spewing from the bottle even before the ghost was completely visible. "Prelandora, don't be hasty! Yes, we agree it's now time to make new plans, but it is not time to go to war!"

Prelandora looked at Ohndrea, dubiously. "I'm glad I finally have your attention. But I warn you, Ohndrea. I can't wait any longer. Wasn't it you who warned I must grow stronger? Well, I'm growing all right—growing tired!"

For the briefest of moments, a look of anger crossed Ohndrea's face, but she quickly recovered and smiled down at Prelandora, benignly. "It's not necessary to warn *me* of anything, my dear," she said.

Prelandora was in no mood. "Well, I'm tired, and you're dead. So, either come up with another plan, or I'm taking over. It is Cedric who is going to rule Tremora, not me! He's all Tremora is talking about, and he's no longer a child. He must be destroyed!"

The temperature in the room dropped dramatically. Ohndrea again looked as if she wanted to kill and devour Prelandora on the spot. "I think it is time we have a truce, you and I," Ohndrea said, menacingly. "Do you forget who called whom for help in the first place? And isn't it obvious? You have yet to acquire the skills necessary to handle all of this black magic I have helped you gather. You need me, Prelandora. You will not succeed without me. Do you need proof? Well, you are in danger of losing everything, including your life right now, and don't even know it. You're not even thinking clearly. Have you forgotten it is fatal to kill the heir to the throne? Even your dark powers would not protect you!"

Prelandora's face drained. "I wasn't actually—"

"Enough. Fortunately, the next steps in our plans are getting ripe, and Cedric's birthday celebration is actually a blessing. It will give us the opportunity we seek. It will expose him for our dragon!"

Prelandora blinked. "What dragon?"

"First things, first," Ohndrea said gravely. "Do you agree with our truce, that there will be no further disrespect? There was a time when even a dog would not bark at me, Prelandora."

Prelandora stood still for several moments and didn't say anything at all. Then, suddenly, she laughed, and the tension in the air was gone. She pointed at the windowsill where the crow had been only hours before. "It's hereditary, Ohndrea; our tempers, I mean. Yes, of course, I need you. And I will behave myself if I must, but only for you. However, you have to understand, I really am finished with all of this waiting."

Ohndrea was only too happy to move on. "I understand, Prelandora, but believe me, the waiting is over. The cozy little world of Tremora is about … *TO CRUMBLE!*"

Prelandora was taken aback at Ohndrea's ferocity when she said this. Her face could not have looked more wicked or determined. *You'd think she was going to become queen herself,* Prelandora thought. Ohndrea gestured for Prelandora to take a seat. Then she ticked off the next items on her fingers, much as she had done before when describing the actions Prelandora would have to take to rule the world. "Your next step is to kidnap the White Witch Fenn's husband, use the dragon to kidnap Cedric, keep the boy safe but hidden, and then introduce your new heir to the throne—the rest of the plan stays the same: You will be on the road to ruling the world!"

Prelandora was again incredulous. *How casually Ohndrea listed the things she must do!* "But how can I accomplish these things?" she cried. "Are you talking about the Witch Fenn who killed you in the cave of the Cyclops—"

Ohndrea inhaled and hissed like an angry snake.

"I mean the witch you forced to flee Tremora, never to be heard from again?" she finished quickly.

"Yes … that Fenn," Ohndrea whispered.

"But, how can I kidnap her husband? I mean, isn't everyone dead from the Age of Magic? And *what* dragon? There are no dragons in Tremora. So how can I use one to kidnap Cedric? And introduce a new heir? I have no son, remember?"

"Am I not here to assist you? These are all parts of our new plan, Prelandora, and they have been thought out thoroughly." She again used her wand to point at her fingers one at a time. "First, as to Fenn's husband—we are going to teach you the secret of the shimmering veil. As to the dragon, let us just say it's a special gift, from me to you. And you will use it to kidnap Cedric. As to a new heir of your own? Well, we need to keep fooling the people for a just a little while longer. Then we'll …"

When Ohndrea was finished, she returned to her bottle, and Prelandora lay back on her bed with her head reeling. She had to think. It's true that there were elements to these plans that made her wonder what Ohndrea was up to, but no matter. In the end, Prelandora was going to rule Tremora! She was sure of it now. And what did she care if Ohndrea wanted her to kidnap Fenn's husband in the process? Or that Ohndrea seemed to have her own private agenda: revenge on Fenn. Why, Prelandora was even going to end up with a brand new pet: a dragon! And, of course, there was the biggest surprise of all: The shimmering veil was real, and she now knew its secret.

After this latest meeting with Ohndrea, Prelandora had set sail for Mesmer Henge. Since she would be breaking the rules of her banishment, she was traveling alone and in disguise to avoid being recognized. Of course she had her wand if there was a need to alter someone's memory or if something more permanent needed to be done. However, there was little chance she would meet any Tremorans where she was going.

As she stood at her ship's bow, she had recalled all she knew of the henge. It was a circle of seven ancient stones that sat atop a tall mesa in the middle of the desolate grass plains of central Tremora. The mesa's steep walls were every bit as formidable as those of a large castle and as effective as a moat at keeping people at bay. One treacherous, switchbacking stairway, carved into the southern face, gave the only access to the top. Legend said giants carried the huge stone monoliths on their backs all the way from the highlands of Farland and heaved them onto the mesa. Then under the direction of a powerful wizard named Mesmer, a stone circle had been was erected, forever known as Mesmer Henge. Its purpose? To read the sky.

It was a long, arduous journey by ship and horseback before Prelandora finally arrived at the base of the mesa. And the climb to the top was equally unpleasant. She avoided most physical activity (except for wielding her wand), so it was not surprising that, by the time she arrived at the standing stones, she was worn out and in a vile mood.

She was early, so she took the time to remove her hat, wig, and makeup and restore her appearance to that of Prelandora. She was about to meet Baakeer, Gatekeeper of Worlds, and wasn't going to appear still disguised as a peasant farmgirl! She then built a fire and hunkered down behind one of the giant stones to get out of the wind and cold and waited for nightfall. It couldn't come fast enough. Finally, after double-checking her notes by the light of her wand and studying the night sky, it was time. She moved to the center of the circle of stones and climbed up on a round stone plinth, shaped like a drum. Once there she took a wide stance and stood with her head and hands raised dramatically to the dark starry sky. Meteors rained down from a radiant in the Constellation of the Sword, and the wind tore through and between the seven stone monoliths, howling and blowing the witch's jet-black hair in swirls around her head. There were only six stones standing. One lay in a crumbled heap.

Ohndrea's directions had been very specific about the time, place, and conditions for Prelandora to call the gatekeeper. It's why she had to leave so soon after their meeting: There was only a brief window every month of a couple days. "This had better work," Prelandora muttered, as she clenched her wand tighter. The euphoria of the adventure was long gone; she was cold and tired and miserable. Then she took a deep breath. "Show yourself gatekeeper. A master calls!" she cried into the night.

She felt a vibration of stone on stone and caught a movement to her right. She quickly turned, crouching with wand ready, to see a door in the face of one of the giant pillars slowly swing open. A very short bearded man, dressed in a plaid shirt, suspenders, khaki shorts, hiking boots, and knitted red seed hat with flaps, stood in the opening. It could have been a dwarf in a costume.

"Well, I was beginning to think I was watching a dead door," the man said as he stepped spritely out onto the grass. He caught sight of Prelandora. "Was it you who called?" he asked.

She stayed crouching and did not answer.

"Well, I am Baakeer, the gatekeeper," the man said. "Does a witch or wizard seek someone from planet earth? If so, state your request."

Prelandora jumped down from her pedestal, marched over, and looked the man up and down haughtily. "*You* are the gatekeeper to the land of Fenn?" she said with scorn.

"At your service," the man said and then looked at his nails absently. "However, I sense an attitude. Perhaps I was mistaken in coming ..." He looked at her sideways.

"Don't be absurd. I was expecting—well, I don't know what I was expecting." Prelandora stepped back and took an authoritative posture. "If you're who you claim to be, then you're here to serve me." She suddenly pointed her wand. "Kneel before your master!"

"Sorry, don't do kneeling," the man said, stepping back and leaning casually against the stone door.

She was incredulous. "How dare you be insolent to me," she cried. Her pointing wand was shaking. "Ohndrea said you must do my bidding! Of course, I have a request."

Baakeer bowed his head slightly. "Ohndrea, whoever that is, is correct, madam. I must do your bidding, but that is not an all-inclusive directive. If you require a summoning, then I am at your service. Otherwise ..." He shrugged his shoulders and continued to study his fingernails.

She became quiet. Then she slowly paced back and forth in front of the man, eyeing him thoughtfully, as she repeatedly tapped her wand into her hand. "I could kill him," she muttered, "but Ohndrea said he was the only one who could bring forth the knight."

Baakeer was unfazed; in fact, even amused, as he nodded his head in agreement.

"However," she continued, "if I dismember him one limb at a time ..." She stopped and looked Baakeer up and down again, this time tapping her chin. "Where to begin ...?" she said.

With that, Baakeer suddenly straightened up. "All right, all right, no need to threaten. It's quite true that I am bound to meet the needs of wizards and witches at this gate between Tremora and Earth. However," he said as he pointed a finger, "you must prove to me you're who you claim to—"

The air suddenly split with lightning, sparks, and a loud explosion. When the smoke cleared, Baakeer stood with black soot covering his face and several large smoldering holes in his shirt and pants. His eyes were red and wide, and his hair was in complete disarray. And one earflap was completely burnt off his hat. "Well, all right then," he stammered. "But, you could have just produced a white rabbit or something …"

"Silence, you pile of dung!" Prelandora shouted, while lowering her wand to her side. "Wizards do not perform tricks … They are not mere magicians!" She glared a long moment at Baakeer and then, "Enough of this!" She turned and strode back to the stone plinth, climbed back up, and assumed her original position; elevated and condescending. "My request is simple, Gatekeeper," she said, once again pointing her wand at him. "There is a Tremoran knight living in your world. His name is Paladin, and he is the husband of Fenn. Find him and deliver him to me!"

Baakeer was finally, but reluctantly, subservient. "Yes, I know of this man," he murmured as he beat at the smoking red embers on his clothes with his hat. "But also know this: This door is for the passage of witches and wizards, not the summoned. Your knight will appear at the next shimmering, but you will have to visit the Stargazer's onyx gardens to find out where and when the next veil will appear. Remember—"

She hissed.

"*Remember*," he said again with emphasis, "once a person passes through the veil, he or she must stay, *willingly*. Otherwise, the person will be of very little use to you as a hero and will weaken and die rather quickly in Tremora."

"I'll take care of that," Prelandora said, and then smirked. *This gatekeeper isn't as smart as he thinks*, she thought. *Does he forget that Paladin is already a Tremoran? Ohndrea said she could go through the door and drag the man back to Tremora in chains if, in the end, that's what was needed.*

Baakeer reached inside his plaid shirt and removed a rolled parchment that grew longer and longer as he pulled it out. "So be it," he said, as he handed it to Prelandora. "Here's a map of the gardens. You'll need it to find the globe of Tremora. That sculpture will give you all the information you need. Your knight will come through the veil at the place and time indicated. It would be wise to be there when he appears." With that Baakeer exited, and the stone door grated closed behind him.

Had she the inclination, Prelandora knew she could have followed Baakeer through the stone door into Fenn's world. But to what purpose? Baakeer would do his duty and fetch Fenn's husband, and she was anxious to visit the onyx gardens. Besides, she had had enough of the insolent little beast to last a lifetime. She jumped down and hurriedly made her exit.

To her, the visit to the stargazer's gardens was even more of an imposition than visiting Mesmer Henge. It required another day of travel on horseback, which she detested, it being beneath her dignity to spend that much time on the back of a hot, sweaty animal, and even though she was going to see one of the true wonders of the world, aesthetics was not part of her makeup: She couldn't care less what was *wonderful and beautiful* about a pile of rocks. She only wanted the location of the next shimmering and then to return to her castle and make her plans.

She was, however, vaguely aware that to a more appreciative audience, the onyx gardens were spectacular. And she was not unaware of their history; she had visited them more than once with her mother who had a fascination for art *and* stargazers. The gardens were located southeast of Mesmer Henge in the middle of the same vast prairie grassland as the mesa. There, scores of huge banded quartz boulders lay strewn across the land, as if thrown by giants playing a board game. And every exposed surface of every stone was carved and polished into fantastic and whimsical shapes.

There were geometric forms from the simplest cubes, cones, orbs, and pyramids to incredibly complex snowflakes and fractals, some small and delicate, some gigantic. There were carvings of trees and delicate plants, both realistic and impressionistic. There were statues of men, women, and children in various postures; some recognizable as human, others not so much, and innumerable animals and strange creatures, all carved out of the stones that legend says fell from the sky.

Some of the sculptures were no bigger than a small knight's chest, others as big as castle turrets. And all were separated by beautifully edged and manicured paths of grass and moss and ivy, with the occasional shallow stream and stone bridge thrown in. And not one statue could be removed, no matter how much the soil was dug up around it. Even the smallest of the small seemed to weigh tons.

Stargazers had been maintaining and protecting the gardens since their first discovery, and it was to their advantage. It was an excellent place to scribe and preserve the secrets of the heavens.

Prelandora finally arrived at the gardens and tethered her horse outside the arched entranceway. She had her map rolled up in one hand and ever-present wand in the other as she pressed forward through the sculptures and statues in long flowing strides, barely noticing her surroundings. Oblivious to the wondrous colors of the chalcedony stone everywhere she turned, she saw only shades of grey.

There was just one thing on her mind: She had to find a large marble globe in all this mess! At a busy carving of birds in flight, she stopped and looked again at her map. She tapped her wand on the parchment and then looked up to her left. And there it was, at the end of a long cobbled pathway. The huge ball was sitting on a circular pedestal. "Ah ha!" she said, as she rerolled the map. She then marched down the path and looked up at the orb intently. It was set in a cupped indention that perfectly fit its polished surface. Water flowed from the paper-thin space between the globe and the base, ran across the top of the pedestal, and fell over the edges, creating a thin continuous cascade of water on all sides. The water then disappeared under a flagstone walkway that circled the entire sculpture. To one side, square stones were stacked on the walkway to form stairs that led up to a clear convex crystal lens mounted on a pole. It looked like a huge magnifying glass.

Painted on the surface of the globe was a map of the entire world, with every continent, mountain, ocean, lake, and stream labeled in spidery writing. She reached up and gave the sphere a tentative push, then yelped and stepped back as the walkway she was standing on moved at the same time in the opposite direction. She watched as both globe and walkway rotated as smoothly and silently as if floating on a bed of oil. The stone steps and crystal lens also moved with the walkway and, after circling a couple of times, came to a stop in front of her with a faint, barely noticeable click.

She saw the familiar shape of the country of Tremora facing her. She quickly dropped her map on the ground, gathered her robes around her, climbed the stairs, and looked through the crystal lens. In the crosshairs of the glass was a spot in the mountains near Fennland. "The Chasm of Dread, and not far from Spreten either! How convenient!" she exclaimed. She then retreated down the stairs and spun the globe again, just to make sure there was no mistake, and it and the stairs came to rest at exactly the same spot as before. "OK, that's the *where*," she said.

Then she climbed the stairs again and looked through the glass and noted the runes scribed beneath the spot in the crosshairs. They spelled out a year, month, date, and time. "And that takes care of the *when*," she declared triumphantly as she straightened up. She turned, descended the stairs quickly, and ran back through the garden and through the gate to mount her horse. One thing was clear: There was no time to waste. The next shimmering was almost upon her!

Chapter Thirty-three

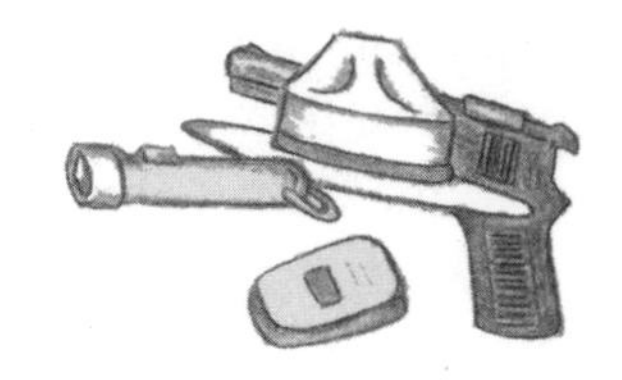

Of Paladin and Mr. Baker

If Prelandora had followed the gatekeeper through the giant stone's door, she would have seen him returning to his log cabin on Founder's Peak. On this side of the door, he was known as Mr. Baker. Once inside his small log cabin, he changed out of his ruined clothes and attended his burns over the kitchen sink. As he applied a salve and fresh aloe to his hands and arms, he thought, *That was close. I think that witch would have actually carved me up! Needs to get some control, that girl does.*

Still, he knew it was partially his fault. Being cheeky just came natural. He knew very well it wasn't his job to question or challenge the witches and wizards who came to him. In fact, he wasn't supposed to comment at all. He and his brothers had been given the sentence of *manning* the seven gates at Mesmer Henge many eons ago when the henge was first constructed. So long ago, in fact, he barely remembered the crimes that caused the punishment in the first place, something about constantly back-talking to wizards or showing disrespect to the wrong enchantress or maybe his and his brothers' habit of appropriating things that were not really theirs. Not that any of it mattered now because the end result was a lifetime sentence of finding and luring people (or aliens, depending on your point of view) to the veil as witches and wizards of Tremora requested—that or the gallows. He and his siblings chose the former.

Little did they dream that a lifetime of gatekeeping was going to be a very long time, indeed.

He was familiar with Paladin and his family, of course. Fenn had been summoned to Tremora twice already on his watch. And the second time, Fenn returned through the henge as a witch and had an unconscious Paladin in tow. But things were better for the two now. The knight recovered fully, and he and Fenn were happily married and had a son named Michael. He had kept a careful eye on them through the years, thinking there was sure to be more traffic into Tremora for *that* family. And he was right. Paladin was a park ranger in this world and luring him to the veil wouldn't be difficult at all. He'd keep an eye out for the next shimmering and then pick up the phone and dial Paladin's number. A cougar sighting should do the trick just nicely.

❦

Paladin stood looking up at the figures on horseback in front of him. A woman with long black hair was sitting on a black steed in the middle of a narrow road looking regal in a bejeweled crown and long black cape. Next to her, a man sat on a white charger with similar attire.

"Welcome back to Tremora, dragon slayer," the woman said.

Paladin didn't answer. He was still trying to establish his wits. Baker had called him early that morning to report a cougar sighting on Founder's Peak. He had set out before daybreak and was closely following the cat's tracks through the forest when he was startled by the strangest sensation. Had a wet branch fallen on his head? He felt drenched but wasn't wet at all. Then he remembered Fenn's stories of passing through the shimmering.

He looked at the woman and creased his brow. "It's been a long time since I was addressed so," he said, gravely. He looked beyond the horses and noted that the dirt road they were standing on disappeared into a forest of giant trees. He could also just catch a glimpse of a long narrow bridge in the distance. Then he studied his more immediate surroundings. He was standing very close to a sheer drop-off into a canyon to his right. He sidled sideways a couple of steps.

He looked back up at the woman in black. "But if I am truly in Tremora, as it seems and as you say," he continued, "then I must beg your pardon. It is not safe for me to be here."

"There is nothing to fear, Sir Paladin," said the woman, quickly. "Your story is well known to us, as well as that of your wife, Fenn. But know that your last time here in this world was many hundreds of years ago. So your fears are moot! This is the Age of Secrets, and black magic is banned now. Any curse you may have suffered in those days couldn't possibly still be working. And your enemies are all dead! No, Paladin, brave knight, be assured. You are being called back to Tremora because your country and king needs you desperately."

"I don't understand."

The woman leaned forward in her saddle. "Our prince has been kidnapped by a *dragon*! And no one can find him, let alone defeat the despicable worm. You must come with us, Paladin. You're our only hope!"

Paladin's face became stern, and his jaw clenched at the word dragon. "But, my lady, surely there are other knights—"

"No, listen; every knight of the realm has been sent out to find the prince, but dragons have been absent from Tremora for a very, very long time. In fact, you yourself may have killed the last one known. No one alive today has the skills necessary to find and slay the dragon and save our Cedric."

Paladin's eyes narrowed. *Could this be true? Was she talking about the witch Ohndrea's familiar, the dragon named Scraw that he slew in his last battle? And, was his curse really gone? He felt fine.* He was fully aware of the time differences associated with the two worlds. Fenn had told her stories many times. He felt a jolt of adrenalin, and old memories and thrills began to course through his body and mind: knighthood, chivalry, adventure … If he stayed and helped these people, he could return to Fenn and Michael before they knew he was even gone! And he did feel OK … in fact, invigorated … younger even. *But are things as they seem?* His cautious nature took over. *Could he trust these two? They didn't appear to be the king and queen themselves.* "Who are you, then?" he asked.

"We are the king's brother and consort," the woman answered, waving absently at her companion. The man wriggled in his seat but remained silent. "I am Prelandora, and this is Lord Pratt. We were sent by High King William to find you and bring you to Tremora Castle." She seemed anxious. "Surely, you are still duty bound, fair knight. You simply must come!" she cried.

"My lady, I don't need reminding of my duties," Paladin said sharply. Indeed, he was quite aware that, as every minute passed, he was slowly discarding the persona of a park ranger and becoming more of the Sir Paladin of his past. But he was still weighing the decision of what to do. And there was something about the king's brother that bothered him—*he's not sitting that horse very well, is he?* he thought. "I must think on this," Paladin said.

Prelandora became obviously alarmed. "No, no, I meant no offense, good knight. Of course, you know your duties. Please, please accept our apologies if I sounded too forward. But, you must know, every minute is precious! We beseech you …" Her voice trailed off, her demeanor changed, and her shoulders slumped. Then she bowed her head and seemed on the verge of tears.

But unknown to Paladin, beneath her robe, Prelandora was pointing her wand.

Suddenly, Paladin was awash with the woman's angst as if it was his own. It was very unsettling; he felt a sudden urge to do anything she asked. He took a step back as if he had just taken a blow to the stomach.

Prelandora kept her head bowed so Paladin would not see her mouth curve up into a smile.

Paladin wiped his brow as his mind became a storm of confusion. *What if Tremora really does need me and I am the king and queen's only hope? As long as I live I am still a knight of the realm. And to be called to rescue a crown prince and fight a dragon—it is what I once lived for!* He faltered. *But, would Fenn understand? Of course she would! Didn't she herself take this risk more than once? And what if it was Michael who was kidnapped? They'd both be desperate, and he knew firsthand the love you can have for a son … The king must be half-mad with worry.* In the end, not only did the arguments stand, but he again wanted to do anything that would please the woman in black. "I will come …," he said, looking up into Prelandora's eyes.

With that and without hesitation, Prelandora pulled her wand and struck the unsuspecting Paladin full in the chest with a stunning spell. Then Flugbark leapt from his horse and, with the help of three wisps who were hiding in the trees, bound the knight tightly. Paladin's hat, tranquilizing gun, flashlight, and other personal effects were all thrown into the ravine at Prelandora's orders. She wasn't sure what all that metal was but didn't want any evidence left on the trail of Paladin's capture or something he could use as a weapon. Then they loaded the unconscious knight on Flugbark's horse and left for the docks of Havenland, there to meet the ship *Abandon All Hope.*

Back in Spreten the wild cackling laugh of the ghost Ohndrea pealed through the passages and halls of the castle.

Chapter Thirty-four

Prelandora Returns to Spreten

Prelandora came out of her reverie disoriented and confused. Then she remembered. She was in the ship's cabin of the *Abandon All Hope* and sailing home to Spreten. And Fenn's boy was running free in Tremora.

Twyla stopped what she was doing, buffing Prelandora's green toenails, and looked up at her master, expectantly. Prelandora swung her feet out of Twyla's lap and dismissed the creature with a gesture of her hand. "Enough," she said. Twyla got up from her stool, scurried to her corner, changed colors, and faded into the background. But, again, she needn't have been alarmed; Prelandora was no longer angry. Her mantra had taken care of that. But she wasn't happy either. She reached for her sandals, put them on, and then sat up straight to think.

Her self-inspection of past events brought her no relief. She still couldn't understand why things were going so wrong. *Because there was so much that had gone right!* In the past two years, the kidnapping of Fenn's husband and Prince Cedric had gone brilliantly. She had to give Ohndrea her kudos: The use of the dragon to grab the boy was pure genius, and the ensuing chaos was wondrous to see. And she was more of her old self again, growing more powerful every day. She had an army and spies, a ship and a castle, a dragon and a prince …

However, she had to admit, one of Ohndrea's original plans didn't work out quite so well: She miscarried and lost her baby soon after Cedric's birth. Was this the beginning of all her troubles? No, she didn't think so. *Obviously, Pratt's genes are not up to muster,* she immediately reasoned, and Ohndrea had agreed. "There will be plenty of mates to choose from once you take over Tremora," Ohndrea assured her on the morning after the mishap. "We just have to fool those in the castle into believing you still have an heir on the way; a good pillow will take care of that. And a prudent use of one of your shape-changers should keep the ruse alive until the right time to introduce a real heir. Then, in with the new, out with the old," she said with a snap of her fingers.

And so far, Flugbark's disguise had worked as planned. While disguised as Myrdain, he was never allowed close enough to the people of the court to be examined too closely; he was usually only seen at a distance on horseback or clothed in concealing garments while accompanying her to public functions.

Then, not long after her visit to Tremora Castle to demand her son Myrdain be named heir to the throne, Ohndrea sat Prelandora down and warned her against something she had no knowledge of before. "Fear not, Prelandora. We are very close. At the summer solstice you will move into Tremora Castle. In only a few years you will be running the country. There are really only two things that you must concern yourself with. First, remember, you must continue to *feed the black magic!* Stay aggressive and grow stronger at every turn."

"Yes, I'm quite aware of this, Ohndrea. I only had a problem when I was stagnating, remember? Waiting for you and your new plans! But, what of this second *concern,* as you call it?"

"There is the danger of the secret of the veil being discovered by the king, and Fenn's son being called into Tremora. The son of Fenn is the only one who can ever defeat our dragon! He must never enter Tremora."

There she was again—the witch *Fenn*; *Fenn's* husband; *Fenn's* son … *Was this the reason things were going awry? Was this obsession of Ohndrea's causing all of this trouble?*

It was the next day that she received the news that the king and the wizard Megan were calling the son of Fenn through the veil.

The warnings rang loud and clear in her head. Yes, everything Ohndrea warned against was coming true: She was getting weaker because her magic did not like failure. And not only was Fenn's whelp here in Tremora (the very thing Ohndrea had said must never happen), but he was proving very difficult to capture or kill. And now, perhaps even worse, it looked as if she wasn't going to prevent the boy from attending the wizard's gathering!

No—things were not going according to Ohndrea's plans now at all. They were going terribly wrong. But rather than succumb to fear, Prelandora got angry. *It wasn't her fault!* She'd done everything asked of her, and more. "Ohndrea got me into this mess, so she'd better get me out," she said out loud. "After all, they need me to succeed as much as I need them!" Yes, it was once again time to talk to great-great-great-granny.

❧

The trip home was otherwise uneventful. Prelandora didn't show her head to the crew again until the ship was docked at Spreten castle. She then swept down the gangplank with Twyla in tow, climbed a long series of wooden steps, and disappeared through the guarded entrance of a round tower in the castle wall. Flugbark and the rest of the entourage were left to their own devices.

Later that night, the moon cast a strikingly bright reflection on the waters of the Spreten Sea, illuminating the frothy foam of breaking waves crashing on the black sands of Sitka Island. Prelandora sat on a driftwood log with eyes wide as saucers and watched the boiling cauldron in front of her. This was not the first time she had gone through these preparations, but tonight everything was taking more effort. Ohndrea's spell book lay open in her lap, and she was hunched over so her elbows could keep the pages from turning in the on-shore wind. She held a flickering candle in one hand and her wand in other. Various live creatures, both hairy and slimy, had been added to the iron pot over the past several hours, culminating in the sacrifice of one of Prelandora's very own creatures: a wisp. She couldn't have cared less.

Twyla and Riella were stirring the lumpy liquid in the pot with long wooden paddles, and they were struggling; the potion was reaching the consistency of a mud bath. Prelandora motioned for them to stop. She looked up at the moon, at the cauldron, and sniffed the air. The conditions were perfect. She then peered down between her arms and moved the candle to see better.

"Lamia Ohndrea defero obtestor per ego," she chanted three times in a low guttural voice. She looked up at the cauldron with eyes wide and expectant. But the pot just simmered and belched rudely. "Now what?" she said, exasperated. This is really getting annoying. "Can anything else go wrong?" She looked back down at the pages of her spell book. "Lamia Ohndrea defero obtestor per ego!" This time her shrill voice pierced the night.

Suddenly the liquid in cauldron came alive. Huge bubbles rose and burst, wet and oily, and a green vapor started to form on its surface. The sisters jumped back, but Prelandora only smiled. "Finally!" she said. They watched as the vapor thickened and grew and cascaded over the lip of the pot to land on the black sand and rush toward the sea.

Prelandora stood up and made a quick gesture with her wand. A thin tentacle formed from the creeping fog and attached itself to the wand's tip. Still smiling, Prelandora slowly waved her arm back and forth, and the entire body of green stopped its movement to the water. Then it reversed direction, formed a cloud, and followed the witch's every movement like the mesmerized head of a swaying cobra.

Meanwhile, Twyla and Riella retrieved a two-handled glass flagon with a long narrow neck and rushed to the witch's side. Grasping the jug with both their hands, they hoisted it high in the air between them. Prelandora pointed, and the fog obediently entered the opening in the top of the container and filled it to overflowing. The sisters then lowered the jug gingerly to the sand and quickly retreated. Prelandora noted their behavior absently as she took a large glass stopper from a pocket in her robes and plugged the bottle closed.

At that moment a huge wave crashed on shore, and the water raced up the beach, just reaching the flames beneath the cauldron for the first time. Steam rose and the fire spit angrily. In a couple hours, the contents of the cauldron would be swept to sea, and the pot scoured clean by the swirling sand and water. Prelandora gave yet another satisfied smile. Any remnants of the black magic she so recently wielded would soon be gone. It wouldn't be wise to leave evidence that she was still practicing the dark arts when her return to Tremora was so near. She abruptly turned and, with her reptilian assistants carrying the precious potion, retreated back to Spreten Castle.

Once safely ensconced in her boudoir, Prelandora sat down on the edge of her bed with the freshly brewed flagon on the floor in front of her. Twyla and Riella had retreated earlier to another part of the castle; the green potion made them uneasy. *Was it the sacrificing of the wisp that always upset them? Did they think they themselves might someday end up in the pot?* At first, Prelandora was amused at the thought but then sobered. She remembered why she was here: She had problems.

She leaned back on the bed, elbows locked, and looked blankly into space. Again, exhausted. She was experiencing episodes of weakness and loss of power she could no longer ignore. At first they were just annoyances, occurring mostly when a plan went awry; she would throw a tantrum and then spend hours before she felt herself again. But, other things were taking more effort now as well. The casting of the spell this evening was a perfect example: It didn't even work the first time! It was no mystery, though, what was happening. Didn't Ohndrea warn her? She looked angrily at the container of green. *But it wasn't my fault! It was Ohndrea's plans that weren't working!*

She stood up, moved to the window, and looked out at the dark Spreten Sea. Again she asked herself, "How did I get into this mess? And how do I unravel this hairball?"

A knock at the door made her turn. *What now?* "Come!" she said.

Riella opened the door slowly and stuck her head in the room. "He speaksss again, my lady," she said meekly.

Prelandora gestured impatiently for her servant to enter. "Tell me!"

Riella took one small step into the room and looked first at the witch and then warily at the glass bottle.

"Tell me, Riella. You have nothing to fear. Unless you waste more of my time, that is."

The reptilian took a deep breath, bowed her head, and looked at a spot on the floor in front of her, all the while licking her face furiously. "Glubscald goesss to Fennland. It'sss all he sssays, my queen."

"Glubscald?" It wasn't really a question. Prelandora knew very well who Glubscald was. But, why is it going to Fennland? Riella had nothing else to say so Prelandora dismissed her with a quick gesture of her hand after ordering her to continue monitoring her husband. Once the door closed, she went back to the window and stood with her head raised and tilted, the better to think.

Glubscald was Flugbark's twin and perhaps Prelandora's most valued creature; he was her mole in King William's court. His specialty was assuming the role of any number of nobles under King William to gain inside information. And his disguises were nearly perfect, even to the king's guards. Thus, she rarely used him as an assassin as she did Flugbark. He was more valuable as her master spy.

Glubscald was at the secret midnight meeting between the king and his followers, disguised as Lord Goth. In this case it *was* necessary to use Glubscald as an assassin; otherwise, there would have been two Lord Goths at the meeting. The information he gathered was invaluable; it's how she learned that the king had solved the mystery of the veil and was calling Fenn's son to Tremora.

But, what was this latest prattling by Pratt? Glubscald goes to Fennland? Wasn't he on the way to Mesmer Henge, still disguised as Lord Goth? She creased her brow in puzzlement. Then it came to her: *The location has changed! They have changed their plans to protect the boy.*

It was time to call Ohndrea.

֍

The heated arguments were over. Prelandora and the ghost finally came to an impasse on who was to blame for all of their failures. In the end, it was Flugbark, Malif, Kalib, the dragon, the weather—anyone and anything other than themselves.

Ohndrea was again advising Prelandora. "Your strength wanes because your power wanes. I warned you! The use of black magic has its price. And now you've pressed your luck again with another shape-changer. It may have stayed incognito in the castle, but it will never avoid detection in that group of wizards, no matter how good it is!"

Prelandora remained silent. It galled her that Ohndrea was right about her shape-changers—especially Flugbark. His flugups were prodigious! She had to admit Flugbark was not Ohndrea's responsibility. And now, even Glubscald was putting her dream in danger. She wanted to put them both back in the pot. "What do you suggest?" she asked.

"You need to get to that meeting, Prelandora. Before another disaster happens. You need to take care of Glubscald. And have a look at that boy. Perhaps you'll have an epiphany. And haven't they unwittingly made it easier for you, by moving their meeting to Fennland? It's a neutral country! Your expulsion has no relevance there. And you have nothing to fear. We've left no footprints. Nothing yet that's happened can lead back to you. But, you have little time. There is only one way to get there so quickly. The dragon! But, you can't be seen together. They must never tie you to the beast. It would destroy our plans entirely. It won't be the black magic that will ensure your demise. The whole world will be against you if it finds out it was you who kidnapped Cedric! But have heart. All is not lost. In just a couple of months, your fake offspring will be named heir to the throne, and you will take up residence in their very home. No, we still have hope. And the plans we are making this evening will make you stronger. I can feel the black magic's excitement. You'll see. So, why not do a spying of your own?"

Chapter Thirty-five

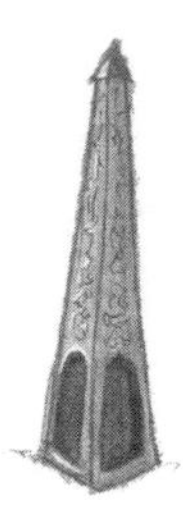

The Obelisk

The sun rose on day nine of Michael's adventure in Tremora. They all stood at the entrance to the bridge: Michael, Tracker, Nova, Pashtook, Joshtook, and Teetook. Joshtook's head was bandaged, and Teetook's hand and arm were in a splint. Pashtook held the troll's bag of gold and precious stones.

"I've taken back my three emeralds, Pashtook, but you'll need what's left in that bag," Tracker said. "High King William will need your services again, I'm sure. Use the money to organize what loyal followers he has left. You'll want to be ready when he calls."

"But what about the troll?" Pashtook asked. Won't it just come back again?"

"I don't think so. That chasm is extremely deep, and it'll take a long time for it to get itself together … pun intended. That head either broke into a thousand pieces, or it's floating out to sea on the Cartook River. Either way, it would have to want to come back up here pretty badly. But the real answer probably lies here." He bent over and picked up ankle irons that were still chained to the bridge. "This troll wasn't working willingly for the witch; it was her prisoner and slave. I don't think it's going to rush back up here just to be chained up again. No, you won't be seeing this troll again for a long, long time.

"However, if it is true that there is another troll at the bridge much farther north of here, then your duty is clear. I've made you captain, and you're a servant of the king now. Use your men, your wiles, and knowledge of the trolls' secrets to defeat it and rid these mountains of these tolls and trolls forever. And especially remember, trolls have to sleep sometime and 'a troll's no good without its head'! Earn your bars, Pashtook. And if all else fails, you can always purchase a camelop! Good luck. The adventure continues."

Pashtook saluted, and he and his brothers turned and disappeared into the woods. Then, Tracker, Michael, and Nova passed single file between the torches and were immediately reminded that this was no ordinary bridge they were crossing. Without warning, it widened enough to accommodate all three of them walking abreast. This was especially welcome to Nova since she didn't like heights anymore than boats, and the swaying of the bridge was already sending her senses reeling. They continued forward with Nova walking gingerly in the middle. About half way across the chasm, Michael told them that the story about the bridge having no supports wasn't true at all. "There're more ropes supporting this bridge than cables on the Golden Gate," he said.

Tracker stopped and looked at Michael curiously. "Whatever are you talking about?" He looked side to side and even went and leaned over the edge of the bridge. "I don't see any ropes *or* cables," he said. Then, he turned to Michael thoughtfully. "You must be seeing through some false reality again. What do you see exactly, and what is that obscure reference to a 'Golden Gate' you just used?"

Michael turned red. "Sorry. Of course you haven't been to San Francisco. The Golden Gate Bridge is famous in my world." He waved vaguely behind him. "I admit I didn't see them at first, but don't you see those huge statues at each end of the bridge anchoring all those ropes? They're holding the whole thing up!"

"Nova?" asked Tracker.

"Nope."

"Michael you're—"

"Yeah, I know. I'm special." Michael laughed. Then he again pointed behind him. "Look, giant statues of a king and queen are back there, and two warriors, a man and a woman, are in front of us. Ropes are wrapped around their shoulders and waists, and they're sculpted to look like they're holding them with their hands …" He stopped and his eyes opened in surprise.

"What is it?" Tracker drew his knife and raised his staff. He looked in all directions but saw nothing.

"Tracker, I think one of the statues is moving!"

Tracker crouched, and Nova snorted. They both stared ahead but saw nothing. "What's happening now, Michael? We can't see what you see!"

Michael leant forward and looked intently. "It's the female warrior. She's definitely motioning for us to continue on."

Nova danced nervously. Michael took her bridle and gave her a reassuring pat on the nose. "I think she's indicating it's safe to cross. Somehow I feel we should trust her, Nova. She's actually smiling."

"Is it a friendly smile or an evil smile, Michael? I don't want us to end up down there with the troll."

Michael looked back at the king and queen. "I think these were very noble people in real life," answered Michael slowly. "I don't think they would have harmed us, but these statues certainly could if they all came to life and yanked on those ropes. Best we hurry."

As they exited the bridge, Michael looked up at the smiling statue and was struck by its familiarity. However, the feeling was fleeting. The head quickly turned and the smile vanished. It was once again a statue of a fierce female warrior.

"Tracker, who were these people?"

"I think you may have answered that question *and* the mystery of who built this bridge yourself, Michael. From your description, they could very well be the king and queen of ancient Farland and two of their knights. I mentioned them in the story of the wazalops, remember? I'm guessing that was a statue of your mother that smiled on us, Michael."

Michael looked back in wonder.

"This bridge must have protected their kingdom from enemies in the Age of Magic. Obviously, some of that magic is still working. We are, after all, on the way to Fennland. I think we've just been approved for passage."

They hadn't traveled far before Tracker again motioned for them to stop. Since they'd passed another night without sleep, he recommended they rest until noon, but with a watch this time. They rested and ate and set out again. That evening around a campfire, Tracker said, "We'll be out of these mountains tomorrow and reach the ruins of Farland Castle by evening. That's where we'll spend the night. From there it's only a couple hours to the wazalops."

Early the next morning, they dropped down out of the mountains and back into the lowlands of Charn. By mid-morning, they reached a fork in the trail. "The way to the left leads to Tremora Castle, the permanent residence of the king and queen. It's the northern route that skirts the Asyr Desert," Tracker said. He pointed his staff to the right. "However, we'll be taking this road. It leads directly north to Gondalor and Fennland."

Hours later, they came upon a tall stone structure standing directly in their path. It was shaped like a narrow tapering pyramid and was covered in carvings and hieroglyphics. There was a plain wooden door in the base on each side. "This marks the spot where the borders of Gondalor, Charn, and Fennland meet," Tracker said. "Each door opens into a different country, and each face of the pyramid has glyphs and writing that give a history of that country's wars." He shook his head sadly, "As you can see there was plenty to write about."

Tracker pointed his staff at the door in front of him. "Obelisks like these are called Pyramids of Giving. This one has been here for hundreds of years and is one of four such structures located in the farthest reaches of Tremora. Originally, their function was to collect alms for the poor. However, today the king also uses them to gather information about traffic at or near Tremora's borders.

"What's unique about this particular outpost is it is also used by the wizards: They made it the only possible entrance to Fennland at the beginning of the Age of Secrets. You can't get to Fennland without going through that door unless you are a wizard, witch, or border guard or have their permission. If you attempt to enter anywhere else along the country's borders, you're blocked by an invisible wall or the Chasms of Dread.

"We'll have to enter one at a time," said Tracker. "You go first, Michael, and I'll follow with Nova. Remember, she is just a dumb pack animal to the rest of the world. Inside, you'll meet one of the king's collectors. He won't harm you. In fact, he's incapable of violence. He'll merely ask you to donate something of value for the less fortunate people of the land." Tracker pulled on his pipe. "Over time, a visit to an obelisk has come to be expected of all Tremorans; kind of a rite of passage. Everyone is expected to visit at least once in his or her lifetime and donate to the poor. But, there's nothing to fear."

Michael entered the door and found the inside of the obelisk far larger than expected. The three stone block walls rose at angles and disappeared into the darkness high above. The floor was tiled and polished. To each side, he could just make out the doors leading to Gondalor and Fennland. Then he noticed a tiny man sitting cross-legged on a small square of carpet in the middle of the floor. Michael cautiously stepped closer. The man was dressed in a simple sleeveless grey garment and was bathed in a blue triangle of light that fell from above like a stage spotlight. The man's long stringy hair glowed silver even in the blue light, and his eyes were large and moist. His arms rested on his knees, and his hands were extended palms up. A silk bag dangled by a pull string from each hand. Startled, Michael realized that the man wasn't completely corporal but, rather, slightly transparent.

"I am the northern collector," the man said in a lilting voice. He looked straight forward, unblinking.

Was he blind? Michael wondered.

"Your journey to Fennland was foretold, boundary traveler. Your path leads that way." He shifted one eye to his left and back. "But first, what will you give up for the less fortunate of this world?"

Michael went into a mini-panic. He was so awed by the light, the huge eyes, the darkness … He stuck his staff awkwardly between crossed legs and patted his clothes with both hands. "Alms? Oh, yeah, of course, I forgot. Err …" *What do I have that anyone would want?* He thought of his knives, especially the gift from his father; he still had some food that his mother packed; food folks in this world wouldn't recognize; his staff, a couple of Y-sticks, some of Tracker's gook, a stuffed fluster bird … *Oh, yeah, wait a minute.*

The man continued to gaze unfocused into space.

Michael plunged his hands into his pockets and found the eggs of the fluster bird. He'd forgotten all about them. But suddenly, he felt unusually possessive. *What did the shopkeeper say? They were full of precious stones or something … Wasn't finding one of these like hitting the lottery?* And then he also remembered: *These were his first very own Tremoran secrets! Why should he just give them up to a complete stranger, and, who knew what they were really worth?* He started to remove his hands.

The collector remained still and stoic.

"*Michael!*" His mother's voice called loudly in his head. "*You must always follow your heart; always follow your heart, Michael …*" He saw her clearly standing in the path. He hesitated. Then a sort of clarity washed over him. *Why am I here anyway? It's not to get rich, that's for sure. What good were precious stones or wealth when all I want is to find my father and return home? Oh, and maybe rescue a prince along the way …*

He also thought about the plight of the poor. *Who better to benefit if these stones are valuable? "There but for the grace of God go I!"* He'd always been taught that the poor were mostly unfortunate victims—that anyone could end up in their shoes; if they were lucky enough even to have shoes!

He slowly removed his hands from his pockets and held one fist out to the old man. Then he opened his hand to show the three dull white eggs. They seemed to glow even more in the darkness of the obelisk. The man fairly gasped. The collector then turned and locked eyes with Michael.

Nope, not blind …

"Please, I will only be a moment," the collector whispered. Then his body faded, and he was gone.

Only days earlier, Michael would have been shocked to see someone disappear before his very eyes. But now, with all of his experiences in Tremora, he expected the unexpected. He looked around the inside of the pyramid impatiently, hoping that the collector would return soon. If he was going to give the eggs away, he wanted to get it over with. His arguments against keeping the stones were starting to sound less convincing.

"You are aware of what these are and of their value, Michael?" The thought came to Michael just as the old man's image reappeared.

"So, you're a Grock too," Michael said, unimpressed. "And, you also know my name." Then Michael's frustration, mixed with his new desire to keep the stones after all, rushed to the surface. This was all too familiar. *Everyone knows who I am, yet I'm hardly ever told anything…* "Yes, of course, I'm aware of their value," he snapped. "What? You don't want them?" He closed the hand holding the eggs and put it to his chest. "I'm sure I can keep them or give them to someone else." His anger was barely in check. But to his consternation, another uninvited image rushed into his head. It was Tralana this time, and she was stomping her foot yet again! *Now, what did I do?* he thought, exasperated.

The old man sat unfazed. He became more visible. "I meant no insult. You're not of this world, after all, and perhaps were unaware," he said, patiently. "And yes, we *are* both Grocks. All collectors are, as are most boundary travelers."

Michael felt justly rebuked and blushed. *Is there something in the air in Tremora? I haven't lost my temper this much in my whole life! How could I have been so rude?* And he was still dealing with the angry image of Tralana. He held out his open hand again with the eggs. "I'm sorry, sir," he said. "No offense taken or given. Please … these are for the poor."

The collector looked at the stones in Michael's outstretched hand and then into Michael's eyes. "You have made a difficult, yet important choice, traveler. And yes, there just might be something in the air here! You have once again proven yourself worthy. Well done."

The collector assumed his distant gaze again. "Now, please put one of the eggs in the bag in my right hand, Michael. Your gift is quite generous. However, we feel you should keep the other two for yourself. All gifts have a purpose, and you may yet need these eggs in your adventure. By the way, it is best you tell no one where you found these. It would put the few remaining wild fluster birds in great danger. Please continue to keep their secret."

"'We feel'?"

"Yes, we. I am but one of four that make up a much larger whole. We project this image for your benefit. Our function is simple: We report to kings. You might, after contemplation, see that much useful information can be derived from each visitor to the obelisks. We pass this intelligence on to the ruling monarch, for example, who and how many people are entering or leaving Tremora, how generous was a person's gift, who is armed and how well. You have passed tests before, Michael, and this is only the latest; there will be more. Again, well done! Please be safe on your journey." The gatekeeper then motioned toward the door to Fennland with his left eye.

Michael turned to go.

"*Wait, Michael. You have forgotten to take* your *gift!*" The gatekeeper held out the bag in his left hand.

"What gift?"

"Ah, the best part of it all," the collector said. "Generosity is not always rewarded in life, Michael. No one who visits an obelisk is ever told that they'll receive something in return for their offering. It's another secret of Tremora. You're expected to keep this secret safe. If a person gives something of him or herself, expecting a reward in return, then the gesture is hollow and dead. These obelisks bestow that important lesson on the citizens of Tremora. If you give generously and from the heart, never expecting praise or thanks, then and only then will you realize the power of that selfless act; the wonders those gifts will return to you will be truly amazing. The kings of old established these monuments for just this purpose. And their lesson will hopefully guide you in your life's journey."

Michael reached out and put his hand in the proffered silk bag. He felt nothing. Was this a joke? He looked at the collector. The old man watched Michael with great interest, but stayed silent. Michael removed his hand. To his surprise, a thick silver ring now adorned his pointing finger. He held it up to his eyes and looked at it closely. It was inlaid with a circle of ivory. Delicate patterns were carved in bas-relief on its surface and bordered with emeralds and thin rings of turquoise. The patterns swirled in a clockwise direction and glowed with a warm inner light.

The gatekeeper shook the bag again at Michael. With some hesitation he reached in the bag for a second time and felt a wad of dry … what? Grass? He grabbed the mass and pulled it out. It was actually a ball of thick fish netting complete with small weights and pieces of cork sewn into the mesh. Michael looked questioningly at the gatekeeper.

"Even we don't know from when or where these gifts come. We do know that these receptacles are very old and from the Age of Magic. Your gifts are perhaps also from that era. Other than that, we can only guess that they'll be useful in your travels."

The old man motioned with his left eye. Michael bowed and exited through the wooden door to Fennland.

❧

When Tracker and Nova saw Michael emerge from the right side of the obelisk, Tracker pushed open the wooden door in front them, and they entered.

"Welcome, Tracker!" "*Welcome Nova!*" hailed the collector. As with Michael, the man sat on his bit of carpet staring into space without looking at either one directly.

Nova was so surprised at being greeted by thought that she immediately sat down on her haunches and stared dumbfounded at the seated figure in front of her. "*H … hello …*"

"A Grock cannot appear undetected in front of us, Nova," the man explained. "This is very fortunate for you, since, without our permission, only a dumb animal can pass the threshold into Fennland unharmed."

Tracker's face blanched when he realized what this meant.

The gatekeeper addressed Tracker. "Fear not, warrior, more people than just you have the safety of your quest in their hands. But, yes, Nova could have been in great danger. The wizard's spell is very powerful. It would never have taken Nova for a dumb animal. Should she have entered Fennland without our consent, she would have ended up quite dumb; *struck* dumb that is."

Tracker turned to Nova. "I'm sorry, Nova. I had no idea. Good grief! Keeping your special gift secret was a strategy to keep you safe, not get you killed."

"*The adventure continues, Tracker!*"

Tracker smiled at Nova's wit and patted her nose gratefully.

"Be assured, Nova was never in any real danger. Our ability to sense other Grocks is for just this purpose. Besides, the king gave you both safe passages long before you arrived. Be calmed."

The old man changed the subject. "Now, you must be anxious to see your companion again, Tracker. I look forward to seeing you both on your return. And I see you still wear the belt given you so long ago. We trust it is still serving you well."

Tracker recognized the familiar banter. It was the same every time he passed through the obelisk, and he knew the next question coming. After all, it had been the old man's job since the earliest of times.

"Though only required once, before I let you go, would you again like to donate to the less fortunate of Tremora?" the collector finished.

"But of course!" Tracker said. "Don't I always? Here's a fresh batch of Bonzo Bugger Gook; easily one of the most valuable gifts I've ever given. Always useful, always useful." Tracker put a corked section of bamboo in the only silk bag held by the old man. Rewards for giving were only meted out once.

"Travel in peace," said the collector. And, just as he did with Michael, he indicated the door to Fennland by shifting his left eye.

Chapter Thirty-six

Corak and Fenn Castle

Michael was looking intently at the hieroglyphics on the Fennland side of the obelisk when Tracker and Nova came through its door.

"I trust the gatekeeper wasn't too hard on you, Michael?" Tracker asked.

"No, no, not at all—though I apparently passed some kind of test. It's a little vague now that I'm out in the fresh air again. But anyway, I have gifts!" He held up the net with one hand and showed off the ring with the other.

"Yes, I know," Tracker said. "It's part of everyone's first ordeal, Michael. But, I think the gifts were part of a secret that you've been asked to keep."

Michael turned red. "Well, yes, but, I mean, it's only you guys. You just came through the obelisk too, and …" He looked from one to the other. They weren't buying it. Seeing no sympathy, he gave up. "Okay, I get it. I'm sorry. I'll remember. But surely we can trust each other."

"Yes, but the problem is … who *else* might be listening?" The voice came from the trees above. They all looked up just as a young man with green skin like Tracker's dropped lightly to the ground in front of them.

Nova leapt and turned to expose her lethal hind legs, and Michael went for his knife. Tracker, however, merely smiled and held up his hands. "Hold on, you two," he said.

The stranger straightened up and gave a formal military salute. Tracker returned the gesture and then strode forward and embraced the man in a warm welcome.

"Michael, let me introduce you to Corak, captain of the border guards from Gondalor."

Corak took a bow. "Welcome to Fennland, traveler."

Michael returned the knife to its sheath and bowed back awkwardly.

"And do you recognize this noble beast, Corak?"

Nova turned to face them, and Corak walked up and stroked her muzzle. "Of course I do, sir. Even in this disguise. Have I not been watching over her for you these past years? It's Novalena." He reached into his pocket and took out a handful of something lumpy and held it out to her.

"*Why it's the brown-sugar man. I recognize him now. He comes to my races and finds me and gives me treats.*" She readily tongued the candy from Corak's palm.

"That particular task has come to an end, Corak," Tracker said. "Nova is now free and traveling with us."

"So I've heard. I'll miss watching her for you, sir. And I'm especially disappointed that I missed her last race."

"I'm sure. And I think your purse missed her as well."

Corak merely smiled sheepishly.

"It's of no consequence, Corak. It was an off duty assignment, after all, and you handled it admirably. Now, I trust your other charge is healthy and well?"

"Yes, sir. Waz awaits you and is anxious to see you."

"Very good. We're on our way to meet him. So, you're relieved of that duty also. But both of those orders would have been rescinded by dispatch, and since there is obviously no need to issue the wizard's warning to us, why are you here, Corak?"

"Megan's orders, sir. I'm to accompany you to the castle. There has been a change in plans."

"Lead on then, lad. It'll be dark soon enough. We'd planned on spending the night at the castle, anyway."

"Good, sir. I've prepared shelter."

They followed Corak in single file. The path led steadily upwards. After a couple hours, they reached the timberline where the barren, windswept land of Fennland opened up before them. They stopped to rest and took in their surroundings. The trail continued on, winding its way up a long gentle slope through random outcrops of boulders and sparse foliage. In the distance, blackened and crumbling ramparts of an old castle stood out starkly against multicolored foothills. And beyond them, loomed incredibly large the majestic snowcapped Seven Sage Mountains.

"The ruins of Farland castle," Corak said, pointing at the collapsed stone walls for Michael's benefit. He then pointed back over their heads. "And behind you, one of the most beautiful sights in the world!" They turned and saw a spectacular panorama of ocean, forests, islands, mountains, and desert; all gilded by the setting sun.

Michael's gaze wandered from the view to the castle ruins to the mountain peaks. His mother once lived here, he now knew, and fought battles in these very hills and defended those very walls. Some of the carvings on the obelisk depicted her in her glory. "Thank you," he whispered.

The others looked at him. "Just a habit. My family often gives thanks to the wonders of our lives." He then turned to Tracker. "What happened to my mother's people, the people of Farland, Tracker? How did their castle get destroyed?"

"I'm afraid it's an all too familiar tale from the Age of Magic, Michael; from the time of Fenn's second visit to Tremora. In those terrible times, a dangerous form of magic was released on the world. At first it appeared as nothing more than an enhancement to simple illusion and conjuring. But then a magician named Rostoff started performing feats of magic that were far beyond smoke and mirrors or sleight of hand: He was casting spells, and the magic he used was black."

Corak looked at Tracker, anxious to move on. Tracker nodded. "The short version of the story is this, Michael: Rostoff found the black magic by accident; became consumed with its power; was tortured for his secret by a coven of witches; and then they themselves became very powerful, indeed. Imagine thirteen witches and warlocks ruling the world! But they soon found they couldn't contain their newfound power any more than Rostoff could: It spread like a plague. At one time, virtually every Tremoran could cast some kind of spell, and everything from the simplest argument to major wars was resolved with the use of black magic; and there were many wars. Then, not surprisingly, infighting among the witches and warlocks also became rampant. The black magic had a life of its own; the more it was used, the more powerful and evil it became.

"Of course, power often corrupts, especially in the hands of the non-discerning, and the people of Tremora came close to annihilating everything and everybody, even without the help of the gang of witches and warlocks. In the end, white wizards, with the help of Fenn, defeated the enchantress Ohndrea, the most powerful witch in the coven, and found and destroyed the original source of the scourge; but by then most of Tremora was in ruin. Fennland castle was destroyed by a warlock who was completely mad. It's one of the stories inscribed on the obelisk."

Michael began to speak but was interrupted by Corak. "Best we continue on," he said, pointing to storm clouds gathering in the east.

Tracker sniffed the wind and estimated the distance to the ruins. He patted Corak on the back. "You're right. We'll just make it if we leave now."

As they neared the castle, the path widened and became an overgrown cobblestone road. Darkness fell quickly, but there was no need for torches; massive lightning strikes tore the sky in shorter and shorter intervals. They sprinted the last hundred yards to the remains of the gatehouse as thunderclaps boomed and shook the ground.

"There's no protection for Nova here," shouted Corak over the din. "Follow me. I've made a shelter across the way. We can build a fire."

He led them across the outer courtyard and through a gaping opening in the inner wall. They made another short sprint across the inner bailey to a wide carved archway and then up a flight of stairs to a large chamber room: the castle's great hall. A long stone table ran the length of the room. It was fairly intact compared with the rest of the rubble. High-backed chairs were overturned and strewn across the floor or lay smashed and crumbled as if struck by a powerful blow. The hall was bordered on three sides with broken arches and columns; very little of the roof remained. They no sooner arrived than the lightning subsided, and it became very dark.

Corak untied his pack and removed two small torches. He handed one to Tracker and then lit them both with a small flint and steel. "Straight ahead, but be careful. There's another level beneath us, and there are openings in the floor." They wound their way through the rubble along one wall toward a lean-to made from animal skins on a raised dais at the far end of the room. They arrived just in time. The sky opened up and the rain fell in torrents.

There was plenty of room for all of them under the shelter. They stayed relatively dry because they were situated under a part of the roof that was still intact. However, the wind was blowing and swirling, and it was wet and icy cold. Tracker and Corak wedged their torches into cracks in the stones, and Michael removed Nova's bundles. Tracker went through the supplies and found food and blankets for all of them, including Nova, while Corak built a small fire from kindling. It was just big enough to keep their hands and feet warm. Michael put on his parka.

"It's raining too hard to build a bigger fire out in the open," Corak said. "We'll take care of that later." The three then hunkered down with their backs against the stone wall, their hoods up and blankets wrapped tightly around them. Nova knelt into a sleeping position and also leaned against the wall for support.

It rained far into the night, and then the storm abruptly broke and disappeared. The moon cast highlights on every wet surface of the ruins, and stars sparkled so bright Michael felt he could easily reach out and pluck them one by one off the black velvet background of the sky. They found themselves all awake at the same time; probably awakened by the complete silence that followed the chaos of the storm. Michael marveled sleepily at the shooting stars while Corak rose and built a bigger fire. Nova was the first to drop back off to sleep, followed closely by Michael and Tracker. They felt safe within the walls of the castle and welcomed a full night's rest.

Corak waited till they were all sound asleep and then scribbled a note on a small piece of parchment. He set it near Tracker's head, under a stone. He then shouldered his gear and quietly struck out across the cracked and broken floor, disappearing through an archway into the darkness.

Chapter Thirty-seven

An Unexpected Change in Plans

A castle in its glory is majestic and powerful; a castle defeated and in ruins assaults the senses. Michael opened his eyes slowly. He didn't stir. He just sat looking across the ruins of the great hall, now lit by the early morning sun. He was expectant. He awoke feeling the same sensation he had felt at the veil and on the bridge—he felt magic. His mind began to fill with vague images of battle and the sounds of men at war. He soon realized without knowing how that he was being shown the castle's last days—the desperate last stand of its defenders and the ruthless efficiency of its victors. Blood ran between every cobblestone. And then, his mind's eye began to reconstruct the ruins: the bastions, the curtain walls, the arcading—he reset every boulder in its proper place. There was a roof on the great hall now, and regal processions filed in, and its royal members took seats at the long table or on the raised dais. It was a happier time. He saw magnificent banquets and heard music and watched entertainment as if he was an observer at the royal table. Then the images suddenly changed, and he was again watching scenes of war and hearing voices whispering tales of court intrigue; snippets of secrets hundreds of years old. Now, vivid images of torture and poor souls chained to walls in dungeons …

A loud snort brought him out of his trance. The images were gone. He turned to Nova whose eyes were wide open. "Did you see it too, Nova?"

"Yes, Michael. It was horrible. I think the walls were talking."

"They certainly were," Tracker answered. Nova had instinctively included Tracker in her thoughts. He was also sitting with his back to the wall and staring across the hall, trance-like. "You broke the spell though, Nova. But there wasn't much more to tell; just more blood and gore. I've seen this story before. I had forgotten that visitors to Farland castle are often shown its violent history in this way. It's the castle trying to ensure immortality. After all, nothing is completely dead until the last memory of its story is finally gone."

Tracker noticed the small stone and parchment on the ground in front of him. "Did anyone see our friend leave this morning?" he asked, as he looked at the note curiously. Michael and Nova hadn't even noticed that Corak was gone.

"It says we are to wait here until Corak returns. He is running another errand for Megan … hmm. And we're not to be alarmed if other visitors arrive while he's gone."

Tracker walked a few steps away from Michael and Nova and struck his familiar pose. He lit his pipe and stood gazing blankly into the sky, thinking. Then, he gave a start. "Did you hear that?" he asked, turning back to them and pointing a finger in the air.

Michael stood up and strained his ears but heard nothing. Nova also rose to her feet. She perked her tiny ears forward and turned her head slightly to the side. It was totally silent except for an occasional drip of rainwater off the overhanging roof. Tracker came back to them.

"I think our plans have changed. If I'm right, this is going to be an interesting day, indeed. Now listen, and we shall see what we shall see." He looked intently at the sky through the open roof.

Pshshshshtt!

They all heard it this time, but very faint. It sounded like air being forced out of a bellows in one quick short spurt. Then complete silence. Tracker crouched with one hand held out behind him like he was stopping traffic. He motioned to Michael and Nova not to make a sound. They hardly breathed.

Pshshshshtt!

This time it was much, much closer.

"Look!" Tracker exclaimed, pointing.

A bright arc of orange was rising silently over the wall to the right. An impossible thought struck Michael. Is that a second sun rising? Of course not, but whatever it was, it was getting a whole lot bigger.

Pshshshshtt!

Michael now saw that the orange arc was the top of a monster's huge head! It rose up slowly and scowled over the wall with blood-filled eyes and a gaping mouth full of fangs. It glared down at them threateningly.

But something wasn't quite right. As the monster kept rising and looming larger, Michael realized it wasn't a real face looking down on them at all. It was a very large, crudely painted, multicolored balloon, and it was silently rising up and moving toward the castle.

"It's an air balloon!"

"Yes, Michael," Tracker said, straightening up. "I thought so." He then gave a short laugh. "You're about to meet a most interesting fellow. His name is Lorenzo, and he is a white wizard. As you can see from his marquee, he has a rather strange sense of humor."

The balloon hovered just beyond the wall. A bearded figure stood in the hanging wicker basket with one arm extended above his head grasping a wooden handle at the end of a long metal chain. The man waved enthusiastically. Then he pulled down on the chain. Pshshshshtt! A flame flared and shot up into the opening at the bottom of the balloon. The balloon rose another couple of feet, gliding forward, just clearing the roof with hanging ropes trailing over the walls and through the rubble. Tracker, Michael, and Nova all strained to look up as the balloon stopped almost directly above them. It was eerily quiet. A hot air balloon makes no noise when the blast valve is closed and the propane burner is off.

The man's head appeared over the edge of the basket, and he looked down at them smiling. "Hallo there!" he called. His voice echoed around the enclosure. "Give us a hand there, Tracker. Just grab the ropes and secure them like a good lad."

Tracker waved Michael to help. They both skipped down off the dais and grabbed the dangling ropes and tied them to large rocks.

Once the balloon was secured, a rope ladder unfurled, and the man in the basket nimbly descended and dropped to the ground.

He was short, plump, and bald on top like the image on the balloon, but his real face was round and friendly. What hair he did have was grey and long and hung down beyond his shoulders. His cloak and robes were as colorful as his balloon. He had a thick ornately carved staff and a large beaded bag slung over one shoulder. Perched on the opposite shoulder was a small tamarin monkey with a long tail and large eyes set in a startling blue face. Its face was framed in a mane and beard of golden hair. Its tiny leather collar was attached to the man's wrist by a long silver chain.

"Well, I seem to be the first to arrive!" the wizard said, giving the surroundings a quick look.

"If you're not counting us, that is!" Tracker said. He greeted the man with a bow and a smile. The wizard also bowed, and as he straightened up, the monkey jumped and landed on Tracker's shoulder. It wrapped its tail around Tracker's neck and then took his face in both of its tiny black hands. It licked and kissed Tracker's face with great fanfare before returning to its master's shoulder.

"Hello, Tamara," Tracker said laughing. He wiped his face with a handkerchief.

"You were always her favorite, Tracker," Lorenzo said. "There's no need for her to mark you every time she sees you, but there you are." The monkey leaned its head against the wizard's neck and patted his cheek. Lorenzo reached into his bag and removed a live wriggling worm with finger and thumb. The monkey took it in both hands, pulled it in half, and threw each piece up in the air one at a time before catching it in its mouth.

"Of course, you all count, Tracker! You're why we've been summoned, after all. So glad you are safe. And now, please, this must be the mystery guest."

They both turned to Michael, who was watching the monkey with great interest and delight. He had immediately recognized the animal as being very similar to one in his own world called the golden lion; it was one of the rarest primates on earth. He learned all about them in school and had even given his allowance once to a cause dedicated to saving them from extinction.

"Of course," Tracker said. "Michael, this is Lorenzo and his familiar, Tamara. He is one of three wizards that form the White Triad."

"As am I," said a falsetto voice. It came from nowhere and everywhere.

Poof! A cloud of white smoke engulfed them all and had them gasping and wiping their teary eyes. As the cloud dissipated, a second figure stood among them. He was also rather portly with green skin and black hair that he wore in a long ponytail. His eyes bulged slightly and his lips were puffy and shiny. Tattoos covered his bare arms, and he had many straps and bracelets on his wrists. A leather cape was clasped at his neck and fell back over his shoulders. Over his head floated (or swam) a multi-colored, thorny puffer fish.

"Oops!" the new arrival squealed. "Cut that one a little close. No permanent damage, though. Just a little residue, that's all. Jasper! If you please?"

The puffer fish quickly darted from one person to the other like a minnow in a pond. It puffed up three times its size and blew the dust from their faces and hair quick as a wink.

"Greetings, brother!" Lorenzo said. He went and gave the new arrival a long heartfelt hug. Tamara jumped up and down on both their heads, trying to reach the puffer fish that was now swimming in circles just beyond its reach. "Good timing! Tracker was about to introduce me to Michael."

Everyone turned to Michael. "This is Lorenzo's brother, Pacco, and his familiar, Jasper," Tracker said, introducing them all. "Lorenzo and Pacco are twins. Fraternal twins that is, the kind that don't look alike."

Michael stepped forward to shake both of their hands. Tamara leapt and ran up his outstretched arm like she was walking a tightrope and gave Michael the same welcoming embrace and kiss as she gave Tracker. Jasper darted here and there making a sound with its lips like an idling motorboat.

Lorenzo gathered Tamara up in his arms while Pacco made a pantomime of reeling Jasper in with an invisible fishing pole, only it worked just like it was real because Jasper swam back in jerks as if caught on a line and returned to her position over Pacco's head.

Tracker looked at Michael. The boy was laughing. He wasn't sure if he had seen Michael laugh the whole time he'd been in Tremora. At first he'd worried whether the quest would be too much for such a young boy. A further complication was the story of the boy's father also being in Tremora. But Michael's resilience had been proven many times already. And here he was laughing as only the young can do, forgetting for a moment the weight he carried on his shoulders. *I only hope you will find more time to enjoy Tremora, Michael,* he thought. It was good to see him relaxed, even if only for a short while. His laugh was infectious.

Michael reached out and petted the forehead of the puffer fish. It was the only part of Jasper that didn't have the sharp spines sticking out. "Very glad to meet all of you," he said. He looked at Tracker. "But, why do you call their friends f*amiliars*, Tracker? What does familiar mean?"

"Ah, yes. Well that might take a little explaining. For now, just think of Tamara and Jasper as special companions. They are part of something else I haven't had time to explain. It's called a frenada. You'll know much more about them and it tomorrow."

Michael was too entertained to be upset about another put-off. He just gave Tracker a "Yeah, yeah, whatever," reply, and continued to pet the puffer fish.

Tracker turned to the brothers. "But, if you two are here, then surely Tashlman can't be far behind," Tracker said looking around.

"Oh, he's here all right … or very near," Lorenzo said. "I passed right over him just a couple of minutes ago."

As if on cue, an elephant's trumpeting split the air. They all turned to the far end of the hall, and there stood a huge white elephant on its hind legs with its trunk extended straight up in the air. It was decked out in leather and metal armor and had long tusks that ended in sharp metal tips. Standing next to it was a tall, fierce looking figure with a white turban and knives of all sizes and shapes strapped to his body. He raised a hooked staff and waved. The elephant crashed down to stand on all fours and the floor shook. Small stones tumbled from the walls. The wizard then took the hook and nudged the elephant behind its front leg and they both started forward.

"Watch out for the holes!" Michael shouted, sensing disaster.

Tracker reached out and put a hand on his shoulder. "It's OK, Michael. Watch."

Michael first looked at Tracker in confusion and then watched as the new arrivals started to come farther into the room. With each step the elephant shrank in size! By the time they both joined the group at the dais,the elephant was no bigger than an average dog. Michael looked at them sheepishly.

"Do not be embarrassed. Your concern was admirable. How could you have known? We are at your service." The tall wizard bowed deeply to Michael while crossing two small swords in front of him. He resheathed the knives, bent down, and swept up the elephant that was the size of an apple, and set it on his shoulder.

"Michael, this is Tashlman and his familiar, Crong," Tracker said, "the third member of the White Wizard Triad. Together they are known as the Wizards of Calandera."

Michael bowed. "Ah, yes, well, pleased to meet you as well."

Tashlman studied Michael a long time. "So, Michael, where do you fend from? You've been quite the conversation lately."

"Well, err," Michael looked at Tracker for help.

"He is the king's guest as are you—," started Tracker, but he was not given the chance to finish.

"All will be revealed in its time, Tashlman!" Again, a strange new voice sounded in the hall.

They all turned, and standing at the entrance to the hall this time was a tall, plainly robed man leaning on an ivory cane. The hood of his cloak was pulled back to expose a wise and ancient face. His eyebrows were bushy, and his beard long and thin. Tremoran locks matching the color of his cane were parted in the middle and fell to his waist.

"Megan," Tracker said.

Chapter Thirty-eight

Megan and Waz

Megan surveyed the open area before speaking. He took no time for pleasantries. In a measured tone that demanded attention, he said, "The king will be here soon." He strode forward and gave instructions without raising his voice. "Lorenzo, why don't you deflate and stay a while? Please prepare the fires. Food and drink are arriving even as we speak." He pointed at the broken table, chairs, and debris and, without breaking stride, "Tashlman, your skills can be used on all of this cracked and damaged soapstone." He looked around the room. "The Prassian Triad has yet to arrive," he observed. He then reached the group in front of him and motioned to Pacco. "There's agate crockery in the buttery. There you'll also find onyx goblets and additional accoutrements fit for a king's table."

The three wizards jumped into action without hesitation. Lorenzo untied the anchoring lines to the balloon, scurried up the rope ladder with Tamara, and steered off over the walls. Tashlman attacked the large broken table with his knives, and dust and chips flew. Crong grew to the size of a bull and up-righted chairs with his trunk, and Pacco hurriedly disappeared through a hole in the floor near the entrance to the hall.

"And now! Tracker, my friend!" Megan gave Tracker a hearty hug and then backed off, giving a military salute and two-handed handshake. "Well done, warrior. You have completed your task admirably. Your adventures should make for interesting storytelling this evening." He then turned to Michael and Nova.

"Welcome to Tremora, Michael. You have the look of your mother. You will have many answers before the gathering comes to an end. Although, I fear they will only lead to more questions that have *no* answers."

Michael started to speak, but Megan had already turned to Nova. *"Noble beast! Have you guessed what your role in all of this is?"*

Nova looked steadily back at Megan. Although she had never met him, she was not surprised at all that they could communicate. He had an aura and presence that foretold many unexpected moments. *"I'm not sure, sir. But, I think it may have something to do with the quest to rescue the prince."*

"In this, you are correct. Are you so willing to embark on this dangerous adventure?"

"But, what if I am the only chance the prince has? Of course, I'm willing! And besides, Michael needs me."

Megan smiled and stroked Nova's nose. *"Good. I will inform the king."*

"Megan, sir," said Michael impatiently. It was obvious that the wizard had been communicating with Nova (it was old hat now; so many Tremorans spoke with their minds), but he couldn't contain himself any longer. "I don't mean to be rude, but was it you who called me? Do you know of my father? He is here, isn't he?"

"Yes, yes, and yes!" Megan stared hard at Michael and let the answers sink in. "But you really must wait for the wizard's gathering. Then, you will be involved in an important ceremony and learn of your quest—the *real* reason you are in Tremora, Michael."

"Yes, yes, I know about the prince, but—"

"I'm afraid you know very little."

"But—"

"I'm sorry, Michael, but for now, you must live with what you've learned from Tracker."

Tracker flinched.

"It's all right, Tracker," Megan said, turning. "Your decision to give Michael more details than we had planned was necessary, given the changing circumstances, but it has led to the very confusion and angst the king and I had hoped to avoid."

Tracker still looked rueful, and Michael's face did, indeed, look confused. Megan looked at them sympathetically. "Take solace, both of you. The good news is you are both safely here now, and the wizard's gathering will start in just a few hours. What is done is done, and as always, the adventure continues … Now, I see you have an interesting ring on that finger there, Michael. May I?"

Michael felt surprisingly relieved by Megan's words, even if, once again, he was turned off like a spigot. After all, he thought, a couple of hours wasn't that much longer to wait. He let the wizard lift his hand.

Megan tapped his right temple with his wand and half glasses appeared on the end of his nose. He looked long and hard at the ring, then pulled a small crystal from his robes and held it up to one eye like a jeweler's loupe to study the carvings on the ring's ivory. He spun the images and noted the glow. "This is very ancient. It is similar to royal rings of lore. But where did you—oh, of course—it's a gift of giving from your visit to the obelisk. This is, indeed, a mystery, Michael. Have you felt any magic?"

"No—no magic," Michael said hesitantly, "but it won't come off my finger, and the light gets brighter when the ivory spins. Perhaps it's a light for the dark?"

"Perhaps, perhaps," Megan said slowly, still studying the ivory images. "But, if it's a royal ring, as I suspect it is, a Tremoran king would have no need for such a light in the dark." He flicked at his own hair absently to make the point. "I think it is much more than that. We shall see." He turned to Tracker. "Any ideas?"

"Maybe in a different place, it will reveal its secret, but no, I've never seen the like." Tracker then looked at Michael. "I think you have a second gift to show Megan."

Michael jumped. "Oh, right." He reached into his pocket and removed the ball of netting.

Megan took it from Michael and looked at it with a smile. "Now I *do* recognize this. But I haven't seen one of these for many, many years. They come from the Age of Magic. They're called imp-ridders. They were woven by gypsies, and many a treasure was exchanged for one of these in its day; they were very powerful. They were the only cure for when your home was infested with magic pests or annoying imps, which was quite common back then. In fact, it was suspected that the gypsies also specialized in creating the problem, but who can say now? Anyway, the amazing thing was, nothing could hide once these nets were cast. An offending imp or screaming slug was easily caught and paralyzed by the netting and then disposed of. But their usefulness faded once black magic was defeated because magic house pests and vermin also disappeared. Interestingly, for a while, the nets were also used for fishing. Once thrown on a body of water, any fish nearby was quickly stunned and snared. Eventually, though, gypsies no longer supplied the nets, and the magic in the old ones gradually weakened and faded away."

Michael took the net back and looked at it thoughtfully. "Do you think this one works?"

"Gifts of the obelisk are never fully understood, Michael. I suspect your imp-ridder will come in handy someday. Best to keep it safe and secret is my advice."

Just then, the air started to vibrate. Tracker's face lit up as a low humming sound filled the open hall. Unexplainably, Michael felt as if he'd just hugged a puppy. He looked around, and there, in the archway, was Corak standing with the strangest creature Michael had ever seen. From Tracker's descripton of the wazalops, it had to be a sentry-herder. Even so, Michael wasn't quite prepared for what he saw. The creature stood taller than Corak on two long, spindly legs with ostrich feet and the body of an unshorn sheep. Instead of wool, though, it was covered in masses of Tremoran locks. It was stooped over slightly, with hands that looked like paddles hanging down loosely at the end of long arms matching its legs. It had a huge nose, lopsided ears, and large, extremely intelligent and sensitive eyes. There was a saddle on its back with bridle and reins to match. The creature reminded Michael at once of an ostrich, a kangaroo, a sheep, and a little camel thrown in for good measure. He guessed it was Tremora's version of the duck-billed platypus.

His musings were interrupted when the creature crouched and launched itself forward. *Definitely part kangaroo*, Michael thought, as it bounded toward them with outstretched arms. It went directly for Tracker. The two rolled over and over on the ground while the wazalop made sounds like an excited dog greeting its master. Then Tracker jumped to his feet and playfully pushed his friend away.

"Sorry to be away so long, old boy, "Tracker said. "Michael, Nova, this is Waz., *my* familiar and best friend."

Waz turned to them, pursed his lips, and purred. He tilted his head and studied Michael and Nova with his wide, piercing blue eyes. It was like looking into the face of a large friendly dog.

"Michael, this could be the most dangerous creature I've ever met," Nova said, unexpectedly. *"He doesn't speak or think in any language that I can understand. He's using those strange sounds at a different level of consciousness. I think he's actually controlling our moods ... Have you ever liked someone this much so soon? Already, I would trust him with my life."*

"Oh yeah ... Waz is a magical creature all right," Michael said smiling, as his right hand disappeared into Waz's huge paws. He was sure Waz had just visited his mind, found things to his liking, and given a stamp of approval to Tracker with a melodic whistle.

"I think we have both been sized up and filleted quite nicely, don't you?" Nova observed with admiration.

"Yes, Nova, Waz has accepted and approved of you both," Tracker agreed. "Of course, there was no doubt in my mind, but Waz makes his own decisions as to who befriends our *frenada*, and it would have been rather awkward if he found your characters wanting. We don't always look at people the same way, we two, and he doesn't always embrace my more unsavory friends ..." He looked at Michael and Nova and winked.

Nova and Michael then looked at each other. Waz was no longer making any sounds, and the feelings, fleeting as they were, of happiness, puppiness, and euphoria were now completely gone.

Tracker explained. "Waz can cause your emotions to alter—change anger to calm, for example, or even strike uncontrollable fear—but only fleetingly. As you can see, it can be a little unsettling but very effective, especially in battle. Remember the story of the wolves?"

Waz straighten up just then and cupped his larger ear. His throat vibrated.

"Yes, Waz," Tracker said. "There are still others to arrive." Tracker looked at Megan. "I think your Prassian Triad is at the door."

This time, three women stood under the arch. The oldest, standing very tall and straight with long gray hair, held the reins of a unicorn. The younger two, slightly shorter with long silver hair, were similar enough to be sisters and stood next to magnificent white striped tigers. All three had their hoods up and their faces partially hidden in shadow. Bands of gold gleamed on their foreheads, and they wore large looped earrings of silver.

Megan waved them forward. Scantily dressed female servants appeared and took possession of the animals. The threesome then carefully wove through the rubble and around Tashlman's work area. He acknowledged them with a bow and banging of knives. When they reached Megan, they came forward one at a time and kissed him on both cheeks.

"We have little time, my friends," Megan said. "The king is on his way." He turned to Tracker, Waz, Michael, and Nova. "Let me introduce you to the Prassian Triad. They are a very powerful combination, indeed."

Both groups looked back and forth at each other. There was some awkward bowing and mumbling, especially from Michael and Tracker. The older woman decided to break the moment. "We are Masha, Tirene, and Carrie," she said, as she pointed with a bejeweled and manicured hand to herself and each of her companions. "We look forward to a more opportune time to talk." Her voice was soft and hypnotic, and Michael found it difficult to look away from her steady gaze.

"And these are Tracker, Waz, Novalena, and Michael," Megan said. "You have already heard of Tracker and Waz, of course, and I think you may have heard of Nova—she is the most famous racing animal in the world. And this is Michael. You will learn more of him later at the gathering. He has been called to complete the king's quest."

The women pulled back their hoods and loosened their hair. They were the most beautiful women Michael had ever seen. Each stepped forward, shook Michael's hand and kissed him on each cheek as they had done to Megan.

Michael felt his skin tingling where the hooped earrings touched his cheeks. The perfume and sweet breath of each woman lingered on and engulfed his senses.

"Well, now you know why they are so powerful, Michael. How does it feel to be enchanted?" Nova asked.

"Wonderful, Nova," he answered dreamily. *"I could feel like this for a thousand years and be perfectly happy—"*

Nova snorted and butted Michael's head with her own.

"Ouch! What the …?" he said, rubbing the spot. The euphoria was gone.

All three women snapped their heads to look at Nova. "So—it seems Novalena is impervious to our powers *and* Michael's protector," said Masha, surprised.

"And, she's the most famous racing camelop in Tremora to boot!" added Carrie.

"And quite possibly a Grock!" exclaimed Tirene.

"We are impressed," Masha said, as they all eyed Nova.

"Yes, yes, you will find there are many secrets and surprises in this group," added Megan. "But, as I said, we must all be patient and wait for the king. Now, would you all please help with the preparations for this evening's dinner?"

"As you wish, *Master*," answered all three at once in melodic voices. They curtsied and bowed their heads, but there was a twinkle in their eyes that told Michael that Megan might not actually be their master at all.

"Enough of your impudence," Megan said, but he was smiling. "No need to practice your wiles on me. I will leave it to you to create the proper atmosphere."

The enchantresses bowed, gave three enigmatic smiles, and turned as one and returned to their familiars. Then Megan motioned for Tracker and Michael to follow him. He led them to a flight of stairs and up to the inner curtain wall of the castle. From there, they looked down on the activities below.

Lorenzo and two helpers were just finishing folding his air balloon and putting it into the woven basket. The bailey was full of carts and horses and tents and campfires. Servants scurried everywhere like ants.

Megan pointed down the valley along the path leading to the castle. "Can you see the banners? It's the king's lead entourage. The flags have been unfurled. There is no need for concealment now that the king is in Fennland. When we received your message, Tracker, that the gathering at Mesmer Henge was known to our enemies, we changed the meeting place to Fennland's castle. There are only a few locations that are safe and designated for such a gathering. This place hasn't seen such an assembly for many, many, years, and it's been that long since the wizards have had a gathering also. There will be a lot to catch up on over the next several days."

Michael felt exhilarated. All this excitement! And his father was here! And it was Megan who had called him into Tremora. And wasn't attending the wizard's gathering the main focus from the very beginning? It was where he would find out why he had been called to Tremora. Well, here he was. But, Michael still had his own agenda. He had been in a daze since Megan had told him he knew of his father. And maybe now Michael would find out where in Tremora his father was and why Megan and the king thought only *he* could rescue the prince.

"Everyone's going to be busy for a while," Megan said, "In the meantime, the king and I found a room on our last visit that should be of great interest to you both. He has given permission to show you."

Chapter Thirty-nine

The Room of Glimpses

Megan, Tracker, and Michael climbed back down from the castle tower and set off across the great hall toward the arched entrance. Once there, Waz and Nova joined them. Megan then led them down the same hole in the floor the wizard Pacco had used earlier. It was a tight squeeze for Waz and Nova, but they would not be left behind. The group soon found themselves on the first floor of the keep in the huge castle kitchen. An open stone oven was built into an entire wall. The fires were burning, food was on the spits, and cauldrons were boiling—a king's feast was being prepared. They wove their way slowly through the food preparation area, enjoying the savory smells and delicious aromas that attacked their senses. Someone called out, and two young servants rushed up with samples of dripping meat and vegetables for each of the new arrivals to taste. Megan, Tracker, and Michael were given pieces of pork on a fork, and Nova and Waz were given dollops of pureed greens on wooden planks that were set on the floor.

"If you left without a taste, you might die of anticipation," shouted Lorenzo from across the room, waving a wooden spoon.

Megan smiled and waved back in thanks. When they finished eating their tantalizers, Megan led everyone to the back wall of the kitchen and through an empty larder to another, much larger room, octagonal in shape with eight entrances. Megan held his staff aloft, and it glowed softly to show that all the doorways but their own were blocked with piles of crumbled masonry or bricked intentionally shut. There was a gaping hole in the center of the floor at least twenty feet across, and Megan walked to it, pointing his staff. They all moved forward cautiously and examined the opening in the dim light.

The hole was the top of a deep vertical shaft, lined with round, multi-colored stones and mortar. Wooden beams with rusted pulleys crisscrossed the gaping hole, and a single lantern hung down into the darkness on the end of a chain. Hugging the shaft's walls was a descending staircase, circling right to left, with treads large enough to support both Nova and Waz easily. Megan reached into the opening with his staff and lit the hanging lantern. The additional light was still not enough to see all the way to the bottom. "As you can see, this shaft is quite deep, and descending those steps can be dangerous—there's no railing. It would be wise to tread softly from here on," he instructed. "And whatever you do, don't wander into any of the rooms at the bottom of these stairs. I'll explain once we get there." Then Megan stepped down onto the first landing and beckoned for them to follow him into the abyss.

Michael ended up last in line and hesitated at the lip for a just a moment. He looked down and watched in detached amazement as Megan, a white robed wizard, descended the curving stairway of the shaft with his lighted staff held high, followed closely by Tracker, a short, green skinned, warrior; Nova, a telepathic camel; and an incredibly unique creature named Waz, that could control the feelings of those around it. Their shadows danced crazily on the stone walls as they reflected the orange lights of the lantern and Megan's torch. He thought of Dorothy's famous quote, "Toto, I don't think we're in Kansas anymore," and came up with his own: "Michael, this isn't zip code 98296 anymore!" He took a deep breath and stepped into the hole.

Eventually, they all reached the bottom safely and found themselves in a large cavern with three identical arched doorways, looming darkly in front of them.

Megan went to the wall near the end of the stairs, pulled down a torch that was mounted there, and lit it with his wand.

"Did you notice that the stairs circled counterclockwise on the way down, Michael?" Tracker asked, as they all gathered around Megan.

"Well, yes, now that you mention it …"

"It's a clever bit of engineering actually. Any enemy that pursued castle defenders down those stairs would have to fight using their left arms. In a battle every advantage counts."

Unless you're left-handed like me, Michael thought.

"And now you're about to see another example of that cleverness," said Megan as he motioned for them all to follow him to the middle door. There was a very unpleasant stench coming from inside. Megan carefully thrust his torch into the darkness to expose a dome-shaped room while holding his other arm out to prevent the others from getting any nearer. The light barely reached the highest point of the ceiling. He lifted his flame higher. They all looked up and saw hundreds of pairs of eyes reflected in the firelight.

Michael gasped. "Bats!"

"Yes, bats. And another excellent line of defense against thieves and invaders! Anyone entering that room unawares will immediately sink several feet into very toxic bat guano and disturb our sleeping friends up there. Then, as the unfortunate intruder looks up he will become blinded by a downpour of even more of the animals' waste. The bones of many an unsuspecting thief lie at the bottom of that room."

Megan then moved to the door to the left but stayed far back from the entrance. The flame on his torch bent toward the opening. "If any of us were to enter this tunnel, we would never return. As you can see, there is a suction that starts out ever so faintly, but the farther in you go, the stronger the pull—until not even the strongest man can stand against it. No one knows where you eventually end up; perhaps the world sucks you down to its very core—or out its top!"

Michael shuddered visibly, and Nova's skin quivered all over as if trying to rid herself of a thousand flies. Even Waz gave a concerned whistle. These were very unpleasant ways to die.

Tracker however, realized at once the importance of what Megan revealed and why he lit a torch in spite of already having a staff to light their way. "But don't you see? These are keys to picking the right passage in a pinch and may help you survive in dark places.

Just remember to watch your flame, beware the flicker, and look for the eyes of the bats!"

"Yes, Tracker, a good bit of advice, and even more important when you realize that these archways are not always in the same order. There is a lot of magic still left in this old castle. This knowledge has been lost or forgotten for some time. Even the king didn't know the secret to choosing the correct entrance. It was your mother's journal, Michael, that ensured the king and I took the correct door from here to the catacombs."

Megan then turned to the third arched doorway with his torch held high. Michael noticed a squiggly red symbol above the entrance. The wizard made a gesture toward it with his wand. "And now remember, we must stay together. It would be dangerous, indeed, to get separated in this maze," Megan warned. "And try not to make a lot of noise. Don't want the roof caving in ..."

They entered the third archway, single file, with Megan leading, followed closely by Michael, Nova, Tracker, and Waz in that order. They soon found themselves navigating a long meandering dark, dank, and slippery tunnel shored up with sagging wooden timbers. Once, Nova's hump hit a crossbeam, causing rocks to fall and kick up dirt and mud. She was quickly relegated to last in line. From then on, if Megan saw a low hanging obstruction, he would send a message to Nova to keep her hump down.

Metal sconces with dripping wax candles were stuck in the walls at regular intervals, and Megan lit them with a wave of his torch as he passed them by. The candles then extinguished themselves after Nova passed. *The light,* mused Michael, *hardly seems necessary since Tracker and Megan's hair, Waz's coat, the hair on Nova's back, and Megan's beard and staff all glow enough to light everyone's way.*

Soon, rooms full of mining tools and ore buckets appeared on either side of the tunnel. They had to go slower because the floor of the tunnel now had steel tracks, making the footing even more treacherous. Then without warning, the shoring disappeared—it was no longer necessary as the passage way was carved right out of the living stone. As they moved deeper into the mountain, large chambers appeared where minerals and rocks were mined and removed from the walls and floor. At times, they were forced to walk across rickety trellises that traversed larger excavations or black voids where a thrown rock was never heard to hit bottom. It was as if the mountain was made of myriad ore deposits and the tunnel sought them out and bored right through them. They passed through whole sections lined with precious metals, agate, crystal, onyx, marble, granite, limestone, and many, many other ores that sparkled and glistened and even hummed softly as if alive.

Michael was awestruck.

"A sight few have ever seen," Megan said as he called a halt. "You are looking at the Lost Mines, which many believe are just a fable. But as you can see, they are very real and another reason Fennland is a protected and forbidden land. Just the knowledge that these mines really exist would be enough to start wars. However, it would be a hollow victory for the victors: After all, this entire cache is cursed. "

Out of curiosity, Michael had begun to reach out to touch a vein of gold. But at Megan's words he hastily retracted his hand and rubbed it on his pants. "Cursed?" he muttered.

"Yes, Michael. In order to ensure thieves, slaves, and those who worked these mines never removed anything valuable for themselves, the earliest rulers of these highlands put a curse on any ore taken from the mountain without permission. Only a member of their clan could remove anything mined from the mountain safely *or* void the curse. Unfortunately, the only surviving person in the lineage of those original highlanders was killed by the Mad Warlock at the same time Fennland castle was destroyed. The secret of the curse died with him. No one today can remove even a pebble from these mines without suffering horribly when he or she hits the light of day."

They carried on, and once again, the way became dark and dank with wooden bracing in the walls and roof. Then, suddenly, the tunnel broke through into a huge natural chamber of stalactites, stalagmites, and silent pools of water—some large enough to launch a boat on. Here and there, the minerals encased in the natural pillars absorbed the light from Megan's torch or the group's locks of hair, resulting in softly glowing pink, green, and blue lighting. And in every direction, there were identical gaping black entrances to more passages and tunnels—it was the center of a fantastic labyrinth.

The group stood in awe at the immense size of the cavern. From somewhere, there came the sound of rushing water. "Now you see what I mean," said Megan. "It would be very easy to get lost down here. It is another example of the castle's inner defenses." Then Megan turned and cast the light of his torch behind them. "And here's another …"

At first no one noticed. Then, Michael gasped. "Our tunnel is gone!"

Megan nodded his head. "Yes, Michael. You can only pass through these tunnels in one direction. So, when you get here to the center of the mountain, the tunnel you used disappears. If a thief was lucky enough to pick the correct entrance at the stairwell, or if an enemy pursued you through the mines, they would end up here—and they would never find their way out again. There are many entrances but only one exit from the center of this mountain—and it's not found by going back the way you came. Every one of the tunnels you see throughout this chamber but one eventually leads you right back here to where you started. It's a maze of death."

Megan then led them across the vast stone floor, skirting the still pools of water and strangely shaped formations, to a tunnel that looked no different from any of the others. The sound of rushing water was louder here, and Michael was curious.

"Where is all that moving water?" he asked, looking around. "It sounds like a river." The echoes in the vast chamber made it difficult to pinpoint where the sound was coming from.

"Beneath us," Megan said. "In just a moment, I'll show you."

Megan then pointed his wand at the tunnel entrance in front of him, and Michael saw the squiggly red symbol again, glowing dimly above its entrance.

"Is that red character some kind of guide or something?" he asked.

Megan looked at Michael, surprised. "You can see it?"

"Well, yeah. Aren't I supposed to? There was another one back there at the entrance to the mines, right?"

"Yes, there was another. The wizards of the Age of Conflict put them here in the mountain to guide defenders of Farland safely to the catacombs. Without these markers, they would be just as easily lost as any enemy. However, the symbols were supposedly hidden from all but the castle's guards and wizards, by a spell..." Megan looked questioningly at Tracker.

Tracker took a step forward and looked at the entrance. "Yes, I can see it, Megan. Not surprising, since Mazalon Warriors would have been on that list back then. As to Michael, that's no surprise either; he has been seeing things cloaked in magic since he got here."

Megan nodded his head and looked thoughtful. "This is most interesting. I look forward to hearing more about your abilities, Michael. But now is neither the time nor place." He again held his torch aloft. "Come," he said and led them into the tunnel.

After a few twists and turns, the walls and ceiling became lined with limestone blocks, and the floor, polished marble. In time, they came to a section of the tunnel that was damaged. The walls were cracked, and the marble floor had small fractures and holes that gaped open. The floor still seemed solid enough, but it was obvious the tunnel had shifted from its original path at some time in the distant past. *Perhaps an earthquake?* Michael guessed.

Megan was gesturing. "This should answer your question about the water, Michael," he said. "Come look." Megan knelt down on one knee and held his torch over one of the holes in the floor. The flame bent forward and his beard and hair were also pulled at, as he peered into the opening.

Michael got down on all fours and cautiously crawled to the edge of the hole and looked in as well. And there, rushing by beneath him was a very fast-flowing, underground river. There was snow and ice floating on the water's surface as it sped past in a blur; the cold on his face was so extreme it almost made icicles on his nose. If the hole was bigger, he felt the air currents created by the raging water would have drawn him right in.

"It's runoff from the mountains, Michael," Megan said, as he rose back up. "Many of the rivers of Tremora start right here beneath the slopes of the Seven Sisters."

Megan helped Michael to his feet and, after warning all to watch where they walked, stepped gingerly through the damaged section of the passage, continuing down the dark tunnel with his torch again held aloft.

The walls soon became smooth again and coated with plaster and, farther on, were decorated with colorful, painted frescos. Michael noted that the illustrations were similar to, but much more detailed than, those found on the obelisk.

"The history of the castle and the kings and queens who sat on its throne," Megan said as if a tour guide. "Tapestries with these exact same images once hung on all the walls of the castle, but they are long gone now. And, by the way, there are no more markers to show the way to the exit. These passages were built by Farlanders, and the secret to getting out of this maze, although known to every person in the castle, was never revealed to outsiders. They carried the maps in their heads."

Megan continued on, sometimes taking a right turn at a fork, sometimes a left, sometimes doubling back—Michael was completely lost. As if reading his mind, Tracker patted him on the back and said, "Do you forget you are with a Mazalon Tracker, Michael? I could find the way out of here with my eyes blindfolded. Even if there is only one exit, I can find it. But that won't be necessary; Megan would never abandon us."

Just then, Megan vanished from sight around another corner. Michael believed Tracker in every sense but speeded up to catch the wizard, anyway. In spite of Tracker's assurances, wasn't it also true that, if for some uncontrollable reason he was left on his own, he would have no light—*his* hair sure wasn't glowing down here! And wasn't that the purpose of this entire maze, anyway? To get people lost—forever!

He hurried around the corner with Tracker, Waz, and Nova following close behind, and there stood Megan, pointing his torch. "The castle vaults," he said. Thick steel-covered wooden doors lay strewn and broken on the ground in front of three large rooms. The granite walls of each enclosure were lined with empty recesses carved directly into the rock as shelves. "In spite of all of the tunnels and walking we have done, we are still almost directly beneath the castle. This is where the coin of the realm and crown jewels were once stored," Megan said. "Unfortunately, a lot of Fennland's treasures ended up ransacked in the castle's final days."

"But how could that happen?" Michael asked. "How could an enemy find these vaults or steal the treasures without getting lost or dying of the curse?"

"No curse protected this hoard, Michael. It was mostly made up of precious cut jewels and coins that belonged to all of the people. When Farland was alive and thriving, there was a stairway that led directly to these vaults from the castle, as well as to the catacombs. It wouldn't have been difficult to find the treasure in the castle's final days. Sadly, the walls of that passage caved in long ago. Believe me; it would have been easier to get here via that route."

Megan then led them into the middle vault and cast the light of his torch on the back wall where various animals and birds were carved and painted in bas-relief. He pushed on an image of a fluster bird with his cane, and the outline of a door appeared. He knocked on the door, and it made a hollow sound. "Only a king can open this," he said, turning to them. "Not all of the treasures of Fenn Castle were plundered," he said with a grim smile. "The contents of that room come into our story later."

Next, he led them through another maze of tunnels to a long, straight, wide corridor, lined with openings that gaped large and dark. The walls were once again adorned with frescos depicting kings and queens and scenes of daily life in the castle.

"The catacombs of Farland," Megan said reverently. His voice echoed softly and disappeared in a whisper.

He led them past several of the openings, clicking his staff at each as if counting. Then he stopped and thrust his torch into a room on his left. "Yes, this is it," Megan said, pointing. They gathered around him and looked in on a room that was entirely covered in panels of carved amber. He ushered them in and extinguished his torch. The effect was dramatic—the amber's translucence absorbed and reflected the collective light of the Tremorans' hair, and the entire room took on the color of a burning ember. The middle of the room was taken up by two granite crypts with sculpted images of a reposed king and queen on the lids, and the figures glowed a soft yellow. They all crowded around and gazed down in wonder.

"Why, those are the king and queen that were protecting the bridge at the chasms of dread." Michael whispered.

"Yes, they are King Arland and Queen Astoria. They were your mother's adopted parents, Michael, and *your* adopted grandparents. This room and these passageways are centuries old. The many kings and queens of Farland are all buried here in these catacombs. King William and I were standings here, just as we are now, when we noticed light coming from the king's sword. It was just as Fenn's diary indicated. It seems the sculptor wove strands of the king's hair into the blade. As a result, this chamber is never in complete darkness. Let me show you."

Everyone backed out into the passage way again and peered one at a time into the now darkened crypt. Not only did the king's blade seem faintly lit, but light also emanated from the end of the sword and focused directly over the king's shoulder on a spot on the wall.

"Now, you will see what we found."

The beam of light was focused directly on a carving of a fluster bird with three eggs. Two were painted brightly, but the third was left the color of the walls. Megan pushed the plain egg with his cane as he had done with the carving in the vault, and this time an entire wall of the crypt soundlessly and slowly rotated open. It exposed a large room carved out of pure marble onyx with swirling colors of green, white, red, and brown.

The room was circular in shape with a low roof, polished walls, and a tiled floor, inlaid with mosaics and complicated diagrams. It was easily big enough to hold them all. Megan had them enter and stand just outside the borders of the floor design, against a section of the wall where he pointed.

"You are standing in Farland Castle's Room of Glimpses, the secret room that Fenn mentioned in her diary," Megan said. "Every castle in Tremora has one. It's where a royal family is privy to visions of the past, present, and possible future. And, also, according to Fenn, it's where the secret of the veil was hidden.

"The first secret of this room is in the floor. I copied the patterns much as you would a brass carving, by rubbing soft stone over patches of leather. In that way, I had a complete copy of the floor to study later. It turned out the patterns contained an exact replica of the monoliths at Mesmer Henge and, more important, a map of the onyx gardens on the Strempshire Plains. Also, there are symbols and diagrams here that reveal the standing stone's secrets. Without them, we would never have been able to call you to Tremora, Michael. Again, your mother's journal was the key to solving the veil's secret.

Megan then moved to the center of the room and pressed another fluster bird egg painted on the floor in front of him. The rotating wall slowly closed them in. "When the king and I first discovered this room, there was a problem. King William was a different king from a different time, and as feared, this Room of Glimpses was very different from that of Tremora Castle. He didn't know how it worked … He lit those lamps on the wall, paced the room, and studied the floor, but nothing was familiar or showed him any images. And nothing about a veil! We even closed ourselves in this room for a night, hoping for a dream, but nothing. In frustration the king again looked to Fenn's diary in the light of the candles, and to his immense relief and surprise, it fell open to pages he had never seen before—pages that apparently could only be read once the room was accessed. They contained instructions on how to make the room come alive.

"But his elation was short lived. The room would not reveal all of its secrets without three precious stones of the egg of a fluster bird. You see, the people of Farland captured and coveted the fluster bird, just like the wazalops that Tracker told you about, Michael, to the point of almost total extinction. Even today, the plain egg of the fluster bird is the rarest thing a Tremoran could find. The egg is never laid in captivity, and wild fluster birds just might be extinct—it's been so long since anyone's seen them outside of the king's aviary. Even King William has never seen a plain egg."

Michael suddenly blanched. *Should I tell him I have* two *of those eggs right here?* He gulped, feeling a sense of panic. *But, the gatekeeper said to keep the fluster bird story secret … And I've been warned over and over about the Age of Secrets and, and … But surely Megan and Tracker could know,* he scolded himself, perplexed. Then he actually started to speak, but Megan was in the middle of telling his tale and, *It would be rude to interrupt,* he quickly countered. In the end, the argument to stay silent won, and the fluster bird eggs stayed hidden in Michael's pocket.

"But there *was* hope," Megan continued. "The diary mentioned that fluster bird eggs were once stored in the castle vaults. So, following

Fenn's maps, we searched for and found the same vaults we just visited. We were, of course, dismayed in the ransacked and empty rooms and thought all was lost until I noticed the same carvings of the bird and eggs that was on the wall of the king and queen's crypt. Unfortunately, pushing the image did nothing but outline the same door I showed you earlier.

"I tried every opening spell I knew, but to no avail. Then King William pushed me aside and gave it a try. Obviously the door was designed to be opened by a king because he easily solved its riddle by chanting the simplest of spells. We opened the door with high hopes, but the contents of the vault were very disappointing. It was basically a room full of purple velvet cushions! And there, in the center of the room was one egg nestled on top of one cushion. When we searched all the other hundreds of cushions stacked and stored in the vault there were crowns and jewels and sundry rings and bracelets and such—mostly personal items of the royals—but there wasn't one other egg to be found."

Megan pointed to the three silver sconces mounted on the curved walls. "We returned with the egg and reread from Fenn's journal the detailed instructions on how to awaken the room. There is a hollow crystal enmeshed in the metalwork of these candleholders. In order for glimpses of a possible future to appear, a king or someone of royal blood had to carefully transfer the contents of each fluster bird's plain egg into the crystals. Once the tiny gems were in place, the candle light and the reflecting silver dishes would supposedly combine to project three images of a possible future onto on the opposite walls through the stones.

"But, of course, we only had the one egg. Would the room show us *anything* with only one egg? What could we do? There was nothing left but to give it a try, so King William broke the egg and poured the tiny stones into one of the crystals as directed. We looked at the opposite wall expectantly, but to our disappointment, only pretty colors appeared on the wall. We couldn't discern anything. Our hopes were dashed. In frustration, the king lifted the crystal egg from its setting and shook it to jumble the gemstones around and then set it back in its cradle again. The combination must have been correct this time because the result was, indeed, magic as you will see."

Megan then then lit the candle in front of him. The wall opposite suddenly lit up, and a vivid flickering picture appeared like a movie on a screen. They all stared.

"*Michael, that's you!*" sent Nova in surprise. Then, "*No, that's us … And, and, Michael, am I dead?*"

Michael looked at the picture, and there he was (albeit boxy and roughly represented)—sword in one hand, knife in the other, standing defiantly over the body of a camelop that had to be Nova's (it had a rope muzzle!). He was looking across a chasm of flames into the face of a large red dragon with wings spread wide, mouth shooting flames, and yellow eyes blazing. Behind the dragon, a dark haired boy, younger than Michael, was watching wide-eyed from behind a marble pillar.

Michael flashed on his messadge from the king. "A companion must die willingly to complete your quest. Will this life be lost for naught?" It was obvious now where the king got that idea.

Nova read his mind with alarm.

Michael quickly held up his hands to calm her. "Nova, Tracker says to remember, not everything comes to pass that the king foretells. And that goes triple for this room. The reality might be something quite different from what you see or think.

"Was the room finally giving us a hint at what must be done to defeat the dragon and rescue Cedric? Perhaps, but remember, this was only one of three possible outcomes and we had no way to determine if this was the true future being revealed. We spent a lot of time trying to make sense of the image. Who, for instance, was this boy in the background? Was it supposed to be Cedric? But Cedric's hair is blond, not black. And who was the hero? Another unknown boy! And where were we to find him? Not to mention Tremora's most famous camelop somehow would play a role. Unfortunately, these rooms give glimpses not answers. Of course, we were chasing the secret of the veil, so it was no stretch to guess where the hero *might* come from … But how were we to find you, Michael, and use the veil to bring you to Tremora? A few of the many riddles the king and I still had to solve. Fenn's journal said the lamps would show three visions of a *possible* future … We were only privy to one. Was it any use to us at all?"

"Couldn't you just get another vision by re-shaking the egg?" Michael interrupted.

"No, I'm afraid not. Once the combination is met on a lamp and an image is projected, the heat of the flame melts some of the softer minerals in the mix, and the whole thing solidifies. It then becomes a curious piece of jewelry—valuable, albeit—but no longer magical or useful because it always projects the same image. One egg—one image—one piece of royal jewelry. Only another egg can give us a new glimpse. And, as you can see, there are two other candle holders, but—"

"Megan, I—," Michael started but was interrupted again. For just then, everyone's attention went to the revolving wall. It was opening. They turned and watched as a man stepped into the room. It was Tarbak.

"The king requests your presence," he said. "The gathering has begun."

Chapter Forty

The Wizard's Gathering

"We must go then," Megan said, waving Tarbak into the Room of Glimpses. He pressed the fluster bird image on the floor, and the door swung closed. He then motioned everyone to move to the center of the room. "Remember when I said there is only one way out of the labyrinth?" he asked. "Well, stand together as close as possible. You're about to make your exit!" He reached up with his staff and pushed on yet another image of a fluster bird centered on the low ceiling. The floor began to rise. At the same time, the ceiling rotated, and an opening appeared in the same way as the iris of a camera lens. Michael was used to elevators, of course, and wasn't nearly as startled as the others.

After climbing the dark shaft for several minutes, the lift came to an abrupt halt. They were back at the surface in a remote corner of the castle. Everyone stepped away. Megan reached out with his staff and tapped the fluster bird again. The floor disappeared in a rush.

"This is only an exit. No one can enter the Room of Glimpses from here," said Megan as the hole in the ground closed up on itself and vanished.

Tarbak then led the group across the inner bailey to the steps of the main hall. They had been in the labyrinth and catacombs for several hours, and it was now nightfall. The dark sky, as usual, was full of shooting stars. A freezing breeze blew fitfully within the enclosure, and Michael felt the chill to the bone, even with his coat. He was also hungry. He hadn't eaten all day, and he looked at the orange-yellow glow coming from the hall's entrance in anticipation.

Music and blunted conversation were coming from within, and Michael looked at Megan questioningly. "The ceremonies will not start without us," Megan said. "But the wizards are exchanging stories, nonetheless. It's been many years since they've been together. And, Michael," he said, grabbing Michael's elbow and lowering his voice, "do not make eye contact with the king's escorts. It is very important."

Michael nodded, thinking it probably had something to do with protecting the king—Tremora's version of Home Security or something. Just another secret …

The group entered the hall and lined up side by side to take in the scene in front of them. The ruined hall had been transformed into a well-lit chamber with walls draped in colorful tapestries and flowing silk drapes. The top of a large striped tent overlapped with the fabric of Lorenzo's hot air balloon to provide a billowing temporary roof, and the long stone table that the wizard Tashlman had repaired earlier now ran down the center of the room, chock full of guests.

A king's banquet was in progress, and the smells of savory meats and spices permeated the air. Several servants, both male and female, were serving food and beverages, while simultaneously dancing to the beat of the mellow music of the lyre and drum. At the far end of the room, the king and his queen sat on a raised dais that ran at right angles to the main table. They were flanked by two standing noblemen with long hair parted in the middle and armed with swords slung behind their backs. A seat to the king's right was empty as were the first two seats at the main table nearest the royal couple.

For warmth, small fires burned in low braziers spaced evenly throughout the room, and clusters of white candles lit the tables. All the wizards that Michael had met earlier were seated with their familiars, and their servants either stood behind them or sat cross-legged, backs against the walls. At least a dozen men and women that Michael hardly had time to notice were also in attendance and seated at the food-ladened table.

Although a feast was in progress, the gathering was far from boisterous or chaotic as might be expected. In fact, the music and dancing and the serving of food and drink were purposely low-key so as not to interfere with the unique entertainment being provided at both ends of the banquet table. There, two large circular slabs of marble slowly rotated like a lazy Susan, and everyone was watching the turning disk nearest him or her in rapt attention. A three-foot-high image of a two-masted ship appeared to be floating in the center of each one. The sails on each ship were aflame, and several miniature flying dinosaurs mounted by riders with spears and helmets circled the vessels from above. Both displays were identical.

Michael was as spellbound as any guest in the hall as he watched the sea-battle being waged on the disk in front of him. The miniature ship pitched up and down on a stormy sea as tiny sailors scurried over the decks and rigging to shoot arrows and blunderbusses at the diving attackers. The sailors were under the command of a tall, regal-looking woman who stood on the forecastle deck with legs wide apart and right arm raised high, holding a wand. Michael recognized the woman as the wizardess Masha. Just then, she turned to her right, pointed her wand, and one of the winged creatures with its rider burst into flames and fell to the table beyond the turning base, disappearing in a puff of dust. Barely audible cheers went up from the ship's crew.

How wonderful, Michael thought excitedly. It's just like watching a 3D movie or the holographic talking heads in the Haunted Mansion at Disneyland. He turned to his companions and saw that they were watching the display as fascinated as he was.

The battle raged on, and more and more of the flying creatures hit the table. It looked as if the battle was going in favor of Masha and the sailors until a sea serpent's head rose from the water and grabbed and swallowed the wizardess in one huge gulp.

There was a collective gasp from the room, but the real Masha, who was now standing and smiling, held up a finger. She pointed at the sea monster.

The creature's head and neck were still high and visible next to the ship, and the flying dinosaurs were circling the serpent with their riders shouting and raising weapons in triumph. But then the expression on the serpent's face changed. It started out grinning, changed to quizzical, and then went to startled surprise. It shook its head violently from side to side, and the flying soldiers scattered. It reared back, and bright lights flashed behind its eyes as if lightning was striking inside its head. Then it opened its mouth wide in obvious agony and bellowed in pain. With a start, it went stiff and stock still. From the depths of its throat, Masha appeared and ran to the end of its tongue with wand blazing. She held her hands above her head and then bent and jumped on the tongue as if on a diving board. On the second bounce she launched forward, turned a summersault, and landed back on the deck of the ship.

The stunned crew of the ship then broke out in loud cheers and celebration, and even louder cheers as the head of the serpent disappeared back into the sea in a circle of smoke and sparks and flames. With renewed effort and much help from Masha's wand, the last of the flying dragons also perished in puffs of smoke and flame. The real Masha then opened her arms wide and took a bow as the king and queen and all of the guests in the room broke out in applause.

The king then looked up and saw the group in the doorway. As he rose, the room went quiet. A nod from the king, and Masha quickly pointed her wand at the spinning disks; the ships and sailors faded to nothing, and the marble trays came to a simultaneous stop. Everyone turned and followed the king's gaze to the new arrivals.

The king made another softly spoken request to Masha. Masha nodded and, with a clap of her hands, sent servants to escort Michael and Tracker and Megan to the head table. Waz and Nova, of course, followed; impervious to whether they were invited or not. Tarbak took an empty seat near the door.

Once lined up in front of the king, first Megan and Tracker, then Michael bowed on one knee. The king acknowledged them and motioned for them to rise.

"Welcome to our table, travelers, and welcome to the wizard's gathering."

Chapter Forty-one

More of the Memory Disks

"Please, be seated," said the king, indicating Megan should sit next to him, and Michael and Tracker should sit at the end of the long banquet table. Nova and Waz took up positions behind Michael's and Tracker's chairs. Food and drink immediately arrived for all, including the animals, and the king encouraged them to eat. "Before we begin," he said, "I want you to partake of the feast. It's best we start this long evening on full stomachs." He then raised his glass to the rest of the guests and encouraged them to continue with their meals as well. Everyone went back to eating and the hall buzzed with conversation.

Michael was, of course, glad of the king's decision to eat first. He couldn't remember the last time he'd had a full meal. *The Flying Fare Inn, maybe? Or the fair food at the Bearcamp market?* All he knew was he needed vegetables and was really hungry. So he readily tucked into the food in front of him, and Tracker and Nova didn't hesitate to dive in either.

After a short while, Nova raised her head from her food and nuzzled Michael's neck. "*Michael, Megan says to remember his warning.*"

Michael looked up and saw Megan watching him. "*Yes, Nova, he doesn't want me to look too closely at any of the king's body guards.*" Michael took a sip from his goblet and raised it to Megan to acknowledge he'd gotten his message. Apparently, like Tracker, Megan's ability to communicate silently was limited to animals and royalty.

"He must think you'll see something," Nova said, looking at the guards behind the king and queen curiously. *"But I can't see anything unusual. Although, you do see things others don't ..."*

"Let it be, Nova!" came Megan's stern warning. Nova snorted and returned to her eating.

When Michael and Tracker appeared sated, Masha gave the signal to clear the tables. She then reached forward and tapped her wand on a crystal centerpiece carved in the shape of a whooping crane. It trumpeted loudly, and the room went quiet.

The king rose to his feet. "We will now more formally welcome our new arrivals," he said. He looked at Tracker and motioned for him to rise. "Fremoran Tremelan, Mazalon Warrior, and trusted servant, once again you have served your country and your king. You were given a most important task and have performed it brilliantly, as your countrymen have done since the beginning of ages. We are grateful." The king glanced at Queen Lelana, who nodded her head and smiled.

"Well done, Tracker," she said warmly, using his common name. "We look forward to hearing the details of your journey when it is your time to spin the disks."

Tracker blushed, made an abbreviated bow, and quickly sat down.

"How interesting," observed Nova to Michael as she looked at Tracker's face. *Green plus red makes brown!"*

The king next looked at Michael who hastily rose to his feet. "Michael Tull, son of Queen Fenn and Sir Paladin the Dragonslayer—welcome to our table and welcome to Tremora."

There were murmurs around the room at this, but Megan, seated behind the king, used his hands to signal everyone to be still.

Michael was also surprised. *Dragonslayer?* He'd never heard his father referred to as dragonslayer *or* Sir Paladin. "Your Majesties," he mumbled and bowed awkwardly.

The king continued. "As you are now aware, you were summoned through the veil to help Tremora in its hour of need." The room again broke out in sounds of disbelief, but William held up his own hand this time. "Yes, the shimmering veil, the fabled gateway to other worlds. This night Megan will tell the tale of a secret that had been lost for over five hundred years." Turning back to Michael, he continued, "You will soon be given a quest, a quest that will be extremely dangerous and, in the end, test your very soul. But for this you were chosen." The king once again glanced at Queen Lelana, and their eyes met briefly.

Michael also looked at the queen, but her expression was stoic and unreadable. Regardless, he was sure there were secrets shared in that exchange with the king.

"Nova? What's going on?"

"I don't know, Michael. The elves told me it is never permitted to read the minds of royals without invitation. These two are definitely blocked. But I, too, sense something ..."

This Age of Secrets thing was getting on Michael's nerves. Out of habit, he raised his hand to ask permission to speak. The king nodded. "But, sir, please excuse me, I don't understand. Your world must be full of brave knights and warriors." Michael motioned vaguely toward Tracker. "I mean, of course, I will help and all that—if I can. But how can I possibly be any help in saving the prince? I'm just a boy ..."

"You are being modest, Michael. Does not the blood of a queen and a Tremoran knight run through your veins?"

Michael was suddenly alarmed. *Tracker was right. These people actually believed he was some kind of warrior-hero or something.* "But my lord, I didn't know any of this until only days ago. And, and, with all due respect, sir, being the son of a dragonslayer doesn't make *me* a dragonslayer."

The king looked at Michael kindly. "We know you have many questions, not the least of which is why you are here. But for now, know this: Prince Cedric cannot be saved without first finding and defeating the dragon, and your role in this was foretold in the Room of Glimpses."

Michael was at a loss. *The king had a point; where did that picture of him and Nova come from?* And it appeared there was no arguing with these people when it came to the Room of Glimpses. He stood silent, waiting.

But instead of explaining anything further, the king motioned for Michael to retake his seat. The king then looked down the table and addressed the room. "Look around you. You are all carefully chosen guests. Unfortunately, the last time I called a meeting of trusted friends; there was a spy in our midst. We were careless. I will not make that mistake again. Tonight, secrets will be revealed that are not to be shared beyond these walls. In attendance, are wizards from around the globe, from countries many have never seen, trusted nobles of my court, knights of the realm, and leaders of my guards. A wizard's gathering is seldom arranged unless one of our countries is in dire need of help and advice. And Tremora is in such peril as you will see … Let us begin." The king looked to Megan and sat down.

Megan stood and pointed at the disks on the table for Michael's benefit. "These are memory disks. They work quite simply. Masha has been using them for the last hour to show us the current events of her distant land. They are used to represent a story being told. As you watch them, you may realize you have your own unique knowledge of the event being depicted. The disks will then reflect your knowledge as well. In this way a more complete story will unfold."

Masha gave a hand signal, and servants moved fire screens to partially block the glow of the braziers, and others blew out candles to dim the light in the room. The disks then began to turn, and a perfect miniature image of Castle Tremora emerged on each one. Each disk was bathed in its own light.

"It is time to dismiss the servants and musicians, Masha," said Megan.

Masha again made a hand gesture, and with a rustle of silk and jangles, her people disappeared into the open stairwell leading to the kitchen and larder.

Megan waited until Masha gave the all-clear and then pointed to the disks. "And here the story begins," he said. The images on the disks distorted and re-focused. A portion of the castle's curtain wall enlarged, and a young smiling boy with fair hair could be seen waving from a gap in the parapet to a crowd gathered below him in the inner bailey. "Many of us were present that day for the birthday of the prince," said Megan, noting the admiring crowd looking up at their future king. The people were singing and cheering. Then the joyous sounds of the crowd turned to gasps and screams as a dragon appeared from nowhere and swooped down, flying off with the boy dangling in its claws. The image zoomed out, and knights on horses galloped out across the drawbridge in the direction of the gesturing crowd.

"The prince was kidnapped on his twelfth birthday," Megan's voice narrated. "No one has seen Prince Cedric since."

Michael looked at the royal table. Queen Lelana's face was blanched and expressionless, but the king's brow was creased in anger.

"Knights and Mazalon Warriors and volunteers have searched the world for over two years without any trace," Megan continued. "And now, events are happening at a rapid and barely controlled rate. A pretender to the throne is about to make his claim, the kingdom is in turmoil, and black magic has re-emerged in our land."

Images of heroes exploring caves, traveling the sea, climbing mountains, and braving extreme weather appeared and disappeared on the disks as Megan spoke. Then images of wisps, Prelandora, Lord Pratt, assaults and muggings, faces full of fear and anguish, and other dark events blinked in and out until the disks finally stopped, becoming bare and silent.

Megan looked up. "Such is the state of Tremora today."

He looked back and the king nodded his head to continue. "We will now fill in the story with details that few if any in Tremora, other than the king and I, know. I will show the events that have led us to this meeting and describe the quest that will hopefully save our land."

He turned to Michael. "The shimmering veil, your presence, and especially the reason you were called to Tremora were supposed to be kept secret, even from you. It was for your safety and the protection of the quest. However, in spite of our best efforts, your presence was discovered on the very first day you arrived in Tremora. And from that moment on, you were in grave danger. And yet, here you are. Tracker, of course, played no small part in overcoming the attempts on your life the past several days. But it can't be ignored that your own innate ability or extreme good fortune also contributed to your evading the enemy. All the more reason to believe that the image we saw in the Room of Glimpses will come true."

Michael knew it was futile to argue.

Megan again addressed the long table of guests. "First, I will tell something of the veil and Michael's family. Some of this will be familiar. For who doesn't know the legends of Queen Fenn of Farland or the witch Fenn and her husband, Paladin, of the Age of Magic?

"But what no one has known till now is the two Fenns that are so much of Tremora's history are one and the same person—a person who was summoned to Tremora twice in times of need, a person from a place called Earth, and a person who is the mother of our boundary traveler, Michael. There is no question this is true, for it came from the mouth of Lady Fenn herself."

Michael sat up, startled.

"Yes, I have passed through the door to your world, Michael, and have talked at length with your mother." He again addressed the room, "When Fenn left Tremora to return to her home at the end of the Age of Magic, she was accompanied by her grievously ill husband, Paladin. In her world, she was able to nurse Paladin back to health, and they eventually prospered and had a son. And that son sits before you."

Everyone's eyes shifted to Michael. He gulped uncomfortably but kept his gaze on Megan.

"But, Michael isn't the only one of his family visiting Tremora at this moment; we now know that his father also came through the veil over two years ago."

Megan paused, knowing the effect this would have on his unsuspecting audience. He didn't even try to quiet the noise in the room this time.

Pacco was the first to see the obvious. "But if you didn't call the dragonslayer through the veil, who did? Surly, he was called by *someone* to kill the dragon and save the prince?"

"You are correct, Pacco. We did not call Paladin back to Tremora because we did not yet know the secret of the veil. As to who did call the dragonslayer—for that we will need some assistance."

He looked to the end of the table and called, "Baakeer, it is time!"

A short man rose from a seat near Corak and removed his curious looking hat.

Michael gasped. "Mr. Baker!"

"Yes, Michael," said Megan. "Your Mr. Baker is also known as Baakeer. He is a gatekeeper. His job is to transport wizards and witches through the portal to your world when ordered and to direct people of earth to the shimmering."

Almost as one, all eyes and heads turned from Michael to look at Baakeer. Another mythical character at the table!

"At your service," Baakeer said, bowing. "And hello to you, Michael. Glad to see you're doing well. But I must complain, Megan. This is most unusual, and I'm not sure my sentence covers this type of service. The doorway stands unmanned."

"You will be dismissed shortly, Baakeer, and you can then return to your duties. However, if you wish, your crimes could be reviewed by this august body, and the rest of your sentence could be spent in the dungeons of Tremora Castle."

"Well, no, no, that's not what I meant," Baakeer stuttered. "Just wanted to make a point, is all," he hurried on. "Anyway, I actually have a soft spot for the Lady Fenn, and if this will help her and her family get back together again—well, then, I'll not challenge you any further."

"Thank you, Baakeer," Megan said, with a smile. "I appreciate that."

Baakeer didn't catch the sarcasm, but others at the table did, and there were muted laughs around the room.

Baakeer shoved up his sleeves and took an aggressive stance. "So, how does this work, again?"

"Just start with the day you were summoned by the witch Prelandora, and envision the events as you saw and heard them. The memory disks will do the rest. Now, everyone, please watch and listen."

Baakeer looked at the disk dubiously and then at Megan. Megan motioned with his hands to go ahead.

"Well," Baakeer began, "a rather rude witch called me that day …"

A perfect model of Mesmer Henge materialized on the slowly revolving disks, and a door opened in one of the standing monoliths. Baakeer jumped out onto the grass. "Well, I was beginning to think I was watching a dead door," he said. "Who was it that called?"

And with that, Baakeer's meeting with Prelandora unfolded in every minute detail.

It was Michael's first look at the witch, Prelandora, and he watched in amazement as she demanded that Baakeer summon his father. Once Baakeer went back through the door in the monolith, the disks cleared and a new image appeared. It was Baakeer's head only, and he was on a cell phone.

The real Baakeer looked up at the questioning sounds coming from up and down the table. The disks stopped like a freeze frame. "It's a device for talking to people through the air on the other side of the veil," he explained, guessing that no one outside of Michael and Megan knew what he was holding up to its ear. The wizard Pacco was especially impressed.

"Thank you, Baakeer," said Megan. "Please continue."

The disks again began slowly to rotate. "There is a good sized cougar roaming Founder's Peak," Baakeer said into the phone, "And one of my hunting dogs is missing, and the others are raising holy heck right now. Could you give it a look, Mr. Tull? … Right, right, I understand, but there've been young hikers on that trail all week … OK, I'll meet you in about an hour."

Then, Baakeer was standing on the porch of a crude log cabin with two dogs on leashes and a double-barreled shotgun broke open over one arm. Coming up the path was Michael's father in full ranger gear.

Michael stared, barely able to breathe. This was the very day his dad had disappeared!

Nova moved forward and nuzzled Michael's neck. "*He's very handsome,*" she said. She felt his emotions and wanted to comfort him. Even Waz tried to help as he sensed Michael's pain. He filled the air with a barely audible sound that caused Michael's heartbeat to slow and feel a sense of calm.

Michael's father was speaking. "OK, let's get this over with. It's my son's birthday, and I don't want to be out all day." Mr. Baker and his dogs came down off the porch, and they all set out on a path through the woods.

The image faded, and as a new scene began to appear, Michael reached back and stroked Nova's muzzle and looked gratefully at Waz. "Thank you, both," he whispered. "But, I'm all right, really. After all, I'm finally learning what happened to my father."

Even so, Michael wasn't quite prepared for what came next. A familiar thin veil was obscuring the scene on the disks now, and behind it were images not quite in focus. Baakeer was apparently looking through the shimmering at Paladin's back and two figures on horseback. The conversation among the three, however, could be heard clearly. Baakeer's version of what happened next unfolded, and finally, when Paladin was jumped and thrown over a saddle, Michael also jumped, and then his face became hard.

The final image of the witch, Pratt, Paladin, and the wisps crossing the bridge faded, and the disks came to a stop.

Michael remained silent. Now he knew.

"Baakeer?" came Megan's voice. "Before you leave, we would appreciate your thoughts on what you witnessed."

"Well, sir, it seems to me that someone name Ohndrea gave the secret of the veil to this here witch, Prelandora. They were way ahead of you on that one, I'd say. And she just lied something awful because she made it sound like the king called Paladin to rescue Prince Cedric. But we know that's not true. And then she up and carts poor Paladin away. I'd say she and Ohndrea had something up their sleeves, or maybe Prelandora was preventing *you* from calling Paladin, in case you figured out the veil's secret for yourselves—you know, him being a famous dragonslayer and all ..."

Megan looked thoughtfully at the dwarf. "Thank you, Baakeer. You have been a great help this evening, and your insights are very interesting. Your sleeping quarters have been prepared, and there will be a horse and rider available for you in the morning for your journey home."

Baakeer nodded, beaming. He was used to taking and following orders of wizards and witches but had never been asked for his input or opinion on anything. And certainly never told his services were appreciated! He was quite chuffed.

Baakeer took his seat, and Megan continued. "When the king and I first heard Baakeer's story, we came to many of the same conclusions. But Baakeer doesn't know the extent of Prelandora's evil as we do. We think we know who Ohndrea is. Prelandora was referring to the black witch that reigned in the Age of Magic; the same Ohndrea who was defeated by Michael's mother.

"We guess Prelandora, in her study of the dark arts, found a way to communicate with Ohndrea's ghost. But we also wondered, like Baakeer, why Prelandora would use the veil to summon and kidnap

Paladin. It was a troubling question that we felt needed answered, and in the end, it was Fenn herself who provided the answer: Revenge! Through Prelandora, Ohndrea was getting back at Fenn for defeating her at the end of the Age of Magic. What better way than to abduct her husband?"

"Then we have to go to Spreten and save him," cried Michael, standing up. "He needs to be rescued! And then, don't you see, with his help we can easily save the prince!"

The king and Megan remained silent. Tracker's face was expressionless.

Michael looked at each in turn, not understanding; even the queen unexplainably dropped her eyes.

Megan held up a hand as if to calm and said, "Michael, we're afraid there's more to the story of your father. He made a serious mistake in believing *anything* Prelandora told him when they met on that trail in the mountains. Tremora was not safe, the king did not call for him, and Ohndrea's spell was not lying dormant …"

Michael's face went white. "Then he's dying? You said my mother had to take him out of Tremora to save him from that terrible spell."

"That is true. But, regardless, we are sure your father is still alive. And therein lies the problem: Saving your father cannot take precedence over first saving our prince."

Michael sank back into his seat. *So that's why they wouldn't tell me where my father is,* he thought. *They were afraid I would try to rescue him and disregard their own crisis. Well, they were right! And, yet …* For a moment he flashed on Prelandora and her wisps and her shape-changers … And then, with clarity he had never known before, Michael knew if they had told him about his father before, he would now be dead. He looked to Megan, and their eyes met. In that instant he felt the wisdom of the Magus.

Tracker reached across the table and covered one of Michael's hands in his own. "Fear not, Michael. We will save the prince *and* your father." He stared into Michael's eyes with the fierceness he had shown at the Bearcamp races. "I swear it."

And I! shot Nova.

Waz snorted and twirled his tongue.

Megan watched Michael and his three companions, and a grim smile briefly crossed his face. "It is what we hope for …" He then came around the table and stood near Michael. "We will now continue with our tale, and you will soon know all we know."

And the disks began to turn …

Megan and the king were on horseback leaving the gates of Tremora Castle. As they traveled, Megan filled in the story of how the king found Fenn's journal and how he himself was called to the king's side. The scene on the disks cut to Fennland Castle and the doorway to the kitchen larder. From there the journey to the Room of Glimpses sped by quickly.

Michael noticed that some scenes were left out or only stayed for an instant. He thought he understood why when it came to the lost mines and the secret passages. Not everything was for public consumption, even to this select group.

"Fenn's journal gave us the secret to accessing her world, the Room of Glimpses showed us a picture of Michael and the dragon, and the floor gave us maps of Mesmer Henge and the Onyx Gardens," Megan said. "The room told other tales as well. Runes carved in the walls told of not one but seven worlds that border our own; one of which was the source of the black magic that troubled Tremora all those years ago. The portal to that world was destroyed by Fenn and white wizards. When the king and I returned to the surface, we set out for Mesmer Henge, armed with enough knowledge to visit the world of Fenn."

The disks turned, and the king and Megan were again on horseback, traversing a vast open plain with grass reaching their animal's shoulders. "We must figure out who that boy was in the picture, Megan," said the king, turning and talking over his shoulder. "But how can a mere boy rescue Cedric? Read me Fenn's instructions again."

"Call to Earth's gatekeeper during the meteor shower in the zodiac of the Sword; he will assist you in summoning your traveler."

"But we don't know whom to summon!"

"There are many mysteries to solve here, my lord. I think we must first use the gatekeeper to find Fenn. She will surely help us."

The king and Megan scaled the walls of the henge and pitched a tent against the cold. Then they stood side by side at the edge of a sheer drop off and watched a magnificent sunset over the plains far below. The orange-red light caught the hairy humps and rumps of vast herds of grazing plains animals. The land appeared on fire.

The next scene showed the king standing in the center of the henge, calling out to Baakeer. As before, the gatekeeper stepped out of a door in one of the monoliths. "Another summons from Tremora—and so soon!" He looked at Megan and the king. "Well, we seem to be in rare company this time!" he said. "I am Baakeer, gatekeeper to the world called Earth. Do you seek a traveler? If so, state your request." He squinted up at the king and then swiveled to look at Megan.

"I am Megan, gatekeeper, head of the wizard guild, and Magus to the Age of Secrets. And this is William, King of Tremora. We seek the door to Fenn's world."

Baakeer nodded his head. Then he looked quizzical. "You are summoning Fenn? I'm afraid that's not possible. No human can survive going through the veil a third time."

"Why not?"

"A human body can only take so much, you know. Don't really understand it myself. The wizards said it has something to do with all those time changes … Not really my business."

"Well no matter, Gatekeeper. We need only talk to Fenn before we tell you who we seek. Can you take us to her?"

"You already know what this door is for, or you wouldn't be here. And you must also know I am bound to do your bidding if you are a wizard or a king. Of course, I can take you to her. But be aware; to walk the paths of this world is more difficult than you think. You may find your journey a bit *heavy*, he said with an enigmatic smile. "Come!"

"Stay a while, Baakeer," said the king. "We would first speak with you. You say you have had other requests recently?"

"Well, that's a problem," Baakeer said, appearing to seriously ponder the question. "It's not my charter to tell tales, after all. And even if you are a king—"

"Danger, Gatekeeper," Megan interrupted. "There is a lack of respect in your voice that is very unwise to use. Regardless of your position or perceived importance, insolence will not be tolerated in the presence of the King of Tremora!" Megan raised his wand as a warning.

Memory of the burns meted out by the witch, Prelandora, must have flashed in Baakeer's mind. "Sorry, sorry. Darn my mouth. It does seem to get me into trouble," Baakeer mumbled while backing away hastily and eyeing the wand. "OK, OK, no harm in telling you. Plus, I don't owe that witch anything anyway, now do I? Teach her to disrespect me. Now, what do you want to know?"

"Everything!" answered Megan.

Baakeer then described Prelandora's visit and, under the scrutiny and questioning of Megan and the king, also described the story of Paladin's capture.

Baakeer stood by patiently while Megan and the king held council around a small fire. "Perhaps Fenn can unravel these riddles, my king," said Megan, finally. "Why would Prelandora call a dragon-slayer to kill her own dragon? I think it is time to seek the counsel of our own witch."

"Shall we?" asked Baakeer, sensing the discussion was over. He gestured toward the stone door.

The king stood, but Megan held out his arm. "No, you must stay here, my lord," said Megan quickly. "You cannot leave your kingdom's borders, unless to do battle. It only follows that you should not travel to other worlds either, my king. Nay, I will visit Fenn and return as soon as possible. It's best you stay."

The king did not appear happy. "I do not need reminding of my duties as king, Megan," he snapped. Then his irritation vanished as quickly as it appeared. "But, of course, you are correct. Once again, your council is sound. Go! And I need not remind you how important it is that we bring forward the boy." Megan bowed and followed Baakeer through the monolith's door.

As Michael watched the scene change on the disk in front of him, he again thought how surreal this whole experience was; he was now looking at his cabin and a miniature image of his mother!

Fenn stood in the cabin's doorway with one hand holding the screen door ajar. She was staring coldly at Baakeer. "So, Baakeer, you have been avoiding me for almost a year, and now you knock at my door at this hour. Are you finally going to tell me of my husband? I was expecting a visit from you long before this."

"It was not my place to tell you of your husband. I am under strict orders as to my duties, as you are well aware. I am but a humble gatekeeper …"

Fenn looked barely in control of her anger. "Yet, you let us think he was dead all this time. But your presence now confirms what I've always thought, what I hoped for. He's in Tremora isn't he? And you led him to the veil!"

Megan interrupted. "Perhaps we can come in, my lady?"

Fenn looked at the wizard for the first time. "You are a Tremoran. And a wizard, by your attire. You even have the look of the magus, Frankland. Do *you* have word of my husband?"

"Each age has a magus, my lady. I know of Frankland. I am the Magus Megan from Tremora's current Age of Secrets."

"You have not answered my question, Megan. Do you know of my husband? And does that mean you know of me?"

"Yes, I know something of Paladin now because of the gatekeeper. And, of course, I know of you. You are very famous in Tremora. But these things are better discussed inside, don't you think? Please?"

Fenn hesitated and then nodded her head. "Yes, perhaps you're right. Even in this world, there are eyes and ears that can't be trusted." She glared at Baakeer and then opened the screen wider.

Megan turned to Baakeer. "It's best you remain outside. But don't disappear. I'll need your assistance in getting back to Tremora."

Fenn stood aside, and Megan entered the cabin. Baakeer pulled up a chair and leaned back against the porch wall. He seemed perfectly happy to remain outside, away from Fenn's wrath. Fenn gave him a last angry look and then turned and closed the door. She led Megan through the cabin's front room and into the kitchen.

"May I offer you tea?"

"I would accept, but I doubt I have the strength to lift my arm. I've felt very heavy from the moment I entered your world."

"You'll get used to it," Fenn said, pointing to the kitchen table. "Please have a seat." She then went to the stove and put a kettle on for two.

Before Megan sat down, however, pictures on the fireplace mantle in the front room caught his eye. He went and examined a family photograph of Fenn, Paladin, and Michael.

Fenn appeared with two steaming mugs, and Megan returned to the kitchen and took his seat. Fenn sat opposite.

"You have a son?" asked Megan, glancing back at the mantle.

"Michael? Yes, he's asleep. It's late at night in our world, Megan. Now, what is this all about?" Her face suddenly grew anxious. "What do you know of my husband? He must be in Tremora. But, I've heard nothing."

"As is often the wisest path, let me start at the beginning. I did not know your husband was in Tremora until Baakeer's story just moments ago. We called to Baakeer because the king of Tremora and I are seeking a boundary traveler to rescue our prince ..." Megan glanced again at the picture on the mantle. "And I now know it is your son we seek."

Fenn gasped. Then she rose and gazed out the kitchen sink window. "Paladin and I wondered if this day would come. We've never told Michael of Tremora. We hoped in some way he would never have to visit that world ..." She turned. "You say you know of my visit to Tremora? Do you know of both of them?"

"Yes. It was your journal, written as a young girl in Farland, that gave the king and me the secret of the veil and led us to Mesmer Henge."

Fenn again stared long and hard at Megan. "You say you knew nothing of my husband being in Tremora until this evening. I find this more than strange. A man like Paladin would not go unnoticed for long. How can he be invisible—unless he is locked away in some dungeon?"

"Lady Fenn, you may very well be correct. I do not mean to upset you. But the gatekeeper said it was a witch named Prelandora that called your husband through the veil. Then she kidnapped him. He has not been seen by anyone else in Tremora that I know of."

Fenn's eyes became unfocused. She leaned back in her chair and looked far away. "A witch you say?"

"Yes. Someone named Ohndrea apparently showed her the secret of the veil."

"Ohndrea," Fenn said softly. "I haven't heard that name in a long, long time." She gave a shudder and came back to him. "I fear the worst, Megan. But come, tell me your tale. A prince needs rescue?"

"It started when a dragon snatched our prince from Tremora Castle's very walls—"

"A dragon," whispered Fenn.

"Yes my lady, a dragon. And we think Prelandora must have used black magic to conjure the beast."

A painful look crossed Fenn's face.

"I see your distress, my lady. It's true; the black magic that you and the white wizards defeated over three hundred years ago is once again growing in Tremora. But, why did the witch call and kidnap Paladin? Was it to keep us from finding him first? After all, he was known as a famous dragonslayer."

Fenn's face became sad. "No, that was not why he was called to Tremora. But, please, continue, Megan. When you are finished, I'll tell my own tale."

The disks suddenly stopped, and everyone in the hall looked at Megan questioningly. Michael, however, knew exactly what was going on. More secrets! He was sure his mother's conversation would be kept from him. And he was right.

"Fenn and I talked long into the night," Megan said. "We discussed all that you have seen here and more. Suffice to say, she agreed she would not stand in the way of Michael entering Tremora."

Then Megan abruptly changed his tone. "It is time to hear Michael and Tracker's story."

Tracker rose and, after lighting his pipe, started his account from the moment Michael appeared on the paths of Golan. Michael saw a miniature version of himself standing in the forest and then realized that Tracker's image, rushing towards him, had to be coming from his own memories of that day.

As Tracker finished describing the encounter with the fake Tralana, Megan interrupted. "And Michael, you were not fooled by the shape-changer's disguise?"

"Well, at first, I think yes, I was. But, the more I looked at the girl and the more she talked, the stranger it all became … Finally, it was pretty obvious something wasn't right."

Megan glanced at the king, and Michael was sure a silent communication of some kind was again exchanged between the two. More secrets …

"Please go on, Tracker," Megan said.

The disks next showed the encounter with the real Tralana. The king seemed especially pleased with the behavior of his favorite messenger. Michael and Tracker's adventures sped by, yet it was more than an hour before the disks came to a stop. At each revelation of Michael's abilities to run fast or show strength or see through magic as he did with the shape-changer and the troll's bridge, Megan would stop and interrupt and clarify. Even Michael was starting to admit he might have abilities he wasn't aware of.

Finally, Tracker brought the story to an end. As with Megan, Tracker did not reveal all, or more than necessary, when spinning his tale. For example, if Nova's abilities as a Grock were to be revealed, then it was up to Megan and the king. And Michael chose to keep his memory of the fluster birds to himself as well.

Even so, enough was revealed of the trip to Fennland's Castle to make everyone look at Michael and Tracker in awe: In spite of the attempts on their lives, a fairy prince was rescued, two wisps were dead, a mountain troll was defeated, a crooked merchant was destroyed, slaves were freed …

"Tracker, you have spun your tale skillfully," Megan said. "Thank you."

Megan then looked at Michael. "It will take weeks to hone your newfound skills, but with the help of the wizards that are here, you will learn much before you embark on your task. It is another reason we are gathered here. We couldn't possibly send you off to fight a dragon and save our prince without all of the weapons and skills with which we can supply you. The White Triad will teach you, Tracker will teach you, the Prassian Triad will teach you, I will teach you.

"Now, let us continue. When the king and I returned to Tremora Castle from Mesmer Henge and saw the unrest and corruption that had escalated in the short time the king was gone, it couldn't have been clearer; it was time to act if we were to survive a complete rebellion and thwart Prelandora's plans to take over Tremora. So, we held a meeting …"

The disks turned to show a room in the castle with a small group of people standing around the king at a circular table. It was a gathering of the king's last remaining loyalists. Megan and Tracker were there, as well as the two lords now standing behind the dais.

The king was speaking and reminding the men of the sad fact that the forthcoming acknowledgement of Lord Pratt's bastard was only months away. Then he said, "There's an elaborate plot to take over Tremora behind all of the troubles in our kingdom. We are now certain that Prelandora, Lord Pratt's witch, was behind the kidnapping of Cedric. If we do not rescue the prince, when Prelandora's bastard becomes king, it won't be he who rules Tremora; it will be the witch."

Nods and grim faces greeted the king's words. "Prelandora has been very clever. Not one action of evil over the last twelve years can be traced back to her, including the kidnapping. And the naming of her son as the heir apparent is completely legal. And she has not been idle. She has built up an army of spies and wisps and soldiers and a ship … and recruited followers in every part of our land. Up to now, we have been helpless to stop her. Up to now …." Then the king told of the veil, of plans to call a hero, plans for a gathering of wizards, plans for war.

The disks stopped, and Megan turned to the royal table. "Lord Goth, perhaps we can borrow your memories for the next part of our story."

One of the armed figures at the king's back started, then reached his hand to the hilt of his sword. "My lord?" he said, looking at the king. "I don't understand …"

Megan made a gesture, and Lord Perth, the second standing lord, moved into a position, separating Goth from the king.

"Oh, it's quite simple," continued Megan as if nothing unusual was occurring. He pointed at the disks. "As you can see, our meeting at the castle is finished and adjourned. We would like to follow your memories of what occurred next, is all." He looked at Goth expectantly, but just then there was a disturbance at the opposite end of the room. Megan glanced back over his shoulder.

Michael also turned and then gasped along with everybody else. For there, standing tall and menacing in the entrance to the hall was the witch, Prelandora.

Chapter Forty-two

Everyone Gets a Taste

For a heartbeat, time stood still; and then several things happened at once. Lord Goth saw Prelandora standing in the doorway, and his eyes opened wide. He then gave a cry and lunged at the king with his dagger. But Lord Perth was ready and parlayed the thrust, suffering a glancing blow to his shoulder. There were loud shouts as the king backed away, shielding the queen, and several people rushed toward Goth; jumping over the king's table, knocking over candles, and crashing plates to the ground. In the middle of it all, a lightning bolt that boiled the air, flew down the table from Prelandora's wand and struck Goth in the middle of the forehead. Perth and others reared back in astonishment as Goth's body crumbled and fell forward with a crash. Stunned silence filled the hall. The only sound heard was the thrashing of the would-be assassin sprawled across the table.

Then a guard gasped and pointed. "Look!" he said. For Goth's body was changing shape, and it was a horrific sight. Goth's head reared up and back, as he contorted and changed into a large, slimy, green toad-like creature with lolling tongue and bulging eyes. The gross spectacle ended when the creature collapsed back onto the table, apparently dead, with a loud sputter of air escaping its warty behind.

No one dared speak. It was Prelandora who finally broke the silence. "Well, it looks like I arrived just in time," she said. "Yet I get no thanks?" She held both hands out to the room as if asking why. "That shape-changer was about to commit regicide right in front of your eyes!" she said accusingly.

"You couldn't be more wrong, Prelandora," came Megan's measured voice. "There was no danger to the king. Several of us were aware of the spy in our midst. In fact, all you did was stop us from learning this man's allegiance. How convenient …"

"Do you dare accuse me of having something to do with this? Do you know who I am? Who I will be?" cried Prelandora.

"And do you forget I am the Magus, Megan, head of the Wizard's Council? I know very well who you are, Prelandora. And I have every right to question the lethal use of your powers."

"Enough!" said the king. "What are you doing here, Prelandora?" he demanded.

The witch spread her arms. "Well, isn't this a wizard's gathering? Am I not a wizardess? Perhaps you forgot to send my invitation? Oh, and Lord Pratt sends greetings to his loving brother, by the way." Her eyes panned the room and a sneer crossed her face. "Or perhaps something more sinister is going on here that involves Tremora's future king?"

"Would you dare accuse this gathering of treasonous activity, Prelandora? That would, indeed, be dangerous territory, even for you," said Megan. "This is a wizard's gathering, true. But, the attendees were hand chosen. This meeting is not all inclusive as you would see if you looked around you." Megan immediately realized his mistake.

"Well, don't mind if I do," Prelandora said as she stepped into the hall. She posed regally and made a grand performance of inspecting the hall. "Yes, I see. Hmm, there *are* some unfamiliar faces here," she said. Then she noticed Baakeer cringing in his seat. A look of surprise crossed her face, but she instantly recovered.

"Perhaps I *was* mistaken, Megan," she said, seductively while tapping her teeth with a finger. She began to move.

Her voice was melodic, and her movements were as graceful and alluring as a dancer. All eyes watched her as she glided leisurely down the table.

"Perhaps, perhaps," she continued. "But, who is this I see? Lorenzo, Pacco, Tashlman … the famous White Triad?" As she came abreast of the three, Pacco's familiar, Jasper, dived into the wizard's pocket; Tamara jumped behind Lorenzo's head and wrapped her arms tightly around his neck; and Crong shrunk to the size of a gerbil and dropped into Tashlman's hood. The three wizards themselves took no notice of anything but Prelandora.

Prelandora chuckled and moved on. "And look at this!" She stopped in front of Masha. "Could it be the Prassian Triad as well? The lovers of beasts?" She wrinkled her nose as if smelling something unpleasant.

Masha started to rise, but Prelandora casually held out her open hand and, without making contact, pushed her back into her seat. Masha made no further effort.

"And you say, Megan, this meeting has nothing to do with the coming summer solstice?" She laughed and ticked off more names as she passed each person by.

She approached the end of the table.

Megan stepped forward into Prelandora's path. "Come no further, Prelandora," he warned. "You are obviously quite aware that we are in neutral territory here in Fennland. Otherwise, you would be in chains by now. But, do not push the limits of those provisions. Use of weapons is a criminal offense in the presence of your king and queen, not to mention black magic. And not everyone here is under your spell." Tracker and Waz were now forming a barrier between the witch and the king and queen.

"I know nothing of this black magic you talk of, Megan. But the use of weapons to save the lives of the king and queen?" She raised an eyebrow. "Hardly an offense, Megan, when I saved their lives," she said dismissively. But she did come to a stop. It wasn't Megan's warning that made her halt, though; she wasn't even looking at Megan as she talked. No, it was Michael.

"Now who could this be?" she asked, making an exaggerated spectacle of eyeing Michael up and down.

Michael looked back at her defiantly. "You kidnapped my father," he forced through clenched teeth. Was it his anger that kept him from cowering? Her gaze had the power of radiating heat.

"Now, whatever gave you that idea?" Prelandora said, not taking her eyes off Michael's face. "Has someone been telling tales, hmmm?" Her eyes shifted down the table toward Baakeer.

"Enough!" Megan said, suddenly. "Who is present at this meeting has nothing to do with you, Prelandora. It is time for you to leave. Would you prefer to be escorted?"

Prelandora finally turned and looked at Megan. "I think I have seen all I need to see," she said. She then looked at the royal table. "I shall look forward to seeing you at the summer solstice, my King. And good luck in finding Prince Cedric," she added, looking at Michael with a smirk. She then bowed, and with one final parting shot for the king, she pointed her wand at the dead shape-changer. "And by the way, you're welcome ..." The corpse turned to ashes and then disappeared entirely.

Prelandora strode out the hall and into the night.

Most of the guests felt as if they just returned to the surface from the depths of a deep pool. There were gasps and coughs and sputters and several goblets of drink were quickly drained.

Tracker rushed to Megan's side and put his hand on his shoulder. "Shall I follow her, Megan?"

"No, Tracker, I'm afraid even with your skills it would be futile. She is in possession of magic that you have no defense against. You would be in great danger."

Megan then raised his voice so everyone in the room could hear. "Take heed, all. That was not the same Prelandora that was banished for boiling caldrons and simple enchantments. She is almost unrecognizable with her power now. It would have taken all of our strength to stand against her this evening, and she knew it. Not to mention the foolishness of doing any harm to the mother of the future king! But let us not be fooled. She was here for two purposes. One was to stop the spy from being caught and actually giving the first proof that she was plotting to usurp the crown, and second, she now has seen and confirmed what she perhaps already knew: Despite all of her efforts to keep it from happening, the son of Fenn is in Tremora, safe, and in allegiance with the king.

Chapter Forty-three

The Quest

It was midnight, and the hall was once again transformed. Instead of one table running its length, the room was now dominated by several stone tables arranged in the shape of two concentric circles. The makeshift canvas and cloth roof from earlier in the evening was gone; leaving the area open to a moonlit, meteor-filled starry sky. Elevated metal braziers bordered the circles for warmth and light. Their flames danced and snapped in the swirling breeze.

The king, queen, Megan, and the six wizards sat at the innermost tables, while guards, lords, knights, Corak, and others filled the seats of the outer. Michael, Tracker, Waz, and Nova stood in the very center of it all, facing the king.

The king rose and addressed the gathering. "Now you know our enemy. You've felt her power and experienced her cunningness. It was not planned, but we could not have impressed you more with our plight."

The king looked to Michael. "There is only one way to defeat the witch and her evil plans to rule Tremora: Rescue Cedric and return him to his people by the summer solstice. That is your quest, Traveler. It is a heavy burden for one so young. Yet, even at this late date, you may refuse your task. You must again make a choice. You may return with Baakeer to Mesmer Henge tomorrow where he will escort you through the portal, never to return to Tremora again, or accept this most difficult quest, risking your very life.

"Before you decide, you should know that you will not be alone in your quest should you decide to stay. Tracker and Waz and Nova will accompany you on your journey. They would not be left behind. And although Megan is desperately needed here at home to keep Prelandora at bay, I think he may yet play some part in your adventure one day."

Waz hummed, Nova snorted, and Tracker put his arm on Michael's shoulder. Michael looked gratefully at his friends and then sobered and looked back at the king.

"And, as mentioned by Megan, the wizards you see seated before you will share their gifts with you. You will leave this castle with all the weapons, and wisdom, and powers that Tremora can possibly give."

Collectively, the wizards nodded their heads or made other gestures of agreement. Tashlman rattled his knives.

"And you will need it all," King William said loudly, to bring the room's attention back to him. "You will be asked to accept or reject your quest at sunrise tomorrow, Michael. You will need that much time to confer with your comrades and others whose opinions you trust. For there is one more grave condition you must consider.

"Prelandora cannot kill Cedric without sacrificing her own life. So, she has our son hidden. The journey to that place will be perilous enough, but once you have found Cedric, you will have to face the dragon. And that's why you were summoned. Dragons only have one natural enemy, Michael: their own young. Have you not guessed the truth? The dragon, Michael, is your father …

End of Book One